PRAISE FOR *THE PETS*
BY BRAGI ÓLAFSSON

"Dark, strange, elusive, compelling, and oddly charming. . . . Ólafsson's English-language debut is part Beckettian or even Kafkaesque black comedy, part existentialist novel in the Paul Auster mode, and part locked-room mystery."—*Kirkus Reviews*

"The best short novel I've read this year. . . . Small, dark, and hard to put down, *The Pets* may be a classic in the literature of small enclosed spaces—a distinguished genre that includes 'The Metamorphosis,' *No Exit*, and a fair amount of Beckett."—Paul LaFarge

"Dark, scary, and unbelievably funny. . . . How long do we have to wait for English versions of Ólafsson's other books?"—*Los Angeles Times*

"Delightfully funny and unexpectedly complex, *The Pets* introduces American readers to a fresh voice and perspective."—*L Magazine*

"An artful mystery about dead animals, mundane objects, and disobedient people."—*Believer*

OTHER BOOKS BY BRAGI ÓLAFSSON
IN ENGLISH TRANSLATION

The Pets

THE AMBASSADOR

BRAGI ÓLAFSSON

TRANSLATED FROM THE ICELANDIC BY LYTTON SMITH

Originally published in Icelandic as *Sendiherrann*
Published by agreement with Forlagið, www.forlagid.is

First edition, 2010

Library of Congress Cataloging-in-Publication Data:

Bragi Ólafsson, 1962-
[Sendiherrann. English]
The ambassador / Bragi Ólafsson ; translated from the Icelandic by Lytton Smith. — 1st ed.
p. cm.
Originally published in Icelandic as Sendiherrann.
ISBN-13: 978-1-934824-13-9 (pbk. : alk. paper)
ISBN-10: 1-934824-13-5 (pbk. : alk. paper)
1. Poets, Icelandic—Fiction. 2. Middle-aged men—Iceland—Fiction.
3. Vilnius (Lithuania)—Fiction. I. Smith, Lytton, 1982- II. Title.
PT7511.B66S4613 2010
839'.6934—dc22
2010028002

Printed on acid-free paper in the United States of America.

Text set in Goudy, an old style serif originally designed by Frederic W. Goudy (1865–1947).

Design by N. J. Furl

Open Letter is the University of Rochester's nonprofit, literary translation press:
Lattimore Hall 411, Box 270082, Rochester, NY 14627

www.openletterbooks.org

This book is dedicated to the memory of my father,
Ólafur Stefánsson.

THE AMBASSADOR

. . .
. . .
. . .
. . .

og við leitum uppi tungu-
mál hvort annars
til að týnast í orðunum
til að þýða hvort annað.

. . .
. . .
. . .
. . .

Á leið sinni af trjánum
niður á kalt yfirborð haustsins
eru laufin jafn lengi og það tekur okkur fólkið
að taka hina stóru ákvörðun.

Þegar við svo setjumst hvort við annars hlið
og speglumst í djúpi dimmunnar á barnum
munum við hvorugt hvaða orð við völdum
—hvað þau þýddu á tungumáli hins.

(From a poem by Liliya Boguinskaia, "Pilies-stræti" (Pilies Gatvé), in an Icelandic translation by Sturla Jón Jónsson, after an English translation by Dora Mistral.)

. . .
. . .
. . .
. . .

and we search for the tongue
of each other's people
to get lost in the words
to translate one another.

. . .
. . .
. . .
. . .

On their way from the trees
down to the cold autumn ground
the leaves take as long as we people
take to reach the big decision.

When we sit down next to each other
and reflect in the deep darkness at the bar
neither remembers the words we chose
—what they meant in each other's tongues.

(From a poem by Liliya Boguinskaia, "Pilies-stræti" (Pilies Gatvé), in an English translation by Lytton Smith, after an Icelandic translation by Sturla Jón Jónsson following an English translation by Dora Mistral.)

PART ONE

REYKJAVÍK

BANKASTRÆTI

It is made from particularly durable material, 100% cotton yet feels waxy to the touch. And the seams will last a lifetime. The exterior is like a laminated dust jacket—"something you'll appreciate, being a poet"—which makes the item totally waterproof, the perfect design for the weather in this country, or, to put it more accurately, any country where you can't take the weather for granted. Even when a day begins without a cloud in the sky, you can't guarantee that dust and dirt are the only things that'll have fallen on you by the time night comes. The color, too, is a key attraction: it doesn't garishly call attention to itself yet is likely to invite quiet admiration, even perhaps—"though of course one shouldn't think such thoughts"—envy. The fact that it was made in Italy is insurance against the price one would have to pay for it, a price that'd clean out your pockets, as the saying goes.

And, on the subject of pockets, one of the nifty little inside pockets is made-to-measure for a cell phone. Or for a cigarette packet, if perhaps the owner doesn't use a cell phone and is instead one of those few stubborn people out of every hundred who smokes, who don't care about smoking's effect on their health. The other inside pocket is also worth mentioning: small, designed perhaps for a wallet, it contains a small, dark blue, velvet bag (that's one of the things that makes this item unique, a bag made from velvet) and in this charming little bag, which you draw closed with a yellow silk cord, are two spare buttons, for the unlikely event that the owner managed to lose the originals and had to replace them. But there's little danger of that happening, since the stitching is, as was mentioned earlier, guaranteed to last a lifetime.

With these words—or something along these lines—the salesperson in the coat department of the men's clothing store on Bankastræti describes the English-style Aquascutum overcoat to Sturla Jón. Sturla had decided to buy this coat a long time ago; he'd even re-ordered it after it sold out. The sales attendant has no idea Sturla Jón had made the order—Sturla hadn't spoken to this employee, who seems to be new, before. So it takes Sturla pleasantly by surprise that the sales attendant recognizes him, though perhaps Sturla should have expected that a person whose job involves paying close attention to clothes might also pay close attention to the people wearing those clothes. On the other hand, it's possible another employee had pointed out, when Sturla entered the store, that this was Sturla Jón the poet, maybe adding: you know, the one who published that book, *free from freedom*.

Sturla had first set eyes on the overcoat in the store back in February. At that time it had been too bitterly cold and stormy for him to justify buying an unlined overcoat, even if he could have afforded it. And when he remembered to take another look at the overcoat later, in June, when there was a marked difference in his financial outlook, the three or four coats that were there before had disappeared from their hangers; they'd all been sold.

"There was a guy in here the other day who must have tried on every single suit in the shop," the sales attendant is saying. Sturla isn't sure how to react to this information. "Perhaps you know him," continues the man. "I think he's a painter, or some sort of artist."

"Did he buy anything?" Sturla asks.

"I'm an artist myself, as it happens," the sales attendant adds, doing his best to sound nonchalant. Sturla repeats the question.

"He couldn't find anything that suited his style," answers the sales attendant, smiling. "We don't have anything in stock that comes with dried mustard on the lapels."

Sturla is surprised to hear a young man like the one standing in front of him use a word like *lapels*.

"The jacket he was wearing had a crusty old stain on it," the sales attendant offers by way of further explanation. When he describes how the customer's mustache was like Adolf Hitler's and adds that it had been difficult at first to tell whether the yellow of the customer's shirt was the original color or a color the shirt had acquired over time, Sturla is fairly certain that the customer was N. Pietur, the visual artist and composer, an old friend of his father. He begins to wonder whether it is appropriate for a sales attendant in a store of this caliber to gossip about other customers. When the attendant adds that, naturally, it isn't just anyone who buys "such expensive and elegant clothes," referring to the range of clothes in the store, Sturla is convinced that if anyone should be allowed to sound-off to a complete stranger about the delicate relationship between employee and customer, in which one person offers another merchandise and that other person has to accept or reject those items, then it should be the customer, not the salesman. Sturla reckons it isn't a great idea for this young employee to be talking to a potential customer about interactions he'd had with a different customer, even if—or precisely because—the former customer hadn't bought anything, despite having asked the salesman to go to a lot of trouble.

His thoughtlessness notwithstanding, the salesman was right to suggest not everyone could afford the clothing this store sells, especially the item Sturla has his eye on. You'd have to say this Italian-made,

English-style overcoat is expensive or, more accurately, over-expensive. But many years ago Sturla Jón, who made it a rule not to spend much money on clothes, had seen a coat like this, somewhere between a mackintosh and a trench coat, and it had occurred to him that, just this once, he should break his usual clothes-shopping habits. So he'd set himself the goal of acquiring the overcoat, almost regardless of the price: the goal of allowing himself, this one time, to buy something expensive, something he knew would afford him more pleasure to wear than the other clothes he owned, clothes which cost no more than they had to.

And as Sturla declares that he is going to take the overcoat, he realizes he is wearing a broad smile on his face—the smile of a man at peace, he thinks, but then he worries it might come across to others as though he is uncontrollably proud of himself, like a child or teenager who is about to fulfill his wildest ambition. "I'll take this one," he says decisively, trying to wipe the smile from his face. The salesman nods gravely, as if an important decision has been reached by all, and says, "Good choice."

At first, Sturla thinks he heard him say "Gotcha!" and he stares at the salesman in astonishment as he folds up the item, which, thanks to the stiffness of the cotton, rustles the way weighty, good quality paper does.

"Was there something else you wanted?" asks the salesman, seeing the look on Sturla's face.

"No, that's all," replies Sturla.

"Gotcha," the salesman says, and they go over to the checkout which, as is customary, is located in the middle of the shop floor, around a square column. Next to the till is a gleaming coffee machine—from the same country as the overcoat—and an artistic display of bright white coffee cups.

"Have an espresso while we're ringing this up," the employee offers, shaking out the creases from the overcoat.

Sturla sets one of the white cups under the nozzle he knows the coffee is supposed to flow from, and he gropes blindly about the machine until the salesman rescues him by pushing a little button, which is the same color as the machine itself and has a picture of a coffee cup on it. While the coffee is brewing, Sturla looks in his wallet and counts out thirteen 5,000-kronur bills.

"It's not often you see this much cash," the man says, and Sturla asks whether there is a discount for paying cash.

"Not for cash, but there's a five percent discount with plastic." The salesman takes the notes from Sturla's hand and puts the coat on the counter next to the coffee cups. He licks his thumb a few times while counting the notes, and has to start counting again when he gets distracted by Sturla, who is taking off his windbreaker and unfolding the coat in order to slip it on. The salesman puts the notes in the till and, smiling a little, watches his latest customer's awkward attempts to struggle into his purchase. He hands Sturla a bag with the store's logo on it so Sturla can put his windbreaker inside, a bag so beautiful Sturla fears he will have to pay extra for it. The bag is a rich brown color, made from thick, waxy paper, a texture not unlike his new coat; it has orange cord handles.

While Sturla is stuffing the windbreaker into the bag, another employee calls the salesman over; a young married couple needs assistance. The couple had caught Sturla's eye when they entered the store: they are a well-known couple from the world of theater, and he had recently heard his father's friend Örn Featherby speak rather scornfully about them in connection with a play one of them, possibly the woman, or perhaps it was the husband, had sold to one of the two major theater companies in town. While Sturla drinks his espresso, he watches the couple and the salesman; they all seem to know one another, and they launch into a conversation that immediately breaks out in laughter. From the husband's gestures, Sturla judges that the topic of discussion is some project the young couple is involved in. Glancing around, Sturla sneaks his hand into a white bowl full of light brown, cylindrical sugar packets, and grabs several. Looking down at them in his palm, he counts them and sneaks them into one of the side-pockets of the overcoat.

By the time he leaves the store, it has begun to rain. It's cold rain, one step shy of sleet. Sturla buttons his overcoat and thinks about how the salesman commented on a prospective buyer's likely uses for this item of clothing. This customer, Sturla Jón, is not a cell phone user but a smoker. As if to prove to passers-by that that is exactly the sort of person he is, someone who wouldn't want to be disturbed by a phone ringing while he is out in the open air, someone who instead expresses his independence with the guilty pleasures of smoking, he pauses on the sidewalk of Bankastræti, right outside the store, fishes a packet of Royales from his inside jacket pocket, taps out a cigarette, and, after lighting it, slides the packet into the made-to-measure inside pocket, but not without difficulty; the packet only just fits.

He goes down Bankastræti in the direction of the Útvegsbanki building on Lækjartorg, a bank which no longer exists. Sturla had actually worked there for nearly two years before going abroad to study; he'd been in the department that handled foreign exchange. A young woman from New Zealand had worked beside him in the bank, and her name now appeared right in front of him, on a vertical, red sign standing on the south-west corner of the old stone house at Bankastræti 3: *Stella.*

Sturla comes to a sudden halt directly under the sign. He looks around to see if anyone has paid any attention to him or is at all surprised that he stopped so suddenly, and he takes another few steps forward before turning to contemplate the *Stella* sign as he inhales the stimulating cigarette smoke. He'd stopped because a question occurred to him: Had the sign been there when he was a young man, or is it a new addition? And, along similar lines—and this flabbergasts him—how on earth can he not know for sure? One voice in his head tells him that the shop has been around at least as long as he has, that it is one of the oldest shops in town; another voice insists that the apparent age of this sign is nothing but a figment of his imagination, the subconscious mind's way of implying that the other, New Zealand Stella—whose slender, feminine fingers had, a quarter-century before, sent amounts of money overseas on the next telex machine to his—had felt for Sturla exactly the way he had longed for her to feel at the time. It was entirely possible that, despairing at some point over whether the woman from New Zealand had any feelings for him, Sturla had looked out of the window of the Foreign Exchange and, gripped by a poetic flight of fancy—which he of all people might succumb to, since he is, after all, a poet—his eye had alighted on a sign on Bankastræti bearing her name, like a message from above, like the sun rising in the east.

Sturla turns back to look at the old Útvegsbanki building and confirms with a smile that the windows of his long-abandoned workplace hadn't faced Lækjartorg; they had instead looked out onto Austurstræti. There was no way he would have been able to look along Bankastræti, at least not at the odd-numbered houses. He continues on his way, but stops again almost immediately to look at two rust-red, life-sized statues of people that rise up from the sidewalk, standing face to face. Only the torsos of the sculptures have been designed to resemble the human body; the lower halves consist solely of a perfect cube, which might represent nothing more than a cube but which might also symbolize the artist's intention for the work. Whether there is a particular significance to these statues or not, they give Sturla the impression of suffering and fear. One of the statues is looking down, bowed by a weight the passing pedestrian can only guess at; the other has thrown its head back and is wearing a pathetic expression, as if inviting the viewer to cut its throat. Sturla looks between the statues, along Bernhöftstorfan in the direction of Skólastræti, and contemplates the corrugated iron roof of Reykjavík's Grammar School in the distance. Four lines from his newly finished book of poems, *assertions*, come to mind:

the house on the hill
which we face towards

the mother, the window
the darkness of the shadows

Sturla—the purported author of the poem—isn't sure whether these lines actually describe the very educational institution he is now looking at or whether they describe another kind of institution: the mother who sees everything, a dark figure in the kitchen on the other side of the window's glass, standing and watching her progeny play on the sidewalk.

Is there a connection, indeed, between the first two lines and lines three and four, between the house and the mother? Does the house symbolize the father? In my Father's house are many rooms: Sturla's father's flat, at the top of Skólavörðustígur, opposite the church on the hill, is a one-bedroom which, besides the living room and bedroom, has a hall, kitchen, and bathroom (which Sturla is planning to use when he drops in on his father after running a quick errand on Austurstræti). In this case, the son, Sturla, has even more rooms than the father, since Sturla's apartment on Skúlagata is technically a two-bedroom.

Suddenly the rain gets heavier. Sturla stubs out his cigarette, puts up the collar on his coat, and presses on in the direction of Lækjargata. As he goes past the Prime Minister's office a sharp gust of wind blows from the north. The weather, in all its bitterness, emphasizes the warm practicality of Sturla's new overcoat, an overcoat that is only lined with thin, red-patterned cotton yet offers considerable protection from both wind and water, and which—as the name of the coat implies, no less significantly—would protect one's shoulders from the dust which falls from above, the way a dust jacket protects a book.

SKÓLAVÖRÐUSTÍGUR

"You're all wet," says Jón Magnússon as he lets his son, Sturla Jón, into the apartment on Skólavörðuholt and watches him remove his wet overcoat in the hallway before draping it over the back of a kitchen chair, in front of the oven.

"May I use your bathroom?" asks Sturla. His right hand is dripping wet from running it through his hair, and he looks as if he needs to dry himself off before doing anything else.

"*May you?* You're in your own father's home, Sturla."

Sturla goes apologetically into the bathroom and locks the door.

He has come from a bookstore on Austurstræti, having bought himself a hotdog and a cold Pepsi from the kiosk opposite Lækjartorg. At the bookstore he bought a folder to keep printouts of ideas for stories he intends to write. Now that he has published his latest collection of poetry he has made a deal with himself, or so he describes it in his head: he won't write any more poetry. Instead, the lines on his page will reach the margin and form blocks where previously there was an irregular collection of uneven lines pointing towards the margin but never quite touching it. And, on the way back up Bankastræti—as if to suggest the folder is going to come in handy straight away—Sturla Jón has an idea for a story, a short-story. It was, he thought, basically about everything he'd done in his life in the past fifteen minutes: a middle-aged poet goes into a bookstore to see, for the first time, his newly-published book sitting with all the other newly-published books, tightly-wrapped in glistening cellophane, on display with its price tag facing the literary-minded folk and other customers of the bookstore. This book has become a commodity to be bought and sold, the value it acquires destined to be measured not against a price tag stuck on a copy, but against each individual reader's opinion as to whether it was a worthy item or not.

In Sturla's opinion, there is an irony to this that results from a deception the poet himself perpetrates: when it comes down to it, his value is only ever evident from the price tag on the book, and every year will bring a new sticker and a lower price until, in the end, when the last copies of the book finally sell at the Icelandic Discount Book Fair, twenty or thirty years later, the price on the sticker will have dropped under 100 kronur, down as low as double-digits. Because of this, and in order to make the distance between the author and his subject matter clear—or else the reader might somehow start imagining he was describing his own experience—Sturla had come up with an idiosyncratic character, a poet, who gets very angry in the bookstore because his newly-published book isn't on display at the front of the store with the other brand new books. Instead, it has been placed in the back, among books from a year, or even two years, ago: on its left is an Icelandic translation of Gogol's Petersburg stories, and on its right a selection of poems by an older Icelandic poet which Sturla believes came out three or maybe four years ago. Sturla had prized this poet highly as a young man but had been ready to dislodge him from his respected pedestal—ideally unceremoniously—ever since Sturla recited his work with him at a poetry event in Kópavogur several years back. The older poet had shown Sturla Jón a complete lack of respect: he stood up in the middle of Sturla's reading to get a coffee at the bar—and not just an everyday Icelandic coffee, mind you, but one of those special coffee drinks (he was eighty-something years old) which necessitates the use of the espresso-machine and which created an incredible racket. This had happened right in the middle of a poem, and continued for the rest of it, so that Sturla's reading went down the drain, lost in all the coffee-making noise.

As Sturla had headed from Bankastræti into Skólavörðustígur, a heavy downpour suddenly broke out, and in order to protect himself, and his new overcoat, from the downpour, he'd slipped into a nearby doorway, into Háspenna, one of the gambling and games halls run by the University of Iceland. He'd debated going into the spick-and-span fishmonger's next door instead, but Sturla chose the games hall over the fish shop since he'd been given a lot of change when he bought the folder at the bookstore, and it occurred to him that, rather than straining his overcoat pocket, he could use the change to support the university, an institution which, among other things, has as its mission fostering in the youth an ability to appreciate and interpret exactly the sort of texts Sturla himself has published. What's more, he worried that stopping in at the fishmongers would cause his new overcoat to soak up the smell of fish—though this fashionable fishmongers, which only offered freshly cooked dishes, never really seemed to smell of fish; the smell was suffocated by cooking the fish in all kinds of seasoning and oils, unlike traditional fishmongers who sell ordinary fresh fish, which somehow always give off the sweet smell fish have.

Often when Sturla reads or hears about fish or fishmongers, it brings to mind an image of a Portuguese fisherman dragging a light blue boat up onto the yellow sand, brimful of gleaming, newly caught fish which a short time before thrashed about as they fought for their lives. Sturla no longer knows whether this picture originally came from a poem he'd read or from a painting or a photograph, but it always conjures up the phrase "Art of Poetry," capital A, capital P. The fish represent the idea the poet captures, the image which moves restlessly in real life until it can be fixed onto paper; from then on it is firmly held in place for the reader to resuscitate later. Sturla knows his analogy for the art of poetry isn't new or especially fresh, but he still thinks it is beautiful; it illuminates the art for him, just like the flashing, brightly-colored slot-machines which shone in the darkened space of the games hall.

The place had a comforting feel, something that wasn't a new discovery for Sturla. He'd been here before; the building had been built about twenty years ago to replace a wooden structure that years before had housed a second-hand bookstore, "The Book." Sturla had been a regular customer of that store as a child and young man, and he owed the foundations of his own library to it, the pillar, as it were; it was the place where he began choosing books for himself. First, it was books like *Prince Valiant* by Hal Foster; after that, he'd picked up all kinds of translated thrillers, and moved on from those to educating himself in the classics—in books that have long been known as the classics. During high school, towards the end of The Book's existence on Skólavörðustígur, Sturla had purchased books by Halldór Laxness, Þórbergur Þórðarson, and the Icelandic poets, like Jóhannes úr Kötlum and Steinn Steinarr. He'd devoured these books with such enthusiasm that in recent years he'd come to believe he'd gotten burned-out from throwing himself into their writing with such admiration; he ended up losing interest in the poets he once absolutely adored.

With the exception of the old poet he'd read with in Kópavogur, he continued to respect the old Icelandic poet pioneers. He often had reason to remind himself that those poets had enriched and deepened his view of the world; they had doubtlessly improved the quality of his lyrical palette, though that spectrum couldn't compare to the complex electric rainbow of slot-machines that greet punters at Skólavörðustígur 6. He could, though, say that the used books of Þórbergur, Jóhannes, and the others he had bought at The Book were among the last purchases of Icelandic books he had made; from then on he almost exclusively bought books by foreign authors, in English and Danish.

On the right side of the entrance to Háspenna was a Gevalia-brand coffee machine. On the front of this was a very visible sign inviting customers to get themselves a free sample in a paper cup before heading into reception to get their bills changed to coins, or simply going on down two steps to the games hall. Although Sturla had only recently drunk a rather strong espresso in the clothing store, and as a rule didn't drink more than one cup of coffee after midday, he still obeyed the Gevalia machine's silent command: he put a paper cup in the tray under the coffee nozzle and pushed the cappuccino button. While he waited for the jet of coffee he watched the university employee behind the glass counter: a dark-haired, thin man who Sturla thought looked like he had as a young man. He had a thick book, the spine firmly creased, and was deeply absorbed in reading it, though he took time to nod his head to the middle-aged man who'd just come in.

There was no one in the games hall. Sturla preferred the place that way.

Sturla had four hundred kronur in spare change in his pocket. He disturbed the supervisor from his reading and gave him the small change, telling him he wanted hundred-kronur coins in exchange. He also changed a thousand-kronur note for some coins. Then he followed the path of lights down to the carpeted games hall and sat on a high stool in front of a machine in the far corner, where there was a view out the window along Bankastræti. Before slotting the first hundred kronur coin in the machine, he looked at the traffic on Skólavörðustígur: a car, a woman, two men, another woman, a few more cars, two young boys, a woman with a dog, a black Hummer which idled at the crosswalk in the street below. As soon as the first coin disappeared into the machine the Hummer began moving along Bankastræti, and by the time it became clear Sturla was a hundred kronur poorer, the gleaming black monster had vanished from sight.

Seven hundred-kronur coins later, Sturla's gamble paid off, and a few coins could be heard dropping into the winnings tray; Sturla had got five hundred kronur back.

While he kept feeding the slot machine with coins he recalled a conversation from fourteen years ago between his father and Hallmundur Margeir, his father's brother, which had taken place one Sunday in front of the old brick house at Skólavörðustígur 4. The conversation was etched in his memory like an engraving in stone. Sturla had been at a children's matinee in the old cinema with his father, Jón, and his late brother, Darri Örn. They had seen *The Adventures of Huckleberry Finn* and as they were going along Skólavörðustígur towards their home at Mánagata (where the boys' mother, Fanný, was busy preparing Sunday lunch) they met Hallmundur and his son, Jónas. The two were on their way to a five o'clock showing at the same cinema, a movie Sturla knew was only for children older than sixteen. Perhaps that fact—given that his cousin Jónas was only twelve at the time—had stuck in Sturla's mind along with, almost word for word, the brothers' fairly ordinary conversation, in part because they talked without their sons saying anything at all to each other. After Jón and Hallmundur exchanged a few words about the movies they had seen or were about to see, Hallmundur had started talking about the house at Bankastræti 7 (one of the houses Sturla had walked past half an hour ago, after he bought the overcoat). What had aroused his uncle's interest in the house was the image he had of the owners, when, in 1932, the house had first been built and they'd looked around the empty rooms. Hallmundur found it quite magnificent to imagine Icelanders from the early thirties looking around the brand new, empty, two hundred square meter stone apartment house; he didn't, though, think his image fit the time period, since Reykjavík's inhabitants lived then, by and large, in hovels of various sorts, as he put it. The conversation had ended with Hallmundur saying that, of course, the bank always ends up possessing anything that has any value—value in material terms, that is. The bank directors of Samvinnubanki were even now sitting at desks on the upper story of this magnificent house, with its view over Bankastræti, moistening their fingers and counting through all the bank notes they receive from the cashiers on the ground floor.

Suddenly a flood of hundred-kronur coins crashed into the coin tray. Sturla had been too immersed in the past to notice three oranges line up in a row on the screen of the slot machine, and he'd not realized that he only had one hundred-kronur coin left in his hand. He looked around instinctively, mainly to determine whether the young student who was supervising the place had heard the rattle of the coins, but in order to see for sure he had to get up and take a few steps across the carpet. He looked with some embarrassment at the shower of coins in the tray, slipped off his chair, and tiptoed carefully out onto the middle of the floor. The service booth was empty; the young man had probably gone to the bathroom. Sturla hurried back to the slot machine, picked the plastic bag from the bookstore up off the floor, and began counting coins into it. There were seven thousand kronur. What's more, he still had the one remaining hundred-kronur coin in his sweaty palm; he slipped the coin into the slot and pressed the button, setting the fruit wheels in motion. He peered into the carrier bag, as if to reassure himself that his winnings were still there, and at the same moment he looked up from the bag he heard a now familiar noise: another consignment of hundred-kronur coins falling into the coin tray, not as many as before, but, at a quick glance, another few thousand kronur or so.

The first thing that came to Sturla's mind was an analogy with the student Rastignac, would-be suitor to the daughter of Old Goriot in Balzac's novel, who had won twice in a row at a roulette casino in the Palais-Royal neighborhood: seven thousand francs followed by an additional thousand francs—enough to pay off Madame de Nucingen's debt at the dressmaker and a large enough sum to buy her affection.

Would the money that had found its way to Sturla be enough for him to buy something equivalent to the affections of Goriot's pretentious daughter?

Without taking time to count the money, Sturla swept the coins into the plastic bag, took the paper cup, now half full of coffee, down from the slot machine, and left the room. Although the young man was still missing from the booth, Sturla looked in the direction of the counter as he went past, and he gulped down the leftover cold coffee before he placed the cup back beside the Gevalia machine. He had been too occupied with the slot machine for the last few minutes to pay attention to whether the weather outside had changed; it had gotten worse, with large hailstones that descended on him like . . . like . . .

He was much too confused at that moment to complete the simile. "His words surrounded him like scales on a fish": he satisfied himself by recalling, as he went past the fish shop, Maxim Gorky's description of his comrade Lenin.

His father's house on Skólavörðustígur was no more than two or three minutes walk away, but in that time the sleet was able to soak through Sturla's overcoat and turn his dark brown hair even darker. He was also weighed down by the suspicion that his actions had somehow robbed the university: he'd gone into the place expecting to lose fourteen hundred kronur, but he'd won at least ten thousand kronur from the school, without giving the school the opportunity to win the money back.

"In other words, you've profited by the five thousand kronur bill I lost there the other day," says Jón, when Sturla had come out of the bathroom and told his father about his winnings from the games hall. "Plus another five thousand some old codger lost in that black hole."

Sturla had intended to show his father the new overcoat he'd hung on a chair in the kitchen—if he hadn't already noticed it for himself—but with his unexpected windfall as food for thought he clean forgot.

"I only hope you'll use the money to good effect, my fortunate son," Jón says as he begins to make coffee, even though Sturla had turned down the offer, saying he would make himself a cup of tea. "It is indeed a considerable responsibility to have ten thousand kronur," continues Jón, and while Sturla watches his father shovel coffee powder into the paper filter, he toys with his cigarette packet and lighter, asking himself whether all men in their late sixties communicate with their sons using the same sarcastic tone as his father—whose routine more often than not reminded Sturla of a younger man pretending to be nearly seventy:

Of course, you'll throw your sense of responsibility overboard and use your swiftly made profit to buy an hour with some prostitute in Lithuania. Something like that won't cost more than ten thousand kronur, I reckon. And most likely you'll have some money left; you could offer the lady some champagne.

I'm not going on a sex trip to the Baltic, if that's what you think. I'm not a soccer hooligan or some investment banker.

Ha, what do you know what'll take place once you've arrived? You can't say for certain that some woman with big, rolling breasts isn't going to come up to you—perhaps when you're completely lost in the city—and offer to accompany you to your hotel, since, naturally, she knows the area better than you, and then she'll show you some motherly concern once you've arrived. I'm not sure you know beforehand how you'll react to such kindness. You do know, however, that there's ten thousand kronur in your pocket you haven't done anything to earn, and you also know that you won't need to explain it to anyone if the money disappears as suddenly as it appeared.

I don't think you know your son particularly well. Besides, I didn't win quite ten thousand kronur in the games hall; I've yet to count it, and the fourteen hundred I put in needs to be subtracted from that total.

Maybe that's true. But, that aside, you haven't been close to any woman since you and Hildur separated, am I right? What have you been up to since then? That was six or seven years ago.

What do you know about it, Pop? Would you like me to introduce you to every woman I get to know?

Perhaps you shouldn't get too close to womenfolk in general; it's not worth taking the risk of ending up with a sixth little bastard.

All at once Sturla Jón comes to his senses, standing in the kitchen doorway and half-listening to Jón; he'd been imagining the whole conversation. He wonders whether his father would really call his grandchildren—Egill, Gunnar, Grettir, Hildigunnur, and Hallgerður—bastards, but he gives Jón the benefit of doubt and answers his own question in the negative.

"When are you going to Latvia?" Jón asks once he has finished preparing the coffee and is waiting for the kettle to boil.

"I'm going to Lithuania," Sturla corrects him, trying to remember whether Sæunn, the young woman he had been in a brief relationship with three years ago, ever met his father. They probably never met, but it startles Sturla that he can't be sure about it. Is he getting too old to remember whether or not he'd introduced his young girlfriend to his father not long ago?

"And what exactly are you are going to do there?" Jón wants to know. "In . . . Vilnius."

"Both in Vilnius and in a little town some place near to Vilnius. I am going to read my poems. It's a poetry festival."

"You've gone to one of these festivals before, right?" Jón's question is laden with disapproval at his son's dalliance with poetry, but Sturla decides not to let that get on his nerves. He'd learned to rise above his father's needless sermonizing about the "minor art form" that is poetry. Poetry was a reminder that the son was currently working in his chosen artistic medium, while the father, the internationally educated film director, hadn't come close to completing his "great form," the movie, for three-and-a-half decades; the nearest he'd gotten was arranging some books about directors and movie-making in the library in Hafnarfjörður, where he worked. That said, he'd recently mentioned that an old schoolmate of his, a chemist, was going to finance a movie which Jón and his friend Örn Featherby had been planning for quite some time, but Sturla took the news with a large pinch of salt.

In answer to the question about whether or not he'd gone to poetry festivals like the one he was going to in Lithuania, Sturla curtly replies that he's been both to Belgium and to the Faroe Islands roughly ten years ago.

"But you weren't impressed by the festivals, correct?" his father asks.

"No, I wouldn't say I was," comes the response, and as Jón is asking, in a surly tone, why he expects this festival to be any better than the others, it occurs to him, from somewhere in the depths of his brain, to use the coming trip to Lithuania as material for an article he could write for Jónatan Jóhannsson's literary magazine, *From E to F.* Why not expose the things that would take place at the international festival *before* they took place, and set up the possibility of writing a second article about the same material after the festival ends, in light of what *had* happened—in other words, what he actually experienced. The idea, which Sturla at once becomes convinced is a fabulous idea, reminds him of that famous story from the world of cultural journalism in Reykjavík, about a music critic at an Icelandic newspaper, a man better known as a composer—indeed, rather well known as one—who published a review of one of his colleagues' concerts in the paper, a concert which had been postponed at the last minute and didn't take place until after the review appeared.

But while this critic had so clumsily deceived his readers, people reading Sturla's article, on the other hand, would be just as aware as its author that it deals with future events, that it presents honest speculation about how things at the poetry festival would turn out. It would really be no different from what you find in the mass media every day, with people predicting what will happen in sports or the stock market. Following from his thoughts about the article and the composer's advance "review," it occurs to Sturla to tell his father how he'd been in a clothing store earlier and had heard a story about N. Pietur, the old acquaintance of both Jón and Örn Featherby who, firstly, happens to be the half-brother of the editor Jónatan Jóhannsson and, secondly, is the very composer about whom the premature review was written. But Jón breaks the silence first, asking Sturla whether he is going to read from his new book in Lithuania.

"They are translating some poems from it, yes," answers Sturla. "But I'll read mainly from the older books." He tells his father that in addition to the ten or eleven poems which had been translated from Icelandic into Lithuanian (by a Lithuanian who had lived in Iceland for half his life), one of the poems from the new book, "kennslustund," has been translated into Lithuanian via Sturla's own translation from Icelandic into English, "the lesson." The translator, a Belarusian poet from Minsk who was also participating in the poetry festival, had in turn sent Sturla one of her own poems, translated into English, which he had then hastily translated into Icelandic.

"And the point of this was?" asks Jón.

"To foster some personal interaction, so the festival's participants know each other a little before they meet up," Sturla replies, thinking he's given his father a good answer.

"But you are not your usual self in this new book," Jón says, almost accusatorially, and when Sturla asks him to explain what he means by this, Jón replies that the tone of some of the poems seemed to him a little out-moded. It wasn't so much that he felt Sturla was composing in the fashion of the older Icelandic poets, but more that some of the poems sound like they were written by a young poet from thirty or forty years back.

Sturla looks thoughtfully at his father and lights a cigarette. "Do you have any particular poems in mind?" he asks, blowing out a cloud of smoke.

"I don't know how to answer that. But which do you think I prefer," asks Jón, looking meaningfully at his son, "pipe smoke or cigarette smoke?"

Sturla lets his father answer his own question:

"Pipe smoke. Örn comes here with his pipe and pipe-cleaner and all the accoutrements of pipe-smoking, and though there is often a revolting odor when he draws the pipe-cleaner out of the cylinder, I'm now more able to enjoy pipe smoke than the acrid cloud which comes from a cigarette."

Sturla looks off into space, then glances back at his father and smokes.

"There are a few lines in one poem which I put a definite question mark next to," Jón continues. "And they are, I think, the only lines which rhyme. Or seem like they rhyme, at least." He reaches out for Sturla's book on the sideboard and contemplates the image on the front cover for a moment: a rather blurry picture of an old-fashioned document folder lying on a table; a fountain pen lies open on the folder. While Jón searches through the book he mumbles its short title, *assertions*, and he repeats it twice more until he finds the page he is looking for. He reads aloud: "the mother, the window / the darkness of the shadows." Glancing up, he asks, "What were you aiming for in those lines? Why not go all the way, if you were going to rhyme? Why didn't you say, for example, "the mother in the window," or "the mother *at* the window, dark in the shadow?"

As Sturla explains to his father how he'd deliberately avoided the rhyme—how he looks upon rhyme in serious poetry as a foreign body (he didn't, of course, use the word *serious*)—he suspects the quoted lines were strong and vivid after all; it seemed quite clear they were able to move the reader, given that both author and his father had thought of them on the same day, less than an hour apart.

"Did you find something strange about this half-rhyme?" Sturla asks. "Did you find it stuck out like a sore thumb?"

"*Half-rhyme?*" asks Jón.

In Sturla's mind, a positive response to his own question about the half-rhyme hadn't been totally out of the question. But if he is honest with himself, he has repeatedly found something peculiar about these lines, without being able to put his finger on exactly why, or to convince himself to either cut them or ignore the issue altogether.

"What does it mean?" continues Jón, who hasn't understood the term "half-rhyme." "Or does it mean anything?"

"I'm implying that the person at the window, looking out, is the mother," answers Sturla, "and what are shadows made of, other than darkness?" When he realizes that his father isn't satisfied by this response, he continues: "I didn't set out to explain the poems in this book."

"So it isn't supposed to mean anything specific?"

"No. That's exactly what it's supposed to mean: nothing specific. The reader asks himself what it might mean. I'm not publishing a book of poems in order to force meaning on people."

"Perhaps then it's Norman Bates' Mother, this mother in the window?" asks Jón with a smile. And when Sturla doesn't say anything, Jón repeats his question: "Well? Is it her? You know I met Anthony Perkins once."

Sturla lights himself another cigarette.

"I still don't understand why, all of a sudden, you've started rhyming," continues Jón. "Or half-rhyming, as you put it."

His father's smile always reminded him of the American movie actor Robert Duvall. It had some fine, intelligent irony that caught Sturla off-balance: he had not expected his father to show any enthusiasm for his poems—though it was rather ironic to call his observations "enthusiasm"—or to reveal his worry that his son might not be on the right poetic path. Sturla hadn't yet told Jón that he was done writing poetry, that he was intending to turn to prose, but regardless of that, he found his father's observations quite unnecessary. He was interrogating him about the significance of a lyrical metaphor, which Sturla had let stand in the book—and, on top of all this, he was questioning lines about the mother which weren't really *his*, they were *someone else's*. And at the same time Sturla is reminding himself that these lines are *someone else's*, his father quotes the very poet who had, after his death, built his reputation in large part on assertions that he was actually *someone else*.

"One must be modern," Jón says, and once again the shape of his mouth makes him look like Robert Duvall. "So says your father, and so said the foremost poet of the poetic renaissance of the nineteenth century."

Sturla places his cigarette down amidst the unsmoked pipe tobacco that is in the ashtray, and looks at his father who comments, seeming very pleased with himself, that he can make out the aroma of Prince Albert tobacco.

Jón Magnússon is only sixteen years older than his son Sturla Jón Jónsson. Jón was in his second year at the Grammar School in Reykjavík when Sturla Jón came into the world, but he definitely wasn't going to let that interrupt his studies, as Sturla remembered his father advising him when he himself started Grammar School. Jón and Fanný Alexson, Sturla's mother, still lived at that time with their parents, but shortly after the birth of their son they moved into a little apartment on the east side of town which Fanný's father, Benedikt Alexson, at that time a politician and later an ambassador in Oslo and Stockholm, rented for them. When Sturla was born Fanný had completed one year at the Business School of Iceland. She'd intended to continue her studies, but she wasn't able to fulfill her ambition: Fanný and Jón acquired another boy, Darri Örn, two years after Sturla was born; Darri was born the day Jón graduated from Grammar School. When he was one month old Benedikt bought a little apartment on Mánagata for Jón and his daughter, an apartment they lived in throughout their cohabitation, twenty years in all, and which they sublet during the three years they spent in Prague while Jón was studying film.

As Fanný had told Sturla, something in Jón Magnússon's character had touched a sensitive nerve in her shortly after they had met; she had begun to sense a kind of mental imbalance, a malaise, which among other things made her almost pathologically dependent on Jón. It led her to develop a great impatience about all kinds of minor details in her relationships with other people, especially Jón. She had never before displayed such neuroses, and they began to swell inside her like a malignant tumor, having a growing influence on her behavior towards others, no matter whether they were close relatives or complete strangers at the supermarket checkout. That "devilish condition" of hers, as Jón described it long afterwards to Sturla, increased dramatically following the birth of Darri Örn, and in their last months in Czechoslovakia Fanný and Jón's relationship unraveled because of these notions hidden inside her, feelings someone who shared a roof with two young kids shouldn't entertain. Jón had for his part already withdrawn from Fanný and the boys, moving deeper and deeper into a private world he was creating with his graduate project—a rather strange story, to say the least, about an individual who is faced with eleven doors—but fortunately Jón and Fanný were wise enough to make an agreement to separate for a time; that was their way of saving the relationship, a relationship which became marriage a year after Jón came back from Prague, and lasted, at least on paper, until 1977, the year Sturla Jón graduated from Grammar School, two years later than his peers.

During Fanný and Jón's separation, it was her habit to make up theories, theories that Jón believed later came to poison every single moment of their relationship. That habit culminated in her idea that one day during their time together, in June 1957, she had had a son who came to nothing—that is, he died—while Jón was on an all-night bender with his friends, celebrating the completion of the very exams she'd never allowed herself to take because of her children, "the most idiotic stupidity a person can get mixed up in," as Sturla later heard his mother say when Hulda, his ex-wife and the mother of his five children, was pregnant with their last child, Hallgerður.

Fanný had been placed in a psychiatric ward three times, due to what Jón called "chronic daily confusion"—once while she lived with Jón, and twice during the three years she lived with another man—but since she had decided to live alone, and had moved into a little basement apartment on Nýlendugata where she still lived, she had managed to maintain a mental balance "with the help of the liquor which I never touched during the twenty years I lived with Jón Magnússon," as she described it to her son. It was, however, a balance that anyone who didn't know Fanný's past would be more likely to call a chronic imbalance.

Wasn't it somewhat unusual, Sturla thinks, as he and his father sit facing each other in Jón's living room and Sturla runs his eyes over the bookshelves, that at nearly seventy years old his father is occupied by the relatively new art form of the cinema—with all the enthusiasm of a childlike quest for learning—while it could easily be said that Sturla is overburdened by old-fashioned literary interests, which his father maintains need reinventing in the spirit of that young man who famously gave up poetry one-and-a-half centuries ago. Among the books on Jón's shelves is the newest edition of the Time Out Film Guide, a thick-spined book about the 1001 movies the reader ought to see before he dies; a biography of Billy Wilder; and a long row of black paperback screenplays from Faber and Faber. However, most of the space on the shelf is taken up by videocassettes and DVDs. On the coffee table lie a few oversized books about the movies of Pasolini and Milos Forman, and two smaller books by the Japanese photographer Nobuyoshi Araki. Sturla has no doubt that his father consciously chose to put these particular books on display as a demonstration of his antipathy to what one always sees in architecture magazines: the handsome coffee-table books in people's living rooms—books which are meant to suggest highly-refined taste.

One of the photographs in the second Nobuyoshi Araki book was a black and white image of a hooker in Tokyo; she sat, wearing a depressed expression, her thighs wide open, her hands bound at her feet, her eyes staring despondently at an electric dildo which someone else—perhaps Nobuyoshi, imagined Sturla—had placed in her vagina. Another picture was of a huge, steaming pool of piss on the floor of a train station; others variously depicted distressed female sex-workers (usually naked) and their fully clothed customers; or tired-looking office-workers on board the express train. A few pictures were images of the photographer's wife; in one she was alive; in another she was lying in her coffin, her final resting place. Sturla had flicked through the book the last time he visited the house at Skólavörðustígur 46. This time, he satisfies himself with placing it on the table and contemplating the color photograph on the back cover, an image of a younger Japanese woman in a kimono sticking a blood-red slice of watermelon between her lips, a slice shaped—or so Sturla Jón thinks—like an erect penis.

His thoughts turn to the Mother. With a capital M. And for a moment the word *myrkur*, darkness, occupies his mind. Although thirty years have passed since the publication of Sturla's first book, *The Flip Side of Words*, he is still troubled by his decision to use capital letters at the beginnings of poems and after periods; in some of the poems he'd gone so far as to imitate that peculiar custom by which English poets put capital letters at the start of lines. Except for the title of the book, Sturla still considered his first collection a worthy part of his oeuvre—although some of the poems were juvenilia, on the whole there was nothing to be ashamed of—and for that reason he was disturbed that the orthography of the book—his use of capitalization, etc.—hadn't been in keeping with the rest of his publications. But he knew he wouldn't be able to change that, even if this first book of his was one day reprinted. Long ago he had set himself the rule that he wouldn't change anything in his work once it left his hands. Only a few weeks after the publication of *The Flip Side of Words* Sturla had found out that, to put it baldly, using capital letters in poetic verse was wrong, as every word—two letter conjunctions as much as nouns or verbs—had equal weight and one shouldn't visually isolate words from their neighbors with these larger characters.

But now, when he thinks about the mother—his own mother and the one who stood by the window and stood for darkness and stood in the shadows—he discovers that the shape of the words calls for capitals, contrary to his *assertions*, and when he goes over in his mind the conversation he's just had with his father about poetry, the following imaginary exchange takes place, which he finds just as important and just as worthless as his life's work at this very moment:

STURLA: There are no more than forty-two people in this country interested in poetry. And not many more in other places.

JÓN: Are you sure? Only forty-two?
STURLA: Forty-two or forty-three, the difference isn't important.
JÓN: Then why are you stubbornly writing what you call poetry? Why not trick these works of yours into other kinds of text? I mean texts that call themselves something other than poetry.
STURLA: I am no longer stubbornly fixated on one or the other. I let others do the verse writing for me these days.
JÓN: But why don't you just quit?
STURLA: I have quit.

But Jón would be totally unaffected by Sturla's declaration. He wouldn't hear it. If you were to compare the two things, then Bezdomny's decision to stop writing poetry, in Bulgakov's novel, would doubtlessly affect Jón more deeply than his own son's decision to do the same; the latter was not a character in a novel by a Russian writer; he was not even a character in a novel. And to avoid irritating himself further over his father's lack of interest, Sturla thinks about the new overcoat he has hung on the chair in front of the oven in the kitchen. He imagines how the color of the overcoat will look against the color of the apartment building he lives in on Skúlagata when, or if, a photographer from a newspaper makes him stand in front of the white building and shoots at him like a madman, as photographers tend to, snapping photos as if this is the last subject they'll ever get to shoot in their careers. These wouldn't be snaps of just one more poet staring at the camera, like someone with absolutely no interest in being photographed or talked about on the pages of some rag. But when Sturla measures the beige-colored overcoat against the white walls of the apartment building, he feels like cream has been splashed on caramel pudding, a splashing that's accompanied by some splurting sounds which remind him of something—he isn't sure exactly what—from the kitchen, or from the cowshed of the farm he'd lived on one summer when he was a child. Sturla hates all metaphors from the world of food for their bad taste, especially when someone describes a work of art as being hard to swallow or digest. Sturla always ends up picturing the process of digestion, and more than once had been prevented from enjoying a work of art because someone had smudged it with a metaphor from the digestive system.

"Let the matches be," Sturla suddenly hears Jón say, interrupting his thoughts by indicating to his son that there is no need for him to use up the box of matches he has been playing with.

"Why do you have these matches out here?" asks Sturla, closing the box and setting it away from him on the table.

"Örn left them here yesterday," replies Jón, and when Sturla asks how things are going with the script he and Örn Featherby were working on—are they still working on the same script Jón had talked about before?—Jón stands up from the chair and asks Sturla to wait; he is going to get him a drink, they need to drink a toast of schnapps before Sturla goes to the Baltic.

"Have you talked to Fanný?" Jón calls from within the kitchen.

"I'm planning to drop in on her tomorrow," replies Sturla Jón, opening the box of matches again. "I'm going to let her have another copy of my book; she wants to make a gift of it. She's not in very good shape at the moment."

"'Not in very good shape?' You can be so old-fashioned, Sturla!"

Sturla considers it inappropriate for his father to speak to him that way (especially right now, just after he's finished criticizing the outmoded style of Sturla's poems). He's never gotten used to his father's need to always refer to his mother by her first name, rather than simply saying, "Have you talked to your mother?"

While Sturla lights another match and Jón repeats from the kitchen that the matches are Örn's, so he isn't allowed to light them, Sturla thinks about how the name Fanný conjures up in his mind the image of some woman out about town, a woman from the west side of town, on Nýlendugata. And as if to correct the formal wording which his father had mocked him for using, as though he were a small boy, he keeps on talking about his mother when Jón returns to the living room with shot glasses and schnapps. He decides to tell his father about the new methods Fanný is using to get alcohol, incomprehensible methods that the most ingenious of engineers or developers could be proud of, but Jón answers that this doesn't surprise him. Even though Fanný is Sturla's mother and she and Jón were married for twenty long years, the two of them, father and son (though he doesn't use the words "father and son"), will never understand anything that Fanný does or thinks. How could you explain, for instance, Fanný locking her husband in the bathroom for four hours? While Jón shakes his head over the memory, stands up and goes to the bathroom, Sturla recalls his father's account of the time he was shut out of family life in his own home, while the other family members moved freely about the small but roomy apartment on Mánagata. Sturla, who was only ten or eleven years old at the time, well remembers the atmosphere at home created by the following course of events:

MÁNAGATA

It is Saturday. The family has borrowed a car from Fanný's older sister Anný, and is planning to use the opportunity to drive to Hveragerði to see the monkey in the cage at the greenhouse restaurant, Eden. The idea, which had been discussed the previous evening, is to set off around noon and stop for lunch on the way: hotdogs at Litla kaffistofan, the coffee shop on Hellisheiði. This all took place shortly before Jón started working in the library; at the time, he was working as an assistant cameraman for the newly-established State television station. During the previous weeks he had been listening to Debussy's opera, *Pelléas and Mélisande*, with an eye to studying the atmosphere of the work and writing a script for the movie which would become his first production since he completed his film studies in Prague.

The mysterious and impenetrable French opera music has resounded through the apartment practically every minute Jón is home over the past weeks, but on this Saturday morning Fanný finally tells him she's had enough of this Symbolist sound world. She longs to hear some light music, some pop songs: they are, "for God's sake," about to go on a car trip out of town, which isn't an everyday event, and she doesn't want to sit in the car with the weight of French opera on her head. Jón's reaction to Fanný's complaint is initially positive. He says he will stop when this side of the record is done playing, but when Fanný asks him to stop at once, arguing that he doesn't reasonably need to listen to such music on a Saturday morning when the family is about to go and do something fun together, Jón replies that he doesn't want to remove the needle during the middle of the record; Fanný will have to wait ten minutes or so to get her way.

But she doesn't. Without any further warning she storms from the kitchen into the living room. She goes straight to the record player and yanks up the lid. And when she jerks the arm from the record there is a fearful screech of destruction: she has not only lifted the arm up but she has actually liberated it from the player. Fanný stands there for a few moments, looking at the narrow, oblong object as though she has no idea what purpose it serves.

With his long and trying experience of Fanný's tantrums, Jón sits still in his seat, looking at his wife as she holds the torn-off arm with its diamond needle, a needle which just moments before was releasing the sublime music of Debussy from the black vinyl. She declares—making it sound like she'd had a purposeful plan based on a rational appraisal of the right and wrong of the situation—that this (and by "this" she means what she's done to the record player) is what happens when someone isn't listened to, when that person's patience is taken as collateral for some ten minutes of opera music.

Sturla's reaction to this sudden household war is much the same as his father's. Sitting at his writing desk in the bedroom (they had one bedroom between them, which shared a wall with living room) he immediately knows what has happened, and he also knows that it pays to show self-control. Once Fanný gives up waiting for her husband to react—after they have both given themselves sufficient time to think about it, Jón in the easy-chair, Fanný standing in the middle of the floor—she puts down the arm and the needle and goes back into the kitchen. Just then, Sturla hears his father clear his throat, and shortly afterwards the sound of the bathroom door being locked.

This has happened before: his mother would stop something with her hands, something which could have been more easily stopped with words, and his father would disappear into the only room in the apartment that could be locked with a key.

A few minutes later, when Fanný has finished with the provisions, she bangs on the bathroom door, tugging at the handle and demanding that Jón produce himself; she will have the record player repaired. Sturla can't detect any great remorse in his mother's words, but whether it is there or not, she has no success; his father wants something more, perhaps something else from Fanný or perhaps simply more time and space alone in his locked bathroom. By the time he has been in the bathroom for fifteen minutes Fanný has finished getting everything ready for the car trip. The only thing missing is the driver. But whatever she tries, she gets no response, either to her repeated apologies or to her beseeching, and when another quarter of an hour has passed it becomes clear what is happening: Jón intends to remain there in peace and quiet, which isn't a surprising outcome when you think that all Fanný wanted was peace and quiet.

Fanný's next move is to tidy the living room; she whistles some pop tune as she cleans, as though declaring she has nothing remarkable to think about, but then Sturla hears her moving the furniture around. This evidently requires some effort, and as if to cement the dynamic that has been created in the household, she sets the chair which Jón was sitting in just half-an-hour ago against the bathroom door; she then places the coffee table between the chair and the wall opposite the bathroom. As a result of her labors, going through the hall now means climbing over a high chair-back then along the full-length coffee table, which extends most of the way towards the front door (which opens in); this makes it impossible to leave the apartment, unless you move the table further into the hallway, closer to the kitchen. The next thing Sturla hears from Fanný is an indirect order to go out and play by himself: You shouldn't hang about inside in such fine weather.

Nothing more was said about the trip to Hveragerði; that topic of conversation wasn't taken up again until the day's events were recalled much later, after Jón and Fanný had separated, when those peoples' worlds—as Sturla describes it to himself, sitting in his father's living room on Skólavörðuholt—had changed completely. But in order to go outside (as he'd been told to), Sturla had needed his mother's help to move the living room table away from the front door: he got outside by climbing over it—without creating a way to open the bathroom door (which, unlike the kitchen door, only opened outwards).

Later, Sturla would connect this peculiar memory about his childhood home to a poem he'd once translated from English, a kind of hotel poem by some Eastern European poet (he had entirely forgotten the name) in which an ageless gentleman (he especially remembered the word "ageless") walked into his closet (which was how the poem described his hotel room) from the rainy street outside. Later, another ageless person entered the poem, an elegant woman who was emptying a laundry basket while the gentleman threw his cigar into the street, and together they entered another closet off from the rainy street, a closet which had a curtain, a washing bowl, and a hook. Although Sturla had long ago lost the translation, and it had never been published, the poem remained in his mind, not least because he could compare the image to the outside of the bathroom door at Mánagata, which had an iron hook. Fanný was always intending to remove this (but never getting round to it) because Hallmundur, Jón's brother, tended to hang his overcoat on the hook when he came to visit. Every time Hallmundur had left, Fanný always complained—Sturla remembered clearly—that she hated having an overcoat hanging on the wall between the bathroom and the kitchen.

About three hours later, when Sturla comes home because he has fallen out of a tree and given himself a bloody cut on the leg, Fanný has to move the chair and table away from the bathroom door: the child needs a band-aid and she doesn't have any rubbing alcohol handy to disinfect the wound; both these items are kept in the closet above the bathroom sink. Jón strides out of the bathroom, gets himself some milk and cookies from the kitchen, and covers himself with a blanket on the living-room sofa.

For the rest of the day, silence reigns. Fanný looks after Sturla and, to make up for missing the monkey in Hveragerði, she calls Hallmundur, Jón's brother, and gives the two young friends, Jónas and Sturla, money to go to a movie at the theater on Snorrabraut. But although what happened that day seems to have been for the most part forgotten, especially after Fanný comes home one day with a new record player—a better model than they'd previously had—one thing stands out like a neon sign: a few words Jón wrote in lipstick on the wall above the bathtub, words which stuck fast in Sturla's memory, for he'd managed to read them when he went into the bathroom with his mother to get a band-aid and rubbing alcohol. She hadn't gotten him out of the room quickly enough. Long afterwards, Sturla would associate a piano sonata by Domenico Scarlatti, which he heard by chance on the state radio station when he was younger, with his father's message on the bathroom wall— a message which, even as a child, Sturla had thought pretty childish. And this had played a huge part in his beginning to feel that it was worthwhile to create things which at first glance didn't seem to have any value, either for him or for those around him.

"You make it sound like you were listening to *Dýrin í Hálsaskógi* or *Peter and the Wolf*," Fanný calls out to Jón once she has cleaned the words off the wall and come out of the bathroom.

Her comment immediately lodges in Sturla's mind because two years before the whole family had gone to a performance of the Thorbjörn Egner play at the National Theatre, and Sturla has considerable difficulty connecting Lilli the climbing mouse and his companions with the music that had screeched out from the record player in the living room four hours earlier.

And so Fanný stands in the doorway of the living room and asks brusquely: "Murder which child?" But she doesn't receive any response from Jón, who is now lying under a comforter in the living room.

FRAKKASTÍGUR

"You're visiting her tomorrow, you say?" Jón asks, snapping his son out of his revery.

"Yes, I'm planning to stop by tomorrow," replies Sturla.

As often happened after Fanný was mentioned, they fall silent for a while. But just when Sturla appears to have lost himself in the book about Pasolini which was lying on the table, Jón inquires about the journey to Lithuania and advises him—without being asked—to buy himself a cell phone before going abroad. His new book has just been published, and it is important first of all because it is likely someone will want to get hold of him—something even Sturla has to admit, if only to himself, is an astute observation—and, what's more, he'll be able to get in touch with home from wherever he is, without having to rely on extortionately priced hotel telephones or that phenomena which is rapidly vanishing from the streets of the world: phone booths.

"You also ought to take some U.S. dollars with you," continues Jón, and when Sturla points out to him that in the independent state of Lithuania people aren't any better off waving American banknotes around—there are no longer two bars in the hotels, one for domestic currency and another for foreign—Jón interrupts, arguing that this isn't true: a society which has spent fifty years believing that its own currency is worthless needs another fifty years to persuade itself of the contrary; whether Lithuania was a self-governed state or not, Sturla should nevertheless travel with some U.S. dollars. Moreover, he will need a suitcase on wheels. Jón could get a case like that for him from his friend Örn, which he never uses anyway, but hearing his father's suggestions, Sturla realizes he's had more than enough advice.

"Relax, pop," he says, asking whether he can't instead lend him some movie or other to watch this evening; he has a brand new suitcase at home for the little luggage he plans to take overseas.

Jón stares at his son as if he's trying to guess what movie might suit this fifty-one-year-old man who he'd had a hand in shaping. That, he concludes, will be a movie from the library by an Iranian director, a pretty smart movie which he actually needs to return to the library the following day (it has been reserved). It would be fine for Sturla to stop by with the video around 10:00 tomorrow, since he won't take the bus into Hafnarfjörður before 10:30.

Sturla picks up the video and reads the text on the back of the case. Apparently, the movie is about a middle-aged man who decides to commit suicide, and has to find someone who will bury him after he's accomplished his task.

"An uplifting movie," quips Sturla, but Jón doesn't see any reason to respond. "Everyone tries to get him to change his mind," Sturla reads from the case, and his father nods his head in agreement. Sturla puts the movie in his plastic bag.

"When were Gogol's Petersburg stories published?" he asks his father as he takes his overcoat from the back of the chair in the kitchen and strokes the surface to see whether it has dried.

"I reckon that must have been around 1840," replies Jón.

"No, I meant the new Icelandic translation. The one that came out last year or the year before last."

"Wasn't it published last year or the year before that?"

"That's what I think, yes"

"Well, there's the answer to your question," says Jón, watching Sturla put on his overcoat.

They say their goodbyes. Jón wishes his son safe travels, but Sturla reminds him that they will be seeing each other tomorrow when he returns the movie, so he says he'll hold off on a proper farewell.

The weather has cooled since Sturla came in to the warmth of his father's house an hour earlier. As he goes past the Hotel Leifur Eiríksson on Skólavörðustígur then down Frakkastígur in the direction of Laugavegur it begins to snow. Snowflakes float lightly to earth in the twilight, an image Sturla tells himself he hasn't seen for many years; he feels like it hasn't snowed like this in Reykjavík since he was a kid. But just as he is wondering whether the weather in the Baltic will be like this, his foot slips on the wet sidewalk and he almost swings the plastic bag into a couple of kids who are walking towards him from Njálsgata. The hundred-kronur coins from the casino jingle in time with the quick motion of the bag, and after Sturla apologizes to the pair he reminds himself to go to the bank on the corner of Laugavegur and Barónsstígur before heading home.

He decides there and then to use the money he has received, these coins, to buy himself something special in Lithuania, something that will always remind him of the trip, the way he suspects the new overcoat will. In a book he read about the Baltic countries, Sturla had learned that in Vilnius sophisticated people bought jewelry made of amber—that was the local specialty, designs and creations made from fossilized resin—but he doesn't have any use for such things, other than to give it to someone, and in the future a knick-knack he gave to someone would hardly remind him of a trip he'd taken on his own.

LÆKJARGATA

The soft winter sun lights up the classroom. Jónas Hallmundsson looks out of the window over Lækjargata and appears not to be listening as the teacher, Armann Valur, begins joking with his pupils that they are now one month into the new system of dating time, a system that began with the eruption on Vestmannaeyjar, the Westman Islands, on January 23rd of that year. He starts talking about the time he stayed in the town of Westman Islands ten years ago, when he visited a schoolmate of his from "this very school, this distinguished school," and stayed at his parents' house for a few weeks. At that time, in 1961, he'd been sure a huge volcanic eruption would take place there, and even though Surtsey Island had erupted a couple of years later "in that vicinity," he'd never lost the faith that the Devil would bring the blesséd Westman Islands to world attention by spewing his powerful essence over the place.

"And because of that," he continues, "I'm now giving myself permission to invite you up to the board, one at a time, and ask you a few questions about these famous islands of the Westmen, the Vestmannaeyjar." He turns back to them, flexes his shoulders and stretches his arms out on both sides. Then he lets them fall quickly down to his sides and calls the name of a girl in the class, asking her to be so good as to "trot up to the blackboard." The girl's name, Ljótunn, always had an effect on her classmates, the girls no less than the boys: everyone would look up or show some other indication that they had heard her name mentioned, not just because it was an unusual, embarrassing name but because it was so ironic: her facial beauty—not to mention her physical beauty—was undeniable (if you can describe beauty in such terms). Just as people tend to look at the light rather than the dark, they tended to look at Ljótunn rather than the person next to her, if they could.

"How many islands comprise the Vestmannaeyjar?" asks Armann Valur when the girl has come up to the board and stands facing the class. "Do you know?"

"Aren't there fifteen?" replies Ljótunn.

"That's what I'm asking," says Armann Valur, smiling. "You have to answer."

"I guess it's fourteen."

"The number gets lower," says Armann Valur.

"There are twelve." Ljótunn corrects herself; her final answer.

"Not bad," says Armann Valur after thinking for a moment, and addresses the girl by name again; he enjoyed saying her name. "Not bad, Ljótunn; there *are* exactly twelve. When you fly over them. Seen from land, there are perhaps no more than one or two, but when someone flies over them, I mean on a big iron bird, he needs the fingers of both hands, plus two of the fingers of the person sitting next to him, in order to count them. There are exactly twelve." He asks the girl another question which she can't answer, then he asks her to sit back down. She is now out of the game, this is a knockout round.

As Ljótunn goes to her desk and sits down, Armann Valur follows her to her seat with his eyes, even though he knows the other pupils will notice if he indulges his temptation to watch her. Then he scans the room and settles on Jónas Hallmundsson, who is still busy thinking about what is happening down on the street outside the school building.

"Jónas Hallmundsson," says Armann in a commanding tone. "Would you like to be next in our Vestmannaeyjar quiz?"

Jónas nods his head and glances at the person sitting next to him, his friend Brynjólfur Madsen, who shakes his head, as if to say that he wouldn't take part in this nonsense himself. Brynjólfur looks away from him to Armann Valur as he begins asking Jónas his first question:

"What is the temperature of a simmering lava field?"

Jónas looks out the window.

"You won't find the answer out in Lækjargata," says Armann Valur, his arms folded and an amused expression on his face.

"A hundred degrees," replies Jónas.

The picture which Armann Valur made of himself, with his arms across his chest and a boastful expression on his face, momentarily calls to mind Benito Mussolini on the balcony of the Palazzo Venezia in Rome, talking to his people. "Very good, very good," he says, nodding his head quickly. He removes his arms from his chest, and when a pupil in the next row starts to make a comment about Jónas's reply, Armann stops him with a wave of his hand. "But tell me this, Jónas: How many inhabitants lost their lives when that awful eruption took place on the islands?"

"Everyone," replies Jónas, without hesitation.

"Everyone, you say?"

"Everyone but one."

"The number keeps getting lower," says Armann Valur, smiling.

"Then I'll subtract the one," Jónas says, repeating his original answer.

"You're exactly right, as ever," says Armann Valur cheerfully, indicating to one of the rows of students that they should quiet down. "For the Islanders, the most wonderful thing about this astonishing eruption is that none of them was killed. They can thank their God, Betel, for that, the ones who survived."

Stifled laughter can be heard from the back of the room. Armann Valur casts a meaningful glance at two longhaired boys who are sitting side by side, his eyes questioning whether he has said something funny, whether they have found a reason to start giggling like little girls. Then he turns back to Jónas Hallmundsson who is once again looking out the window.

"And now we come to your third question, Jónas. If you answer it correctly, then you're in the final. That, I reckon, would be a great victory. The prize—so you know now there's definitely something to strive for—is a plane trip for one to the Vestmannaeyjar; a plane-trip, obviously, which the victor has to take in his imagination, because as you well know the principal has lately disapproved of schoolteachers sending pupils out of the country, even in the service of knowledge. But the question is–" Armann looks at Brynjólfur leaning towards Jónas so he can whisper something to him, and he jabs his index finger in the air to add emphasis to his next words: "Now, Brynjólfur, you aren't allowed to slip him the answer before I pose the question."

And both Jónas and Brynjólfur smile at their teacher.

"The question is this," continues Armann Valur. "What nickname do the island boys have for the puffins they kill? And do they use their stately animal, the puffin . . . ?" He hesitates a few moments while he works out how to continue. "This question has two parts: What is the nickname the Westman Islanders have for the puffin, and do they use it—that is to say, the bird, once they have stuffed it—to promote their islands abroad? I must admit this is a complicated question, but we are at the Grammar School in Reykjavík, where things tend to be complicated."

Jónas looks thoughtful. Armann Valur reiterates to Brynjólfur that he isn't allowed to help his companion, and then Jónas answers:

"'Professor.' They call the puffins 'professor.' And yes, one could say that the stuffed puffin is a kind of ambassador for the people who live on the island."

Armann looks at his pupil. He takes off his glasses, breathes on the inside of the glass and puts them back on. "Perhaps 'provost.' But 'professor' . . . I'm not of the opinion that professor is a better name for this strange bird. This wonderbird."

"I'd be fine with provost," says Jónas.

"Yes, no, well, we should think a little about 'professor.' Let us—those of us who are gathered here in this room at the Grammar School in Reykjavík—decide that the island boys' stuffed puffin is called 'Professor.' That's quite logical, since those island boys and girls are a well-educated bunch." Armann Valur clears his throat and traces his index finger in the air to summon his pupils' attention. Then he starts speaking as though he's giving a lecture: "In the Vestmannaeyjar everyone has a university degree. The young as much as the old. At any given moment one-quarter of the residents have doctorates in this and that from the university on the mainland. It may be that they call their bird provost when it's alive and on the run from the pocket nets of the over-educated islanders. But when it's stuffed, that black-and-white bird of wisdom—which is the type of bird we are now considering—is better called professor. It is a professor of taxidermy, to be precise: it has studied its own stuffing. After all, it knows all about the straw which is packed in its head as soon as its brain has been removed. It yearns for its eternal existence on a plinth of lava; every movement of its wings, every single take-off, it is always aiming to achieve its fate as soon as possible."

A pupil towards the end of the middle row raises his hand to ask for permission to speak but Armann Valur continues without stopping:

"You have to find out for yourself," he says, and then directs his words straight to Jónas, who is busily taking notes on a sheet of paper while obviously having difficultly holding in his laughter. "I notice that you are taking notes, Jónas. That is good. Notes can find you in surprising places—they're not tied down the way they would be when they're written into paragraphs." He hesitates and weighs his words. "Because we are not simply written words. Við erum ekki . . . 'We are not the stuffed men,' to quote the poet. To *mis*quote the poet. We don't get an eternal life on a plinth of lava." He glances around, clears his throat again and turns back quickly to tell Jónas, "You will have a career in the diplomatic service."

Jónas has a questioning look in his eyes.

"One day you'll be a representative for our people. And possibly for the Vestmannaeyjar too."

Jónas Hallmundsson is the Icelandic teacher Armann Valur's favorite student, as is evident from the way his classmates react to this declaration: they, especially the boys, are irritated. Besides, Árman has a closer relationship with Jónas than he has with his other pupils.

Armann had once invited Jónas to his place, to his apartment on Rauðarárstígur. One afternoon immediately after final exams at the end of Jónas's second year at the school they had met by chance on the upper part of Laugavegur, and after talking together and realizing that Jónas's uncle, Jón Magnússon, was Armann's former classmate and an acquaintance, Armann seized the opportunity to invite Jónas home to see photographs of the old friends when they were at Grammar School. And to make sure that his young pupil accepted the offer, Armann said he wanted to give him a small volume of poetry written by another friend of his; he was sure Jónas enjoyed poetry.

This was true, though Jónas barely indicated it—it was almost as if he wanted to hide his interest.

The host's generosity exceeded what Jónas considered appropriate for a teacher to his pupil. After Armann had offered him a pilsner (which he stored on the windowsill), showed him some photographs from a drinking party (with the face of Jónas's uncle, Jón Magnússon, smack in the middle of them), and given him a faded photocopied booklet of poems by Jónatan Jóhannsson (whose nickname was Jójó), he absolutely insisted that Jónas let him buy them a meal at Matstofa

Austurbæjar, a cheap and cheerful diner close to the corner of Snorrabraut and Laugavegur. Jónas had to use considerable skill in turning down the invitation, but Armann reacted with no less cunning by making his guest promise that he could invite him to Matstofa some other time—he considered it an honor and felt that, in the natural course of mentoring his promising pupil, they ought to share a meal. They kept that promise, but not until much later, about a year after Jónas had graduated from the school, when he met Armann in the Lindargata liquor store one Friday and went with him to Hressingarskálinn, where they had coffee (with measures of schnapps) and Danishes.

Jónas later told his cousin Sturla Jón about that afternoon over coffee at Hressingarskálinn, after Jónas had stopped in to visit Sturla at the Útvegsbanki one lunchtime. The conversation had remained with Sturla Jón; he would remember it every time he went into the McDonalds that was later installed in the building which formerly housed Hressingarskálinn.

"And you, Brynjólfur Madsen," says Armann Valur after he'd informed them all that Jónas had reached the final. "I'm going to ask you the next question, since you're sitting beside Jónas. What are the letter markings those Islanders put on their ships?" There is no doubt that Armann Valur gets some satisfaction out of pronouncing the name "Madsen," though the way he exaggerates the Danish sound of it is entirely at odds with the bearer of the name. But before Brynjólfur can answer, Armann jumps in with a sudden gesture, saying "Forgive me, Brynjólfur, but I believe it's better to ask your colleague Völundur Ermenreksson this question." He turns to a boy who had been trying to join in the quiz a moment ago and says, "Völundur Ermenreksson, you should be able to tell me what letters they use on the prow of their fleet, the Westman Islanders."

He has barely spoken when the school bell rings.

Armann Valur, who stopped teaching at the Grammar School in Reykjavík the year after Jónas graduated, went on to teach Icelandic to Sturla Jón at the university, where Sturla began studying the same year he stopped working at the bank. And that same winter, in April 1978, Jónas Hallmundsson took his own life. It happened the same day—possibly the same hour—that Sturla Jón bought himself a used (and very badly treated) copy of a record by the English electric folk band Steeleye Span, All Around My Hat, in a collector's shop on Laugavegur.

Even though one could say, without hesitation, that those two contemporaries and cousins, Sturla and Jónas, had been brought up almost as brothers until they were twelve or thirteen years old, Jónas's suicide didn't effect Sturla the way he felt it should have, given that Jónas was a close relative. During their high school years they began to grow apart, and even though they had common interests in their formative years, not least an enthusiasm for poetry and politics, other aspects of their personalities began to clash, which led to a greater and greater rift between them. This rift was deep and difficult to overlook in the eyes of their fathers, the brothers Jón and Hallmundur, on account of the friendship and close relationship they had shared since childhood. The insurmountable gap was formalized when they each registered for graduate study: Jón at the Grammar School in Reykjavík and Sturla in the Icelandic Business School.

In fact, they didn't really understand this—least of all Jón Magnússon—because the Icelandic Business School was an unexpected choice for Sturla Jón. When he was questioned, often jokingly (why did someone who couldn't tell the difference between kronur and aurar, dollars and cents, need to know which was debit and which credit?) Sturla would answer that he bore a grudge against the complacent and arrogant Grammar School; he wanted to associate with a different kind of people, so he was throwing his lot in with the enemy. Additionally, there were cute girls in Business School; the daughters of company owners went there. But whether or not Sturla learned to arrange sums of money in columns marked "debit" and "credit," he completed the final exams at Business School. Though studying there didn't get him into the apartment of the daughter of prosperous parents, nor did he sneak himself into the enemy's confidences, he managed to learn that he ought to avoid everything in life concerned with money, for as long as possible, and he also learned to type—something which he later used when writing and which made a difference in the work he was able to get at the bank once he'd completed his studies.

Soon after Sturla started "working with money," as he described his business with the telex machine at the bank, Jónas showed up suddenly one morning in the doorway of Foreign Business Transactions, wanting to invite his relative for coffee at Hressingarskálinn. Although it wasn't the appropriate time to take a coffee break, Sturla got permission from his supervisor to step out. Apart from meeting once in a while at family gatherings, which were rare events, and running into each other in the city center while they were in school, the cousins hadn't really talked since high school. Even though it turned out that Sturla had to pay for Jónas's food and drink at Hressingarskálinn, he still appreciated that Jónas had decided to drop in on him.

But the renewal of their friendship soon made Sturla unhappy. When Jónas started dropping in on him regularly during office hours (instead of visiting him at home, since Sturla was living with his father at the time) and when the motivation for a friendly visit was more often than not to ask Sturla for money, it became clear to Sturla that the cousins had nothing in common, and he began to wish that his connection to Jónas could be more like the imaginary acquaintances he'd had with characters in novels that were in vogue that year, promising unfortunates who seemed to despise everything around them, but who mostly just hated themselves. It became clear that Jónas was drinking more than was healthy, and what sat even worse with Sturla was that Jónas, somewhat passive-aggressively, looked down on his cousin Sturla's fledgling attempts at writing poetry.

As for the "financial aid" he gave his once lost, now found-again cousin, Sturla was quite sure he had, to put it baldly, provided the capital for the liquor and pills which Jónas used to put an end to his life in April, 1978. He had loaned Jónas five thousand kronur two days before he died, and if what Sturla had heard was correct—that there were two empty bottles of Black Death and two empty containers of Magnyl painkillers on the table by the bed where Jónas was found—it was difficult to imagine anything other than that the fatal dose had been bought with the five thousand kronur. Fanný said she had seen Jónas going past her kitchen window at Mánagata the day before he committed the deed, and he'd been holding a black plastic bag, which meant he'd come from Ríkið, the state liquor store on Snorrabraut, on the way home to his rented basement room on Meðalholt. Fanný was, in other words, the last family member to see Jónas alive, and news about his suicide had dealt her such a blow that she didn't trust herself to go to Jónas's funeral, something which Hallmundur and Þeba, Jónas's mother, never forgave her for.

Sturla often thought about his father's comment that he couldn't understand why Fanný hadn't knocked on the window as Jónas went past that day—why she hadn't invited him in, given how enamored she was of their young nephew and how much she longed to have visitors in her solitude on Mánagata.

As cynical as it sounds, Sturla had calculated a rather simple math problem—a relatively clear debit-and-credit situation—in which, as a repayment of all those little amounts of money he'd loaned his cousin, he deserved to inherit a particular item Jónas had possessed, something which originally belonged to Sturla's maternal grandfather. Fanný had given the item to Jónas when her father died, and it was something Sturla had longed to own. He'd always thought he would inherit it himself, never imagining that anyone else would lay claim to it when Benedikt died—or that his mother would think to give it to her brother-in-law's family. The item in question was a high-quality light-brown leather folder which the ambassador Benedikt always kept on his desk in the embassy in Oslo and later, after he moved home, in his office on Reynimelur. It wasn't so much the tired, strange beauty of this Norwegian document folder that had attracted Sturla when he was a child peering into his grandfather's office: what he had found thrilling was that Benedikt, the esteemed public servant, had used it as a base when he wrote letters and reflections, and he put all kinds of papers into the leather folder, papers that, in Sturla's mind, were certain to contain crucial information about relations between the Island in the North and the Rest of the World.

Jónas had probably admired the folder too when he and his parents visited Benedikt and Anna at Reynimelur, but Fanný's decision that he should inherit it was indicative of her nonsensical belief that he was the promising intellectual in the family: such a jewel ought to be in the hands of a thinker. It was true that Sturla ended up making use of some of the ideas Jónas had thought up and kept in the folder, and it was also true that Sturla's grandfather's folder had contained those ideas, but in other respects Jónas's life turned out to be a poor model. He never became the promising and self-assured ambassador Armann Valur had predicted he would in the classroom on Lækjargata the year Heimaey erupted. He was never sent overseas on behalf of his country.

SKÚLAGATA

The clock shows seven minutes on the way towards 12:00 when the telephone on Sturla's nightstand rings. He was up until about 4:30 in the morning; he sat at the kitchen table, practically without getting up, from 10:00 in the evening until 2:00 in the morning, drafting a narrative of the poetry festival. And then, between 2:00 and 4:00, he sat in the room with the printed text in front of him on the table, only moving to get a beer from the kitchen. He later listened to some John Martyn songs while he drank his last beer and collected his thoughts, before falling asleep on the living room sofa and waking around 9:00 to go to the bathroom and from there to the bedroom. He is not particularly well rested, therefore, when his father wakes him by calling.

"You never came by with the tape," are the first words Sturla Jón hears said on this bright October day. And immediately he runs through the mental to-do list he had prepared for his next-to-last day before going to Lithuania. He'd meant to get into the list earlier in the morning: he plans to buy a cell phone (Jón had told him that before starting to use such a phone one would need to charge the battery for a full twenty-four hours); he plans to talk to Jónatan Jóhannsson, Jójó, about the article for the magazine; and he plans to visit his mother at Nýlendugata—he knows she will be devastated if he doesn't go to say goodbye before he leaves.

"It got stuck in the machine," Sturla answers, watching his alarm clock change to 11:08.

"What do you mean, stuck in the machine?"

Sturla Jón gets out of bed and starts dressing himself while describing to his father how the tape of the Iranian movie had held his attention for half-an-hour without him actually getting to see any of the movie. He'd put the cassette in the VCR (the way a person puts a cassette in the VCR) and after the tape had played for a few seconds it stopped, and didn't just stop: the tape had been wrenched out from the black plastic case into the bowels of the machine, and so there was no way to get the tape out of the machine without cutting it or taking the machine itself apart. Neither option had seemed promising.

"There's a man here waiting for the tape," Jón says, and he reminds Sturla of something he already knows well, even though he is poorly rested and has a headache: he had planned to return the tape to his father at Skólavörðustígur before he went to work.

"Didn't the library only just open?" And Sturla asks himself a question he hadn't really thought much about before: shouldn't his father have retired and be collecting his pension, now that he is in his sixty-eighth year?

"Yes, it opened ten minutes ago," answers Jón.

"Isn't the time in Hafnarfjörður the same as in Reykjavík?"

"You ought to have someone untangle the movie from the machine for you, if you can't do it yourself," says his father, scoldingly. "He's waiting here for it, that man."

"What type of person waits for the library in Hafnarfjörður to open in the morning to get himself an Iranian movie?" Sturla asks his father, realizing straightaway that this remark has only managed to slip out because last night's alcohol is still in his bloodstream, and that there's a chance drunkenness might have played a role in the powerful inspiration which had gripped him when writing his article.

"There are people, even in Hafnarfjörður, who are interested in movies which aren't American or British," replies Jón. The man who was waiting for the movie had ordered it from the library yesterday; he should have known it was a total mistake to lend Sturla a movie that someone was going to borrow the next day.

Sturla says he will take the machine to get repaired this afternoon; Jón will have to give the man a different movie instead.

"Did you just wake up?" asks Jón.

Sturla glances at the clock and tells himself it is absurd for the sixty-seven-year-old father to scold his fifty-one-year-old son for not waking up early enough. Without it having occurred to him before, Sturla begins thinking about another father and son relationship, and he answers his father's question by saying that he wrote his Judgment last night—his own *Urteil*—which took him exactly the same amount of time it took Kafka to write his, from 10:00 in the evening until 2:00 in the morning. He is going to let Jójó have the text for his magazine before he leaves for Lithuania. It is in a way a "departure" from the things he has written before: it isn't only a judgment against himself but it's also a well-reasoned, constructive article about the current state of poetry.

Without making a dig at his son's accomplishment—without even making a sarcastic remark about the editor Jónatan Jóhannsson, as Sturla expected him to—Jón tells him to have the movie ready by tomorrow. Then he says goodbye, hangs up, and immediately calls back to remind his son to buy a phone, as he advised him the day before. "I can show you how it works when you bring me the movie in the morning," he adds.

Sturla sighs deeply and shakes his head. When he goes out of the bedroom into the living room, buck-naked, he notices the living-room table is covered in white sheets, books, and empty beer bottles which he'd arranged at one end of the table. "Two hours away from the city." He strokes his stomach and then his hand travels down to scratch his crotch. He picks up a sheet of paper from the table and reads aloud: "Two hours away from the city. By Sturla Jón Jónsson." Then he goes back into the bedroom and puts on dark blue, rather baggy chinos, a wine-red shirt, a brown cardigan, and white socks. He goes to the tall living room window and looks out at Akrafjall mountain, Esjan, and the gas station on Skúlagata, and he repeats to himself, quietly, the title of the article, Two hours away from the city.

He gets himself coffee and cookies. Next he clears the beer bottles from the living-room table, disconnects the VCR and places it in a plastic bag. He stands for a minute in front of the coat hooks, debating whether to go out in his new overcoat or his blue duffel coat, and after looking at the weather out of the kitchen window he opts for the latter, wrapping a striped scarf once around his neck before he leaves.

When Sturla comes back home from town roughly two hours later, having taken the machine in for repair on the east side of town and having bought himself a cell phone on Laugavegur—that least expensive one he could find—he finds in his mailbox, along with the daily newspaper which gets delivered free of charge, an envelope from an institute called the International Biographical Center in Cambridge, England.

"That could make a good scene in a novel about me," he thinks as he looks at the envelope while waiting for the elevator. When he reminds himself that he still hasn't written a novel—hasn't even made up his mind yet what sort of novel he will write—he argues back to himself that the scene he has just experienced would be perfect as a key moment in the story he feels sure he will write, eventually: the protagonist one day receives a letter from overseas which unexpectedly casts a new light on his life; in the reader's mind, this establishment would offer a complete contrast to the character. "I, the superintendent of an apartment building, the person the residents of other apartments rely on when something goes wrong in the building, am waiting for the elevator while holding a letter which I have received from the International Biographical Center, *alþjóðlegri ævisagnamiðstöð*." He translates the sender's name on the envelope into his own language and, as he is wondering whether it is only by mistake that a letter from such an institute could be sent to Mr. Sturla Jon Jonsson, Skúlagata 40, 101 Reykjavik, Iceland, one of his neighbors appears, a man of a similar age who—going by what Sturla has read on his mailbox—is married with four children.

"Hey," says the man.

Sturla returns the greeting and notices that his neighbor is holding the handle of a broom—a broom Sturla bought on behalf of all the residents a few weeks ago to keep in the basement laundry room; he'd received complaints from one apartment in the building that they didn't have anything for sweeping away snow in winter.

"Listen, tell me something," the man says, "how is it that . . ."

As Sturla waits for him to continue he ponders whether the man is planning to take the broom up to his apartment permanently or whether he will return it afterwards. But nothing more comes of the man's question; the elevator door opens and the man—who Sturla remembers is called Þorlákur—points at the plastic bag in Sturla's hand, asking whether he has bought a phone.

"Yes," replies Sturla, and he asks himself whether the residents of the building think it is perfectly normal to ask their super what he is up to. Wasn't it a little bold of the man, who doesn't know him at all, other than in passing, to inquire about the contents of the bag he is carrying into his house? Does the man know, for example, that Sturla is a poet? Had it come up at one of the tenants' meetings Sturla is required to attend? No. He is not listed that way either in the phone book or on his mailbox. Even though the attendant in the clothing store the day before—the man on the street—had known his line of work (that is, his other job, not as a super) Sturla reckons it unlikely that many of his neighbors know he is involved in writing poetry.

He likes that idea: living alone in a huge apartment block in Reykjavík and sending out a body of literary work which, perhaps, none of the people from the building had any idea could be bought in the bookstores.

What's more, he isn't just a poet who has published some books: he has been selected on the merit of those books—and probably because of his character, too—to be sent to another country as the appointed representative of the people. This fact is foremost in Sturla's mind when his neighbor asks:

"A cell phone, if I'm not mistaken?"

"Yes, that's right," Sturla answers.

"I don't know where we'd be without those phones," the man continues, asking Sturla with his eyes whether or not he pressed the right button.

Probably in the same place, Sturla thinks to himself: here in a lift on the first floor, about to ascend to the upper floors. But instead he says, without pause: "I only got this phone just now, because I'm going overseas."

"And where are you traveling to?" his neighbor asks.

"To Lithuania."

"Lithuania?"

"It'll be cheaper to use a cell phone abroad than to use the phone in the hotel room," Sturla adds. He realizes immediately that he's just given his neighbor, who's practically a stranger, the mental image of him lying in a hotel room, far away from home.

"A hotel in Lithuania?"

But before Sturla can decide whether he ought to confirm the picture which has clearly popped up in the man's head, there is a new question:

"Isn't Lithuania some place near Russia?"

"It's by the Baltic Sea."

"Yes, it's by the Baltic Sea," says the man.

"It's between Poland and Belarus."

"Belarus?"

"It's like a part of Russia," Sturla hears himself explain. "Or of the Soviet Union, to be precise. It was part of the Soviet Union."

"Lithuania? Didn't the Icelandic people sign a petition on behalf of Lithuania not that long ago?"

"I couldn't say," answers Sturla.

"Three hundred thousand signatures. I think that our Foreign Minister went over there and delivered it to the president of Lithuania. Or the prime minister."

"What was the reason for the signatures?" asks Sturla. "Did you sign?"

"No, not me."

"I didn't know anything about it," says Sturla. "It's rather unlikely that there were enough Icelanders for three hundred thousand signatures, if both ours were missing, right?"

"That's true. Unless I've got it backwards, and Lithuania signed something for Iceland."

Although Sturla is quite content to keep talking about topics on which he, Sturla, is clearly better informed, he decides to steer the conversation away from geography and the collecting of signatures for petitions and towards something his interlocutor will surely know more about: "You could say I'm going on a business trip of sorts," he says, looking around nonchalantly, as if the business he is going to conduct isn't at all remarkable.

At that moment the elevator door opens, but the information Sturla has just announced makes his neighbor press the button that holds the door open and turn to Sturla; he looks like someone who has just been told something he long suspected.

"You're going on a business trip to Lithuania, you say?"

"Yes, kind of," replies Sturla Jón, realizing that the explanation "business trip to Lithuania" suggests he is involved in a drug deal or prostitution, or maybe both. He feels he'd better correct the misunderstanding, but he doesn't want to directly state that misunderstanding—in case there isn't one. But his neighbor jumps in first, accompanying his words with a smile that is clearly meant to be ambiguous:

"Then it's what's called in English 'business and pleasure?'" And with that he releases the button and waves his open hand as he leaves.

Sturla doesn't feel that this is the way he wants to end the conversation, but when he hurriedly adds that the business in Lithuania concerns his job, his everyday affairs, his comment is cut off by his neighbor bidding him goodbye with the words: "Well, enjoy the trip." And it immediately strikes Sturla that Þorlákur (if that is his name) has the impression that he is headed to a conference of supers, or something of that nature. He decides to make it quite clear, before he leaves the man on this floor, that he, a poet, is not going to be part of a congregation of supers, whatever that peculiar assembly is like.

"I am going to a book festival," he blurts out, and he imagines that he looks like a dog who has heard his owner calling.

Sturla's words have a magnetic effect on the man: his free hand, the hand which isn't holding the broom, thrusts out to block the open elevator door from closing, and he asks, surprised:

"What did you say? A book festival?"

"A poetry festival, to be precise. An international poetry festival."

"Listen, don't go anywhere," says the man; he stays in the elevator and once again presses the door hold button so the elevator won't move. "I just remembered I'm supposed to get the laundry from the dryer for my wife. Is it okay if we head back down?"

Sturla has no idea where he stands anymore, and because he doesn't know how he ought to reply he simply says, "Yes, okay," and so the elevator goes back down, when it ought to instead be going two floors up, to Sturla's floor.

"So you write poetry," his neighbor wants to know.

"That's what I've been up to, yes."

"And have you published anything?"

"My new book was published a few days ago."

"Your first book?"

"I've published a few books," Sturla answers, looking searchingly at the man.

"I clearly don't keep up very well," he says, apologetically, and asks Sturla what the book is called, saying that it isn't out of the question that he might have heard about it. "No, I don't recognize the title," he says when he has thought about *assertions* for a few moments.

The elevator comes to a halt.

How long did the tormented pianist Ryder, the character in Ishiguro's novel, spend in the elevator during his first elevator journey on his mysterious concert tour? Sturla recalls how irritated his colleague and friend, the poet Svanur Bergmundsson, was with Ryder: how he, Svanur, had practically pulled his beard out (he was, indeed, bearded) because of his bewilderment at the way the author had allowed a character to have a conversation with another character for what seemed like half- or even three-quarters of an hour, even though the actual time they spent conversing, according to the narrative, could only have been a minute or two at most. Could it be that poets—with Svanur Bergmundsson at the head of their ranks—wouldn't put up with novelists playing around with and twisting the concept of time; is poetry alone allowed to challenge the reader's perception of logic? Does this particular method mean that the novelist's work falls to pieces, that it doesn't hold water in the eyes of a perceptive reader, one who feels that he deserves—as compensation for the effort and generosity which reading a long book requires—not to be sent out into the wilderness and abandoned there, alone, insecure, and lost?

At that moment—as Sturla thinks about the information he has given his neighbor about his published books—he has the quite amazing realization that the whole flock of books he's published under his name (if you can call seven a "whole flock") are in circulation: in libraries, on the shelves of literary-minded people, in bookstores (at least his two most recent books). But has he contributed something to that form, a form he has by now spent roughly a quarter-century devoting the bulk of his spare time and energy to—or is it a formlessness (which one could also say about time and energy)? How widely held, for example, is his father's opinion that if he really wants to continue with poetry—composing, as he'd called it—then he should ball the poetry up into one continuous text and hide it there, because this impatient world no longer has the appetite or attention span for irregular linebreaks and for words that come in outfits which remind one of frayed rags (prose, on the other hand, wears a carefully-cut, broad-shouldered suit)—in other words, for a dense, weighty book wrapped in a beautifully designed jacket which will protect the poet's work from dust, from the passage of time, and from use.

One moment Sturla feels there is depth and purpose to his writing but the next—and this is something which has been happening more and more often—he, the poet, starts to think that he can't see anything in the production of poetry but emptiness and the surface emotions that still lifes offer: more or less beautiful textures, at best, things better suited to being the subject of a watercolor on the wall of a room. In those gloomy moments when the latter feeling grips him—like the moments when he allows himself to delve into the work of his favorite authors for writing inspiration—he looks at and thinks about certain poems which he has loved more than others, poems that one could say left him exposed as a poet and—paradoxical as it sounds—made him greater and lesser at the same time. One of those poets who "opened and shut" Sturla's creativity in that way was the same poet his father Jón referred to the day before, when he criticized Sturla for verging on old-fashioned forms of poetry by rhyming—or half-rhyming. And yet that reactionary innovation in Sturla's poetry didn't originate with him, though these days he isn't able to look into the eyes of the person from whom it came. The image Sturla's father had mentioned originally had used perfect rhyme, accompanied by alliteration: "the mother in the window / the murk of the shadow." To better fit the words to his own style, and also because rhyme was a somewhat fussy custom that irritated him, Sturla altered the lines so they read, "the mother, the window / the darkness of the shadows." He'd downplayed the subtle symmetry of the lines in favor of the necessary friction that makes the art of poetry something more than just form.

But how long is it possible to fill out the same form? Is the form of poetry infinite? These and other questions bob about in Sturla's mind as he stands in the stationary elevator. His neighbor, on the other hand, has another question as he holds the elevator doors open:

"What do people do at a book festival?" And he apologizes at once for not having introduced himself; he is called Áslákur, nicknamed Láki—though of course they'd met at a tenants' meeting. He knows Sturla's name well, and he too has a cousin with that revered name, a friend who is, in fact, actually called Sturla Snorrason. He also apologizes again for having asked if he, Sturla Jón, would travel down to the laundry room. He just needs to get the laundry and then they can go back up in the elevator. It will only take a moment.

Sturla has nothing against the unexpected digression that is this elevator journey. He is interested in finding out what this so-called Láki wants with the broom—a question he ultimately doesn't get an answer to because Láki sets it down in the laundry room while he takes things out of the dryer and forgets to take it with him when he gets back in the elevator.

During this stop on their trip to the laundry room, the neighbors have the following conversation:

"So, what do people do at these book festivals?"

Sturla realizes that to some extent he needs to answer this question carefully; it is as though something important rests on it. "What do people do?" He gives himself some time to reflect. "People meet and chat together. And they give readings. That is generally the purpose of such a festival: people read to other people."

"So that . . ." Láki pushes open the door into the laundry room. "It's a kind of holiday for authors? After they've finished writing their books?"

"I wouldn't call it that," Sturla answers, but as he is setting out to convince this man about the significant energy and organization that goes into the travel of the majority of authors, he is asked another question:

"So you've been to this sort of festival before?" Láki puts the broom against the wall, opens the dryer, and looks over at Sturla, who is standing with his back to him and staring out the window.

"I've probably been to two or three," answers Sturla, turning around. And while he recalls the two he's previously been invited to, in Belgium and the Faroe Islands, he realizes his neighbor isn't listening while he takes the laundry out of the dryer. And thinking this, he wonders whether he ought perhaps to revise the way he'd described his first trips to poetry festivals in the article he wrote last night, the article that imagines The Season of Poetry, which is the name of the festival in Lithuania. Although it should be very clear to the reader of the article that Sturla is joking in his, as it were, advance review of the festival, he isn't sure everyone would understand the disparaging remarks he'd made about past festivals, which he'd included mainly to underscore the frustrated tone of the article's narrator, the character Sturla invented as the voice of the piece. Sturla begins to realize that people like this married man, Áslákur, a father of four children, weren't likely to comprehend that behind the personality who appears in the text lives another character: the omniscient author who can allow himself to turn everything upside down.

"I've recently begun writing a little story myself," says Áslákur, after a few seconds have passed without Sturla saying anything. "But I'm not sure it counts as literature," he ploughs on, stuffing the laundry into a red plastic tub.

"Why do you say that?"

"It's an altogether different thing to be a real artist who carefully puts together well-rhymed and well-alliterated poems," replies Áslákur and closes the dryer.

At around the same time the day before the salesperson in the clothing store on Bankastræti had contrived to tell him he painted. And though Sturla had found a need to let this stranger, his neighbor, know he was going to a book festival (not to a gathering of supers), generally speaking Sturla didn't have any reason to let people know out of the blue that he writes poetry. When it seems that Áslákur doesn't have any more questions about the poetry festival, Sturla starts to suspect Áslákur asked him down to the laundry room because he doesn't like being there alone. As it turns out, he doesn't seem to have the interest in Sturla he had so genuinely shown. Sturla offers to help with the laundry baskets but Áslákur declines; his expression changes as though to suggest that he has forgotten why he invited Sturla to the laundry room in the first place. When they get back to the elevator Sturla studies the envelope from Cambridge—partly to see whether the mail will arouse Láki's interest in the poet—but once they are in the elevator and Áslákur doesn't say anything, Sturla suspects he's occupied with the little story he mentioned he is writing. Perhaps he is lamenting his missed opportunity to be a published author, like his fellow traveler in the elevator.

When they part ways, with Áslákur saying goodbye to Sturla somewhat curtly as he launches himself out of the elevator, Sturla is beginning to wonder why this fifty year-old man is home alone in the middle of a weekday. He supposes that his wife and children are at work and school, but what does this curious—and seemingly moody—man do in his apartment when it gets to be two o'clock in the afternoon? Does he start looking for something that he knows doesn't exist, something which he can't be sure about, something concrete and intangible at the same time—and is he sorely disappointed when he doesn't find anything other than what existed in front of his eyes every single day?

The first thing Sturla does, on the other hand, when he enters his place is open the envelope from the Biographical Center. In the upper right corner of the letter is a red logo, a simply sketched image of the earth, and below the logo are the initials of the sender: IBC. A little further down was a drawing of a church building in Cambridge.

Sturla begins to read the English text:

Dear Mr. Jonsson

2,000 OUTSTANDING INTELLECTUALS OF THE 21ST CENTURY

The Oxford English Dictionary defines intellectualism as the "doctrine that knowledge is wholly or mainly derived from pure reason" and it follows by saying that an intellectual is a "person possessing a good understanding, enlightened person."

Surely, therefore, this definition is the reason for your selection to be included in this prestigious publication which is due for release in early 2007. I invite you to take your place within its pages. Only two thousand intellectuals can be featured from across the world and I therefore urge you to complete the enclosed questionnaire as soon as possible.

He takes a break from reading and lets himself scan the rest of the text with his eyes. Is he being mocked, or has he ended up on a list of world intellectuals because of some kind of misunderstanding? Could it really be the case that the recipient has to act fast to avoid being excluded from the two thousand people there is room for in the volume? Who'd had the idea of sending him—Sturla Jón Jónsson—this letter? The name of a Nicholas S. Law is written below the body of the letter, his signature looking rather like the lines of a cartoon EKG; what on earth could this man have been thinking as he put down his pen after signing the letter? The postscript asks the recipient to recommend someone he knows who deserves to be in the book by writing their name in a special box on the reverse side of the letter. Here is the answer to why Sturla received the letter: some spiteful individual from the crowd of Icelandic writers had also got a similar letter—at the recommendation of another spiteful author—and he had added Sturla's name to the list of suggested recipients. The person had thought they should add, "of course, the inferior poet Sturla Jón

Jónsson—who has never had any thoughts that have had any influence on other people—he ought to be very much at home on your list of the two thousand most vital thinkers on earth."

Sturla would without doubt have done the same thing, if he'd been able to step outside himself and look from a distance at the mediocre poet Sturla Jón. In fact, his first thought is to return the letter with the words to the effect that he isn't worthy of or able to accept this honor which has been offered to him, but he can instead recommend the bearded Icelandic poet Svanur Bergmundsson, the same person who had, in conversation with his fellow poet, friend, and countryman Sturla Jón, described how the Japanese-English author Ishiguro (or Japenglish, as Sturla can't resist adding for his own benefit) had shown complete disregard for his loyal readers by allowing three-quarters of an hour to pass inside just two minutes during one of his novels.

But perhaps a similar letter has already dropped into Svanur's mailbox.

Suddenly Sturla is depressed at the thought of how little these colleagues, he and Svanur—and also their fellow Icelandic poets of a similar stature—have contributed to world literature; their contribution even to Icelandic literature is pretty modest. And on the heels of this thought he begins thinking of his neighbor Áslákur, and an even greater gloom descends over him; in all the apartment buildings in the country—in all the high rises in the world—life goes on in exactly the same way as inside the residences of Skúlagata 40 in Reykjavík; how pathetic it is, how miserable. Weren't fathers of numerous children all over the world fetching brooms from laundry rooms of apartments, only to return them to the same place later? Is there anywhere in the world where you can't find insignificant men struggling to write some insignificant texts which are of no use to anyone but themselves—in other words, useless products that actually prevent the people who write them from being human beings of any value.

Or are they?

Doesn't the piece Sturla wrote yesterday have any message? Could it be that the actual message of his damning, sarcastic critique of poetry festivals is self-deception, which springs from his discomfort and dissatisfaction over his own impotence and uselessness? That's all very plausible, but he isn't able to shake the feeling that this decision to make the leap from poetry to prose—a personal change of form—has aroused something entirely new inside him, something which really means something, for him or to others. He decides to fix himself a drink, and on his way into the kitchen (where the drinks are), he puts the newest Richard Thompson album, Front Parlour Ballads, on the CD player.

Isn't this something that happens to him at regular intervals, these reflections and this doubt about his occupation? After having gulped down two shots of vodka and persuaded himself, by scanning his eyes briefly over his article from yesterday, that he is on the right path—that he couldn't be on anything but the right path—Sturla rings the editor Jónatan Jóhannsson.

"I think I've written you an article," he says, letting Jónatan know he will swing by in the morning with it; he is heading abroad on Friday.

"Is it a short-story?" the editor asks and continues noisily eating something he'd picked up while Sturla was saying his name at the beginning of the conversation.

"Not exactly. It's more in the family of narratives of events which have yet to happen."

"More in the *family* of?"

"This is what it is: a narrative of something which isn't."

"Sounds peculiar. Is it speculative fiction? Is it science fiction?"

"No, I wouldn't really call it science fiction, not exactly."

"I've got to apologize to you, Sturla: I don't take any sort of 'invention fiction' for the magazine. If you're planning to give me science fiction, I'm going to have to turn it down."

Sturla laughs into the handset; he isn't sure whether his father's old friend is joking or not.

"Listen, something's changed about you," Jónatan says cheerfully, and when Sturla keeps quiet Jónatan continues: "It's hard to believe you're still the same person, given the size of your nostrils."

"What on earth do you mean?" asks Sturla.

"You know, I'd never realized before that you had such big ears," the editor continues, and for a moment Sturla wonders if there was something wrong with him, if he was crazy, even.

"What I've got for you is a report from the future," says Sturla, and after hesitating briefly to see if Jónatan will interrupt him and continue with his convoluted description, he adds: "What I mean by this is that this thing that I am writing about, the thing that's going to happen," and Jónatan lets him barrel on unimpeded, "is a poetry festival that I am on the way to in Lithuania in two days, and the article I'm going to let you have in the morning has to do with that festival—it gives an account of what happened at it."

"So in other words it's a kind of prophecy?" asks Jónatan.

"We could perhaps call it speculative fiction," offers Sturla. "I am writing about something which hasn't yet come to pass, but in a way that . . ."

"Just send it to me," Jónatan interrupts, giving Sturla his e-mail address, jójó@frometof.is. "I'll be in touch once I've managed to read it."

"I will, of course, have headed to Lithuania by then," replies Sturla, feeling fairly certain the article will surprise the editor when he reads it; he can hardly be expecting such a merciless autopsy of the state of poetry as he will find in the article. "But I'll have a cell phone with me," Sturla adds, asking Jónatan to wait while he looks for his new cell phone number. When he gives Jónatan the number, Jónatan repeats the digits like he's never heard a row of numbers placed in an order before, as if placing one numeral next to another is a foreign concept. It is, Sturla thinks, smiling, indicative of his antipathy to numbers which begin with an eight, the way all cell phone numbers do.

"Now, are you going to let the newspaper know about the mistake with the picture?" Jónatan asks when it comes time to say goodbye.

"What picture?"

"Of that brother poet of yours."

"I'm no longer sure I follow what's going on in this conversation," Sturla replies, and he tells Jónatan again that he'll receive the article the next day.

"Didn't you see the newspaper today?" asks Jónatan. "Did you see the announcement?"

"What announcement?"

"You've published a book, right? Your father told me that you published a new poetry book. You told me about it yourself when we spoke the other day. I even know the title. And I know that because it was in the paper today."

"I didn't know they had written about it. I haven't looked at the newspaper. Did they include the wrong picture with the announcement? An image of my namesake, Sturla Jónsson?"

"It don't think it's the first time it's happened," answers Jónatan, happily. "That seventy year-old writer of quatrains becomes more and more well-known as a modern poet every time *you* put out a book."

Sturla asks Jónatan to wait while he grabs the paper (he had picked it up at the same time as the letter from Cambridge) but the editor says he can't, that he will wait to hear from Sturla in the morning.

While Sturla looks at the picture of his namesake Sturla Jónsson, a farmer and politician, he asks himself how Jónatan could have been the first to point out this announcement to him. It is late in the day; someone who knows him better must have glanced at the announcement and the picture—even his children should have seen it.

But they aren't in the habit of calling him; it would take something more than the publication of the wrong picture in a newspaper. And as Sturla gets himself another drink from the kitchen he asks himself whether he ought to bother giving them a call before he goes abroad.

NÝLENDUGATA

"You're wearing a new overcoat," is the first thing Fanný says to Sturla Jón after she opens the door on Nýlendugata.

For a few moments now he has been standing next to a meter-tall, weather-beaten statue of a gnome that is on the sidewalk in front of the door, waiting for his mother to invite him in. When no invite seems forthcoming it occurs to Sturla that perhaps she is in a state of mind where she is amused by watching her son stand beside a garden gnome; perhaps she wants to enjoy the sight as long as possible. The expression on her face doesn't indicate this, though, and suddenly she declares she should get rid of him; and when she adds that she means that miserable-looking smurf by the door, Sturla is relieved. The image before him in the doorway, on the other hand, brings to mind the same reflections as every other time he has looked at his mother, this sixty-seven-year-old woman who looks like time divorced her in her seventh decade and left the least possible mark on her countenance.

She is a pretty woman but her facial features always remind Sturla that a skull is right under the skin, and although he's a little ashamed of letting it pop into his mind, the following metaphor surfaces, a metaphor he wishes he connected with someone other than his mother, who is "a picture of death, if it were possible to photograph death." But as badly as she treats herself, with liquor, smoking, medicine and "an incessant lack of activity," as she herself describes it, it is as though nothing can spoil her outer beauty. She still uses some clothes which she has owned for twenty or thirty years: well-made clothes she allowed herself to buy while she was married to Jón Magnússon, despite the fact that she and Jón had limited funds; clothes which still show off how shapely her body is, and how dignified and graceful her movements are, an impression which stands in sharp contrast to her personality—she is liable to be absolutely unpredictable, not only under the influence of liquor or medicine, but also when she yearned for but didn't have any liquor or medicine. The make-up on her face is always in the right place, and in the right amounts, and her hair always looks as if she's just come out of a hairdresser's: light gold, glistening, and carefully brushed.

Sturla stands facing his mother outside the basement door on Nýlendugata; her apartment is two steps below street level, and he can't get used to having to look down on his mother when she opens the door, a further two steps down. In spite of the decline she'd chosen in her life—or which life had chosen for her—she has a certain dignity that should at least be accompanied by a few steps that go up.

"You're wearing a new overcoat," she'd said, and Sturla nods his head; yes, he is wearing a new overcoat. He takes a step forward to kiss his mother. She on the other hand moves away from him and continues talking while she beckons him to come in: "Beautiful." She means the overcoat.

Based on Fanný's demeanor, it seems like she hasn't started drinking yet. But it's more than possible that she'd had a drink with breakfast and a few drinks after that; nothing is the way it seems where

Fanný Alexson is concerned. For example, her apartment is only thirty square meters, at least ten square meters smaller than Jón Magnússon's apartment on Skólavörðuholt, but when you enter it from outside, the tastefully-decorated kitchen and living room immediately give the impression of wealth, the impression that you've entered some rich person's attractively decorated home. The only things which aren't immediately visible are the small bedroom off the living room and the tiny bathroom off from the kitchen, on the left-hand side of the front door. Originally, when Fanný bought the apartment nine years ago, the only place to wash was a shower cubicle in the laundry room, which she shared with the family who lived on the second story of the house. But because Fanný could never adjust to having to stand up to clean herself—something she'd never needed to put up with other than during the three years she and Jón lived in Prague—she got permission from her upstairs neighbors to put a bathtub in the laundry room; after this, it was impossible to use the room for laundry. As a result, their laundry facilities, both the upstairs family and the "family of Fanný" (as she called her own company), had to be moved into their kitchens. Therefore Fanný got the laundry room all to herself, although she allowed (gladly) the daughter of the couple upstairs to use it whenever she wanted; her parents didn't seem to have any need for a bathtub. This seventeen-year-old girl had immediately become close to Fanný, and in many ways she had become a surrogate daughter to the ambassador's eccentric daughter—much to the chagrin of the girl's actual mother.

"What matters most is that it is made out of good material," Fanný says when Sturla lets her examine the overcoat. "And of course good needlework," she adds when Sturla repeats the sales assistant's claims about how the seams were sewn so they would last a lifetime: he is going to own the overcoat until he is ancient, without ever needing to get it repaired. Fanný asks Sturla if he has eaten anything, and he says he has, though he doesn't mention that he got himself a hotdog on Austurstræti (hotdog number two in just three days). "Well, it's okay to get you a wine glass, then," she says, as if she'd wanted to make sure he doesn't start drinking on an empty stomach, and when Sturla accepts the offer but says he'd prefer white wine, if she has any, his suspicions that she has an open bottle handy are confirmed: "I've only got this open bottle of red wine from yesterday. Halla, my girlfriend, came over around noon yesterday, and I invited her to have a little red wine."

But no-one had visited Fanný around midday the day before; over the phone yesterday she'd told Sturla that she'd been waiting for the plumber since midday (there was a leak in the kitchen) and she'd thought it was the plumber when Sturla called around four to postpone his visit until today. She'd called the plumber three or four times, and she'd let him ruin her day; she hated waiting, because she found herself unable to do anything else with the time but wait.

Sturla takes the red wine and offers to look at the kitchen sink. As he turns on the water, Fanný asks him to leave it alone: she doesn't want him, a poet, to start messing around with something like that.

"You're forgetting that I'm a super," Sturla says, smiling. "A super ought to be able to deal with something like this, right? Or at least try to look as if he does."

"You don't know anything about it," Fanný contradicts him, and Sturla, knowing she is right, turns off the water, taps the faucet, and looks at his mother with an expression that is meant to indicate he should be treated like an expert, though he hasn't a clue.

"You're going abroad," she says, rather abruptly, and looks out of the kitchen window, through the thin nylon window screen, at a huge black station wagon that's driving lazily past the house.

"I am going abroad, yes," answers Sturla, and takes a drink of red wine before setting his glass on a cloth coaster on the kitchen table.

Fanný looks at Sturla for a brief moment and their eyes meet in silence.

"I am leaving tomorrow morning," Sturla says to break the silence, and he looks towards the living room window at the black car going slowly past as if everything outside is moving at a different speed from inside.

"Are you going to take your camera with you?" Fanný asks. She goes to the kitchen table, both hands around her glass, and looks in the same direction as Sturla for a moment. She sits at the table once the black car has finally moved past the living room window, sipping her wine.

When Sturla replies that he doesn't own a camera Fanný asks whether she's told him about the photograph of herself, the one which is going to be in the exhibition.

"What exhibition?"

"He sent an old picture of me which he took many years ago, he's intending to include it in—"

"Who?" interrupts Sturla. "Who sent you a picture of yourself?"

"Helgi Haraldsson. He is an old school friend. An old friend of Örn Featherby."

"I don't know who this Helgi is. What is the picture of?"

Sturla is pleasantly surprised to see his mother smile.

"I never got accustomed to that name, Featherby," she says, shaking her head and still smiling to herself. "But I've known Örn a little longer than almost anyone else still living. In some ways longer than your father."

"What photograph exhibition are you talking about?"

"Helgi H. Haraldsson is going to hold a photography exhibition, and he intends to show the picture he took of me. And to mark the occasion, I want to invite you to have a shot of Danish schnapps which I got from my Halla yesterday. You're going abroad tomorrow, after all."

Sturla decides to let his mother take charge of things; he realizes that he won't be able to stop her from mixing a strong drink with the red wine. He also knows that at some point she will explain the photograph she mentioned, that it is pointless to push her. And yet he asks her what it is a picture of.

"I'm bare-breasted in it," answers Fanný, turning her head to look at Sturla as she stands by the kitchen sink pouring schnapps into two little shot glasses.

Sturla has taken the cigarette packet from his shirt pocket but remembers his mother doesn't like tobacco smoke; she always asks him to smoke by the open front door. But on this occasion, as Sturla goes to the door, asking as he passes her what she means when she says she is "bare-breasted" in the picture, she invites him to smoke at the table; she doesn't want the cold to get in. She means that the picture, which Helgi H. Haraldsson took of her when she was a young woman, is of her head and her breasts—when her breasts were also younger.

"And . . ." Sturla doesn't really know what he should say. "Did he ask you to do that?"

"*I* didn't ask him to do it," answers Fanný, moving the shot glasses over to the kitchen table.

"And he's going to show it now? In public?"

"Helgi H. Haraldsson has never had a photography exhibition before. Helgi H. Haraldsson is a biologist."

Sturla glances skeptically at his mother. "Does dad know about this?" he asks.

"That was why he took the picture of my breasts."

"What was?"

"Because he's a biologist."

"And does dad know about this?"

"Why do you think it's any of his business if an old lover took a picture of my breasts some forty years ago?"

"Lover?"

"Old lover."

"While you and dad were . . .?"

"While your dad and I were, yes."

"And dad didn't know about it?"

"No, your dad didn't know about it. And *doesn't* know about it. What's more, it's none of his business." She takes a sip from her shot glass and moves it in Sturla's direction to clink glasses before she sets it down.

Sturla lifts his shot glass to touch hers.

"Have you seen him recently?" asks Fanný when she has finished her drink. "I want to show you the picture," she adds, standing up.

"I don't need to see it," replies Sturla.

"You don't *need* to see it? I know you don't *need* to see it but I want to show you it anyway." She goes into the bedroom and comes back with a black plastic folder which she places on the kitchen table before she fetches the cold bottle of schnapps from the counter by the sink. She sits down while she takes a black and white photograph from the folder—it's of a young woman with light, wavy hair and small but beautifully-shaped breasts; there is no doubt it is Fanný, and no doubt that the model had warm feelings for the person holding the camera.

Sturla takes the picture from his mother's hand and looks at it a little while. And as if to show that contemplating his mother's naked chest doesn't make him uncomfortable he lifts his cigarette and sucks in a long drag of smoke while he examines the picture. Then he places it on the side and gives his mother—and, in the process, the photographer—his opinion that it is an elegant picture. "But when is it being exhibited?" he asks.

"You'll have to ask Helgi," Fanný answers, smiling absent-mindedly, as if she wants to recall the feeling she remembers—or imagines—having felt when the picture was taken. "I don't know anything more about it, other than that he intends to ask our little Örn to write something for the exhibition program."

"To ask Örn to write about the pictures?" Sturla tries best as he can to make her understand, without using so many words, that this isn't a particularly good idea.

"Yes, what can I say? I'm just the model," says Fanný in a dramatic, cloying way, which suddenly annoys Sturla; he finds the whole thing quite disagreeable.

"I don't like it, mom." He finds it strange to hear himself say the word "mom" to his mother. "Örn and Dad meet almost every day."

"And what about it, my dear son? Did your father turn you into such a great prude? Don't blame that on me."

"I don't want to have anything to do with this."

"But you are pleased with the picture, right?"

"Yes, mom, it's an elegant picture, you look beautiful in the picture."

"Those are the very same breasts you suckled at when you were little," says Fanný smiling, and she waves Sturla's cigarette smoke away from her. "When you were little. When you were a shrimp. Newly born like a . . . infant."

"Do you remember the folder you gave Jónas?" asks Sturla, replacing the photograph in the plastic folder.

"You always looked away when I pointed you towards my breasts," continues Fanný, though she takes back her words, saying she was only joking. "Why should you have been shy about such matters? You who ended up having five children, a whole kindergarten, and who was present for all the births, isn't that right?"

"Do you remember the folder you gave to Jónas?" Sturla repeats, replacing the black plastic folder by the wall at the end of the table.

"Do I remember the folder? What folder?" Fanný picks up the plastic folder, takes the photograph of herself back out, and contemplates it as though she'd forgotten to scrutinize some particular detail.

"The one grandfather had," says Sturla. "The folder he always kept on his writing desk. It was a leather folder you could open up; there were some compartments in it, almost like envelopes, and inside it was some sort of dry, thick paper which was designed to be an underlay for writing on."

Fanný sets aside the photograph and takes off her glasses, which are lime-green in color and also shaped like two horizontal limes or lemons. She bends her head and strokes her temples like she is trying to hide some pain that she can't keep the lower half of her face from revealing. Sturla watches her replace the picture in the folder and put it on the kitchen chair at the other end of the counter.

"Why are you bringing this up?" asks Fanný when she has put her glasses back on. "What about this folder?"

"Don't you remember giving it to him?"

"Are you sure I gave Jónas some folder?" She drinks from her red wine glass and dries her lips with a napkin from the counter.

"I know it because, among other things, I was quite upset that you gave it to *him*."

"And what about this folder? Why on earth would you be upset about some folder?"

"Because I had always wanted to own it. But right after grandfather died you all of a sudden gave the folder to Jónas. Because he was such a wonderful student."

"A wonderful student?" Fanný smiles half-sadly, and looks around pensively.

"All I wanted to know was whether you remembered this. Not that it makes any difference now."

"No, my Sturla, it doesn't make any difference at all. How many years has it been since poor Jónas died?"

They are silent for a while. Then, when Sturla says that it mattered a lot, that it matters even more to him today, Fanný suddenly loses her patience.

"Sturla. If you want a folder exactly like that, you can take this folder here." She indicates the plastic folder on the kitchen counter. "I don't need a special folder to cover my breasts. They will be on public display anyway soon. I even think the show will be at the Art Museum of the Icelandic Federal Labor Union, or whatever it's called."

"Mom, I'm not mentioning the folder because I need a folder. I've had grandfather's folder ever since Jónas died."

Fanný shrugs her shoulders, as if to show there is no need to discuss the matter further.

"I am talking about it now because there were things in the folder that belonged to each of them, both grandfather and Jónas. There were papers from grandfather from when he was in Norway, and some photographs, and a whole manuscript . . ."

"I remember pictures of you and Jónas which your grandfather had on his desk," interrupts Fanný. "You were on a swing in the playground across from Freyjugata."

Sturla looks disappointedly at his mother, who continues:

"I always went there with you, when I was looking after you boys those years Þeba worked at the office. Don't you remember the photo?"

Sturla says he remembered it.

"I took it myself using your father's camera. The one he never allowed me to use. You were on the right swing and Jónas on the left and behind you was that nurse who killed herself."

While his mother spends a long time telling him—perhaps it seems longer because Sturla has heard it all before—about how the young nurse at the kindergarten on Freyjugata cut her life short; about how Þeba, the wife of Hallmundur, Jón's brother, made her family very unhappy by taking a job (even though Hallmundur earned more than enough for the family); and how it fell to her to care for the young Jónas as well as her own children, Jónas who fifteen years after the picture was taken at the playground cut his own life short using the very same method as the woman who had stood between him and Sturla in the picture—the whole time Fanný's narrative grows from moment to moment like a dark and sinister flower, watered by the wine, Sturla smokes one cigarette on the heels of another and has another two shots of schnapps; he doesn't make a fuss when Fanný opens another bottle of red wine, though it isn't yet five o'clock. He regards this woman, recalling the conversation he'd had with his father two days earlier, and is amazed that he almost described to her what the folder she gave to Jónas contained. Why on earth would he tell her about that? He must never tell anyone.

"Get yourself a little more red wine, or I'll drink it all myself," says Fanný, pushing the bottle towards him on the table. But Sturla knew as well as she does that once he leaves she'll open another bottle; he can see her taking one to the bathtub in the laundry room. He imagines the young girl from upstairs coming down to the basement and sitting on the edge of the bathtub beside his mother; he imagines the girl in the bathtub instead of his mother; he imagines himself getting into the bathtub with the girl—and Fanný suddenly asks, making it sound like she is saying goodbye to him, as though she'd prefer to lie down in a hot bath than to have her son stay any longer:

"And you're definitely going?"

"Going where?"

"Aren't you going abroad in the morning? I was only asking whether you're definitely going."

"I think so, yes," answers Sturla, continuing, "I think, therefore I go."

"Yes, of course you're going," answers Fanný. "You don't need to think any more about it. You're going in the morning. Have you got your ticket already?"

"Yes, mom, of course I already have my ticket."

"Then everything's ready. You only need to remember your passport."

"I'll remember my passport, mom."

"Do you need a passport in the country you're going to?"

"I don't expect it will be enough to show them my poetry."

"Your poetry?"

"I am going abroad to recite poetry."

"I know that, Sturla."

"Yes, and I know that I need a passport to get into Lithuania."

"Thanks for the book, Sturla dear. I will look at it more soon."

This is the first time since he gave her his book a few days ago that Fanný has mentioned it. He remembers at once that he'd brought another copy of the book with him, like she asked him to, but he decides only to let her have it if she mentions it without being asked.

"I hope you enjoy it," he says. "It was written using that folder I was talking about. You could say that the book actually came out of grandfather's folder."

"I don't remember father having a folder," says Fanný, as though the word folder has just come up in their conversation for the first time. "But that is a beautiful picture on the cover of your book," she adds, smiling weakly.

"That's a picture of that folder I was telling you about," explains Sturla, but he doesn't want to bring this topic back up: his mother clearly doesn't want to discuss it, or to remember it, even though she admits remembering the folder once she more closely examines the cover image on Sturla's book.

"I remember this," she says, but she doesn't have anything more to add except to suggest that Sturla must eventually have gotten hold of the folder, and one can't ignore the fact—as she puts it—that in order for him to obtain it, his cousin and contemporary had had to off himself.

Sturla acts as if he hasn't heard her. But he wonders if lying behind her observation is the phrase "one person's death is another's life" (is he trying to be as tasteless in his choice of words as she was?), and he thinks of the mother in the poem, the one living in the darkness of shadows—as he interprets that shadow. She'll stand by the window when he goes out the gate to the sidewalk, for sure, and she'll wave to him as he heads past. He gives her his cell phone number (explaining why it starts with the number eight, since she's never seen that sort of number before) and they say goodbye in the doorway, somewhat brusquely. Fanný says she can't stand outside in this cold, that she isn't suited to living in this cold, damp country; in fact, she ought to go overseas with Sturla to the sun and warmth.

As Sturla had predicted, his mother stands inside the window, behind the nylon screen, but the way she moves her hand when he goes past the window feels wrong, as though it doesn't belong to her. It's too fast: it reminds him of a duck beating its wings to get out of the way of a car on the road. He waves back and begins walking faster; he wants to hurry home to Skúlagata to read over his article for the magazine. While his mother's monologue about the past had been going on and on he'd been remembering the newly-written text, and he is beginning to get the feeling—perhaps influenced by the wine he's drunk—that the article is not only very well executed, but also marks the start of a new period in his life as an author: his settling of accounts with poetry (which, he thinks, will get a final farewell at the end of his visit to Lithuania) and the seeds of what lies ahead. That said, he will need the limited time he has left to touch up the text before he sends it to Jónatan Jóhannsson. There is nothing else he needs to do before going abroad the next morning except what he'd put off doing the day before: calling his children, who all happened to be with their mother at Egilsstaðir at the moment, which was unusual; tidying up the apartment a little so that it will be cozy to return to; packing; and . . . he suddenly thinks, now that it is too late, of course, that he'd meant to pick up the VCR so he could return the Iranian movie to his father.

TWO HOURS AWAY FROM THE CITY

by Sturla Jón Jónsson

> Poetry lives in all things. That
> is the chief argument
> against Poetry.
> —Miroslav Holub

"The trip scheduled from Vilnius to Druskininkai takes just two hours. The Czech poet Nezval wrote about the five minutes distance from the town but here we are dealing with a longer distance. From Vilnius to Druskininkai, it is a two-hour trip by coach.

Vilnius? Why talk about Vilnius? And what in heaven's name is Druskininkai? What does the unintelligible name Druskininkai signify?

Well, I have been invited to an international poetry festival in a little village in Lithuania called Druskininkai, which is southwest of the capital city Vilnius and directly south of the ancient capital city, Kaunas, where the Dalai Lama once went when he visited Vilnius. No other Icelanders have been invited to the festival in Druskininkai; I'll be traveling alone and I am supposed to show up in this country in mid-October.

It is certainly tempting to state the obvious and say that Druskininkai is an absurd name for a village, even taking into account that the village is in Lithuania, a country where anything goes when it comes to giving names.

But such temptation is too obvious for a poet to give in to it. And no less so when we are discussing a poet who has reached the stage in his art where he believes he has nothing more to accomplish as a poet.

Druskininkai means the same thing as Salzburg in Austria. Although Salzburg isn't considered a very happening place at the moment, still, it is hardly possible to say that nothing good has come from there.

"I am called Dainius Navakas and I come from Druskininkai." This doesn't sound convincing though there is evidence of an individual with the name Dainius Navakas who lives in Druskininkai.

After I received an invitation to the poetry festival, I looked up information about Druskininkai on the Internet and found, among other things, the name Dainius Navakas. From what I understood from the homepage of the town of Druskininkai, this Dainius Navakas works as some kind of information official.

But now to the poetry festival. The last thing I want to do is seem ungrateful towards the people who organized it, but at the same time I have to mention that I was astonished when I saw the first event would be a recital by three American poets.

I discovered this information in the documents about the festival that were sent to me by e-mail. Actually, the three women poets are supposed to read in Vilnius itself, in the cultural center at the American Embassy, and although that will take place before the festival formally starts, I notice on one page of the documents which were sent to me that their reading will signal that the festival has begun.

All this is a reason for even more amazement, when I think about how the international poetry festival in Druskininkai is originally Nordic, certainly not American or Anglo-Saxon.

If I've learned anything from my past experiences of poetry festivals of the sort we're discussing here, then I know that nothing will prevent these three American poets from reading at the opening of the festival. Neither a bomb attack on their embassy in the city, nor unforeseen deaths back home, be that in Wyoming or Nebraska, will prevent them from being at the podium at the designated time.

No doubt it will surprise people that I react to the matter like this, by declaring my opinion that nothing will prevent the American trio from doing what they're supposed to, yet in reality the plans of the people who devise the program for a festival of this caliber seldom go wrong. I speak from experience in this matter.

For example, I don't foresee that, instead of these three American women, three male poets from Finland who no-one is expecting to be in Druskininkai in October will suddenly jump up from nowhere. Three very fat and dead drunk Fins with everything showing, in all senses of the phrase.

No. Nuh-uh, as people say out in the country, people who have no idea that a gathering like the Druskininkai gathering exists anywhere in the world, and who wouldn't give a hoot if they did.

If something unpredictable were to happen at a poetry festival like this, it would be along these lines: a few minutes before a reading, somebody would notice that the texts from one of the foreign participants, which have been translated into Lithuanian like everybody's else's poems, are not actually his own poems, but some entirely different pieces which are totally unconnected to poetry.

An obituary about a deceased relative? A letter to a newspaper which the party in question wrote to protest the planned organizational changes to the city center in the town where he lives?

The poet accidentally e-mailed the wrong document overseas, and the translator, who had naturally never read anything by the poet, and so had no sense from reading the article how it ought to sound, hadn't noticed anything wrong, and so translated the whole caboodle without hesitation, trusting that the continuous and somewhat lumbering text is just one long and rather detailed prose poem.

Lithuanian is a very old language. The oldest in Europe, if Icelandic is not counted. I've read works in Lithuanian and heard it spoken on board a ferry to Norway, and I really think it would be exaggerating to describe the language as beautiful in either texture or sound.

I, at least, can't make it work to lyrical ends. It needs some great changes to become a useful tool in the hands of the poet, at least those poets who have developed any feeling for sound and rhythm.

According to the program of the Druskininkai festival, some domestic poets will be showing off. I can already hear the rattle when all the Antanases and Vytautases begin booming loudly into the microphone in the festival hall.

That will be an unbroken hour of torture and we'll have to listen to it. And then the reading will continue with the translated poems of the participants, with the proud translators rising up from their chairs and reeling off the obituaries for deceased friends and the newspaper articles about planning matters, and then one will deeply wish, just like the young student Rastignac—when he stood before Monsieur and Madame de Restaud, having dropped old Goriot's name—that the earth will open up and swallow him.

But let us assume everything goes as it should as far as the translation of the foreigners' poems is concerned. Let us allow the natives the benefit of doubt in this respect.

There is still, on the other hand, the question of whether one will be able to actually read one's poetry, even though that is the reason for the trip to Druskininkai.

Three or fours years ago, I was invited to take part in a comparable festival in the city of Liège in Belgium, although that festival was perhaps on a considerably greater scale than the one I will be attending in Lithuania.

Despite the fact that I stayed in Liège for four whole days, and though the organizers were good enough to see to everyone's needs while we were there, it turned out, when it came down to it, that there wasn't enough time to read my poems.

In the first place, so many poets had been invited to the festival, from every corner of the world, that there were very few poets left in the countries they had come from; it would have caused serious problems if the invited poets hadn't returned to their native countries. And secondly, the program in which I was included stretched so far in excess of the time limit that, when it was time for me, the time set aside for the reading had already run out.

The festival organizers announced the immediate departure of the coach that was going to deliver the participants from the reading hall back to the hotel.

At that very moment I was beginning to get dry in the mouth, out of nervousness at having to read in front of such esteemed people from so many countries.

There was no way, apparently, to make the coach wait. The driver needed to get home. And the question I asked one Belgian poet, a young man who I had talked with earlier, during one of the many midday breaks, was this: "To his home where? Is his home so far away that the organizers of the festival need to worry about him getting there in good time? In good time for what?"

For my part, I'd come all the way from Iceland to read poems in Belgium, and because this Belgian driver, who had been hired to drive me and the other poets home to a hotel after the recital, needed to get home right now and go to sleep, there wasn't time for me, the next-to-last poet in the program.

Nor for the South African poet, who was last in the program.

It seems the poetic democracy they have in Belgium is like the freedom of speech in the Parliament of the Communist party in Moscow: the Chief Secretary and his comrades from the Party's Executive Branch Committee reported, in a speech lasting many hours, all the magnificent qualities of the red power and the Party's mercy, but the people's delegate to Parliament was only given three minutes to make his own recommendations.

The difference, of course, is that the black South African and I didn't get a single second to showcase our excellent abilities.

We could just as well have stayed home; he in his faraway Johannesburg (if that's where he lived) and I in Skúlagata, in my cozy little Reykjavík.

And so I've still never read my poems in Belgium. Even though I was sent there for four days for precisely that purpose.

The only thing I got for my trouble in making that journey to Liège was a daily meal with the other poets in the assembly hall of the conference center where the festival was being held.

And wine. There was certainly unlimited wine with our food, both during the festival and in the evenings.

The food itself was nothing to complain about, although some poets, at least one from Iraq and another from Cyprus, did have some criticisms, particularly about the relative portions of meat, fish, potatoes, and salads on their plates.

This all begs the question, of course, as to whether something similar, that is, in terms of the amount of time for reading, is in the cards for Lithuania.

"In the cards for Lithuania?" That reminds me of the story of a man whom I met by chance in a restaurant in downtown Reykjavík two or three years ago. He had been invited to Lithuania, but unlike me was he on a business trip (although in a certain sense you could say that my dealings with that country are a little business-like in character).

While I earn my living as a superintendent and a poet, this man works on the other hand for a wealthy firm in Reykjavík, and the hotel which he stayed at in Vilnius, located on the main street in the city center, was, according to his account, the best of the many hotels he'd stayed in.

It was comparable to the best hotels in New York and Paris. There was a roomy Jacuzzi, a thirty-inch flatscreen on the wall facing a California King-size bed, a DVD player, and not just a box of assorted chocolates laying on his pillow on the bed, but also a little bottle of champagne and a cloth bag containing orange-flavored chocolate.

I can't help but suspect I'll be thinking about the magnificent description of this hotel when I step over the threshold to the dormitory, or hostel, or shelter, which is were I assume I'll be staying in Druskininkai and Vilnius.

Unbelievably, that is in fact the usual situation for invited guests if you make your living as a poet. Even the Faroe Islands, the one nation out of all nations which ought to comport itself well towards Icelanders, is no less apathetic when it comes to dealing with Icelandic artists and literary folk.

A few years ago I went to a kind of "culture week" in Þórshöfn, where poets, visual artists, and musicians from all the Nordic countries and Greenland come together, and it was not until the small welcoming committee greeted me and the other Icelanders at their poky little airport in Þórshöfn that I found out I wouldn't have a private room at the hotel. I wouldn't be based at the hotel at all, but instead in a boarding house at the edge of town.

I ended up sharing a room with a Norwegian who had come over from Norway and spoke the absurd children's language nýnorska, or New Norwegian, and who was purging himself through some kind of detox, letting nothing pass his lips the whole week except lemon-flavored water.

It was, evidently, incomprehensible that this miserable individual should choose exactly this week for his self-centered cleansing ritual. The smell emanating from his mouth every time he opened it (which wasn't infrequently) was the sourest halitosis I have ever experienced from anybody.

That we were roommates made other participants at this Faroese poetry farce look at me with compassion for having to share a room with this New-Norwegian phenomenon, but also with ironic glances, which I interpreted as indicating they had formed an opinion that I, the Icelander, deserved to spend the darkest hours of the day in Þórshöfn in an atmosphere transformed by the cocktail of lemon juice, water, Norwegian exhalations, and unused digestive fluids.

I am not saying for certain that the same thing will happen in Lithuania, but, given how the program is organized for the Friday, with the recital of the American poets, I don't exactly have high hopes.

It will begin with the farce the American trio have prepared for us. Kelly Francesca, Daniella Goldblum, and Jenny Lipp.

The first day proper of the festival is Saturday. All right, I say. All right. Nothing wrong with that.

But that the first item in the program is called "After Midday with German poet Günther Meierhof" is not only typical but even an inevitable discrimination against poets who speak and write in minor languages; that seems to be a given at festivals like this, whether they are held in England, Sweden, or Iceland.

This so-called "After Midday" with the German poet (a poet no-one outside of Germany has ever heard of) goes on for two hours, and then, only then, does someone else get a turn.

First up are the domestic poets, and things proceed with them offering some outlandish play, no doubt some sort of "lyrical" play—I can't understand why people haven't seen through this phenomenon long ago, since the theater has nothing whatsoever to do with poetry.

There seems, in fact, to be something missing from the program on Saturday: it ends after this "performance" and participants are simply left afterwards in an empty space. There is not even any mention of supper.

The second day starts with the formal registration of participants at something called the Dainava center at 16 Maironio Street.

Why on earth do the people who organize these things assume that we all know where Maironio Street is? Most of us have come to Druskininkai for the first (and last) time in our lives.

But at the end of the registration period (which I don't expect will be any better; I imagine we'll get some kind of card with our name on it, which we're expected to wear hanging on our chests) we suddenly jump into a recital by some poet from Wales, some totally unknown poet who has decided to go by the name Niphin Bush, absurd as it sounds.

It doesn't take a powerful imagination to predict that such people are more accurately called drinkers. A poet bearing the same last name as an American president doesn't deserve to be taken seriously as a poet.

I don't intend to cast specific aspersions on the job of the American president—haven't we had enough of that grumbling?—but trying to make a career as a poet who shares a name with George W., Jeb, and George the elder is about as clever as sitting in the driver's seat of a truck that's going at full speed only to find the steering wheel is missing.

I perhaps shouldn't be allowed to make assertions about people I've never met. But if anyone is allowed to do this, then I think I should be the one.

Before I went to the poetry festival in Liège, the one I mentioned above, I carefully read the documents about the festival which I'd been sent, and one participant caught my attention: a fifty-something poet from Ireland (exactly the way you'd describe me, if you changed the "r" in Ireland for a "c"). This person has published an incredible number of poetry books, as well as some books on the art of poetry in general (as if there aren't enough books about that already).

Although I didn't have a picture of this person, I immediately knew he had to be a drinker, and I was also sure his sole purpose in visiting Liège was to sample the Belgian strawberry and cherry beer.

Indeed, I had a very vivid image of this person in my mind, long before I met him, and in that image he was sitting at a Belgian beer bar with a huge glass of light-red strawberry beer in front of him, and beside the beer were two or three whisky glasses which he had gulped down between mouthfuls of beer.

And then I met the man: the only thing wrong with my prophetic image was his preference for Irish rather than strawberry beer; he drank Guinness with whisky. But his main purpose in turning up at the poetry festival was, as he himself put it: "One has poetic license to drink more than one usually drinks on a working day at home."

I don't know whether I should recount the other items on the program for Sunday. To tell the truth, what most attracted my attention in the program was the midday, coffee, and supper breaks, which could be more frequent, based on a quick glance at how compressed the poetry program is.

There, at least, you get some nourishment, something you don't get from all the Nordic drivel which will be poured over us by the bucket-load at the festival.

And barely have I got my head around the term "creative writing" than, between one o'clock and half-past three on Sunday, we're offered a lesson in this sort of writing.

I am fairly sure the trio of American poets will do really well at that gathering, shouting interjections in the form of pretentious-sounding questions which have no value besides disturbing the moderators of these so-called lessons from their attempt to share their limited knowledge with the simpletons who go in for the creative-writing lark—a group which definitely won't include me.

And that about covers the major points of the Lithuanian program, which I have here in front of me, except for the Sunday night, when they've planned some universal gathering of poets. And, following that, there's an item in the program with the embarrassing name "Night of the One Poem."

Monday, the last official day of the festival, naturally begins with breakfast. Some people won't exactly be bright-eyed that morning.

Then there is some ridiculous performance planned for the tired, ready to depart participants, some nonsense called "The disagreement between fire, water, air, and earth."

I'm going to make myself disappear while this torture takes place.

At the end of all this, there's a festival publicity event to introduce a festival poetry collection which is being published on behalf of the festival.

The only good thing about both the presentation and the publication is that—mixed in with all the stillborn poems by Jespers, Bengts, and Kláuses—you can find my own poems in the collection, the poems of a poet who has turned his back on poetry.

Actually, the poems will be in the odd Lithuanian language, but nevertheless they will be there, and as far as I'm concerned it will be enough that people know the poems were originally written in the one Nordic language you can definitely describe as having a somewhat lyrical tone: the Icelandic language.

And then, as a way of concluding this tragicomic presentation, all kinds of reading groups take over the program. We poor devils will be arranged into groups according to some rigid system one of the festival committee members has been devoting months to, and I'm assuming that these groups will perform an autopsy on one of the poems.

I wouldn't be surprised if we end up choosing a messy effort by one of the American housewife-poets, or by the Meierhof Phenomenon; it certainly won't be a poem by that drunkard Bush or by me, who is from the back of beyond.

And finally, when we've all been over-stuffed with the art of words, the organizers will reveal to us who is the idiotic winner of the poetry contest they announced on the first day of the festival.

At this moment, I will be asking myself why in the world I accepted the invitation to this strange festival. Especially as I'm already thinking about, eagerly anticipating, the moment I get to take off in the airplane from Vilnius, free from all that crap, at least until the invite to the next festival arrives.

Nevertheless, I am going to go there in mid-October; not long now.

Indeed, I got my tickets in the mail this morning. Keflavík—Copenhagen—Vilnius and back. The tickets were sealed in a stupid envelope which was so tight a fit that I tore them on one corner when I tried to get them out.

It felt to me like I was playfully tearing banknotes in half. The feeling was painful and tender at the same time.

I imagined some crazy rich rapper in Los Angeles excitedly setting down his gun and beginning to tear dollar bills apart in front of a photographer who has come to visit him.

Why don't they invite this sort of larger-than-life guy to Lithuania for the festival?

Someone people know. Someone who can compose on the spot and actually has something to say about the situation in the world. Or the situation in South Central.

I can imagine this rapper sitting at the breakfast in Druskininkai, his baseball cap on backwards and thick gold chains dangling into his oatmeal.

The organizer of the festival is standing outside the breakfast room, and he has taken up smoking again."

PART TWO

VILNIUS

A STAIN ON THE CARPET

When he opens the door to room number 304 in the Ambassador Hotel in Vilnius, it's not the television set which seems to hang from thin air high above the curtains, but a darkish stain on the light brown carpet in the entryway that Sturla first locks eyes on. The stain is the same size as the hazelnut Sturla had earlier slipped into his overcoat pocket while he was waiting to be picked up from the airport. It was a beautifully shaped and colored natural object, something that would serve as a kind of lucky charm while he was staying in that country.

Sturla had been told in an e-mail from the organizers of the festival that a person by the name of Jonas would meet him at the airport. "One of our most renowned poets" had been included in parenthesis in English after the man's last name—a very strange name which Sturla had not tried especially hard to remember. At first, Sturla wasn't sure what he ought to feel about the fact that his welcoming party had the same name as his long-dead cousin poet, but when he had shaken this Jonas's hand, after the latter had eventually found him on the sidewalk in front of the airport terminal, he felt it was appropriate that a poet with this name would welcome him to his final week as a poet, or so he told himself.

"Nice to meet you, Jonas," Sturla had said, and Jonas replied, "Nice to meet you soon, Mister Jonsson."

Just as with Jonas's last name, Sturla had difficulty remembering the name of the woman who was with him, a dark-haired, striking woman in her forties who kept her eyes hidden behind unusually large, coal-black sunglasses. Jonas the poet's appearance didn't give any indication that he was a writer. He wore a short, light gray leather jacket, jeans of some unknown origin, and his unkempt hair looked like it was full of plaster or dust. Sturla saw why when they got into the car: it was a twenty-year-old red Datsun which appeared to have long been used for some sort of construction jobs.

Other than his greeting when they met, Jonas seemed unwilling to trust himself on the slippery ice of English; the woman handled the introductions. She started by apologizing for Jonas, who spoke German but not English; Sturla would have to ask her if he wanted to know something, and then she immediately said something strange about Vilnius: "But what is there to know? It's only a city."

Sturla shrugged his shoulders; he wanted to ask something so that it didn't seem like he was agreeing with this woman's opinion of the city, but nothing came to mind. She asked Sturla a few polite questions about whether his flight had been okay and what the weather was like in Iceland, then turned her undivided attention to Jonas; they seemed to be in the middle of a discussion, and forgot him completely for the quarter of an hour it took to drive to the hotel. In the meantime, Sturla listened to the Lithuanian coming from their mouths—a language which maybe wasn't as stiff-sounding as he had assumed in his article's jokes about the festival (in a disrespectful fashion, he now realized)—and he wondered whether or not finding a hazelnut on the bare concrete at the entrance to the airport terminal was a little strange. Wasn't such an unlikely occurrence on his arrival in the country a sign that something unexpected was going to happen, something that would never happen on, say, Skúlagata?

As soon as Jonas and the woman finished their conversation, Sturla was going to ask them whether they could guess what the little hazelnut had been doing in the concrete airport landscape. He imagined the question as a humorous little remark which would allow him to perhaps form a very tiny connection with these people: truth be told, he found it a little uncomfortable that they didn't pay more attention to him, a newcomer to their country. But Jonas and the woman (Sturla thought she might also be a poet) didn't stop talking for a single moment until the three of them arrived at the hotel reception, where a long and seemingly complicated discussion took place between the woman with sunglasses and the hotel employee, a young red-headed woman in a dark blue uniform who ended the conversation by turning to Sturla and saying, in English, "I will take care of you now." This declaration appeared to lift a heavy load off Jonas and his lady friend; they smiled—something Sturla realized he hadn't seen them do yet—and Jonas suddenly remembered to give Sturla an envelope with information about the festival. They said their goodbyes, and Sturla found he was relieved to be out of their care.

"You're in room number 304," the red-headed woman had told him, and she had then told him several things about the hotel, pointing out the stairs with her index finger and telling him, apologetically, that there was no elevator; he would need to climb two flights and then go to his left.

Sturla was therefore still out of breath when he stepped over the stain on the carpet of the hotel room, with his suitcase in tow and his briefcase in his hand. When he was past the stain and stood beside his bed, what drew his attention next—other than that the room was cramped—was the lamp on the bedside table between the narrow beds; it had an orange-colored plastic shade which seemed to have come from a pizza parlor he once ate at in Budapest exactly twenty years ago; he'd stayed there with Hulda for a weekend, after visiting an old, distant aunt of hers in Vienna. But when Sturla switches on the lamp, and dims the overhead light, there is a soft and pleasant glow in the room, which reminds him of a particular habit he'd adopted when traveling abroad: the first thing he would do on entering a hotel room—even before turning on the television—was pour himself a shot of whatever alcohol he'd bought in duty-free.

As if welcoming himself to the new place.

On this occasion, Sturla had bought himself a half-liter of twelve-year-old scotch whisky. He lifts his briefcase up onto the table below the mirror, opens it by arranging the numbers into the combination 666, and looks at himself in the mirror as he opens the briefcase. He decides to take a shower after he's had a drink, then change his clothes and work out whether or not to order coffee up to the room to refresh himself, before he has another measure of whisky and goes into town to look around. He remembers seeing a door to a cafeteria or some kind of bar midway between the hotel entrance and the reception, and he allows himself to imagine that the young man who was sitting inside, next to a window that looks out onto the street, is one of the festival participants. "I've evidently arrived at some kind of Scandinavian family gathering," Sturla says out loud to the mirror; he decides that the man he'd glimpsed looks like those Nordic poets who enthusiastically recite their works in a dramatic manner, with musical accompaniment; he must be a Norwegian or Swede, Sturla thinks, as he scrambles the numbers on the lock again. Then he takes the whisky bottle from the briefcase (wrapped in a black v-neck sweater he'd bought on his layover at Kastrup airport in Copenhagen), a paperback (which he'd also bought at the airport), a cigarette packet, and the in-flight magazine from the AirBaltic Fokker airplane.

While he fetches himself a water glass from the bathroom Sturla recalls the article he read in the in-flight magazine about the Chernobyl nuclear disaster in April 1986, and he thinks about how close he is to that area at the moment. Chernobyl, which is in the Ukraine, is right by the border with Belarus, itself no more than a stone's throw from Vilnius, and the radioactive material had done most damage in Belarus, both to the people and to the arable land.

Sturla pours some gold-colored scotch into the clear water glass and holds it up to the mirror before taking his first sip.

"Belarus," he says aloud to himself. "Lukashenko. President Alexander Lukashenko." And he tries to imagine how it feels to live in a country which is governed by a person who describes the language of his people, Belarusian, as unsuitable for dealing with important matters; who says that the only great languages of the world are Russian or English. It reminds him of a middle-aged man from Belarus who he got to know a little at the poetry festival in Belgium, a poet and literary critic who Sturla regrets not having mentioned in his newly-written article, which he realizes at this moment casts his hosts, past and present, in a negative light. Perhaps if he'd also added one or two more generous depictions, it might have brightened it up a bit, without sacrificing any of its sting. If anyone is ripe for a generous characterization, Sturla thinks, it is that Belarusian literary guy in Liège. He'd aroused Sturla's admiration because of his rare talent for making harsh critiques sound like they contained some praise. Talking with Sturla and two other poets at the festival in Liège, he had torn apart the unsuccessful organization of the festival in a particularly humorous fashion, but at the same time praised it generously. It had been a splendid example of constructive demolition, of the warmth there could be in sarcasm, a quality Sturla wanted most of all to characterize his own thoughts and actions as an author. And yet Sturla had never come across a more strong and pungent odor of sweat than the one which had emanated from the pithy Belarusian, and he'd done his best to avoid ending up on the same table as him at mealtimes.

Sturla remembers how, while translating the poem by Liliya (the Belarusian poet who he suspects he will likely meet quite soon), his memory of the literary critic's body odor had been quite literally disturbing. If there was something that put Sturla off-balance in close conversations with people, it was the odor of sweat or of halitosis, and if any life experience were likely to stick in his mind, it was being forced to breathe the pollution that comes from the human body.

"Cheers, Liliya Boguinskaia. I'll go back to Belarus with you."

And Sturla toasts the mirror on behalf of the Belarusian poet whose poem he translated and who translated his poem from an English translation as part of the project the festival organizers had instigated in the hope that the poets would get to know each other before they met at the festival. And just as Liliya Boguinskaia has no idea who this Sturla Jón Jónsson is, this guy who has translated her poem "Pilies Street" into Icelandic, Sturla doesn't know anything about her: only her name and that she'd translated his poem "kennslustund," via English, "the lesson," into her own language.

"Cheers to the unknown translator," Sturla says, smiling. He finishes the drink and grimaces at himself in the mirror. Then he goes to the window and draws back the curtains, and as he wonders if Liliya is already in Vilnius and what she looks like—whether she is planning to arrive in the country before the festival begins, since she lives in the vicinity—he faces the whitewashed wall of a house and a well-lit yard between the buildings where two trash cans are laying on their sides and some cars are parked. He notices that all five cars are German brands. It strikes him at once how little people notice in new, foreign surroundings; not just people generally, but himself in particular— someone who is supposed to be a poet, and therefore observant, his eyes open to everything before them; provided, of course that his conception of what a poet should be is correct: someone who is the conscience of language, someone who has the duty of setting into language things that others are not attentive to or aware of.

This thought strikes him because he realizes, with some regret, that on the way into the city from the airport he didn't pay proper attention to what the city looks like and what impression it had on him. The only thing he remembers from the trip are two or three particularly ugly high-rises, a set of dwarf skyscrapers which he suspects were built after the country won its independence from the Soviet Union.

A single glance had stamped these awful structures in his mind as the symbol of long-awaited liberty from totalitarian communist rule for the natives. Those people he particularly remembers noticing from the car on his way to the hotel had seemed handsome and even well-to-do (as his mother would put it)—a complete contrast to the mournful image which the brutal present-day architecture had imposed on the city for the sole purpose of challenging the poet's eyes.

But had he expected anything other than that people here are beautiful?

A WORLD WHICH OPENS ONTO THE STREET

Before Sturla gets in the shower he turns on the television. While figuring out what channels are available, he is surprised at how high in the air the device has been placed, and how unsafe the fixtures seem. When he comes back out of the bathroom, in a cloud of steam that has been created because he thoughtlessly shut the door, there is a discussion about finances on the American news channel CNN. Three men are sitting in three chairs—chairs which Sturla thinks seem to be of Scandinavian design—and deliberating over the possibilities which investment in Chinese business might offer to western investors. The clock shows a few minutes to 10:00. Sturla half-watches the televised conversation while he finishes drying himself, and then he slips hurriedly into underwear, pants, and shirt and gets his wallet out of his jacket to take down to the cafeteria. He looks in the mirror and strokes the still-wet hair on his head so that it doesn't hang over his forehead in that way which always reminds him of Adolf Hitler. He launches himself towards the door a little too quickly to remember the stain on the hallway carpet, which he'd only just managed to steer clear of stepping in earlier. He'd meant to investigate the stain by touching it, first when he initially noticed it and then before taking a shower, but he ends up doing so now; he finds out that the dark stain is wet, that the liquid seems to be oil or some kind of cleaning fluid.

He shivers a little in disgust as he dries his finger on a hand towel from the bathroom. He carefully sniffs his fingertip, as though it might be dangerous to bring it too close to his nose, and he bends back down to the carpet and touches the area around the stain. When he stands back up, he experiences a sudden dizziness, and while he waits for this dizziness to clear, he looks at the television screen: the pope is standing in his car, waving to a great crowd that has gathered in some European city. Before Sturla leaves the room he takes some toilet paper from the bathroom, folds it over, and places it on top of the stain.

He springs down the stairs. He is feeling good. The hotel experience always gives him a special sense of liberty, which he instinctively connects with his first ever trip abroad and with going camping as a teenager. A rented room always makes him feel that something unexpected or thrilling will happen, the sort of thing which seldom happens at his own apartment. Even the stain on the carpet in room number 304 at the Ambassador Hotel makes it somehow more thrilling, more strange—he ought to say more dangerous, he thinks, smiling to himself at this idea as he reaches the first floor.

No, Sturla Jón, the wet stain on the hotel carpet doesn't make the room dangerous!

The red-headed girl in reception has the telephone receiver pressed to her ear with her shoulder; she seems a bit panicky as she searches through some papers on the desk. She still gives herself time to smile at Sturla as he goes by, and he feels like he'd better stop and react to her smile in some way. He has reached the glass doors of the cafeteria by the time he turns back and goes up to the reception desk. The girl, called Elena according to the badge on her dark blue jacket, indicates to him with her hand that she will help him in just a moment, and while Sturla waits he looks over a selection of brochures in canvas pockets on the wall by reception. He has selected three brochures to take with him by the time the redhead speaks his name: Mr. Jonson. He turns around, and the girl, who has taken the phone from her ear, asks Sturla if she can help him with something. He starts by apologizing for having disturbed her and as he listens to himself he thinks how silly he sounds asking if he can get coffee "in there," pointing in the direction of the cafeteria.

"Yes, of course," Elena replies, smiling.

"To take up to my room?" asks Sturla.

"Yes, you just ask for coffee in the caféteria." And the girl smiles again, returning the phone to her ear and apologizing to the person on the line.

The young Norwegian or Swede is still sitting at the same table in the restaurant, a thick book in front of him. He holds a thin self-rolled cigarette and looks out the window at the avenue Sturla was on before, when he got out of the car outside the hotel earlier in the evening, and which is called G-something-or-other prospektas, like the Nevski prospect in Gogol's short story of the same name. (He decides to ask a local, perhaps Elena at reception, how to translate "prospektas" in this context; to one who recognizes the word only from Germanic and Latin languages, using it to describe a street or avenue sounds quite peculiar.) Except for the Nordic contingent—it occurs to Sturla that maybe he should introduce himself, "being from the Nordic lands myself," as he would phrase it—there are two older men in the place, smoking silently at a table in the middle of the room, and four young people who are talking together at high velocity and who seem to notice something funny about Sturla; when he goes past them they all look quickly at him before turning back to one another, stifling bursts of laughter.

It isn't clear whether this place is called a cafeteria or a bar: the chairs, tables, and all the fixtures are more reminiscent of the waiting room in a federal building. There are cakes and sandwiches in a glass case at the service counter and, facing outwards on a glass shelf in front of a mirrored window, long rows of beer and liquor bottles, something which doesn't really match what Sturla notices next: index cards with handwritten information about the breakfast the place serves between 7:00 and 10:30 every day except Sunday.

What do hotel guests do on Sunday mornings? he asks himself. And he considers himself lucky not to need to figure that out: he will be out in the country that day, in the spa town of Druskininkai.

Three young waitresses are standing side-by-side behind the till, wearing reddish jackets which are perhaps more like smocks, and they all stare as one at Sturla when he asks whether he can get a double espresso to take up to his room. The girls don't seem to know what to say, but one makes a decision, the one in the middle: she asks Sturla if he is staying in the hotel. When he confirms that he is, she informs him that they only offer table service, that he won't be able to take coffee up to his room.

"You don't have any paper cups?" Sturla asks, running his eyes over the liquor selection on the shelf, to see if they carry the same whisky as he has up in the room.

The girl shrugs her shoulders, as if she doesn't understand the question, but instead of asking why he wants a paper cup, she tells him that they only have normal coffee cups; he can sit at any of the tables in the room and have coffee.

"There's no way I can take one of the 'normal' cups up to my room?"

"We only serve coffee at the tables."

"But in those cups?" Sturla asks, nodding to a row of water glasses.

"No," replies the girl. Sturla asks himself whether he might have to return to his room without getting any coffee out of the fancy Krups machine which gleams from between the girl who just spoke and the one standing on her right. He asks if he can order some coffee for here, and perhaps Coke in a paper or plastic glass, but that option isn't available: he can have some Coke, but not in a paper or plastic glass.

"Þá held ég að allir möguleikar séu fullreyndir," he says, but none of the girls seems interested in finding out what the words mean. They look expressionlessly at Sturla, who imagines that either they are hiding their amazement—who is this strange guy who wants to take coffee up to his room?—or else they don't really understand what he wants.

The kids who were laughing at the table are now sitting in silence and don't seem to notice Sturla as he goes past them. Still thinking about his failed attempt to order coffee, he looks to see what the Nordic guy is drinking, and isn't very surprised to find that it's tea. Though Sturla had considered saying hello to the man, he now decides not to; he raises his head and pushes open the glass door which swings into the hotel lobby. As he does, he thinks about how a coffee shop like this one doesn't deserve better customers than those who make their own cigarettes and order nothing more than a single cup of tea all evening.

"I couldn't get any coffee to take up to my room," Sturla tells the redhead at reception; she is now sitting and talking with another young woman in an identical uniform who is putting on make-up. She seems surprised that Sturla couldn't get any coffee, and she says she will fix it right away; he can go on up and she will bring him some coffee. Sturla thanks her gratefully and asks her to order him an espresso; he prefers coffee without milk.

What are my children doing right now? he wonders as he goes upstairs, and is immediately amazed that he is thinking about his offspring so unexpectedly, here in this distant place. Is it possible some of them were thinking about their father at the same moment, perhaps worrying that he is alone, so far away from everyone he knows? Are they are also worrying whether he will succeed in the assignment he has been given, an assignment on behalf of his country: to represent it in the narrow but vital world of poetry? No. Hardly. It had not occurred to him once to mention his role here in such grand terms. As he climbs to his floor he begins imagining what his five children are doing at that moment. He pauses and tries to picture them for himself, in the same way the omniscient narrator of a realistic novel would if he wanted to describe Sturla Jón's sons and daughters:

Egill is sitting by the kitchen table with his mother, Hulda, and his girlfriend Puri. It is evening, as it is in Lithuania, but it isn't the same time: there's a three-hour difference between Iceland and mainland Northern Europe. It is uncomfortably bright in Hulda's kitchen: sixty-watt lightbulbs in the ceiling lights illuminate every corner and every surface, but in the window is the deep darkness you find out in the country. Símon, Hulda's partner, a store manager, is probably still at work. Hulda tells Egill how happy she is to have all five of her children at home with her; it doesn't happen often. But Egill, who lives in London and is visiting Egilsstaðir briefly, is immersed in thoughts of Reykjavík: he longs to be in the capital city where he knows—or ought to know, since even his father knows it—that two American neo-country-and-western bands are playing concerts this weekend. The Spanish Puri undoubtedly also wants to be in the capital city, if what Egill told Sturla is true and she is a songwriter and singer who has put out a few CDs—something Sturla knows isn't necessarily any indication of success or fame nowadays.

The interplay of these two facts—that he is enjoying his freedom in a hotel away from home while his son is imprisoned with his mother and Símon—causes Sturla to feel a little guilty; he never told Egill that he and Puri could stay at his place on Skúlagata if they went to Reykjavík before going back to London. But Sturla isn't especially keen to loan his apartment to his oldest son. Three years ago, when Egill came home to Iceland unexpectedly with his then-girlfriend, an Irish artist who was ten years older than him, Sturla was staying in Stykkishólmur, in a house he'd rented through the Writer's Union. When Egill let him know that he was looking for a place to stay for a few days, Sturla was happy to tell him he could get the key to Skúlagata from his grandfather Jón and that he could stay in the apartment while Sturla was away. Sturla wasn't quite so happy when he returned from his trip to Stykkishólmur, more than a week after Egill and the Irish woman had left. Judging by the mess, it seemed like they had needed to abandon the apartment in a hurry, after holding a party. It later came to light that six CDs had vanished from Sturla's collection: three by Incredible String Band, two by Joni Mitchell, and the CD which Sturla considered probably his favorite in his collection: *It's So Hard to Tell Who's Going to Love You the Best* by Karen Dalton. And when he called Egill to let him know that his acquaintances, that rabble he'd invited into the apartment, had cleaned out his CD collection, Egill suddenly remembered he'd borrowed the CDs; he would return them next time he visited.

Notwithstanding the disorder that had characterized Egill's life since he was a young man, and notwithstanding his lack of success in finding his own sound as a musician—a sound he could call his own and which didn't remind him of many other people—Sturla still had faith that his son would eventually "find the right note" and stand out, just as he, the father, had succeeded (at least in the opinion of the so-called literary establishment) with the publication of his fourth book, which came out when he was thirty-five years old. However, the works in that book hadn't been "written themselves" like the poems he'd written until then. Sturla's experience working as a prison warden for two years before sitting down to write *free from freedom* had invigorated his poetry, and his method of describing the prison experience appealed so well to the Icelandic literary scene that not only did the book sell a thousand copies when it came out, but it even continued to sell the next year, better than the books Sturla had published after that. And just as that book, based on his specific experiences as a prison guard, earned Sturla Jón a lasting reputation (even if men like his neighbor on Skúlagata, Láki or whatever he called himself, don't know he is a poet), so Sturla expects something similar awaits his son Egill: he will be able to utilize his own unique experience living in a major city overseas and getting to know people of different backgrounds. Sooner or later he'll work out how to shape that experience into a form people will understand.

Gunnar, Sturla's next-oldest son, had on occasion asked to stay with his father while he was in Reykjavík, and one weekend, when he was flying south to compete in a table-tennis tournament, he'd stayed in the apartment alone. But his interests and sense of duty were so unlike his brother's that Sturla would even trust Gunnar with his work as super if he needed to. On the other hand, their relationship as father and son is a long way from being what Sturla thought the relationship between close family members ought to be. Soon after Gunnar began working for his step-father in the grocery department of the Cooperative regional store, his relations with Sturla had become merely civil—stiff, even. In the four years Gunnar had worked with Símon (instead of continuing his studies, as it had always seemed he would), it would be fair to say his entire world had shrunk to what he had to say about the two- or three-thousand square-meter storeroom of Samkaup Selections, his workplace. As a teenager, Gunnar had shown some interest in his father's poetry, had at least read his books, and had once written a little essay about a few poems from the first one, but in recent years Sturla's next-oldest (or next-youngest) son had expressed his strong disapproval of "that hobbyhorse, poetry," as Gunnar once let slip out in his father's company.

Those words had possibly had a worse effect on Sturla than they should have: the accusation was made at a gathering of Hulda's family, a gathering which Sturla's mother-in-law had insisted he come to, despite (or because) he hadn't seen Hulda's relatives since they'd separated almost ten years before. And although Sturla had generally not spoken much with the mother of his children after the separation, the change which had come over their son Gunnar was motivation enough to talk to her. Hulda, on the other hand, absolutely refused to talk about how their twenty-four-year-old son's behavior and mentality had come to resemble a sixty-year-old grocery store manager's, as Sturla put it bluntly—Hulda was, in fact, offended by Sturla's comments, and possibly reasonably so.

Thinking about how unalike Egill and Gunnar are, Sturla Jón imagines Gunnar coming into the kitchen while Egill, Hulda, and Puri are sitting there with their coffees, talking about music or movies. Gunnar takes stock of the kitchen table: this and that much remain of the two boxes of cookies his mother has put out on the table, so there's no need to order more yet—orders should be made as close as possible to the moment supplies run out. And having made his decision, he disappears from the kitchen with a milky coffee drink in a water glass, without anyone who is seated at the table under the ceiling lights having spoken to him.

The youngest son, Grettir, is currently on the next floor of the house, in his room. He is studying (this strikes Sturla as very plausible). Grettir had begun studying at the Grammar School in Reykjavík, where his younger sister Hallgerður had recently started her second year, but before he finished the first year—after badly breaking his leg and ankle on the steps in front of the school, an injury that confined him to bed rest for a month and a half—he decided he wanted to continue his studies at the Grammar School in Egilsstaðir.

Grettir, who is nineteen, has always been the most sensitive of the siblings, not only physically but also to the words and glances of other people, as Sturla describes it to himself. But though the boy is clearly fascinated by art, especially music (like his brother Egill) and the visual arts, he had never shown any inclination towards creating art: he is happy just enjoying it. This interest keeps him so occupied that little else, his studies included, has any place in his head.

Though nothing directly indicated that Grettir was physically attracted to his own sex—nor to the other sex, for that matter—it seemed, on the other hand, that nearly all his enthusiasm for artists was directed at those artists who were openly homosexual or else radiated something more delicate than their colleagues. Among visual artists, for example, he highly prized David Hockney, Egon Schiele,

Giacometti, Modigliani, and Gustav Klimt, and, for some reason, Francis Bacon, who according to what his mother said stares down at anyone who enters Grettir's room from a huge framed photograph on the wall above his bed. Hulda hadn't told Sturla this because she found it funny but because it aroused her alarm—more even than Bacon's self-portraits did.

Although the description of his youngest son's room had come from his mother, Sturla got regular updates about Grettir's private world—his tiny bedroom—from his daughter Hallgerður. Shortly after hearing about the picture of Francis Bacon, he'd tried to wheedle out of his son what he was listening to these days and what had recently caught his attention in the other arts, but when he had little success—it was as if Grettir didn't want to share his private world with anyone, not even his father—Sturla asked Hallgerður if she could tell him what Grettir's room looked like; if she could "spy a little for him." And when she found out how happy her description of Grettir's room made her father, she began to explain her brother's unusual and sophisticated tastes, and by and by she came to enjoy telling her father about Grettir's newest acquisitions, the things he'd ordered on the internet or brought home from the library.

The conversations between father and daughter, Sturla and Hallgerður, often turned to what was at the top of Grettir's CD pile, or what he had recently discovered in the world of visual art. Sturla thought it was especially funny to hear how a poster of Picasso's *Three Dancers* was hanging on the bedroom wall, a picture which, it so happened, Sturla remembered well because of the shadowy figure who looked eyelessly to the left, an open-mouthed profile in the balcony window, midway between two dancers on the right side of the picture. To Sturla's eyes, that figure was his uncle Hallmundur rather than Picasso's friend who had died while the picture was being painted.

Among the musicians Grettir liked, according to Hallgerður, he listened most to David Bowie, Mark Almond, Morrissey, George Michael, and Scott Walker, but when Hallgerður gave Sturla the news over the phone that she'd seen a CD bearing the name Gérard Souzay, Sturla almost couldn't stop himself from bursting out laughing. He thought it was both endlessly funny and delightful that his nineteen-year-old son at Egilsstaðir had found his way to lieder and opera songs. But, of course, he had to refrain from laughing because, despite the fact that he and Hallgerður liked to smile at Grettir's tastes in arts, Sturla hoped that his daughter would perhaps be a little infected by him.

During the weeks and months after the French baritone singer was discovered in Grettir's room, he added CDs from the library with names like Hans Hotter, Nicolai Gedda, and Benjamin Gigli, and after them came French chamber music—French only. On the other hand, in the last eighteen months Grettir had, according to Hallgerður, completely fallen for singers and lyricists like Antony and the Johnsons, CocoRosie, and the Canadian Rufus Wainwright—names Sturla recognized from the music section of the newspaper but hadn't paid much attention to, except for the last one, which he connected more to his own musical tastes than those of his son, since Rufus was the son of a musician Sturla had prized for thirty years, Loudon Wainwright. This fact had made Sturla want to hear how the young Rufus sounded but after having listened to a few tracks in a record store on Laugavegur he realized that he would be happy enough with the father of the family.

But even though he seemed to have great enthusiasm for, and a strong feeling for, the delicate—feminine, even—when it came to music and the visual arts, Grettir had given his father's poetry no more thought than courtesy required; even Gunnar had expressed himself more fully about Sturla's poetry.

The reason why Sturla thinks about his sons first is not so much because they are sons—nor because of the sequence of their ages—but more because he has unconsciously saved his daughters for last, in the same way, he thinks, that a man keeps the best of the assorted chocolates until last.

He has reached his hotel room by the time he lets his thoughts rest on Hildigunnur, his older daughter, the child he admits to himself he feels the most affection for (though it's forbidden, of course, for a father of five children to have such thoughts; children ought to be—according to what the books say—equal in the eyes of their parents). But more than once—not just twice, but a few hundred times, if not a thousand—Sturla has been amazed at the fact that his eldest daughter, who is certainly a poet's daughter, has chosen to do things which Sturla considers diametrically opposed to lyrical thinking and to delight in the beauty of life, things like weight-lifting, fitness training, and trying to make herself darker than when she was born. Hildigunnur's friend, a very promising swimmer who died at just sixteen years old from an overdose of steroids, had managed to interest her in sports and strength-training shortly before her death. Hildigunnur's newfound enthusiasm had actually increased after her friend's passing and had led, over the course of several years, to a behavior Sturla couldn't think about as anything other than an unconditional worship of appearances and surfaces—a behavior Sturla (and, indeed, Hulda as well) considered unnatural and false, and, even more than that, dangerous to her health, especially her mental health. But the uncompromising program which his older daughter had trapped herself in—and which it wasn't easy to pull her out of—naturally changed nothing in Sturla's feelings for Hildigunnur: she is still the child who he has the most respect for. He can't exactly explain this to himself; it is often the case that what a person experiences most strongly is also the hardest to articulate in words.

Both of Sturla's daughters are somewhat darker than their brothers. It is largely because of this that Hildigunnur's parents have great difficulty understanding their older daughter's resolute desire to improve her skin color by engaging in that dangerous, even life-threatening habit: tanning. Hallgerður, Hildigunnur's sister, actually already has the look their parents (and probably also their brothers) wish Hildigunnur had, and the reason is simply that Hildigunnur had changed herself. She has altered herself through strength training and an almost debilitating competitive temperament which little by little has given her eyes and mouth a determined look; her father—who still wants to picture the face of the girl he fathered—constantly has to wipe the more recent image from his imagination when they talk.

Sturla imagines that Hildigunnur is at the fitness center in Egilsstaðir, and as he turns his thoughts to Hallgerður, to where she might be at this minute, he introduces Símon, Hulda's partner, into the picture. Símon comes into the kitchen and reaches in the kitchen cupboard for the coffee mug with his name on it. Then he blends himself some kind of milk drink with coffee and a large quantity of white sugar from one of those sugar containers you find on tables at country diners and gas stations. His lumbering movements and weary sighs—sighs which sound almost half as loud as the physical labors that cause him to complain—arouse even more hostility in Egill than he ordinarily feels towards this country town; the sounds intensify the uncomfortable feeling which accompanies being seated, motionless, in an overly-bright rural kitchen when he should be in a warm, dark music venue in Reykjavík, among people who have no idea where Egilsstaðir is, who have never been into a co-op. Símon sits down with them, Egill, Þuri, and Hulda, and says something about his job before lifting the coffee mug to his thin lips and beginning to slurp.

Even though Sturla has only met his children's stepfather twice—at Hallgerður's confirmation four years ago and then a year after that, when he went east to stay with his children while Hulda and Símon went abroad—and though he's seen Símon dressed in a black, pinstripe suit, Sturla always imagines him in a white butcher's apron that's stained with blood and viscera from the animals at the meat counter. Sturla pretends not to know that Símon has had nothing to do with meat processing since he began working his way up the company as a young man, when he was completely unaware that he would one day be the surrogate father of five rather good-natured and promising children—instead of father to his own children.

The first thing Sturla does when he gets back to his room is to see whether the toilet paper has managed to soak up the liquid from the stain on the carpet. It turns out that it hasn't made so much of a mark that the paper needs changing. He lights himself a cigarette, pours some whisky into a glass, and acts on his idea of placing one of his shoes on top of the paper, in order to press it down onto the wet spot. While he is up, he hangs his overcoat and suit in the closet in the entryway; he strokes the material of the overcoat, letting it rustle as he does, then fetches the whisky glass, raising it so he can see the color of the twelve-year-old drink against the light brown shade of the coat. The color of the whisky always reminds him of the caramel wrappers in the tins of Quality Street chocolates at his grandfather the ambassador's house, tins which never seemed to get empty. Those were the candies he always saved for last, the most exciting ones. The color of the overcoat, on the other hand, is the color of dry earth: of the rational, of stability, of permanence. As he takes a sip of the drink Sturla realizes how much he longs to have a coffee on the side. A few days ago he was being offered expensive coffee in a clothing store in Reykjavík, but here in the Ambassador Hotel, in the capital city of Lithuania-land—as he calls it at this moment—he seems unable to get any coffee up in his room, even though the cafeteria is open, even though there is a high-quality espresso machine, which looks like it is brand-new, perhaps even unused, waiting to be put to use downstairs.

Sturla slips his hand into one of the overcoat pockets and gets out some of the sugar which he'd taken from the clothing store on Bankastræti. He examines the brown package for a bit and wonders whether he shouldn't be avoiding coffee, since it is so late and a pleasant tiredness is easing throughout his whole body, promising him a good, deep night of sleep. It has been a long day. Good sense whispers to Sturla that he should let the people in reception know that he doesn't need the coffee; he ought to brush his teeth, rest his cheek on the white, freshly-washed linen of the hotel pillow, and let himself disappear into sleep, that one dwelling place in life which you can always count on being the same, as complicated and unpredictable as it is. He decides instead to go on a short stroll around town. He reasons that it will be good to get a generous dose of oxygen into his lungs before lying down for the night. Just as he remembers he'd meant to call his father and let him know he forgot to get the VCR from the repair shop—which therefore will get in the way of loaning the Iranian movie the next day—his phone rings loudly, and it takes him a little while to find the gadget; it is a new experience, answering a phone that isn't connected to a wall.

"Sturla dear?"

"Hi, mom."

"How are you doing?"

"I'm doing well. I'm just waiting for coffee to arrive in my room."

"In your room? Are you going to drink coffee in your bedroom? Are you in a hotel?"

"Yes, mom. How are you doing?"

"Do you need to be at the hotel? Aren't there coffee shops there in . . . ?"

"Mom."

"Why can't I be with you over there . . ."

"I only just got to the hotel," Sturla interrupts. "I'm going to go and nose about town."

"Jenný just left, " says Fanný with a heaviness in her voice. "I think she is about ready to give up on Tobbi."

"Þorbjörn?"

"Þorbjörn Gestur, yes. That damn dog."

"Mom, there's no need to call someone a dog." And to change the topic of conversation Sturla repeats his question about how she is doing.

"But aren't dogs man's best friends?" answers Fanný contrarily, and Sturla lets her answer her own question.

"They were in a summer house up north, Jenný and Tobbi," she continues. "Some teachers' residence Tobbi rented. And how do you think that this summerhouse trip ended? It began with Jenný driving back to Reykjavík, leaving Tobbi back at the house . . ."

"But mom, how are *you?*" He lights himself a cigarette and pours another whisky.

"I am not feeling well as long as Jenný isn't doing so well," says Fanný, and Sturla gathers from her reply that she is quite drunk. She continues her report about her sister and her sister's common-law husband; the story is that Þorbjörn Gestur, the English teacher who has lived with Jenný for several years, had, while staying at the residence, offended Jenny so disgracefully on the second day that she couldn't stand staying another minute under the same roof as him, in "some Scandinavian pine-hut in North Iceland," as Fanný puts it; Sturla thinks this is unlikely to be a direct quote from her sister, a German translator. Jenný drove home that evening, six hours without stopping, but Tobbi remained at the house the rest of the week, and was even somehow able to make his way to Akureyri for wine and some food, to help him drink all the wine. The evening before he was due to leave the summerhouse he wrote a long message in the guest book on behalf of the next guests, a young couple and their family—the woman's father and the man's mother—who turned up at midday Friday when, according to the rules, Tobbi ought to have finished tidying the house and be ready to be gone.

"I think we may count ourselves lucky, Sturla dear, that we don't live with people who don't understand us. You are in Latvia and I am at my place on Nýlendugata; there are no other people to confuse us here, no other people hanging off us and wanting us to live the way we don't want to live."

"I am in Lithuania, mom."

"I know that, dearest. And I am at Nýlendugata."

"But how did Jenný know Tobbi had written in the guest book, since she'd already gone back to Reykjavík?" Sturla asks, admiring the way Þorbjörn Gestur had left this parting message, ranting across the white pages in the guestbook so that the next guests at the house wouldn't need to bother.

"How did *she* know that?" Fanný acts like she hasn't understood her son's question. "She, of course, had to go and fetch the man. She had to drive six hours back and fetch Tobbi, who was planning to stay with those poor people at the house."

Sturla suddenly realizes that he is the one paying for the telephone call, not Fanný, even though she called him. As he tries to get her to understand that they can't talk together much longer, she starts to describe Tobbi's written rant—how odd it was to write something in the guestbook which hadn't happened yet, and especially to do that in the name of complete strangers. Sturla realizes that Þorbjörn Gestur has used the same method he did in his article about the poetry festival in Druskininkai; if Sturla had understood his mother correctly, Jenný's common-law husband had described how those total strangers had spent the days they were about to stay in that very house he was refusing to leave—even though he was required to. In other words, Sturla and Þorbjörn, such different personalities, had both written about times that hadn't yet arrived.

When Sturla imagines how his mother looks at this moment, and pictures her surroundings at Nýlendugata, he remembers the plastic folder and the picture she'd shown him the day before, and he is as amazed as before that she can't remember the document folder she'd given to his cousin Jónas—the folder which revealed, when it came into Sturla's possession a long time later, that it had been storing Jónas's writings, writings which Sturla has brought into his present, where they have become a judgment against him.

At the end of the conversation with his mother, Sturla doesn't feel up to calling his father; he realizes he needs to go out. He decides not to wait any longer for the coffee which he was promised but to get some coffee (or something else) at a bar or restaurant—to do what his mother suggested. He drains the whisky glass, puts on his overcoat, and turns off the television. On the way downstairs he remembers again that he wanted to tell his father the name of the street he is staying on; he thought it would please the socialist Jón Magnússon.

On the sideboard in reception is a tray with cold beer bottles and some glasses placed upside down. With a smile which is meant to make it clear that he is joking, Sturla asks the girl whether the bottles are meant for him—he'd let himself think she might be bringing him beer instead of coffee—but the girl replies apologetically that the beer is for a sick hotel guest who isn't able to come down from his hotel room; she could bring some beer to Sturla's room, but the cafeteria is also open. Sturla apologizes in turn, saying that he was just joking, but that she can still help him with another matter: could she tell him what the word *prospektas* meant in Lithuanian? The girl seems, however, not to recognize the word, or else she misunderstands the question; she shrugs her shoulders and tells Sturla to ask Elena, who was on shift just before.

Sturla repeats the question in vain.

"You must ask Elena," reiterates the girl in English.

"But where is Elena?" asks Sturla, also in English, thinking how peculiar it sounds to ask after people by first name when he's not been in the country more than two hours. "She was going to bring coffee up to my room."

"She is gone," replies the girl, letting him know he will have to wait until the morning. "Will you be staying after tomorrow?" she asks.

"Yes, I will be here," answers Sturla, and straight away the photograph from the back of the record sleeve of *Will You be Staying After Sunday* by The Peppermint Rainbow pops up in his mind: three rather ungainly young men in white shoes, light blue pants, and dark shirts with light blue neckties, and two black-haired, sun-bronzed women in white leather boots and light blue, short summer dresses, the same color as their companions' pants. This makes him think again about his five children—Egill, Gunnar, Grettir, Hildigunnur, and Hallgerður—and when he repeats to the girl at reception, once she has repeated her question, that he will be here the next morning, he smiles to himself, thinking that not only will he find out tomorrow morning what the word *prospektas* means in Lithuanian, but he might also get a cup of coffee up in his room; better late than never. And he delights in the thought that Elena herself will bring him that cup.

He goes past the cafeteria; the Nordic man has disappeared. Presumably he is sleeping after his tea-drinking. Sturla opens the door to the street, and this reminds him of an Icelandic poem which often comes, unbidden, into his thought when he opens an outside door—a poem about the world which "opens out onto the street."

THE DANCE OF THE SEVEN VEILS

When Sturla wakes up the next day he is still thinking about what happened the evening before at a club downtown called the Old Town Erotic Center. The course of events had accompanied him into a deep sleep, and he knows he will always remember, as long as his mind is able to store things, everything from last night, the things he has made up and those he actually experienced. Sturla had enjoyed sleeping on the white hotel linen; he hadn't been so tired in a long time, and now when he wakes from his excellent rest he is glad he didn't have a cup of coffee the evening before, as he had planned; instead, he'd drunk a single beer, then two glasses of red wine at the club, and also the sparkling wine which was included in the cover charge. And when he gets out of bed and goes into the bathroom he is able to think up a title for the memorable events (which he had decided right away to note down in his notebook, with the intention of possibly using them in a short-story later):

"Beneath the Gaze of Salomé."

Soon after he left the hotel the evening before—once he'd spent a few moments breathing in the invigorating atmosphere which larger cities than one's own usually offer—he had gotten himself a beer at a small, likable pub nearby. He had taken a copy of his book *assertions* with him, and, as he often enjoyed doing on a trip abroad, he had sat down with his own book and a beer, and selected some poems to read. As peculiar as it sounds, seeing the poems in print in different settings from those where they'd sprung up gave him a certain distance from his own work. In the case of this new book, which had come to him in an entirely different way than his earlier books, this "foreign" reading affected the poems even more powerfully for him. Between choosing the poems and reading them he looked around inside the pub at the few people who were there, and when he'd just finished the first beer and was about to order himself another he overheard four young Swedes at the next table talking about going to some bar in the old part of town, some really exciting place they had been told about, and he'd decided to follow them, to let them lead him to the old quarter of town.

The Swedes decided to stay at this pub a little while longer. They ordered a round of some strong spirit in shot glasses and toasted themselves: four young men from Scandinavia visiting the Baltic. When they stood up to go out one of them suggested that they should have one more round, and just then—totally without having thought about home—the idea occurred to Sturla that his first work as a prose writer, not counting the article he had written about the poetry festival which had yet to happen, would be a kind of manual for foreigners who were visiting Reykjavík: a work of fiction which in content and appearance would be published as though it was a guidebook that introduced strangers to Iceland's capital city—but it would do exactly the opposite, in fact. It would lead the reader astray and give him a completely opposite, but possibly just as interesting, picture of the more than two-hundred year-old city. Sturla imagined the Swedes were drinking a toast to his new idea as they gulped down the contents of the next shot and either bellowed or shrugged off the bite of the taste. They swaggered boldly out onto the sidewalk.

Sturla followed the Swedes out and trailed them at a suitable distance for about ten minutes. They had obviously gotten Dutch courage from the drinks they'd downed, and their conversations on the way oddly reminded Sturla of the interactions of people in a dance club, a place where no one can hear anything at all but the loud music. In contrast, the noise they were making here allowed Sturla to especially notice how great the silence was that ruled the streets of the city, even though they teemed with life. It all suggested a very beautiful, dream-like condition, the scene in a movie which prepares the viewer for something unexpected, something which alters the perspective of those watching events unfold, like the impact of a well-executed short-story. And just like earlier in the evening, when he was sitting in the car on the way from the airport, Sturla thought about how handsome the Lithuanians were; it was, though, as Sturla admitted to himself, a somewhat fanciful thought. He simply wanted—he felt he had a duty—to be positive towards his hosts.

As he was following his unsuspecting tour guides, they vanished through the door to the place they had talked about (a place which was obviously targeted towards men) and he reckoned that, since these young men—who definitely looked like they'd had good upbringings back home and whose appearance suggested they were a socially acceptable bunch—were allowing themselves (without pause for reflection or preface at all) to step one after the other out of the fully-clothed and safe world they were used to and to head inside, towards the uncertain moment when you find yourself standing, dressed, in front of naked strangers: given all this, it could hardly be harmful for a fifty-something father of five to watch young women taking off their clothes. What's more, he thought, it would be a useful experience for a middle-aged poet who is trying to train himself in a more revealing literary form to get to know the sort of underground cultures in which people pay for nakedness. He'd certainly be able to get himself a table a good distance away from the stage.

That plan turned out not to be so easy: the only free table was right next to the stage. When Sturla entered the club—having gone through some kind of ceremony at the entrance he could only describe as a weapons search, paid the rather hefty cover charge, and read on a placard hanging on the wall in the coat-check that the club's atmosphere was supposed to evoke the Middle Ages—the Swedes had already sat down at a table right in front of the stage, with a direct view of the glistening pole which the dancers would hold onto as they stripped.

As Sturla was looking around the hall at the variously hairy heads of the men who had gathered together there, a young bare-breasted woman in a white miniskirt and black Chinese slippers came up to him, and she indicated politely that he should sit at a table with two middle-aged men by the right side of the stage. Sturla planned at first to decline her offer, but when he saw that all the other tables in the hall seemed to be occupied he reconciled himself to sitting with two men who, to tell the truth, didn't seem to be on their first visit to such a place. The bare-breasted woman asked Sturla whether he wanted champagne or vodka. He said he wanted champagne and when he slipped his hand into his jacket pocket to make sure his wallet was still there the girl told him that the champagne was included in the price; he didn't need to pay anything, she would bring it to him before the show started. Sturla nodded that he understood but told her he nevertheless needed to go and get his wallet from his overcoat in the coat-check. The woman offered to accompany him, as if she expected he wouldn't find the way.

"We have a Salomé night tonight," said the girl in English as they went in the direction of the coat-check. "It's première," she continued, and Sturla nodded his head and felt for a moment as if they—he and this young, pretty woman, who seemed hardly aware of her naked breasts—were discussing a major cultural event (he didn't, of course, rule out that possibility).

"I am looking forward to it," Sturla interrupted the woman, who was beginning to describe this Salomé night in more detail, and while he thought about the similarity between that title and *The Night of One Poem* which he was attending in Druskininkai he told the woman (truthfully) that Salomé was one of his favorite stories; he had read the play both in English and Icelandic—she did mean Salomé, the daughter of Herod, didn't she?

"It's Salomé who makes her father cut the head off Judas," the woman answered in English, and she let Sturla know she would bring him champagne once he was sitting back down; the show would begin any minute.

Sturla thanked her for this and when he allowed himself to look shamelessly at her youthful breasts she seemed suddenly to remember that they were on show for everyone's eyes, and she gave a friendly smile to Sturla and thanked him for—for what? thought Sturla, which left him with a strange feeling: it wasn't sexual in any way, it was more of a tender and affectionate feeling; he had seen something beautiful in this young woman who firmly believed that Salomé had forced her stepfather to behead Judas. While Sturla tried to figure out how a headless man manages to hang himself, he watched the back of the bare-breasted woman as she went towards the bar. He got his wallet from the overcoat, though he was a little uncomfortable leaving the new overcoat in the unguarded coat check.

The men at the table welcomed Sturla back with smiles and raised glasses; it was as though they had missed him in the two or three minutes he had been away. One of them, a rather tall man who seemed to be the spokesman for the companions, told Sturla in English that the show was beginning, but the other man who, without being especially fat in other respects nevertheless had the largest paunch Sturla had ever seen on any man, looked at Sturla with curious eyes and asked him where he came from. They said they were Russian and both seemed delighted to have an Icelander at their table. The tall one raised his glass again and said he would toast Sturla when his champagne arrived; his companion with the paunch said, out of the blue, that he had come to the right place, that this was the place for Icelanders, and he asked what Sturla was doing in Vilnius.

"I am a writer," replied Sturla. "I am going to a poetry festival here in *Lithåen*."

"In . . ." the tall one asked, confused.

"In Lithuania," Sturla corrected himself, and they told him the Russian word for Lithuania.

Suddenly there was a loud noise from the club's loudspeaker.

"I'm a writer too," said the paunchy one, and he looked at the unlit stage.

The tall one giggled a little strangely, and Sturla thought that perhaps he was laughing at the same thing he himself found funny: the heavy Russian accent of his companion, which called to mind images of the grey and glowering Soviet figures in western movies about the Cold War.

"I write decadent books about Russian businessmen," continued the big-bellied man in English. "You know: oligarchs. Not poetry, romans."

"Really?" asked Sturla, sounding as skeptical as the word suggested; had the man meant to describe his books as "decadent," or had Sturla misheard? And as soon as he asked whether the man had published many books the tall one lost control of the laughter that had been simmering under his giggles.

"I said: I write books," answered the author, emphasizing the present tense of the verb "write." He'd clearly been unsettled by the laughter of his companion, who clapped his paunchy friend on the back while he told Sturla that he shouldn't trust his big-bellied companion (though he didn't use the adjective "big-bellied"); it would be, to put it bluntly, dangerous to do so—though in all other respects Sturla shouldn't be frightened; they were not dangerous men. The taller Russian's knowledge of English and his convincing pronunciation had to a large extent thrown Sturla off-balance; with his own grammar-school English and clumsy Icelandic pronunciation, Sturla felt a definite sense of inferiority, but when the Russian continued Sturla thought he perceived an affectation in his word choice and his emphasis, and he decided that of the two parties he was faring a little better than the Russian in his struggles with the English language.

"He has no books under his belt," said the taller one. "He is a businessman. *He* is the main character in the non-existing books he is talking about." And he smiled at the self-professed author who responded to him, looking a little flushed in the face:

"I am *going* to write this book. Not poetry like you."

He turned his eyes to Sturla. "Poetry is good but I am going to write roman."

Then we're in a similar situation, thought Sturla: he doesn't want to speak ill of poetry but he doesn't think he has any need for it. On the other hand, people everywhere around him seemed to have a need to tell him about their own desire to create, whether in the field of visual or written arts: the salesperson in the men's clothing store, Áslákur in the elevator, and now this fat-bellied Russian in the strip club. Could it be that Sturla had the trustworthy countenance of a good listener, that people found they could entrust their secrets to him, tell him about their own personal creations, even before they have been created? If truth be told, Sturla was having some difficulty working out whether he was meant to repay the curiosity his table-companions had shown him and ask in turn what their job or business in Vilnius was—it had occurred to him that responding to questions of that nature might not be something these two were keen to do—and he counted himself lucky when he heard quiet music over the sound system: slow string music with soprano singing, far too loud for the small size of the hall. It was an aria from the opera Salomé, sung by Birgitta Nilsson:

"Jokanaan, ich bin verliebt in deinen Leib . . ."

"Mu*sick*," said the shorter Russian, rather loudly, turning to Sturla with a happy expression on his face.

His companion—who Sturla had decided, at least in his own head, to call Igor, while he called the paunchy one Yuri (a suitably stout name)—shushed him and indicated with a series of hand gestures that he should listen to the music, not talk about it. Igor also turned disapprovingly in the direction of the Swedes at the next table, who seemed to be becoming impatient, or, at least, one of them seemed like he was going to belt out some motivational cheers, not unlike the ones you hear at soccer matches. Soon enough the aria died down and was replaced by the following recorded announcement in English, spoken by a rather overly-emotive male voice with a noticeably stiff pronunciation:

"Tonight is a *Salomé night*. If anyone in the audience is named Jokanaan then he is here on his own responsibility and judgment." (Here there was a little pause, as if to heighten the gravity of what had just been said and what would follow.) "A man's head is a heavy burden but please keep it erected and we will guarantee you your full pleasure and admissional investment. Ladies and . . ." (Now came another, somewhat strange hesitation from the announcer; he heaved a sigh, as if he disapproved of something, and cleared his throat before continuing.) "gentlemen, please welcome and make way . . . give head to Salomé Martysevic from Belarus: our Baltic Salomé with seven veils." Then he suddenly burst into throaty laughter which reminded Sturla of the Hammer Horror movies he had seen at the Hafnarbíó Movie Theater on Barónsstígur when he was a teenager; the taller Russian, Igor, asked himself out loud, very displeased, how in heaven's name Belarus had become one of the Baltic states.

"A man's head is a heavy burden . . ." Where did Sturla recognize that from? When one of the stage lights clicked on to illuminate the dry-ice smoke which was pumped onto the stage from both wings, it suddenly dawned on Sturla, in light of what the voice had said about the heavy burden of a man's head, that it was from some of the most quoted lines of twentieth-century Icelandic poetry. In this light, those lines evidently had some other hidden meaning, unless this meaning was exactly what had been in the poet's mind when he wrote the poem.

And perhaps it was the case that the double-entendre had been further pronounced by a kind of partner to the line: the title which another poet had given to both a poem and a full-length collection, *The Head of the Woman*, a head as different from a male head as can be.

"But please keep it erected . . ." Wasn't that how the man in the loudspeakers had put it? If Sturla remembered correctly, the readers addressed in the poem about the man-head were men, not women—"but yet we must stand upright" went the second line—and with the following line in his mind—"and summer redresses most of our sins"—Sturla allowed himself to contemplate the ugly idea that the poem was an incentive to young students who had filled their heads with serious study during the winter to head into the summer firm and rigid; to let the other sex sense their active libidos without having to ask; such aggression would be forgiven and no-one—no-one but the other sex—would note such brazen behavior amidst the dazzle of summer . . .

Sturla tried to recall more lines from the poem—a poem which he'd been required to memorize during high school—and found the lines which he had buried deep in his brain were eerily well suited to the moment he had reached in his own life: "we left the old dwelling-place behind /—like a daily paper in a wastepaper basket—." Reykjavík was now his old dwelling-place, it was the daily paper in the wastepaper basket, and if he remembered correctly, at the end of the poem was the line "excited and new," exactly describing what Sturla thought he and his companions, the Russians, were expecting they would be offered any moment now: something exciting and new.

Just then a champagne bottle was brought to the table, along with three glasses on a black, dirty tray that was covered in old ring stains from other glasses. "With compliments from your host, Herodes," said the bare-breasted hostess, smiling. It wasn't the same woman as the one Sturla had got to know a little; this hostess was quite a bit older, with massive, rolling breasts, and a confident manner, which she made very clear as she swiftly grabbed Yuri's hand and shook her head in reaction to his clumsy, bullying attempts to slap her on the ass. If Sturla read her glance correctly, he saw the endemic, historical antipathy of Lithuanians towards Russians, which flared up, instead of the submissiveness the club's owner doubtlessly required her to show to customers. Igor seemed to be thinking along similar lines: he smiled at the girl and thanked her for the table service—though he found out soon after that the champagne was only cheap sparkling wine; he would have to order some real "bubbles" when they had finished enduring this piss from Herod.

At the same moment the woman vanished from the table they heard the music again, the same as before, and the Belarusian Salomé burst onto the stage: a rather pale woman of about thirty, not as slender and supple as a stripper might be. She was wrapped head to toe in multi-colored silk veils, and as for her shoes, Sturla couldn't work out whether they were going-out shoes or just sandals with high heels. When she had turned a few circles around the pole on the stage, the aria sung by Birgitta Nilsson faded out, and different music was piped into the loudspeaker, an instrumental piece from the East. The Swede who had already been making a racket was getting steadily louder but Yuri wanted peace and quiet to enjoy watching the dancer; he shushed the bellowing Swede and got a grateful look from his companion Igor as his reward (something he'd clearly been hoping for). The woman on stage couldn't disguise her nervousness, and no doubt the silent concentration which hung thick in the air increased her anxiety; she seemed to understand the great expectation in the eyes of all the men who had come to see what she (and the other dancers who would doubtlessly follow her) concealed under her veils.

As soon as she whipped off the first veil, the one around her neck, her shyness seemed to vanish, and her movements became supple and pliable; she wound herself around the pole like a lithe snake, and her movements earned her praise from Yuri's lips, something in Russian which she heard and obviously appreciated, but which also gave the Swede, who Yuri had shushed a moment ago, license to air his opinions, too. When the next veil was cast to the floor, the one which had concealed her hair, the Swede shouted out, clearly against the wishes of his companions, something in his own language, something which Sturla suspected concerned what she had just revealed of her body. Her hair drew the audience's attention: it was short and cut in layers, with cropped back and sides; a color that looked like cream had been poured over it.

The woman evidently heard this shout, but she reacted differently than Sturla, and no doubt the rest of the audience, expected: rather than give the Swede an ugly glance, she flung herself off the pole, stepped down from the stage and tiptoed in his direction like a cat. The Swede hadn't expected she would come down from her stage, as Sturla described it to himself, but it wasn't easy to judge from his expression whether or not he liked it when Salomé knelt on the floor before him, grabbed his knees, and pushed his legs apart. Nervous laughter gripped his companions, but the smile which had formed on the face of the victim disappeared suddenly when the woman began to tiptoe slowly with her index and middle fingers up from his knees, along his legs in the direction of his crotch. By the time Salomé's fingers had reached the Swede's thighs his companions had stopped laughing and had fallen silent.

Suddenly she stopped walking her fingers, moved her hand slowly and calmly to her shoulders, and quickly jerked away the third veil; now her breasts were showing under the silk. She coiled the veil around the Swede's head and fastened it like a headband with a knot. Shouts of appreciation could be heard around the hall but everyone at that table was focused on keeping quiet; it was as if the four Swedes had succumbed to some kind of shock, that they knew they looked defeated. But when Salomé put her hand back on the victim's knee and began to walk her fingers further up his thigh they rediscovered their voices and called out something which was meant to sound like an incentive but which was entirely unconvincing. And just as suddenly as she had begun, the dancer stopped caressing the unsuspecting Swede: she ran the palm of her hand quickly up his inside leg, grabbing his crotch and letting go afterwards with a smile which was meant to suggest very little enthusiasm. With this she turned her back on him and stepped up onto the stage, to the sounds of general applause.

While she enjoyed the praise which the scene with the Swede had won her, and glided about on the stage, either against the column or unsupported, wearing the four veils which were still around her, a question popped into Sturla's mind: How many male Icelandic authors had at some point in their careers been in the same situation as he was at this moment—at a Lithuanian strip club watching a daring dance which had its origin in world literature (if only in name), in the company of a Russian author of novels who, according to his companion, was not an author of novels at all, while at the next table sat four somewhat shamefaced young Swedes (who Sturla was gradually beginning to suspect were in Vilnius for the same reason he was)? The more he thought about it, the more likely it seemed that these young men were involved with literature or some intellectual activity, especially as the bar where he had first seen them was one of the restaurants that was recommended in the festival's information packet for participants.

Suddenly, while Sturla was taking a sip from his glass of sparkling wine, Yuri jerked him out of these thoughts by nudging him and pointing at the dancer Salomé, who was looking right at him. For a minute or two Sturla had watched her rub herself tightly against the column, but now she had let go of her hold—and Yuri was spot on, she was looking Sturla directly in the face as she stretched her hands into the air, not unlike a flamenco dancer, and let her fingers play with each other, as if they were debating what they should do with the fifty-something Icelander who had evidently come here for the first time. Sturla realized he had tensed. And it didn't help that Igor began to whisper English words to him which sounded like old-fashioned poetry (wasn't he and not Yuri the poet?): "Wherefore doth she look at me with her golden eyes, under her gilded eyelids?"

The Belarusian dancer continued to stare at Sturla, and when she took a step in his direction and slowly lowered her hands, Igor continued: "I know not who she is. I do not wish to know who she is." And Sturla looked around, as if he feared that everyone in the place was expecting that he was going to suffer the same fate as the Swede; when Salomé loosened the fourth veil, the one that was wound about her stomach, and let it fall to the floor, Igor leaned closer to Sturla and whispered "Bid her begone." This sounded like a warning, for at that very moment she was heading in Sturla's direction, at that moment she was just about to step down from the stage—but then, without warning, the drunken Swede sprang up from his seat and leapt onto the platform. From the way his hands were placed on his waist it looked like he was going to dance like a Russian Cossack, but he also looked a bit confused, as though he was well aware that he was about to embarrass himself but had nonetheless resolved to let it happen. Salomé had frozen in place and was looking at the Swede with a startled expression, and before anyone was able to do anything about it the guy—who Sturla was going to have to thank later for taking attention away from him—had unzipped his fly and begun to slip his hand inside. But just as quickly as he had dashed up onto the stage, three others from the audience followed suit: one of his companions, another man (clearly an employee), and also Yuri. Watched by Salomé's frightened gaze they dragged the drunk Swede down from the stage without the slightest resistance. His other two companions at the table had clearly had enough of his antics; they stood up and led him out of the hall towards the bar and the exit, as the employee, a huge, broad-shouldered man in a pinstripe suit, turned at once to the dancer to reassure her and to encourage her to continue now that he'd disappeared.

"Scandinavians," Igor said brusquely to Sturla, a sharp comment which accorded little respect to people from the Nordic lands. "You are not Scandinavian," he continued, sounding as though he'd forgotten to pay attention to his English pronunciation.

To the sound of a noticeable murmur through the hall, Salomé began dancing again, and she seemed—to Sturla's great relief—to have forgotten what she'd been about to do the moment before the disturbance took place. Igor clapped Sturla firmly on the shoulder. "I've known other Icelanders," he said; there had been young students in Moscow in the sixties, lively men whose hearts were in the right place, as Igor put it, and he concluded his positive summary of Icelanders by saying: "And they are not Scandinavians."

"Stupid tourist," barked out Yuri when he sat back down at his table, having watched the Swedes leave. Then he said something in his own language, something Sturla told himself must have hewn closely to his own, rather negative characterization of Nordic people in his article about the poetry festival.

It was difficult to tell whether or not the dancing of the Belarusian Salomé had really aroused the admiration of the men in the hall, but everyone's attention was grabbed when she loosened the fifth veil, the one around her waist. According to the voice which had announced the dancer, and the story of Salomé which the dancer alluded to, there should have been seven veils around her body, but after she took off the fifth there was only one veil remaining, the color of an orange in shadow, and this veil concealed the last part of a woman's body to ever be revealed; it was wrapped around her like a cloth diaper on an infant. Sturla saw that both his companions had noticed the discrepancy, and they exchanged curious glances. Had the girl miscounted, or was the discrepancy intended to make the audience speculate as they waited: Was there a seventh veil underneath?

For a moment, Sturla feared that the pale, naked dancer would decide to come up to him. At least he noticed her looking tenderly towards him for a while as she rubbed herself up against the pole on stage, but then the man in the striped suit came back onto the stage, holding an object about the size of a basketball in his outstretched hands; the object was concealed in a silk scarf. According to the script, this object was supposed to grab the Belarusian's attention—or, as Igor put it, "Here comes Jokanaan," and just then Salomé untied the knot on the sixth scarf, let it fall to the floor, and whipped the veil from the object the pinstripe-wearing guy held out. With that tug she pulled away all the mystery from everything on stage that mattered. In Salomé's assistant's hand there was a tray, and on the tray the head of a mannequin, wearing a slightly-askew wig, its neck blood-red. Salomé held the tray with both hands and led it, and the assistant, towards the audience, all the way up to the edge of the stage, only about a meter from the table where Sturla and the Russians sat.

Then she bent forward, her back to the hall, so that her most private parts were on display to anyone who didn't look away, and when she kissed the decapitated head on the tray, a peculiar expression crossed the face of her assistant, the man in the jacket. It took Sturla a fraction of a second to realize that his facial expression was meant to indicate sexual bliss. Immediately a glimpse of a memory occurred to Sturla, an image from his youth: his mother drunk at Mánagata, at a party which had made an indelible impression in young Sturla's mind because one of his father's friends had dared him, at the age of ten or eleven, to drink a sip of Bols liqueur (the name Bols had stuck in his memory then and never left), and Fanný—who had planned to take Sturla to her sister Jenný's in order to save him from the loud, hectic gathering of his father and his acquaintances, had never left; she had been behaving very inappropriately with his father's close friend Örn Featherby and another of the guests, the accountant Magnús Hall. When Sturla, who was sitting in the lap of one of the opera ghosts (that was what he'd started calling his father's friends), broke loose and tried to get out of the living room, he saw his mother pressing her half-naked breast up to Magnús Hall's face, and thrusting her ass (which might well also have been naked, under her thin nightgown) in the direction of Örn Featherby, who smiled uncomfortably at the frightened child, this boy he had held in his hand while he was baptized and who now ran out of the very same room in which the baptism had taken place, pretending he didn't hear his father, who was standing, glass in hand, at the kitchen-table, in conversation with another of his friends, calling in a drunken voice to "Sturla mine."

"You can tell that she is from Belarus," Igor whispered to Sturla, twitching his head in the direction of the dancer's ass.

Yuri laughed at his companion's comment and declared that now the time had come for a real bottle of champagne. But in spite of his "bubbly" suggestion he couldn't hide the fact that he wasn't comfortable at all; contrary to Sturla's expectations, the uncouth Russian was trying to avoid looking at what the Belarusian woman seemed absolutely determined to display.

Sturla decided he'd had enough. He applauded along with the others when Salomé finally disappeared with her assistant behind the curtain at the back of the stage, then he apologized to his companions and said he needed to step out to the restroom briefly. His real mission was to get his overcoat, leave the Old Town Erotic Center, and relieve himself in some other place before beginning the task of recalling the route back to the hotel. While he put on the overcoat he looked around for the woman with small breasts who had accompanied him to the coat check earlier in the evening, but she was nowhere to be seen. So he headed out, thanking the guy who opened the door for him, a young man in a pinstripe jacket and pants, for a lovely evening. He was a little surprised to hear himself enthuse about how beautifully the place was decorated; the words slipped out of his mouth because he was so happy and relieved to be free of those same fixtures.

And now, the morning after, as Sturla comes out of the bathroom and lights a cigarette, he finds he is still relieved to be free of the place where he'd been the previous evening. And as he draws the curtain and looks out at the yard, where the two trash cans are still lying on their sides and there are more cars, he looks forward to seeing how the city of Vilnius will appear for the first time in the light; he still hasn't seen anything other than its pale backside.

THE DAZZLING BRIGHTNESS

When Sturla comes down to reception, there is a dwarfish man standing behind the desk, wearing the same style uniform the girls had worn the previous evening. They say good morning, and Sturla recalls what Svanur Bergmundsson said when the two of them were on a trip to Italy some years ago: that he was frightened of little people, especially men. He experienced their presence as a bad omen, like a black cat crossing your path on the street. When Sturla is about to push open the glass door to the cafeteria, still thinking about Svanur's crude words, he hesitates instinctively, feeling that he ought to say something to the man at the reception, something other than good morning. He turns back, apologizes politely to him, and asks the little guy if he can tell him what the word "prospektas" means in Lithuanian.

"I am sorry but I am not from here," the man replies. It is difficult to pin down his accent, and Sturla reads the name Henryk on his employee badge. "You can maybe ask in the conservatory," continues the man.

Sturla gets the feeling that maybe there's something to Svanur's fear of dwarfish people, as absurd as it sounds. He himself has just made up a superstition that seeing dwarfish foreigners outside their home country betokens something unpredictable, some kind of mishap, as he puts it, for passersby.

"In the *conservatory*?" Sturla repeats.

Henryk nods his head and points in the direction of the cafeteria.

"You mean the . . . *konditori*?"

"It's the transparent door over there," responds Henryk, smiling good-naturedly to this hotel guest who has just woken up.

Sturla chooses a table in the center of the breakfast room; no sooner has he sat down than the cell phone rings in his shirt pocket. It takes him a moment to answer because he has completely forgotten what button to press.

"Hi, Sturla." It is his father, Jón.

"Hi, Dad."

"You've reached your destination?"

Jón's voice has a serious tone, and Sturla thinks he detects either anxiety or disapproval. The first thing which pops into his mind is that his failure to return the videotape to his father before leaving the country might have cast a long shadow over Jón's workday. In Jón's mind, the thought that the man who was planning to pick up the Iranian movie from the library collection was going to be disappointed would be troubling enough to render the day as good as useless. Although strangers, rather than those close to him, tend to benefit from what little scrupulousness Jón has, Sturla reckons it unlikely that this is what's burdening his father; something else has bothered him.

"I've arrived in Lithuania, yes," replies Sturla, and he says he'd planned to call the evening before, but he'd been so exhausted after his journey through Copenhagen that he went to sleep shortly after going up to his hotel room in Vilnius. As soon as he utters those words, he regrets it; he wants to share with his father everything he'd seen at the strip-club the evening before.

"You say you are in Vilnius?" asks Jón, and there is still some unease in his voice.

"Yes. Listen to this, I wanted to tell you yesterday the name of the street where the hotel is located." Asking his father to wait a moment, he stands up and flings himself quickly out onto the sidewalk to see the street sign which he'd noticed yesterday hanging over the hotel door. A feeling of contentment washes over him at being situated here in the hotel on a sunny day, with a delicious breakfast on the way; happily, he has the whole day and all evening to spend at his leisure in this friendly city, for the festival program doesn't begin until the next day.

"Gedimino Prospektas," Sturla reads from the sign into the cell phone. "The street is called nothing other than Gedimino Prospektas. I don't yet know what "prospektas" means in this context, but I'm probably going to get a private lesson today from a young woman who works here at the hotel." Sturla thinks he probably sounds too eager, the way a young boy sounds when he knows something really exciting is about to happen, and when he tries to respond to his father's lack of interest in his partial description of the street name by telling him about his vain attempts to order coffee at the hotel cafeteria the evening before—how his attempts convinced him that the service mentality of the fine people who lived here was the same as it had been during the era of Soviet rule—Jón interrupts him mid-word by announcing that Jónatan Jóhannsson called him last night and described something he, Sturla, would probably want to hear.

"I don't know what it means," says Jón, "but there is some guy here in Reykjavík who has some thoughts about your new book. And he intends, according to what Jónatan heard from a journalist at the daily paper *Vísir*, to share them with the public."

"What do you mean, thoughts?" asks Sturla, who is back at the table and looking around for a waitress. "Share what with the public?"

"Like I said: I have no idea what it means these days for someone to have observations about a newly published book of poetry. Unless of course you are writing poetry about this man; I don't know anything about that. Or "asserting" something which he feels is plainly false," says Jón, undoubtedly feeling proud about having referred to the title of the book.

"And . . . Jónatan didn't explain it more fully?"

One of the girls who had denied Sturla coffee the evening before comes up to his table and hands him a white piece of paper listing his options for breakfast.

"He didn't know anything other than that this man—he didn't know at the time who he was—was unhappy about something in the book, and had spoken with a journalist at the paper, someone other than the person who'd told Jónatan about this, about sharing something that had troubled him with the paper's readers."

Sturla looks at the menu without taking in what is written there, and continues to do so until his father says that he had simply wanted to let him know about all this.

"Can you find out who it is?" asks Sturla, and when Jón agrees to, Sturla asks whether Jónatan hadn't mentioned anything else; whether he hadn't spoken about an article he'd read.

"Yes, he did, as a matter of fact," replies Jón, and Sturla can tell that what he is about to hear now would be no more pleasant than the story he'd just been told over the phone. "He was quite amazed by the whole thing."

"By the whole thing?"

"He said he'd read the article you gave him for the magazine."

"And what? Was he a little amazed by it?" Sturla looks up at the girl who is still hovering in front of him and indicates with his finger that he wants coffee, orange juice, and toast.

"He said he didn't understand a word in it," continues Jón. "He spoke about how you were tearing strips off some festival which you had been at but hadn't yet been held. What festival were you writing about? I didn't understand what he meant."

"And what else?" Sturla nods his head when the girl points questioningly at the word marmelade on the menu. "Why was he telling you about it?"

"Weren't *you* asking me whether he'd mentioned it? Given the things he told me about this story of yours, it actually sounded to me like the piece deserved some praise: how you were speaking ill of the Nordic countries and poetry and . . ." The tone of Jón's voice becomes a little cheerier, and for a moment Sturla feels proud that an article of his has given him space to criticize things he knows his father doesn't think much of. But immediately after he feels on the other hand anxious that Jónatan might not want to publish the article. "He seemed pleased," continues Jón, "that you were taking some American poets down a peg or two and finished up your article with a dig at African-Americans, or black Americans, as I think he put it, Jónatan."

Through the phone Sturla then hears a young, rather shrill female voice calling to his father, and Jón calls back—though not right into the phone—that he is coming, he is talking to overseas on the phone. Then Sturla hears the female voice shout that she is going, and he allows himself to ask his father who the "young voice" belongs to. The question makes his father happy, while Sturla doesn't really find it so promising to hear and know that his sixty-seven-year-old father has a young girl visiting him. He didn't like to ask who she was or how they had met—he suspects he knows, and his mental image of that liaison doesn't make him happy. And when he imagines the absurdity of his father and the girl watching a movie together in the living room at Skólavörðustígur the evening before, some movie which could appeal to people of completely different natures and of such different ages, he is pretty sure that the girl is the reason his father has forgotten to mention the Iranian movie.

"She's gone," says Jón, after the sound of the door slamming travels all the way from Reykjavík to Vilnius.

"But what was the movie?" asks Sturla, kicking himself for having asked.

"What movie?"

Sturla repeats his question about the owner of the female voice, and he stumblingly asks if Jón was with a student for a private lesson at this early hour of the morning.

"And what would I be teaching, my dear son?"

"But what about the movie?" Sturla asks in response, but he goes straight back to the previous topic of discussion, which seems to be the reason for the phone conversation: the rumor about the poetry book.

"Why is some guy on the street complaining about a newly published poetry book? It's absolutely absurd."

"I don't know anything else about it," answers Jón, and Sturla can tell he is thinking about something else. "I don't know the world of poetry," continues Jón, but he interrupts himself and asks Sturla to wait; she has returned, the girl, and he needs to let her in.

Sturla shakes his head at his father and nods his head to the waitress, who has brought him breakfast. He places the telephone on the table for a moment while he puts sugar in the coffee, and when he returns it to his ear his father is asking if he is there; he will have to call him back, "he just needs to see to his student."

The bread turns out not to be toasted, though Sturla asked for toast. It's actually ice-cold, as if it has just come out of cold storage, and he calls over the woman who greeted him when he first came in, asking her to fetch him some toasted bread. Until she comes back, Sturla plays with the cell phone and thinks about what his father told him; he looks towards the window and forgets he is abroad on a sunny day: he has arrived back in Iceland, there's a gray cloud over the country, and the images which occupy his mind are of the past, Snorrabraut, Mánagata, Meðalholt, the Grammar School in Reykjavík—from there he heads into an imaginary editorial office (Sturla has never been to an editor's office).

"But this is toasted bread," says the waitress when she comes back to the table.

"Are you completely sure?" asks Sturla, then he decides he won't complain any further about the bread—other, that is, than asking why it is ice-cold, literally frozen, if it is toast.

The woman has no other answer to the question than to shrug her shoulders, and Sturla thanks her with a smile; that will be all.

He promises himself not to let what his father told him destroy the bright day that is waiting for him outside the cafeteria window. He eats the other slice of bread, orders himself an espresso (which he has to pay extra for) and smokes a cigarette before standing up. Outside the window he notices that, despite the shining sun, the people who are traipsing along the sidewalk are fully-clad in winter clothes, either coats or windbreakers, and on the way out of the cafeteria Sturla puts on his overcoat; he sniffs at the shoulders to see if any odor has settled into it from the strip-club.

When he comes into the hotel lobby, intending to nonchalantly greet Henryk, a short man with a moustache and a thick, tightly-cropped goatee—a man who is actually quite tall compared to Henryk—is standing in reception, and he suddenly throws up his hands when he sets eyes on Sturla.

"Hello, hello!" he cries in English. "You're the Icelander, isn't that so?"

Sturla says that is correct, and in response the man beams and stretches out his hand towards the Icelander.

They say hello. Sturla is happy to shake this cheerful man's hand. Even though he doesn't need comforting, the man's demeanor is calming to Sturla; for the first time since he arrived in the city he realizes he doesn't have to be on his own.

"Welcome to Vilnius," says the man and strokes his goatee. "I recognized you from your picture." And he asks Sturla if he hasn't been well taken care of, if Jonas and Renata hadn't come to fetch him, if he wasn't satisfied with the hotel-room, and just as Sturla is running out of positive responses to the man's questions, he finally asks one which calls for a negative:

"They managed to show you the Writers' Union, didn't they, Jonas and Renata?"

"No."

"No?" The man strokes his moustache with his index finger and thumb, and then places that hand on Sturla's shoulder. "I asked them to take you there before you came to the hotel."

Though Sturla appreciates the man's friendly manner, he finds his physical closeness a little uncomfortable; he runs his hand through his hair, and this movement is enough for the Lithuanian—if he was in fact Lithuanian—to remove his hand from Sturla's shoulder.

"I'm pretty sure that it's still in the same place," he says with a smile, and proceeds to describe how the Writers' Union is on the next street; he points out the window to a stately house at the bottom of a street which meets Gedimino Prospektas almost directly across from the hotel. Yet it seems like he hadn't forgiven Jonas and Renata for failing to take Sturla there on the way to the hotel: he starts talking about how important it is when you come to a new place—as he assumes Lithuania is for Sturla—that the first building a person enters be someplace worth visiting because it is this building which will stay in your memory: not the airport (the airport is more or less the same wherever you land) but the first building in the body of the town (or, as he puts it in English: the city organism). For example, the first door he went through in the mega-city of London, when he went there for the first time, a few years ago, was the door to an old bookstore across from the underground station he first came out, after his journey from Heathrow airport, and this old bookstore was still in his mind when he thought of that metropolis, London; everything else in the city had been forgotten and buried, even St. Paul's Church was nothing but a basement cellar compared to that entrance to the glorious world on the ground floor of Charing Cross. It is just like when a child first enters the world. His first experience is what he sees when he goes out the narrow door of his mother, and after that, everything up to old age, all his thoughts—whether the child is a man or woman—are about the environment which was first in front of his crying eyes: the navel and everything above and below it.

"No, I'm going a bit too far now," he adds, and he literally bursts out laughing.

"But are you sure a newborn child can see with its eyes right away?" asks Sturla, feeling at once that the question sounds rather pedantic.

The bearded guy seems not to hear the question. Laughing, he again says that he has taken the metaphor about the crying child too far, but his expression suggests that he thinks Sturla is a bit of a killjoy; the guy apologizes by saying: "But we're allowed to say whatever comes to mind, we poets, isn't that so? Whatever rubbish it is."

Sturla nods along with his new companion; he hadn't realized he was yet another poet. Some people are no longer strangers as soon as they look you in the eye: this bearded chatterbox is one of them, and Sturla considers it a possibility that they'll get better acquainted at the poetry festival.

"But it's not every city where the Writers' Union can be seen from the hotel that hosts a foreign poet," he says, and Sturla admires the way he arranges his words in flawless English. "And it's there, later today, at three o'clock, where we're holding a reading, a few native poets, including me . . . Of course, I've forgotten to introduce myself in all my endless prattling-on . . . I am called Jokûbas Daugirdas and I'm one of too many poets in this city . . ." and while he tells Sturla about the program, and continues talking about the reason the Writers' Union of Lithuania got the use of such a splendid old house—a story which he perhaps goes through in unnecessary detail—Sturla contemplates, in light of what Jokûbas maintained about the permanence of a person's first acquaintance with a new environment, whether or not the Ambassador Hotel will live on in his thoughts, and he's quite convinced that it will. At least, he realizes he's already forgotten the appearance of the airport terminal, and he decides to reconcile himself to the idea that, rather than the entrance to the Writers' Union of Lithuania, the reception of the Ambassador Hotel on Gedimino Prospektas will remain in his memory as a souvenir of his trip to Lithuania: Elena's face, the pamphlets in the stand on the way past reception—and an image of the dwarfish Henryk, who he can see just beyond Jokûbas's shoulder at this moment, a friendly guy who it is impossible to imagine betokens bad luck for anyone.

"And it's not every Writers' Union which is also the home of the best bar in the city," continues Jokûbas. While he adds more than a few words about the arrangement—which Sturla finds strange—by which the Writers' Union of Lithuania is licensed to serve food and drink, Sturla tries to imagine what sort of poetry this man writes. He is a man who clearly has a tendency to lose himself in needless details: Sturla pictures him writing long lines and putting lots of them under a single title; he imagines that even his suggestion that Sturla have his morning beer at the Writers' Union bar (it's open at this hour of the morning) has already found its way into one of his poems. Sturla, however, says that he wants to begin the day by nosing around town: he still hasn't had the chance to see downtown Vilnius in daylight, having only been able to see the shadowy side of the city so far. Last night, he'd inadvertently stumbled into a "manly" entertainment spot, as he tries to put it in English, but this confession doesn't seem to pique Jokûbas's curiosity; he begins telling Sturla about a few places in the city which he might enjoy exploring, and he recommends especially fervently an eatery on Pilies Street, a street Sturla realizes he knows about, since he remembers it as the title of Liliya Boguinskaia's poem that he translated, the Belarusian poet who in turn had translated Sturla's "kennslustund."

Before they say goodbye, Sturla asks Jokûbas if he knows whether Liliya from Belarus, Liliya Boguinskaia, has arrived in the city.

"Do you know her?" asks Jokûbas, and when Sturla explains to him that they were asked to translate each other's poems as part of a scheme to get unfamiliar poets acquainted with each other before the festival, Jokûbas tells him he expects she will be at that very eatery around midday today. He met her last night and she had, like Sturla (though this clearly hadn't been the case) asked for a good restaurant in the city. She'd been here many years ago, during Soviet rule, and had actually written some poems about the city; when he directed her to the restaurant on Pilies Street she said she was going to go there today: she remembered the street after having written a poem about it.

"That's probably the poem I translated," says Sturla, and Jokûbas replies:

"My brother runs the restaurant. Tell the waiter that I told you about the place; you won't be sorry."

While Sturla takes the last sip of his coffee, he watches Jokûbas, in green corduroy jacket and baggy blue jeans, going along the avenue, down the street towards the Writers' Union. Sturla's overcoat rustles comfortably when he raises the collar before heading out onto the sidewalk and into the cool October sun. For a moment he pushes away his thoughts about the phone call he's just had with Jón and is pleased with himself for having bought the overcoat before heading to Lithuania: if any item of clothing was right for this climate, it was this Aquascutum overcoat. There's no question about it, he thinks, and then admonishes himself good-naturedly for letting himself—a poet who should be skeptical about everything—be so sure about his choice as to declare that there is "no question" about it.

In contrast to the dazzling brightness of the sun which could be seen shining on the faces of Vilnius's residents, there is, on the other hand, no question that the conversation with Jón has cast a heavy shadow from Iceland; it doesn't fall across these citizens, of course, only their guest, Sturla, who goes along the sidewalk on the sunny side of the avenue, Gedimino Prospektas, towards the cathedral square—that is, if he can trust the city map he is looking at.

THE TABLE IN THE FAR CORNER

According to written sources, the city of Vilnius dates back to 1323. An ancient folk tale tells how the Lithuanian count Gediminas (the forefather of the Jagello family that ruled Lithuania and later Poland for two and a half centuries) loved to hunt in the extensive, dense forest on the tract of land where Vilnius now stands. He lived in a nearby castle in the town of Trakai. At the end of one particularly successful hunting trip in the forest, Gediminas and his retinue set up camp at the banks of the rivers Neris and Vilna, and stayed there drinking late into the night. During the night, Gediminas dreamed a strange dream: that high in the mountains above the river Vilna there stood a gigantic iron wolf which howled with the sound of a hundred wolves. And when Gediminas awoke he sent for the heathen priest Lizdeika, the one who guarded the holy fire, and asked him to interpret the images he had seen in his sleep. The priest read in the dream a message from the gods, requiring Gediminas to erect a fortified castle up on the slopes where the iron wolf had howled. This building should be just as magnificent as the animal had been, and an industrious city would arise around it. This city would be very beautiful, and her glory would be lasting in the surrounding districts, like a wolf with the sound of a hundred wolves. Count Gediminas took Lizdeika's interpretation of the dream seriously and sent invitations to craftsmen and merchants in small towns across Germany to construct buildings in exchange for various privileges, including, among others, complete religious freedom. And so the city of Vilnius was born, the same city that now sounds under Sturla's hard soles as he goes towards the cathedral square wearing his overcoat.

He'd read this story in a booklet in the hotel reception, and as he goes on his way down Gedimino Prospektas he is suddenly so immersed in drawing analogies between the wolf on the slopes and what his father told him about the rumors regarding *assertions* that he doesn't notice the magnificent façade of the National Theater across the street: four very prominent and unmistakable copper figures stretching themselves out over the street and literally shouting for attention with their dramatic facial expressions and hand gestures. Sturla had seen pictures of these silent delegates for the art of theater in some booklet or newspaper, and he would have recognized them if he'd had his eyes open during his walk. But at the moment nothing in his surroundings can attract his attention; the word "wolf, wolf" resounds in his head, and he realizes his father has provided him with a warning, just like the wolf on the hill. He hasn't really thought about what the wolf symbolizes, but Sturla feels that everyday events and objects around him frequently turn out to have been insightful prophecies, and so he makes up his mind that the image of the wolf must be some form of omen—like the dwarf in reception, perhaps—and, moreover, he connects it to the "house on the hill" line in the poem which he fears is one of the sources of the man's thoughts, that man who spoke with the journalist, according to Jónatan.

Could it be that the house on the hill—which had actually found its way into Sturla's poem thirty years ago—was also the castle of this Count Gediminas, long before Sturla had any idea such a castle existed? Earlier in the week, on the way down Bankastræti, he had considered the idea—and, in fact, it seemed to actually be the case, given when the poem was originally written—that the high-roofed house in the poem was the Grammar School in Reykjavík; of course, it could be, as his father Jón had suggested, that the house on the hill was the overcast residence of Norman Bates and his mother, but at this moment Sturla is most taken with the new possibility that the poem was composed about something its writer hadn't yet experienced, just as Sturla has recently written about his experience at the poetry festival before the festival even took place. But it could also be argued that his insignificant lyrical creation dealt with all these, or—and this was perhaps more likely—had nothing to do with any of them. And Sturla thinks this is true of all poems, as far as the much debated but ill-explained definition of the riddle called poetry is concerned: they are about everything and nothing at the same time. The whole world—everything that has happened in the kingdom of nature until now—is contained in every text which, given his aforementioned definition, counts as poetry in Sturla's eyes. As he is approaching the cathedral square he recalls Miroslav Holub's poem, which suggests that poetry is found in everything, a fact that is also the chief argument against poetry, but he immediately begins to doubt the Czech poet's assertion when he observes the white, neo-classical edifice which dominates the square, on the left side of a handsome tower: the cathedral of the city of Vilnius.

The façade of the church boasts a gigantic colonnade, which Sturla thinks looks like it is made out of plastic or cork—like some sweeping meringue, to use a clichéd metaphor from the world of baking. But as he convinces himself that the edifice he is now approaching looks with every step more and more like a department store and less like a refuge where humble mortals confront God, he tells himself it isn't a good idea for him to be forming judgments given the prickly mood he is in at the moment. He isn't in the same cheerful mood as when he woke up two hours ago; he can't shake off the less-than-amusing message from his father. On the other hand, he is fascinated by the white-painted tower in the square. Was it possible that Jónatan hadn't seen the essence of the article? Sturla goes up to the tower to see whether he is allowed to enter, but it turns out he can't. What on earth did the half-witted editor mean by saying that someone had been making comments about *assertions*? Had Jónas lied when he told Sturla thirty years ago at Hressó that no one had ever seen his poetry? There are a significant number of tourists around the tower, and it comes to Sturla's attention that many have taken their winter clothes off; it has warmed up, and he deliberates whether he should head back to the hotel and divest himself of his overcoat before continuing into the old downtown. But just then a cool breeze, like the blast of an air conditioner, plays around him, and he is glad to have a reason to keep wearing his new coat, which he is doing his best not to congratulate himself again for buying.

After taking an hour-long stroll around the friendly downtown Sturla feels much more light-hearted, and he sits down at a likeable restaurant on the city hall square, orders a glass of beer, and smokes a few cigarettes. He realizes he is hungry and asks the waitress for the menu, but then remembers the suggestion of the man who he met in reception earlier that morning, Jokûbas. He decides to find Pilies Street and see whether he might get to meet Liliya Boguinskaia, who Jokûbas had said in all likelihood would be there around midday. It turns out that Pilies Street is only a few steps away; it lies down from the city hall square towards the cathedral square, a very diverting little pedestrian street with an assortment of stores and restaurants (as Sturla imagines to himself it would be described in a tourist brochure).

It is more or less in the middle of Sturla's thought about whether or not buskers play in the otherwise lively downtown that he hears the distant sound of live music. He recognizes the melody, and as he heads towards the sound he remembers it is a tune by Rod Stewart and the Faces, although he can't quite recall the title. The performer is a fairly small man, probably around fifty, wearing cowboy boots, narrow black jeans, a frayed dark-grey suit jacket with sleeves that look rather like they had gone through some sort of shredder, and he is wearing on his head a broad-rimmed hat that matches the boots. He is standing in front of a restaurant and he is playing an acoustic bass guitar with an unusually long neck—an instrument Sturla didn't know existed before he saw his son Egill playing one at a concert in Reykjavík several years ago. Although the raspy singing of this rather gloomy-looking man rises above his bass playing—a surprisingly weak sound for such a huge instrument—all his concentration seems directed at the instrument, and Sturla assumes he can pass by unnoticed, something he is happy about since he has no coins in his pocket to give him. In his overcoat pocket is his hotel key and the hazelnut from the airport—as he searches through his pockets he also finds the ticket for the VCR he took to the repair shop before he left—and it occurs to Sturla that he could of course give the man the nut.

Wasn't it a good idea, giving someone in need a lucky charm? Though perhaps Sturla hasn't gotten his full use of this lucky charm yet.

As he moves past the musician, and makes a sustained attempt to remember the name of the song, the nut in his pocket reminds him of how seriously self-incriminating the book he has just published is. It won't take more than one phone conversation for it to be shoved in his face. He keeps looking out for the restaurant, which he is beginning to suspect he doesn't have the correct name for. When he reaches the bottom of the street he asks a young man where the place is and heads back up the street with him; it is further up, but worth going a little way for, since it is one of the best restaurants in the city.

It turns out that the place they were discussing is the same place the bass player with the hat is standing in front of. As Sturla thanks the young man for the help, he notices that the musician in black is playing a new song, this time one which Sturla recognizes at once: *Mandolin Wind* by Rod Stewart. Sturla thinks this folky song might even be the next track on the same album as the earlier tune he'd half-recognized—a record he probably wouldn't care to have in his collection these days, but which he'd enjoyed listening to since he was almost twenty. He admits to himself that this music cheers him: it reminds him of something good, something from a time in his life when the future lay before him—when the world hadn't yet been revealed to him—and he decides to stop briefly and listen to the tune before he goes into the restaurant. The performer, who has lit himself a cigarette and hooked the filter into the head of the bass's neck, notices Sturla's attention, and rewards his listener by increasing the energy of his performance. Sturla nods to him, without being certain that the extra hoarseness he is adding to his voice is actually an improvement; nevertheless, he decides to oblige him. He fishes his wallet from his jacket pocket, chooses the smallest note he can find (10 *litos*), and puts it in the open instrument case on the sidewalk. But when Sturla moves to enter the door, the singer twitches his head to signal that Sturla ought to wait, and he suddenly pauses mid-song.

"Where are you from?" he asks in a deep voice, reaching out for the cigarette on the neck of the bass.

"From Iceland," answers Sturla, one hand on the doorknob.

"How long are you staying here in Vilnius?"

Sturla wonders whether he ought to give a stranger this information, but when the small bass player points to the open case and thanks him, Sturla replies, thinking it both a little silly and somewhat fun: "I'm heading to Druskininkai in the morning. Do you know Druskininkai?"

"Do I know Druskininkai? I know it as the back of my hand," he replies in English. His expression suggests he knows exactly what he's talking about. And he adds: "Druskininkai is one helluva place," with an emphasis which is as ill-suited to him as the huge bass. "It's a fucking healthy place, you know. Very good for your body. For your body and soul."

Sturla nods his head and opens the door.

"But Iceland?" the man hurries to add. "It's fucking cold, I presume?"

And Sturla asks himself, before he answers, where the man got hold of his English. And when Sturla answers affirmatively, the man shivers as though it has suddenly become freezing cold, and he blows into the air to emphasize his opinion of Iceland. And, before he starts the next tune, he raises his jacket collar around his neck, flashes a smile which gives Sturla an uneasy feeling, and waves to indicate that their conversation is over; Sturla is free to go in through the door of the restaurant, if he wants.

Never talk to strangers, Sturla says to himself, and he remembers suddenly that these words are the name of a chapter in a book he has read, though he can't recall what book that is at the moment. He wonders if this deep-voiced Rod Stewart fan is as ignorant as Áslákur in the lift on Skúlagata, who didn't know about Iceland's support for Lithuania's fight for independence fifteen years ago. Surely a Lithuanian person of this man's age, old enough to remember the events of the past fifteen years, ought to express thanks to an Icelander he meets by chance for their support in making life bearable in his homeland, rather than venting his opinion that Iceland is intolerably cold?

There is no one in the place, and the clock shows it's not much past eleven. The dark brown wood fixtures remind him of something German or Austrian, and the sound of the music which is coming out of little loudspeakers, including one by the coat hooks, is in keeping with the fixtures. Sturla thinks some more about what he read describing the founding of Vilnius: among the artisans who Count Gediminas enticed from the small towns in Germany to settle in the new city, there must have been some musicians, perhaps like the bass player outside on the sidewalk in wide-brimmed hat, tall leather boots, and torn jacket—musicians playing tunes by the Rod Stewart and the Faces of their day and age. Besides the music, the first sign of life that Sturla discerns is an old man in a cook's uniform who trots out one of the doors, which looks like it leads to the kitchen, and in through another, which he guesses is the bathroom. Sturla takes off his overcoat and hangs it on the coat hook in the entryway. Then he goes into the two-room dining room, where finely checkered cloths lie on all the tables, and he chooses a seat in the far corner of the room. He reaches for the breast pocket of his jacket, to check if he's got his cell phone, then remembers the hazelnut in his overcoat and decides to get it; he wants it nearby.

When he turns back from the coat hook, carrying not only the nut but also the overcoat, which he has decided to keep at his table since he is alone, a young waiter is standing in his way. He gives Sturla a friendly smile but also shakes his head, offering another kind of smile that somehow convinces Sturla not to protest when the waiter takes his overcoat, saying he will hang it on the coat hook. He then invites Sturla to sit in the outer room, but Sturla tells him he's already chosen a seat in the inner room—he wants to be more isolated—and he orders a large beer and some good liquor; the waiter proposes cherry brandy.

"That sounds good," says Sturla, and he watches as the black-clad waiter takes the overcoat towards the coat hooks. He goes back to his seat and rests his arms on the arms of the chair, which he feels embrace him like a flesh-and-blood person. He lights a cigarette. He is pleased with the place and resolves not to let himself be affected by the everyday matters his father might later report from Iceland. The lyrical version of reality—no matter how tough he knows the real situation to be—looks much better among these surroundings. This place's walls have certainly never belonged to an American fast-food joint, while the old, traditional eateries in Reykjavík were giving way to cheap, soulless international restaurant chains. That said, the impossible *had* happened: Hressingarskálinn in Austurstræti had gone back to being Hressingarskálinn again after the McDonald's hadn't done very well in that location. But Sturla could still see before him the plastic fixtures of the fast-food franchise; even though the management of the place had changed a long time after he and Jónas used to meet up there, he places himself and his cousin in red and yellow plastic chairs as he recalls (and invents) their conversations about the latter's poetry manuscript and the "northern moors" melancholy which Jónas had said he perceived in the tunes and lyrics of the musician Megas.

It was about two weeks before Jónas died. He had shown up at Sturla's workplace right at midday, to make sure he could catch the bank employee before he went for lunch, and Sturla, who was not especially eager to meet up with his cousin—he was, sad to say, becoming very annoyed at Jónas's visits to the bank—asked him to wait at Hressingarskálinn while he finished some telex-messages which needed to be sent before midday. It turned out that Sturla enjoyed chatting with Jónas on that occasion; he found that his cousin shared numerous details about himself, details which it was natural and healthy for them to share. He even, totally unexpectedly, surprised Sturla by paying for lunch—that had never happened before, and didn't happen the two subsequent times they met up there.

When they'd sat down, well inside the western room in Hressingarskálinn, Jónas said that Sturla's mother, Fanný, had phoned his father, Hallmundur, the day before and asked after him. He added that he didn't often hear from his father (something Sturla already knew) and that they didn't have an especially good relationship (which was no less familiar to Sturla) but that Hallmundur had dropped by his place on Meðalholt to let him know that Fanný had called and that she wanted to talk to him. Jónas didn't have a phone in his cellar apartment. He had no idea what Fanný might want to talk to him about, and Sturla, who thought he knew that his cousin was half-scared of his mother—others were too—told Jónas that it was entirely safe to talk to her; perhaps she wanted to ask him something. Jónas said he would visit her, and he began talking about Norðurmýri: some days he would go past Sturla's parents' house at Mánagata 10, and on sunless days the neighborhood seemed to him to correspond to Megas's first album, to the sweet, cruel mood of his peculiar version of *Come and Look Into My Coffin*, a mood he described as *the gray, shingled eclipse of the mind*;

(Sturla later saw those words typed in the manuscript Jónas had been talking about that time at Hressó.) Going into Norðurmýri from a westerly direction he always recalled the lyrics that came from inside the coffin: *my tongue is stiff it offends no one any more / although the liquor store is close, / I can't make it there or make a purchase.* The State Liquor Store was on Snorrabraut, a relatively short distance away from Meðalholt, and Jónas tended to buy his alcohol there, although sometimes he would go to the Lindargata State Liquor Store—for example, the time when he met Armann Valur, his old teacher from high school, two years ago, and they went to Hressingarskálinn together.

Shortly after Jónas died, Sturla had asked his mother why she tried to call Jónas—Jónas had heard about it from his father—but she didn't remember why. To this day, no one knew what she'd wanted from Jónas.

Discussing Norðurmýri indirectly led Jónas and Sturla to start talking about poetry as they sat in Hressó having coffee and rolls, and it turned out that Jónas had written an entire manuscript of poetry. He had begun it during his penultimate year in grammar school, but he'd never shown it to anyone and didn't expect to find a publisher for it—the manuscript wasn't anything more than some crappy imitations of dusty old modernists, and it consisted in part of ironic attempts to poke fun at the collectivistic, regimenting wise-ass criminality of those commie *Fylkingin* Poets who dominated the poetry scene these days. But perhaps he would show Sturla the mess one day, though he wasn't allowed to laugh at him. "I would be very keen to see the manuscript," Sturla had said. And he still remembered, word-for-word, Jónas' response to his sincere interest: "Perhaps you could use something from it. Some lines might be useful to you." And he had promised to bring "that garbage" the next time he looked in on Sturla at the bank.

Although at the time Sturla hadn't published poems in magazines, let alone a book, Jónas knew about his interest in poetry and knew that he wrote poetry. When the inspiration seized him (meaning: when he was drunk), Jónas would make belittling remarks about poetry, saying that the phenomenon of contemporary poetry was solely for people who couldn't admit they had no talent for other pursuits, for tasks requiring concentration or discipline. Because of this, Sturla was surprised by what his cousin said about sitting on a complete manuscript, whatever that meant.

And yet, it turned out that Jónas never showed Sturla these secret papers—papers which later came out of Benedikt's folder—because two weeks after the conversation at Hressingarskálinn, Jónas was dead. On the two occasions they'd met in between those events, Jónas hadn't been in any state to remember what he'd promised. It was on the latter of those meetings that Sturla lent him the money which he fully believed Jónas had used to buy his overdose: his Magnyl pills, which he probably bought from the pharmacy on the corner of Rauðarárstígur and Háteigsvegur; and the bottles of Brennivín, Black Death, which he must have carried in a black plastic bag along Snorrabraut, through Norðurmýri, and up to Meðalholt.

That Jónas's manuscript—which was surprisingly close to complete, especially given the disapproval the author had expressed about it—ended up in Sturla's hands was in fact the greatest blessing (or the worst misfortune?) that could have resulted from the way Benedikt's leather folder was an inch away from being discarded.

For in fact it had been discarded. A few months after Jónas's death, Hallmundur called Sturla; he said he'd been going through his son's belongings, and he was ready to get rid of those that were of no value to anyone, but he wanted to make sure Sturla got a chance to look at the books, records, and other things which he might have a use for. Sturla had long wanted to find a way to ask his uncle if he could take a look at his cousin's belongings, but he never had. And when he went to Hallmundur and Þeba's house in Breiðholt, into their garage where Hallmundur had stacked the cases with his son's possessions, it soon became apparent that all the loose items—paper, stationery, and other small items—had already been thrown out; among these items was the folder, which Hallmundur remembered had gone into the charity container at the trash dump. Once he'd found this out, Sturla didn't stay in the garage long; he collected, somewhat hastily, a few records (including the first record by Megas and some five or six CDs by T-Bone Walker) and a few books which Hallmundur clearly didn't care to keep. He turned down an offer to have coffee with the couple and took the next bus to the trash dump.

It took quite some toil for Sturla to find the case Hallmundur had thrown into the container, and it was no less difficult to begin to understand how his uncle could have abandoned—in the cold and foul-smelling dump—such a well-treated item as the ambassador's beautiful document folder, something which had not only laid on his son's writing table for many years but which also held all kinds of his personal items: photographs, old report cards, sketches, and, last but not least, the typed manuscript of a book he'd composed. It seemed like Jónas's parents had neglected to look inside the folder, and for a few moments Sturla deliberated whether to collect only the manuscript and folder, and let Hallmundur and Þeba know about all the other things it contained; perhaps they hadn't known that the folder was full of their son's personal effects. But given that they would still not be interested in keeping those things, it would be quite awkward, Sturla reasoned, if he pointed the items out to them. With that in mind, he decided to keep them himself—as well as an old, Russian-made chess timer which lay in the same cardboard box as the folder and a yellow Waterman fountain pen which he remembered Jónas had received as a confirmation gift.

But was it possible that Jónas had shown someone else his poetry, poetry which had caught Sturla so much by surprise on the first read? It was true that some of the poems had borrowed things from the modernist works of earlier times, and that some of the poems showed a clear sarcasm towards the so-called radical poets of the mid-seventies, but Sturla thought he immediately perceived a personal quality in them that he truly believed was valuable. And over time, because he would often browse through Jónas's typed sheets, the poems began to take front seat in Sturla's mind, and he often recalled a line of poetry here and there from the manuscript at unlikely times, until finally Jónas's lines had not only become part of Sturla's lyrical storehouse—as he phrased it—but some of them even ran together with Sturla's own thoughts. Or did he have it backwards: Did his thoughts spring from Jónas's texts? The result was that, almost three decades after Jónas's nameless manuscript came into Sturla's possession, its contents formed the backbone of his latest book, *assertions*.

But was it possible that someone had recognized Jónas's poems in the form in which they were published in Sturla's book? What other reason was there why, at the dawn of the 21st century, someone would question something as innocent as a newly-published book of poems? Of course, he shouldn't rule out that some classmate of Jónas—even perhaps some miserable down-and-out who he had started hanging around with in his last days—had read some of the manuscript, perhaps a few poems, even though Sturla had absolutely trusted his cousin's statement that he would be the first person to read "the whole caboodle."

No more than ten minutes passes between Sturla ordering the food and it arriving at the table. Sturla orders another beer, and while he waits for this and looks at the meat and potatoes on the plate, he hears the door to the place open; it closes again a moment later, without anyone having come inside. He pushes at the hot dish with his fork, using it to release the various aromas: it is the same kind of food as Count Gediminas's immigrant, German laborers would have ordered in his time. This, Sturla thinks, is original food.

The waiter who brings him the second beer is different from the one who intercepted him and hung up his overcoat; he is older and more substantial—is he Jokûbas Daugirdas's brother?

Sturla has no sooner taken his first bite of meat than the telephone rings in his breast pocket. He scrambles to get the telephone as his father's home phone number shows up on the screen. He puts the fork down, swallows, takes a sip of beer, draws a deep breath, and answers.

"Hi, Sturla."

Sturla isn't able to work out what lies beneath his father's tone of voice.

"Has the newspaper arrived?" he asks, without returning the greeting.

"Where are you?" replies Jón.

"You know where I am."

"No."

"I am in Vilnius."

"Where in Vilnius?"

"Downtown."

"Somewhere inside?"

"What do you mean? I'm in a restaurant downtown." He waits for his father to say something and continues: "Is it *that* serious? Should I hold onto something?"

"Jónatan asked me to give you his regards."

"So you're giving me the good news first? But why is Jónatan sending me his regards? Weren't you telling me this morning that he didn't want to publish my article?" Sturla prongs a small bite of meat for himself.

"I think I'm going to have to read this to you," says Jón, and now there is no subtext concealed in his tone of voice. "Although reading it isn't going to make you happy there, overseas" he continues.

Like a flash, a picture of Henryk the dwarf in the hotel reception immediately pops up in Sturla's mind. He runs his hand through his hair with a serious expression; his eyes are full of doubt about whether he is up to his job.

Jón clears his throat and rustles the newspaper, giving Sturla a chance to say something before he starts reading the article. "*Poet Charged with Cheap Plagiarism*. That's the headline." And after that he pauses to let Sturla reply. "The poet Sturla Jón Jónsson, who is well-known for . . ."

"Who wrote it?" interrupts Sturla.

Jón gives him an e-mail address that accompanies the article, and Sturla writes it on the napkin beside the plate. And when Jón continues reading, Sturla interrupts to describe his admiration at the splendid chiastic alliteration, *poet charged / cheap plagiarism*; considering the way the newspaperman exposed himself completely in his headline, you have a classic example of an unsuccessful poet who has become a journalist and is trying to take down someone who'd succeeded where he failed. Then he takes a long sip of beer and asks his father to read on.

"The poet Sturla Jón Jónsson, who is well-known for his book *free from freedom*, which came out some years back, published a new book of poems recently, which he called *assertions*. That an Icelandic poet has published a new book is not, of course, usually considered a story, but . . ."

Sturla once again interrupts the reading. "Is there a picture with the story?" he asks. "Please say it's not a picture of Sturla Jónsson the politician."

Without doubt, Jón has been avoiding mention of it, for the picture he describes to Sturla was a picture that has been published before, in a photo-story the newspaper had published about a party held at the Writers' Union of Iceland on the occasion of the establishment of a center for publicizing Icelandic literature—the same center that chose Sturla as the Icelandic representative to the poetry festival in Lithuania. It is a picture that in Sturla's mind had been completely unforgivable for the newspaper to publish; he doesn't look at all good in it: drunk to the eyeballs and with a baseball cap on his head which a colleague, an unscrupulous novelist and scholar, had placed on him just before the photographer took the picture. "You look like a corpse that's washed ashore and been fitted up in a baseball cap and tie," his father had said when the picture was originally published, and that was exactly the way Sturla had seen himself in the picture: a thrown-together, purposeless character, not someone who was likely to achieve a single thing.

"What do they have against me?" Sturla almost shouts into the phone, and it occurs to him to ask his father to stop reading. "In one newspaper they publish a picture of me as a farmer and rhymer, and in the next paper, which is of course published by the same mob, I'm a drunk in a baseball cap!" Sturla almost makes himself laugh with these words, but the manner in which he barks that his father should continue reading the news suggests he isn't at all happy. And while Jón reads the journalist's story to its conclusion, Sturla forces himself to hold off interrupting, other than to ask who the devil Brynjólfur Madsen is; while the reading goes on he quickly drinks his beer and indicates that the waiter should bring him another one, and another shot of the cherry brandy.

"That an Icelandic poet has published a new book is not, of course, usually considered a story . . ." Jón takes up the thread where he'd been stopped. ". . . but there is more going on when the published volume seems to no small degree to bear the hallmarks of a pickpocket, as appears to be the case with Sturla Jón Jónsson's aforementioned book. This journalist's attention was drawn to the theft in question by Brynjólfur Madsen, the District Court Attorney and a schoolfellow of one Jónas Hallmundsson, who appears to be the real author of the poems which Sturla has published under his own name, and who died before his time in 1978, at only twenty-two years old. According to the conversation this journalist had with Brynjólfur Madsen, Brynjólfur was browsing, quite by chance, through the aforementioned book by Sturla Jón in a bookstore downtown. He soon realized that he recognized things in the book, that he'd seen some of the sentences and images before. Then it dawned on him: they came from poems written by his former classmate, the late Jónas, who happened to be Sturla Jón's cousin, the son of Sturla's uncle, Hallmundur Margeir Magnússon. It seemed, if he wasn't mistaken, quite clear that many of the poems, if not most of them, were largely identical to poems Jónas had shown Brynjólfur at his home in the east part of Reykjavík, around the time the friends graduated from Reykjavík Grammar School. Shortly after this Jónas had actually given Brynjólfur some of the poems, typed and signed, in a beautiful chapbook Brynjólfur still owns and was able to produce in support of his claim. Jónas Hallmundsson had thought about publishing his poetry, but he struggled with mental problems, and he hadn't found sufficient equilibrium to bring his project to fruition. But it is clear that his cousin Sturla Jón came into possession of Jónas's manuscript and thought it would be okay to publish it under his own name, although he waited almost thirty years to do so. On the other hand, it is also clear that he has carried out a few facelifts on Jónas's poems, which it is safe to say were very mature poems considering how young the poet was when he wrote the poems. Brynjólfur Madsen compared the poet Sturla Jón's alterations to his relative's creative work with the surgical embellishments of a certain pop star who transformed himself from a black man to a pink one. It had never been a secret that in many of his poems Jónas was mocking the poetic posturing of his classmates who published in the school newspaper *MR*, and now you could say that Sturla Jón has managed to perfect his cousin's ironic gestures by publishing them under his own name as if they were serious, weighty poems. Brynjólfur said that he was in fact dumbfounded that an Icelandic poet in his fifties, whose books were published by a respected publisher, and who evidently enjoyed grants from the Icelandic State, should be caught engaged in such a prosaic pursuit, and, what's more, within his own family." Jón clears his throat. "That's a terribly written article."

"Is it over?" asks Sturla when it was clear that Jón has stopped talking.

"It is over," replies his father, and Sturla hears those words as if they were the words spoken on the cross:

It is finished.

And he asks: "Did you manage to get the VCR?"

"No, Sturla, I didn't manage to get the video recorder. You never left me the receipt."

"What receipt?"

"The receipt proving that the recorder was in for repair. Without it, I don't even know where it's being repaired."

"I've got the ticket," replies Sturla, standing. "I've got it here in my overcoat pocket, wait just one moment." He ambles through the place's empty rooms towards the entrance, holding the telephone away from his ear. When he sees that there is nothing hanging from the coat hooks he looks around, goes past the deserted bar, and pushes open the door to the kitchen, which smells somewhat worse than a kitchen ought to. The two waiters and a miserable, middle-aged cook are standing inside, huddled strangely close to each other, and they look questioningly at Sturla as he apologizes and tells them he is looking for his overcoat. The waiter who took the overcoat to hang it up said that he had done so and asks if the overcoat isn't on the coat hook.

Then Sturla remembers hearing the main door open without anyone coming in. He repeats his question to the waiter: Is he absolutely sure he had hung up the overcoat? Then he presses the phone to his ear, with a despairing expression, and tells his father that he will have to call back.

"What is the matter?" asks the waiter in English.

Sturla replaces the phone in his shirt pocket and heads out of the kitchen towards the entrance. Even though there is still nothing on the coat hooks, Sturla angrily rattles some of the hangers, and as a few of them fell to the floor with a clattering sound, causing the waiters to come bustling out of the kitchen wondering what's happened, Sturla rushes out the door and is out onto the sidewalk by the time the waiters reach the coat hooks. He throws up his hands when he realizes that the bass player in the hat has vanished, but he doesn't stop to ask about him; he runs down the crowded street. He pushes past people without apologizing and as soon as he has run about twenty meters in one direction he suddenly stops, and then starts running in another direction, with the same urgency as before. It takes him a few minutes to realize that his sprints are useless; there is no point searching for a man who has long since vanished into his own familiar neighborhood, gone without a trace.

When he finally comes back through the door, exhausted and wearing a hangdog expression, the waiters are standing by the bar, and they come towards Sturla with anxious expressions. They try to tell him that they have difficulty understanding how the overcoat vanished: never before in the restaurant's history has an item of clothing disappeared from the coat hooks, and definitely not when the place was empty. Sturla looks at them, completely dumbfounded by their explanation, and suddenly he decides it is best to point out to them that there had been a man with a guitar outside the place, dressed in black—"all black," as he puts it in English. In all likelihood, he was the only person in the world who'd known he was in that restaurant—other than them, that is, and his father, who he'd been talking to on the phone.

When he adds that it seems likely that the man ducked into the place and grabbed the overcoat—he had heard someone come in when no one actually came in—the older waiter answers that it was very unlikely that some colored person came inside just to steal something from the coat hooks; there are very few coloreds here in Vilnius. Sturla doesn't bother to correct the misunderstanding. Instead, he asks the younger waiter why he'd taken his overcoat away to hang it on the coat hooks, why he hadn't let him keep it with him, as he'd wanted. But the waiter doesn't seem to understand the comment: he replies that, here, we don't take responsibility for clothes which are left on the coat hooks; nobody does, not even the more expensive restaurants in the city.

"We are very sorry," says the older waiter, who Sturla is now certain has to be Jokûbas's brother, that wretched man who'd guided Sturla to this restaurant. For a moment it occurs to him that perhaps they work together as accomplices to lure people to the business, and that they share their ill-gotten gains from the restaurant and coat hooks, but

Sturla pushes these thoughts out of his mind with little further consideration. The waiter takes down Sturla's telephone number, the name of his hotel, and his room number. He will let him know, if it suits him, when, or if, the overcoat turns up. Maybe someone—someone who is barely from this world, Sturla thinks—took the overcoat by mistake; it's possible that someone believed they'd forgotten a similar coat the evening before, popped in to get it, and didn't scrutinize it closely enough to see that it was the wrong item.

Sturla can feel his rage bubbling up inside. He strikes his fist on the table, and the waiter—for no other reason, it seems, than to make some kind of response—asks if it was a good overcoat. Sturla is just about to inform the man exactly how much he paid for the overcoat, but he suddenly realizes how absurd it had been to leave such an expensive coat alone by the open entrance to a building where anyone could freely come and go—how stupid it had been, above everything else, to let thirteen 5,000-kronur notes slip through his fingers, all for some winter coat which no one—least of all the disappearing busker—could guess the monetary value of just by looking at it. And he decides there and then to do nothing more than storm out. The plain fact is that the overcoat has vanished and isn't going to re-appear.

Sturla's suspicions about the brotherly connection between the waiter and Jokûbas are confirmed when the former brings Sturla a drink, "to offset your misfortune," as he puts it, and then says that, naturally, it is unthinkable that Sturla should pay for the meal; that is the least they can do to repair the damage. But Sturla can't bear to stay in the place a moment longer; he feels like he has suffered enough in there and shouldn't continue tempting fate. He declines the drink and leaves without saying goodbye.

The midday sun is hot and strong when Sturla walks unsteadily back down Pilies Street, tired and with a heavy head; if truth be told, he is too exhausted to fully realize what has happened in the last few minutes. Jokûbas Daugirdas's description of his brother's restaurant—"You won't be sorry"—echoes in Sturla's head, and though nothing in the world is more likely at this moment to put him in a resentful mood, he suddenly remembers the lyrics to the song *Mandolin Wind*; this song which no doubt Jónas Hallmundsson would have despised, and he would definitely have died laughing if he'd known one of the records Sturla had liked most when he was around twenty—though without ever making a great show of it—had been a Rod Stewart record, *Every Picture Tells a Story*.

PART THREE

DRUSKININKAI

A PACKED READING

Liliya Boginskaia is standing in the lobby when Sturla enters the Ambassador Hotel. He can't, of course, recognize this straight away since he doesn't know what the Belarusian poet looks like, but Liliya—as she later told Sturla—immediately guesses correctly that the person coming in was the Icelandic poet, the author of "the lesson," which she'd translated from English after the author himself had translated it into English. She watches Sturla and listens carefully as he explains things to the employee at reception, no longer the dwarf Henryk but instead a middle-aged woman, a rather sulky woman who reacts badly to Sturla's announcement that he's managed to lose the key to his room. She mutters something to herself, stabs a reprimanding index finger into the air in Sturla's direction, and shakes her head before getting him a new key from a little cubbyhole. Liliya watches, wearing an amused expression, as this irritable character makes Sturla fill out a receipt for the reception key, and she stops him politely as he turns away from the desk and heads towards the stairs.

"Are you Sturla Jón?" she asks, and Sturla is astonished to hear a foreigner say his name the way this poet does: almost flawlessly.

"I am," answers Sturla, and he knows right away that this is Liliya. She is more beautiful than he'd imagined—though how could he have known? he asks himself.

They shake hands.

"I'm glad to make your acquaintance," she says in a rather formal English, and as Sturla feels the warmth of her handshake, she confirms her name: she is Liliya, the one who translated his poem, "the lesson"—she'd really enjoyed doing so. It had also been a nice surprise—and yet, of course, she hadn't expected anything else—that the first Icelandic poem she read had been so wonderful.

"Thank you for saying so," says Sturla, and while he is a little amazed at how she dashes along in her praise of him, he convinces himself that this beautiful and likeable woman is speaking sincerely. He realizes that at this particular moment he is in need of something good from other people, but it isn't just wishful thinking that makes him treat Liliya's words as truthful: something in her eyes stands out.

"I also had a lot of fun translating your poem about Pilies Street," he says. But as soon as he utters the name of that street he thinks he knows Liliya has a better memory of it than he does. And yet at the same time he finds that this person's presence warms him. He contemplates her: dark brown hair, dark eyebrows, dark, stone-like pupils in her eyes and more dark stones beaded on a string around her neck, but everything else in her appearance is bright, the word that best describes her countenance. She is the same age as Sturla; she was born, he thinks, at the same moment.

"You know that this street is here in Vilnius?" she asks, meaning the street in her poem. She smiles, and Sturla feels for a moment that something in the look in her eyes asks something of him, something he longs to know what it is—and longs to give her.

"I've just come from there," he replies, moving the hotel key to his other hand.

"Seriously?" Liliya catches Sturla completely off-guard by taking his upper arm with her hand. "Were you at the coffee shop?" she asks.

"I was at a restaurant which a man by the name of Jokûbas directed me to this morning; he is one of the organizers of the festival." Sturla is at that moment about to explain that the same Jokûbas told him he'd showed Liliya the place the day before, and that she would be there at midday, but he stops himself. It might imply that Sturla had expected to meet her there.

"Jokûbas? Is he the one with the goatee?"

Sturla confirms this, adding that his brother owns the restaurant on Pilies Street.

"He is an interesting man," says Liliya, and Sturla isn't sure which of the brothers she is referring to; could it be she knows them both? He is surprised that she doesn't tell him Jokûbas pointed the place out to her, and in light of what she says next it doesn't seem that he had. "And reliable," she continues. "One of those men who, when you ask about something, you can trust the response. Even though he is more or less drunk all day."

Sturla still doesn't know which of the Daugirdases she means, the poet or the restaurateur. But he advises Liliya not to go to the restaurant; it isn't worth it. And she laughs, saying she knows where she'd go if she fancies going to a restaurant: she wants to show Sturla the place she'd recalled in the poem, not because it had attained higher stature after being mentioned in her poem, but rather . . . She stops mid-sentence and corrects herself:

"Or maybe it did, after I wrote the poem about it. And now you have translated that very poem all the way into Icelandic." And then she continues smiling: "The reading begins in half-an-hour." And she asks Sturla if he is planning to get a coffee here in the hotel beforehand, or whether she can invite him for a beer at the bar in the Writers' Union; it is probably best to get there early: she expects the first official reading of the festival will be well attended.

Sturla explains he needs to make a phone call in his room, and he proposes to meet Liliya downstairs. He'd almost entirely forgotten the reading by the three female American poets in the assembly hall of the Writers' Union. He suddenly gets the feeling that he must seem rather dry to Liliya—in all honesty, he isn't feeling well—and when she lets go of her grasp on his arm, and he is about to head up, he asks her whether she knows these American poets. Liliya says she's read a book by one of them, Jenny Lipp, who lives in Lithuania; she came from Kansas and had made her home in the city of Kaunas. She'd read an interview with her in yesterday's newspaper, in which Jenny recalled how she'd moved to Lithuania three years ago, after getting to know a Lithuanian woman at a poetry festival in San Francisco, and when she found out that the old capital city of Lithuania was called Kaunas she'd resolved to have a home there, even though her friend lived in Vilnius. That way, she could tell people that she had moved from Kansas to Kaunas; it would be ridiculous but true. Sturla can't tell if the last words, "ridiculous but true," come directly from Liliya or from the Kansas-woman, but for Sturla they bring to mind a line which Jónas Hallmundsson had from time to time used in conversation between the two relatives, he and Sturla, as they chatted together at Hressingarskálinn in Austurstræti in the months before Jónas took his own life; a line which he had taken directly from Megas's song about Ragnheiður, the daughter of Bishop Brynjólfur: "but, fine fellows, listen up; it's ridiculous but it's true."

How well these words describe this point in Sturla's life, when he has been exposed in at least two senses of the word.

And though Sturla has to admit that the American poet's eccentric decision, choosing where to live based on how a word sounds, suggests an interesting character—he, for example, had had a completely different image of the American poets when he wrote his article—he knows he has no desire at this moment to go to her and her sister poets' reading, even though he would be in Liliya's company, someone he'd otherwise be keen to get close to and know better. He wants to call the often-mentioned Jokûbas and let him know that his restaurant-owning brother is not so reliable: customers' winter clothes get stolen from coat hooks, even when there is only a single customer. He wants to let him know that he is outraged, but he also realizes he can't let the festival organizers know what the stolen piece of clothing cost: such a figure could only awaken suspicions as to why he, a poet (and superintendent) from Iceland, would waste his money on an overcoat which cost three times the monthly salary of a workman in his hosts' country.

And that leads Sturla to even more definitely resolve not to let Liliya know about the overcoat; he decides instead to face up to the bare fact that the overcoat has vanished. Just as poetry has vanished from his life, so too his overcoat—however much it cost—might as well go the same way.

Liliya repeats that she will wait for Sturla in the cafeteria. He replies he'll be quick and heads wearily up the stairs, with a heavy heart but grateful that he's met this sympathetic female poet from Belarus.

When he looks at the stain on the carpet in the entryway to his room, he curses the fact that he'd kept his lucky charm, the hazelnut, in his overcoat; it's absurd not to take better care of the things that protect one from misfortune. He turns on the television, stretches for the whisky bottle on the table under the mirror, and watches himself as he drinks a decent measure and surfs channels on the screen: two English-language news-channels; a few Lithuanian, Polish, and German ones; and at the end a grayish-black screen which buzzes like an empty factory someone has forgotten to shut down. It is Chernobyl, he thinks, a direct transmission from Chernobyl, twenty years on.

Should he have invited Liliya up to his room? Without thinking, he rings down to reception and asks the woman who got him a replacement key if she can tell him what room Liliya Boguinskaia is in. It turns out she is in room 307, and Sturla peeps out into the corridor and sees that her room is almost directly across from his, probably with a view of Gedimino Prospektas. And now she's sitting in the cafeteria and waiting for me, he thinks.

No, it would probably have been too bold to invite her up to the room. Sturla lights himself a cigarette and takes another sip from the whisky bottle, and while he looks for Jokûbas Daugirdas's phone number in the festival materials, the following conversation plays out in his head:

STURLA: I just want to let you know that I went to your brother's restaurant at lunchtime.

JOKÛBAS: Glad to hear it! I trust my brother treated you well.

STURLA: (*aware that he sounds like he's had a lot to drink, but expecting his interlocutor to be less sober than he himself, if Liliya's words are to be trusted*): Treated me well isn't perhaps the right way to put it. I trust that you get your share of the profits from the valuables stolen from the coat hooks.

JOKÛBAS: I don't know what you mean. You'll be at the reading, won't you? In the assembly hall of the Writers' Union? Yes, I told you about it when we met this morning, didn't I?

STURLA: Yes, you told me about the reading this morning. Before that, you told me about your brother's restaurant. But what makes you think I want to go to some reading when my new overcoat has just been stolen, an item which cost me about what a workman in this country earns in three months? You probably didn't think it was worth so much, and what's more you'll get nowhere near that amount in this country.

JOKÛBAS: It's going to be a well-attended reading. I can promise you that much.

How could he know the reading would be well-attended? Sturla asks himself, and then he ponders another question that he mentally directs to Jokûbas: Do you think it'll be as well-attended as your brother's restaurant?

On what basis could this man so confidently assert that these three American poets will draw the whole world, when Sturla has decided not to attend? This very morning he'd told Sturla he wouldn't be disappointed by his brother's restaurant, the one restaurant in the whole world Sturla is certain he'll never again visit. And during the day he'd claimed the three poets' reading would be so well attended that it would be fair to call it crowded; what other assertions will slip from the lips of this roguish alcoholic now that it is growing dark?

And then the obnoxious ring of the phone clamors from Sturla's breast pocket. He glances at the phone and sees his father's number; he'd forgotten to call him back. Sturla takes another gulp from the whisky bottle and looks at the phone in his hand. He decides not to answer. Had this been his father's plan when he urged his son to get a cell phone before going abroad, a plan to get a hold of him wherever he is, night and day? A man should be able to decide for himself whether he opens the door to let someone in. How many times had those free-spirited appeals to individual liberty in cell phone advertisements struck a nerve with Sturla? He'd always considered these communication devices the perfect fetters to freedom. He'd often imagined himself heading out into nature to let the seeds of some idea grow inside him, something which would later take tangible form in words, when suddenly a phone would ring in his pocket: it had occurred to someone in town that she needed to ring Sturla Jón Jónsson, but this same person hadn't considered that Sturla might at this moment be thinking something that couldn't withstand being broken in two. Now his father has tricked him into renouncing his freedom from this freedom: he has trapped Sturla into being reachable twenty-four hours a day. Hadn't he spoken to him enough for one day? Did he also need to make his son suffer agony over whether to answer the phone? He would call his father that evening, or in a minute; he first needs to let Liliya know that he can't go to the reading. While the phone continues to ring, Sturla splashes cold water on his face in the bathroom, and as he begins rinsing his mouth with toothpaste his father gives up; Sturla imagines him in the apartment on Skólavörðustígur, setting down the telephone.

Liliya is sitting next to the cafeteria window; she has a half-empty glass of beer in front of her and two full shots of something dark and red. The way she reacts to Sturla when he sits down opposite her makes him even more certain that she is a really good person. It occurs to him that he probably didn't take sufficient care in preparing her poem in its Icelandic version; she had without doubt produced a wonderful translation of his "kennslustund" in her native tongue. She smiles warmly at him, glances at the clock as if to let him know that they ought to hurry to get to the reading, and holds one of the shots out to him. It is cherry brandy, ever the appropriate drink for focusing one's powers of observation immediately before a poetry reading. It makes Sturla feel especially bad to let Liliya know he can't come to the reading; he sips from his shot while she empties hers, and he tells her that he needs to work this afternoon—it is ridiculous but yet true—he needs to make corrections to an article which is about to be published in a magazine in Iceland. It can't wait past this afternoon; he has to e-mail corrections by the day's end.

"Perhaps we'll see you this evening." Liliya suggests, and Sturla considers it both good and bad that he can't discern any disappointment in her eyes. She asks what the article is about, and finishes her glass of beer while Sturla tells her it considers the advantages and drawbacks of literary festivals ("pros and cons" is how he puts it in English, immediately regretting the phrase). He does his best to make it sound interesting, feeling uncomfortable that he isn't being completely honest with Liliya, this person who he feels sure is going to enchant him more then he is usually enchanted by people.

"I'll be up in my room," he says. "I just need to send these corrections, then I'll be up in my room."

As soon as he starts going up the stairs to the third floor, he experiences a nagging hunger. He decides to head into town shortly and get himself something to eat; he's not had any nourishment other than the wretched breakfast and those two or three bites of meat he'd managed to eat at the restaurant. Absent-mindedly he watches the news on television, smokes two cigarettes, and pours another measure from the whisky bottle into a glass. Then he decides to go out, and when he crosses onto the shady side of the street he realizes unhappily how valuable the overcoat had been to him—and only now senses how quickly he's been drinking whisky over the past half hour.

When he comes back to the hotel room two hours later—with some new experiences which he wants to forget as soon as possible—the television has for some reason been taken down from the wall and has been placed on top of the closet which contains the empty fridge. Sturla realizes that he longs for something other than whisky to drink—perhaps cold beer or white wine—and he becomes suddenly angry that the fridge in the room is hooked-up although there isn't even a lone bottle of water inside. He is well aware that his nervous system isn't in the best possible shape at the moment, but he resolves nevertheless to go to reception, where the dwarfish Henryk is sitting on a raised office chair, and to ask when the mini-bar is going to be stocked.

"We don't offer that service in this hotel." Henryk responds to Sturla's remark with something to that effect and, before Sturla knows what he is doing, he finds himself over-zealously describing how he is an Icelandic alcoholic and he must have some liquor in his mini-bar or he will need to change hotels.

"I can look into that tomorrow morning, sir," answers Henryk, clearly amazed by this Icelander's self-diagnosis. In fact, Sturla admires the dwarf's calm, collected behavior; he would be justified in treating Sturla with the same roughness as Sturla has shown. Henryk points the clock out to Sturla—it isn't yet eight o'clock so the cafeteria is open. Sturla buys himself two cold bottles of beer to take up to his room, but he doesn't make it to the second before he falls asleep; the bottle is standing open and untouched on the table by the window as his deep snoring blends in with the low, distant sound of an American television channel, and Sturla sinks into a twelve-hour sleep which he really needs before he travels to Druskininkai at 2:00 in the afternoon the next day.

THE PICKPOCKET'S HAND

What happens the next day, other than the bus leaving for Druskininkai from the Writers' Union at around two o'clock, is that Sturla becomes the owner of two new items of clothing, each of which, in a different fashion, replaces the Aquascutum overcoat. One of these items cost him half the amount as he nearly ended up paying a prostitute shortly before he returned to the hotel around 8:00 the evening before. He took the other item with the stealth of a pickpocket's hand, the same hand "that damn Brynjólfur," Brynjólfur Madsen, seemed to believe Sturla had used to steal his cousin's manuscript. According to the Icelandic media, he was Jónas's school companion and was, Sturla suddenly realized (shortly after concluding his business with the aforementioned prostitute), the reason Jónas had quoted time and again, almost obsessively, Megas's song about Ragnheiður, the bishop's daughter: "but, fine fellows, listen up; it's ridiculous but it's true / that damn Brynjólfur, he's the guy who got her fertilized."

On the other hand, the prostitute was the source of an experience Sturla would prefer to forget. That it should have occurred to him to use his profits from the games hall on Skólavörðustígur on an alcohol-addled (or drug-dazed) prostitute is unfathomable to him now, the next day, as he recalls the conversation with his father about how he was not going on a sex holiday to the Baltic. He remembers, too, his decision—the promise of the unreliable Sturla Jón rather than the intelligent Sturla Jón—that he was going to use the money he won from the University of Iceland to buy himself something that would always remind him of his trip to the poetry festival.

But wouldn't a brief encounter with a prostitute—one who had actually reminded Sturla quite a bit of the Belarusian Salomé at Old Town Erotic Center—have become that very memory which would have lived on from these October days in Lithuania? Sturla had never before had sex with a woman who, as they say, walks the streets, and he momentarily recalls something his friend Svanur told him: that it's good for a writer to experience human interactions (or business transactions) which involve the double-edged pleasure of engaging in an intimacy you've paid money for—that is, the suffering and unhappiness that Sturla had gone through the evening before in the alley. Right now, he is glad to see the open beer bottle awaiting him on the table by the mirror. And while he looks at it in his hand, he recalls his relations with the woman on Konstitucijos Street (somehow the street's name has stuck in his memory). He empties the bottle in a few gulps, and the pain which he had woken up with after his troubled sleep instantly goes away.

Has Svanur ever had relations with a prostitute? Sturla wipes his lips with the back of his hand; he doubts it. "Shy men of extreme sensibility are the born victims of the prostitute;" Christopher Isherwood's words have long lived in Sturla's mind, ever since he read them in a foreword to Baudelaire's diaries, but despite the fact that Svanur isn't really an outward-going character and would doubtlessly maintain that he was endowed with extreme sensibility, he could hardly be considered the obvious victim of the hooker.

Sturla had been sitting in the same bar where he'd seen the Swedes the evening before, but he didn't stay long, wanting to avoid the risk of meeting people from the reading—it was definitely a bar recommended to festival participants, though Sturla expected the crowd was more likely to congregate after the reading at the bar in the Writers' Union, a place he'd still not been to. The fresh memory of meeting Liliya a little while earlier warmed him, but it also depressed him: he wanted to meet up with her alone, not inside with all the other participants that he imagined would gather after the Americans' reading, quite literally and noisily rustling their papers—and he decided he would get together with Liliya the next day. It would be clear then whether she was as warm as she'd been when they first met. But after sitting down in another bar, not far from the "Swedish" bar, and drinking a large enough quantity of beer and cherry brandy to discover that he needed some other activity than just sitting alone at a table by himself, he let himself wander through the streets of the old downtown and his imaginary course of action began to include more and more of the Belarusian poet. He was so intimately wrapped up in this that when a young woman suddenly came up to him and without any introduction told him the price of her body, in *litos* as well as euros, Sturla—or so he later thinks, at least—figured that doing business with this woman made sense as the logical next step in the fantasy wandering the streets and drinking had aroused in him.

Judging by her face and hair, it was like she'd been clipped from Sturla's mental image of Salomé, but the woman's appearance and her pushiness struck him as being simultaneously very repulsive and an indication that she was easy prey (or so Sturla described it to himself). For his part, he was drunk and looked tired, but this woman must have begun her day much earlier than he, because it wasn't yet eight o'clock, and she was in such an intoxicated haze that it was almost impossible to imagine she'd be able to complete the task at hand. That didn't, however, stop Sturla from showing some interest in her; he asked her what she charged for a half-hour—and also asked himself at the same time whether he was serious—and he was told that for an hour he'd need to pay what amounted to 25,000 Icelandic kronur. She charged 15,000 for half an hour, and his next question was what service he could get for 10,000 kronur. She laughed—it was a provocative, spiteful laugh—and told Sturla to follow her into an alley between a children's clothing store and a motorcycle store. And when she had dragged him along with her through the alley they came to a paved yard outside what seemed to be the office of a bookshop or a publisher.

Once there, she shoved Sturla up against the wall, out of sight of the street, and she pressed against him, her face so close to his that despite the great stench of liquor which must be steaming off both of them, he noticed a garlicky stink which succeeded in completely chasing away his desire to do this thing in the shady yard for which he was about to have to pay 10,000 kronur. He turned his face away from the woman, and when she hooked her heel around his leg and stuck her hand down the front of his pants, he'd had more than enough of the horrible garlic smell. He shoved the woman roughly off him and instinctively lashed out by calling her an animal, a beast—employing words that were foreign to his usual vocabulary. The woman reacted by grabbing hold of Sturla's crotch, and, tit for tat, he responded by elbowing her, pushing her away from him and onto the sidewalk. She screamed something in her own tongue, and at that moment a window opened in the house above the bookshop. Although Sturla's wasn't able to comprehend the shout he heard from the window, he realized that if someone was accused of violence in this little crime scene he now found himself participating in, it would in all likelihood be him, the foreigner.

A quarter of an hour later he'd headed up the stairs of the Ambassador Hotel clutching two open beer bottles in an embrace and thinking the peculiarly reassuring thought—which admittedly stemmed from a drunken, fuzzy logic—that Jónas Hallmundsson, his cousin and brother poet (if that was the right way to put it) had indirectly warned him against his schoolmate Brynjólfur Madsen. Jónas had in some unexplainable way known Sturla would step into his trap and take advantage of the unused manuscript, which no-one had even seen—no-one, that is, except Brynjólfur. But if that was true, why hadn't Jónas placed the manuscript in Sturla's hand before he quit the stage? Was it possible his cousin had "rushed ahead," as he'd put it in "kennslustund"— and Sturla had let it stand, unchanged—earlier than he'd planned to?

As Sturla puts the other empty beer bottle into the trashcan next to the mini-bar, he remembers how he'd demanded that the refrigerator be filled the previous evening. He'd probably sworn at and insulted the dwarfish man at the front desk, Henryk, who in one of Sturla's versions of what happened the previous day had been a more powerful omen than the hazelnut from the airport. While Sturla shakes his head over this silly need he has to constantly look for allusions in everything, in the past and in the future, he asks himself what will protect him now, now when the nut which ought to bring him luck is no longer among his earthly possessions, now when he has no overcoat to shelter himself. There is, on the other hand, the question as to whether he has any further need of a good luck charm, now that the oracle has been recited.

Liliya pops into his thoughts, and he remembers she had been holding a plain silk scarf in one of her hands while they talked in the lobby; she'd held onto it with the hand she hadn't used to take his arm. And he decides that after breakfast he will look for a scarf of his own to wrap around his neck; he doesn't want to stroll the cool autumn streets of Druskininkai with the collar of his jacket turned up like the penniless poet Martín Marco on the cold streets of Franco's Madrid. And in this context—as he measures himself against Cela's character in the movie by Mario Camus about the poets, the intellectuals, and the prostitutes of *The Beehive*—it occurs to Sturla that he will perhaps be able to get a scarf in the Spanish-owned clothing store, Zara, which he saw the day before on Gedimino Prospektas, next to the Novotel Hotel and diagonally across from the McDonald's he has decided to visit while he's in town. He'd seen a breakfast prominently advertised in the window which, based on the picture, was going to be rather more exciting than the one he'd received at the hotel.

Two hours later Sturla stands outside Zara. He is wearing a stone-grey cotton scarf around his neck, and his thoughts turn to Stella, the shop on Bankastræti, where he'd stood just a few days earlier in a new overcoat which now protects an entirely different person than it was intended to. He lights himself a cigarette, and when he blows out the smoke, he tastes the beer he drank inside McDonald's in his mouth. As he heads towards the Ambassador Hotel, intending to sit down in the cafeteria and have another beer, he sets eyes on a man who is standing outside the shining, well-polished glass door of the high-rise Novotel Hotel; he's wearing a beige overcoat. Sturla can tell, even at a distance—at least, over the ten meters or so that separate him from the man in the overcoat—that it is a well-made, expensive item of clothing, which perhaps isn't surprising given that the owner appears to be a guest at the hotel, which Sturla knows is one of the most expensive and best hotels in the city, possibly the same hotel he mentioned in his article, the one with the Jacuzzi tubs and orange chocolates in the cloth bag. The man in the overcoat, who appears to be around Sturla's age, has a thin, dark brown leather case under his arm. He swaggers out onto the sidewalk, back and forth, like he is waiting for someone, and the way he raises his head, as if he's basking in the sun on this sunless day, suggests a considerable—and perhaps healthy—self-confidence, something which Sturla himself lacks at this moment, even though he is pleased with his new scarf and has managed to placate himself well enough with the five beers he's had since he woke up.

Sturla adjusts his scarf and looks up at the hotel building, with one eye on the man in the overcoat; just then he greets two women who have come cheerfully out of the hotel and onto the sidewalk. They embrace him in a very Southern European way, with three kisses, and then they set off at a stroll in the same direction as Sturla had been heading. The women are somewhat younger than the man. One of them wears a light gray suit; the other a white coat. Nothing about those people—except perhaps the man's overcoat—should give Sturla a reason to follow them, but he doesn't want to let them out of his sight; he finds himself following along the street. He suspects that these well-dressed people come from France or Italy, that they are probably educated people who are somehow connected with the business of art or culture. Just before they reach Sturla's hotel, they decide to cross to the other sidewalk, as if they're reluctant to mix with the wretched appearance the Ambassador Hotel presents to the sidewalk. They are gallery owners or art collectors, thinks Sturla, and it comes as no surprise when he sees them stop in front of the bronze figures on the National Theater. When he, too, comes to a halt, he hears them speaking English: they are American. He hears one of the women say *interesting* in a way that doesn't match other English-speaking regions. The one in the white coat takes a photograph of them, with the theater in background, and they continue along the street in the direction of the cathedral square.

The place they vanish into had aroused Sturla's attention the day before, for the simple reason that its name is Literatu Svetainé. It is building number 8 on Gedimino Prospektas. Sturla hasn't figured out what the word "svetainé" stands for, and he decides to take the opportunity to find out.

Afterwards, he realizes he hasn't any reason to dwell on what happened after he pursued the American friends of the arts inside Literatu Svetainé. He'd sat at the bar, ordered a glass of beer, and loosened his scarf, which was becoming sweaty around his neck. He'd heard the man in the overcoat (who had actually removed his overcoat before sitting down with the women at a table a little way from the bar) order himself smoked salmon and something which sounded to Sturla like Baby Tomato Soup; they also asked the waiter for some chilled Riesling wine and sparkling water. There was no bass player in a hat on the sidewalk outside this tastefully designed place. When Sturla left his half-empty beer glass at the bar and went towards the entrance, five or six items were hanging from the coat rack, but by the time he opened the door to the street and saw that the sun had broken out from the clouds which a few minutes earlier had lain over the day like a plastic wrapper, there were only four or five items left. Sturla took as long as he needed: he buttoned his jacket as he stood in front of the coat hooks; he wrapped the scarf around his neck—though there was no need to since the sun was beginning to shine—and very calmly placed the overcoat he'd taken from the coat hanger over his forearm. He noticed that the texture of the material was similar, if not identical, to the Aquascutum overcoat from Bankastræti. It isn't until he is approaching the National Theatre, having crossed to that side of the street, that he allows himself to peek at the inside of the coat. There, in gilt embroidered ornamental letters on a dark blue silk square he reads: Brooks Brothers; in smaller letters below that: Established 1818.

Sturla nods his head to the bronze figures on top of the playhouse and hurries along the crowded sidewalk in the direction of his hotel. He is hot by the time he goes inside, and can smell in his sweat the stale smell of morning beers. The Nordic guy he'd seen before with a cup of tea and rolled cigarettes is back at the same table in the cafeteria, and when Sturla glances in through the glass door, he sees Liliya sitting there, in the company of some other people. She has a red kerchief bound around her head. He speeds through the lobby in the direction of the stairs, nodding his head to a young woman at the front desk who he has not previously seen, and the first thing he does when he enters his room is slip on the overcoat and look at himself in the mirror.

It is really unbelievable, thinks Sturla, how similar this American's overcoat is to my own overcoat.

My own?

The American's overcoat?

Who owns which overcoat? Which overcoat is owned by whom?

And what has he done? How many minutes have passed since he followed the American into the restaurant with the literary name? Suddenly Sturla has arrived in room number 304 in the Ambassador Hotel—which he just then remembers he needs to get ready to check out of; he is about to leave Vilnius and head into the country—with a beautiful beige overcoat which he'd stolen from a coat hook at a restaurant. He hasn't even had time to wonder whether there is anything in the pockets of the overcoat.

Is there?

He slips his hand into the side pockets and pulls out two rolled banknotes, twenty dollars altogether, and also a folded piece of paper from the Mabre Residence Hotel, on which some names and sentences, in quotation marks, have been written; Sturla doesn't bother to read it. When he looks in the inner pocket on the other side, some rigid paper and two small, bound, rather oblong-shaped booklets come to light. One bears the familiar name Daniella Goldblum, and the other, which he looks at as though time has stopped, has the name of the woman from Kansas: Jenny Lipp. Under the name is a title, *Three Poems*, and when Sturla opens the binding of Jenny's booklet he sees it is inscribed to the overcoat's owner; the date is yesterday, but it is impossible is to decipher the rest of the poet's writing.

Three questions burst into Sturla's head: Was the woman in the suit Jenny or Daniella? Was the woman in the white coat Daniella or Jenny? And would all these people head to Druskininkai after the meal that was conceivably still now taking place at the table?

There is little more than an hour before the bus was due to leave.

Perhaps Jenny Lipp stays at the Novotel Hotel when she comes to Vilnius from Kaunas. Sturla had thought all the foreign guests of the festival were staying at the Ambassador Hotel—or at least in hotels of a similar price range—but it was possible that this American poet who lives in Lithuania had chosen to cut herself off from this group of guests by finding a hotel on her own, thereby showing she knows her way around Vilnius. But although the self-confident American guy with the brown leather case was dressed in almost the same overcoat as Sturla—even the same size, which is a happy coincidence—Sturla doesn't think he is a poet; in fact, he suspects his first guess is probably still the best: that these three people are involved with the art world, possibly the antiques trade. Perhaps they had been invited, through the American embassy, to their compatriots' reading yesterday, and Jenny and Daniella had been so delighted to meet their "fellow Americans" that they'd given them inscribed copies of their chapbooks, which had been printed on the occasion of the festival.

As if to conclude the conversation Sturla is having with himself about the legality of taking possession of another man's overcoat, he convinces himself that, unlike the loss he experienced the day before, someone who is based at the Mabre Residence Hotel—which sounds like it is a few classes up from the Ambassador Hotel (although the Ambassador Hotel's name implies considerable luxury to the uninitiated)—is hardly likely to let such a mishap throw him off balance. His one difficulty will be that he might need to order a replacement overcoat from America—and maybe he won't even have to do that, since, based on what he's seen of the colorful shops and range of merchandise in Vilnius, it is more than possible to get hold of products made by the sort of manufacturer whose name gets sewn onto a silk square in the overcoat lining, a name he really isn't concerned with remembering at this moment, as he stands in front of the mirror, wearing the coat and stretching out his arms to assure himself that the overcoat still fits.

He takes a sip from the whisky bottle but judging from his expression in the mirror the drink is too strong for this time of day, and while he again remembers that he better pack so he can check out of the hotel, he lights a cigarette, gets himself a glass of water from the bathroom, adds a small amount of whisky to it, and decides after a little thought to put the overcoat at the bottom of his suitcase. He will let the scarf suffice, at least until he has made sure that the owner of the overcoat—the previous owner—isn't connected with the international poetry festival which, according to the printed program, will start at six o'clock today in some lecture hall in Druskininkai.

Before he locks the door to the room, he contemplates the stain on the carpet: it hasn't shrunk and it's still wet. He doesn't waste any time checking out of the hotel, and when he comes into the cafeteria, with his suitcase, he sees that Liliya is still sitting at the same table as before, but she is no longer surrounded by people. There is only one person sitting with her now, a Danish man of roughly sixty, who Sturla thinks he hears Liliya introduce as Roger; he doesn't recall having seen his face in the biographies of festival participants.

"And this is Sturla Jón, from Iceland," Liliya says to the Dane, and Sturla has no doubt that she is glad to see him again, although she doesn't mention it.

And even though Sturla is not especially keen on Liliya's dark red kerchief, he shares her unspoken feeling; it feels good to see her again, and he knows that after everything he's gone through he needs to have a person like Liliya to hold on to. And as he asks himself whether the women in Belarus wear scarves or handkerchiefs, Liliya calls to one of the waitresses and points to the half-empty beer glasses on the table, indicating that she wants three more of the same. Then she asks Sturla if she is the first person from Belarus he's met, explaining that she'd intended to ask him this the day before.

"I am, you see, the first Belarusian Roger here has met," she adds, and the grey-bearded Dane—who appears to be perpetually nodding his head, as if he is always in agreement with something—confirms Liliya's remarks; he hasn't even seen a person from Belarus on television, at least as far as he knows.

"No, I actually met a person from Belarus yesterday," replies Sturla, who can't tell if the Dane was joking or not.

"No! Who was that?" asks Liliya, rather expectantly.

"She was called Salomé."

"That's a peculiar name for a human being from Belarus," says Liliya, and Sturla is amazed that she chose to use the words *human being* rather than *person*; their Danish colleague paused very briefly from nodding his head, seeming similarly surprised.

But just as Sturla is telling himself that the person called Salomé would hardly bind scarves around her head, like Liliya does, the telephone in his breast pocket rings, and he apologizes to his companions before fishing the phone out of his pocket and answering it.

It comes as no surprise that it is his father.

"I thought you were going to call back yesterday," says Jón, and the way he says it indicates he's clearly been anxious. And while Liliya leans forward and takes Sturla's scarf between her thumb and index finger, he tells his father that he'd meant to call last night, but he had unexpectedly ended up at a social gathering with his festival companions (as he phrases it) and had momentarily forgotten everything else.

"I'm afraid I have to bring up again what I told you yesterday," Jón says, and the accusatory tone in his voice leads Sturla to stand up and ask Liliya and the Dane to excuse him. Then he moves over to the door leading to the hotel reception.

"It's reached the front page today," Jón continues, and Sturla asks him: What has reached the front page today?

"The picture from yesterday, except now it's on the front page."

"The one with the baseball cap?"

"Yes, the one with the baseball cap."

What amazes Sturla most about the news his father reads from the front page of the paper, and his comments about the debate "this muckraking mass media" is having over Sturla's newly-published book, is that he, Sturla Jón Jónsson (the poet), hadn't only stolen poems from his relative: his relative had also ruthlessly stolen from other poets, especially Dagur Sigurðarson, the Icelandic poet Jónas held in highest esteem. The difference between Jónas and Sturla Jón's methods was that the former had not seemed at all ashamed of filching here and there—he had even told Brynjólfur about it (and, of course, he'd never actually intended to publish the poems)—but Sturla, on the other hand, is so "bent over backwards" about his thieving that he isn't only maintaining a wall of silence about it, he's even chosen to absent himself from the country. This silence surely spoke volumes for the charge that the things Sturla had taken from his relative's estate were, plain and simple, stolen.

Sturla asks his father whether or not he finds it a little odd that a newspaper of this caliber should concern itself with contemporary poetry.

"This is the very same media that maintains that news should be entertainment," replies Jón, and adds that the paper is itself trying to compose poetry; one of the sub-headings in the article, which must be the journalist's own words, is "The Pickpocket Poet."

"And saying that silence speaks—that comes from Dagur's poem, 'Suicide,'" says Sturla. "So today you can find a picture of me, branded as a word-thief who's been caught red-handed, in every grocery store in the country?"

"I haven't been to any of the country's grocery stores today," replies Jón, and Sturla thinks he perceives in this reply that his father believes what the country is being told on the front pages of its newspapers.

"But you can find it on the net," adds Jón, and he mentions that Sturla's publisher, Gústaf, had called last night—Brynjólfur Madsen wanted to speak to Sturla. Gustaf said Brynjólfur regretted having gone directly to the media with the story, and he also regretted the low tone of the discussion. He'd made those remarks before the second article was published, so if his repentance was real, he no longer had a say in what the paper wrote. But, according to Gústaf, Brynjólfur wanted to explain the matter directly to Sturla. Apparently he wanted to tell him something about Jónas, about his last days, something he couldn't say to Hallmundur and Þeba, whatever that meant.

"What a big-hearted guy," replies Sturla.

"But it has to be said that things really aren't looking so good," says Jón, and Sturla, who is looking towards the hotel entrance and trying to persuade himself that he isn't thinking about what's going on in Iceland, asks his father to wait on the phone while he gets the hotel's e-mail address from the woman at reception. Then he gives the address to Jón, adding that he has to hang up the phone: he is heading to "the festival, which is the real reason why I'm here at all."

But the only thing Sturla knows for sure that he is heading towards is the cafeteria, through the lobby. Liliya seems very busy explaining something to the Dane, and although Sturla is delighted to see her—she, at least, lights up one corner of his gloomy thoughts—he is beginning to find the Dane's incessant head-nodding irritating. He can imagine this grey-bearded man nodding his head at his nagging wife; he starts to feel sorry for the wife of this overly-agreeable poet, about whom he knows nothing other than that he is wearing a wedding band on his ring finger, that he is called Roger, and that he is on his way, together with some other mediocre poets of this world, to visit Druskininkai in Lithuania solely because he doesn't have to pay for anything, neither for travel nor for accommodation.

"I'm telling Roger about the restaurant I went to yesterday evening after the reading," says Liliya, and Roger nods his head to Sturla, his mouth caught in an expression that suggests he is in the middle of some great discovery.

As Sturla expected from Liliya's comment, the restaurant in question is the one Jokûbas had recommended; moreover, Jokûbas had dropped by in person later in the evening, to check up on his brother (Sturla imagines, as Liliya tells her narrative) and to make sure he was giving his friends from the poetry festival the red carpet treatment.

"There wasn't a musician standing outside, playing bass, was there?"

"Not that I recall, no. But at some point I need to take you to my coffee shop on Pilies Street. When we come back from Druskininkai." And she asks Sturla whether he was going back to Iceland immediately after they return from the country.

Even though Sturla takes considerable trouble to give her a clear answer (that he has a whole free day in Vilnius after they come back from Druskininkai; he is going home the morning after), Liliya doesn't seem to pay much attention to his response; she still seems to be thinking about the restaurant from the previous evening. And when she begins describing the food, Sturla politely interrupts her, asking her and Roger how the reading at the Writers' Union had been. The Dane, in his typical quiet way, gives it a good review, and Liliya says she really liked the poems of one of the American women, Kelly Fransesca. They'd reminded her of a Canadian poet she thinks highly of, Dora Mistral, who had actually translated some of her own poems, including "Pilies Street"—Sturla had translated from Dora's English version. Also, a few lines from one of the Jenny Lipp's poems had reminded her of Sturla's "the lesson." She is, she remarks, more and more infatuated with this poem the longer she thinks about it. The metaphor of volcanic eruption strikes her as very fertile; she suspects that such a lyrical undertaking (or, as she puts it, a poetic exercise) must have come from a real depth.

"Thanks for that," says Sturla (acknowledging to himself that he isn't sure how to interpret Liliya's remarks) and instead of sitting down at the table, as Liliya invites him to do, he says he needs to take care of a couple of things before they go to the bus; he needs to make a phone call in his room and will meet them outside the Writers' Union in fifteen minutes: "a quarter of an hour," he tells them in English.

The Dane offers to take Sturla's suitcase (he has very little luggage himself) but Sturla turns him down: he needs some papers from the suitcase when he calls Iceland. Unlike the bobble-headed Dane, Sturla mentally shakes his head horizontally left and right while he listens to himself telling strangers his reasons for wanting his own suitcase with him. He drains his beer and when he says goodbye to Liliya and the Dane, he tries to make sure that the farewell doesn't come across as though it will last more than the quarter of an hour he mentions.

"Do you have any rooms?" he asks the woman at the front desk, the one who'd taken his key shortly before.

The woman looks at Sturla doubtfully. "But weren't you just . . . ?"

"Yes," replies Sturla. "And now I want to check in again."

FITNESS TRAINING

He didn't know why exactly, but from the moment he woke up Sturla had had the feeling he wouldn't be getting on the bus to Druskininkai. And now, as he sits by the window in the twin hotel room (number 411), he feels sure the bus has set off from the Writers' Union and that either Liliya or Roger had run from there to the hotel to tell him to hurry—but, as he'd asked the woman at the front desk to do, they would have been told that Sturla Jón Jónsson had left the hotel at about 1:45.

His failure to show up at the bus at the appointed time means that, sooner or later, he'll have to get to Druskininkai on his own, likely rather early tomorrow. Indeed, nothing but his own death could justify another absence.

His own death. Sturla pauses at those words. Just as a person owns his life—which possibly is the only real property he owns—he must be the owner of his death, too, even though other people have to take care of him in that situation. "It's one thing to live, another to die."

Hadn't he brought that sentence to life in one of his books, *free from freedom*, his only book so far that had sold more than the 150 or 200 copies poetry books usually sell? Sturla hadn't thought about what that sentence might signify, something that was true of everything he'd written, but that was precisely what gave his poetry value and life beyond the first reading; he himself, and supposedly other readers too, were yet to find out what it all meant. His latest book, *assertions*, is of a different nature, as it wasn't conceived in the same way as the others. As suggested by the name, the poems in the book are more determined, giving the reader less leeway for his own interpretations—in certain places he is thrown up against a wall. Sturla had feared this would also be true of the poet: it was now clear he had literally ended up against the wall, that all that was left to do was wake up the execution squad.

But since his own death would justify his absence from the gathering that the world, and all his poems, had led him to, he figures he is well within his rights to play hooky from the so-called group bonding that he knows will be in the program today in Druskininkai. "The guy 'no longer' needs an alibi," or so he misquotes a line from a Dagur Sigurðarson poem. Sturla—and, evidently, Jonas, too—had managed to internalize lines from Dagur's poems over time, almost without trying. As he looks around the spacious hotel room, which could easily house another poet too—that is, if not all the poets are on their way out to the country, to The Season of Poetry, as the organizers had somehow decided to name the festival.

Sturla gets a water glass from the bathroom (which is a lot more spacious than in room 304) and pours the remnants of the whisky bottle into the glass. Then he lights two cigarettes. He leaves one smoking in the ashtray, and he holds the other between his index and middle fingers.

What does Liliya think about me? he wonders. About a man who always vanishes from the scene just when things are about to happen. First of all, he doesn't show up at the reading that marks the beginning of the festival, and then he doesn't show up for the festival itself. It must have occurred to Liliya that this Icelandic poet, whose poem she'd translated (according to the wishes of the festival organizers), a poem about dying before old age—about not being meant to stay the course of one's life—doesn't have time to attend the events he's come here to attend. He must be a very busy man, this man who constantly "rushes ahead," as he'd put it himself in his poem.

Hadn't he also stood up from his first full meal in town the day before just as he'd begun eating, and vanished from the restaurant?

Yes.

Were people having a lot of fun on the bus headed towards Druskininkai? All of the participants would be getting to know the people they were sitting next to, if they hadn't already met, and even getting to know the people who were sitting in front of and behind them, or in the nearby aisle seats. Bottles and little hip flasks would be changing hands and occasional bursts of laughter would rise from the continuous indistinguishable babble which from time to time descends into silence while the passengers think up what they ought to say next—and in one such silence Liliya will look out of the window where she sits beside the grey-bearded Dane, and contemplate the forested countryside that's rushing past the bus at 80 kilometers per hour, her thoughts full of questions about the expression on Sturla's face as he said goodbye and disappeared from the cafeteria after having declined Roger's offer to carry his suitcase to the Writers' Union.

When Sturla opens the closet in the entryway to the room he discovers a black suitcase on wheels that the last guest must have forgotten. He wheels the case across the floor and into the main room, where he lifts it up onto one of the beds. Just then the sun lights up the room. Sturla opens the zipper on the case, and then he goes to the window to draw the curtains; he also turns on the television, which takes a little while to come on before weather reports from Australia and New Zealand fill the room. In the suitcase is a stack of neatly-folded men's clothes, and what especially interests Sturla is that at the bottom are fifteen to twenty identical white shirts, all the same, some still in their plastic covering. Sturla considers the suitcase's contents and sniffs a checked sweater that's on the top. He takes a sip of whisky, extinguishes his cigarette, and smokes the other one. Before closing the case he takes out one of the shirts, puts it on the other bed, and unfolds the sleeves to see whether it might fit. Then he calls the front desk and lets them know that a suitcase has been left behind in the closet.

After closing it, he opens his own suitcase, pulls the Brooks Brothers overcoat out from under the pile of clothes and hangs it on the back of a chair by the writing table in the center of the room. Then he folds the white shirt and places it on top of his clothes, which, compared to the contents of the other suitcase, are in disarray. He rolls the black suitcase into the entryway and leaves it by the door.

A few moments later he decides instead to put back what he took. He opens his case, smells his fingers before retrieving the white shirt, and puts it carefully back where it originally came from. Then he opens a black notebook which he takes out of his briefcase.

No more than a few minutes pass before a hotel employee knocks on the door and takes the suitcase. Sturla is talking to his daughter Hildigunnur; he'd called Egilsstaðir from the hotel telephone, listened briefly to his younger daughter, Hallgerður, who wasn't able to stop and talk to him, and asked her to fetch Hildigunnur.

"And you? What are you doing?" asks Hildigunnur.

"I am on this trip to Lithuania. I'm here at a poetry festival in a city called Vilnius."

"So I've begun toning again," continues Hildigunnur, as though she hasn't heard her father's last words. She'd been talking about the red sports car she bought with her girlfriend, and when she suddenly begins discussing what she calls "toning," Sturla can't remember her ever mentioning stopping fitness training—so why did she have to start again? "They built a new place here in Egilsstaðir," she continues. "Do you remember how the old place looked when you last visited? They now have televisions everywhere and . . ."

Sturla interrupts his daughter and tells her that he doesn't remember visiting any fitness complex when he last went to Egilsstaðir; she must be confusing him (her father) with someone else who came to visit the countryside. He doesn't remind her that he hasn't been to Egilsstaðir for four or five years, since Hulda last asked him to stay with the children while she and Símon went on a week's vacation to Copenhagen.

"Isn't there a gym at the hotel?" asked Hildigunnur, and it is almost heartbreaking for Sturla to have to wonder if his older daughter thinks about anything other than fitness training.

"No, not that I'm aware of," he replies, and he is informed that nowadays all hotels have gyms, "except perhaps a few hostels."

As Hildigunnur asks him about "the weather abroad," whether it is hot there in "what was it called again?" Sturla hears a thin voice call from behind her: "Is that your father?"

It's Hulda's voice, a voice he's not heard for several months but had listened to daily for fifteen years, without ever figuring out why she needed to screech the way she did.

"Yes, it's Dad," Hildigunnur yells, right into the phone, and tells her mother that he is overseas.

"Does she want to talk to me?" asks Sturla, thinking the question sounds like he doesn't expect she will.

And instead of answering, Hildigunnur takes the telephone from her ear, and Hulda greets Sturla with a different, more listless voice than the one she'd used to ask if he was on the phone:

"Hi, Sturla."

"She didn't say goodbye," he replies.

"I haven't heard from you in a long time," replies Hulda. "Where are you?"

"Lithuania. Vilnius."

"What are you doing there?"

"Nothing really. It's just that I was sent here by the Icelandic people."

"Are you really on vacation in . . . where did you say, Lithuania?"

"Do you think the Icelandic nation would send me on vacation?

"I've no idea."

"Why wouldn't I be on vacation in Lithuania or some other place?"

"Do they sell holidays to Lithuania?"

"Was Hildigunnur hurrying off to something?"

"They are all always hurrying somewhere," answers Hulda. "You know how life is for them here in Egilsstaðir; there's no rest for the wicked. That's the country, as you said yourself: never any tranquility. Except perhaps for Egill; he's headed south with his Spanish girlfriend."

"Did you see the thing in the newspaper?"

"Yes, I saw it this morning. But what are you doing over there? Are you giving a reading? Are you alone?"

"Of course I'm alone," replies Sturla. And what he says next, in his most ceremonious tone, he does so in a way he wants Hulda to understand as self-pitying. "You know I've chosen to be alone, Hulda. Whether I am in Lithuania or Reykjavík."

"You've always been a hopeless loner," replies Hulda teasingly. "You can't tell me that's news."

"Don't call me a loner, Hulda!" Sturla practically yells into the phone, and he realizes just how much it irritates him that she would describe him as a "loner." "Call me just about anything other than a loner," he repeats, trying to control himself. "Or a gipsy."

"What would you prefer I called you? A team player?"

"Nothing. You don't always need to make it sound like you are trying to explain my character for some damn magazine interview."

"That *I* seem to be trying to explain . . . ? You're being overly sensitive, Sturla."

And his ex-wife's next question makes Sturla think not of the sort of candid magazine interview he feels journalists ought to be conducting with him—journalists who until now have largely shunned him—but instead the words his father Jón left written on the bathroom wall at Mánagata in the mid-sixties.

"Why would *I* explain your character in a magazine article?" is Hulda's next question. "Aren't we just talking on the phone? And yes, I saw the news about your book of poems in the newspaper. And I didn't find it particularly amusing to read, if you ask me."

"The book?"

"The news. By the way, I haven't congratulated you on the book. But maybe you don't care about that. I found it to be an entertaining book, no matter whether it is by you or by . . ." She pauses when Sturla sighs wearily into the phone and continues, "Of course the book is by you, Sturla. How could you get a book published that had been written by someone else?"

"How? Scores of writers across the world publish books that have been written by other people. Why can't I do it too?"

"Then the news is accurate?"

"If you believe it, then yes, it is."

"If I *believe* it? I don't believe one way or the other; I thought you knew me well enough well to know that." And as she continues talking Sturla considers the accuracy of her words: Hulda was not only skeptical of all kinds of religion—a peculiar fact in light of her relationship with Símon the co-op manager, who was himself a staunch believer—but she was also skeptical of everything else in the world until she'd completely tested it. This had the effect, as she admitted, that she didn't believe in anything in the world, something that in Sturla's eyes had contributed to her rather rigid attitude toward personal relationships.

"You could, on the other hand, tell me whether this person is right," Hulda suggests, "this Brynjólfur or whatever he's called."

But to what end? Sturla thinks. Whatever he says, she won't believe him. He answers her with another question.

"Have the children read it?"

"Gunnar asked me about it. You know Hildigunnur doesn't read the paper. And I'm not going to point it out to Grettir or Hallgerður."

"And what did Gunnar ask you?"

"The same thing I'm asking you: whether you used Jónas's poems. You've got to remember that they don't really know who Jónas was; it's been thirty years since he died, if I remember correctly."

"You know how I work, Hulda. You read someone else's work, and inevitably something filters into your work. Jónas understood this too; his writing was peppered with things others had written, just as my poems are filled with things he wrote. Much of what he wrote is borrowed from Dagur Sigurðarson and others."

"But this man is accusing you of stealing whole poems from Jónas—who I didn't even know wrote poems. Which reminds me: your mother called me yesterday, and she wasn't what you'd call sober."

"Did you talk about me?"

Sturla suddenly hears the shout of a booming voice from inside the single family house at Egilsstaðir: "Is that Stulli?"

It is Símon, the surrogate father of his young children, the only person in the whole world, except for some kids from childhood, who calls Sturla "Stulli".

Hulda answers Símon, and Sturla wonders to himself whether asking someone who they're talking to on the phone is some kind of custom out in the East fjords. And while Hulda begins telling him about her phone conversation with her former mother-in-law, Sturla imagines that the accusation (as described in the media) must have made Símon almost as wildly happy as (Sturla imagines) when he manages to catch teenagers shoplifting at the grocery store.

According to Hulda, Fanný had been really drunk when she called. She hadn't heard from her for a few weeks—they'd always had regular conversations since Sturla and Hulda separated—and after Fanný asked for news of her grandchildren, she got right to the point. She said she was devastated by the nonsense which was being stirred up about innocent people in the media, and without naming the informant (Brynjólfur) by name she blamed Jónas for having managed to blacken the name of her son. What's more, she'd added that "right before that thoroughly spoiled boy killed himself, she'd invited him up to her place on Mánagata, but he hadn't been up to the task."

"What on earth do you mean by that?" asks Sturla, lighting himself a cigarette.

"*I* don't mean anything by it," replies Hulda, and she points out that Sturla's mother had said those words, not her.

Sturla stands up, takes the overcoat from the back of the chair, and places it on the floor, where he looks at it while he continues listening to Hulda describing his mother's ill-advised, drunken remarks about her ex-husband's nephew's guilt and her own son's innocence. But when Hulda suggests he should call his mother, he answers by saying that he is actually very busy over here right now; it isn't true, as he'd said, that he is up to nothing—he is at a poetry festival in Vilnius and in a little village a short way from the capital city, and he has more than enough going on right now. He wonders what Hulda would make of the letter he'd received from Cambridge, what her reaction would be to seeing his name (with a short biography and a list of works) alongside the names of two thousand outstanding individuals from around the world, each doing their own thing without shouting about it in the media, without accusing each other over the inevitable influence that one individual has on another.

"Did mother mention anything about a folder?" asks Sturla.

"What folder?"

"You remember my folder, the one I always used at my writing desk; the one I got from Jónas."

"Sturla."

As soon as she says his name in that admonishing fashion he knows exactly what she will say next (even though it has been a long time since this last happened); she will tell him how nothing remains of their past but the five children. She doesn't remember some folder Sturla had hunched over when he should have been caring for the children. And then she adds that she is uncomfortable talking to Fanný because it always reminds her of the atmosphere of the past. She doesn't have anything against his mother, but she feels it is more important that she talks to her grandchildren than to her. The problem was that Hulda, about two years ago, had scolded Fanný for calling while drunk and wanting to speak to the children—not, of course, a good model—and so Fanný had practically ceased talking to them; instead, she'd largely focused her drunken speculations on Hulda, as the previous evening's conversation indicated. Had Fanný needed to tell her, Hulda, something about how she'd tried to invite her young nephew up to her apartment? There was no other way Hulda could understand Fanný's remark that Jónas "had not been up to the task."

And this is also true for Sturla, as he asks Hulda to say goodbye to the children and puts down the phone: he gets himself a glass of water from the bathroom, and then he grabs his wallet and goes down to the cafeteria, where he orders two cold bottles of beer and a double cherry brandy.

On the way back up, cursing the hotel for not having an elevator, he thinks about Áslákur, his neighbor on Skúlagata. That's what a poet does, he thinks, as he remembers his neighbor's curiosity about what poets do at a poetry festival: they fetch a few drinks from the hotel bar, because at the place they're staying the minibar is empty, and they struggle up four flights of stairs with the drinks on a plastic tray because the hotel can't accommodate an elevator.

Sturla is having difficulty breathing by the time he gets to the fourth floor, which leads him to contemplate a ridiculous idea: that perhaps he would benefit from the sort of fitness training his daughter Hildigunnur participates in. When he has reached his room, put down the tray, picked the overcoat up off the floor and set it on the bed, he looks at the hotel information brochure, which is contained in a faux-leather folder. And when he turns the illustrated page he finds, to his surprise, that he'd lied to Hildigunnur: there is a gym at the hotel. In a low-quality photograph one could see a white-painted room with bikes and weight-lifting machines, but what occurs to Sturla about that photograph—and the thought makes him happy—is that this is fitness training for loners. Due to the small size, it's only right for one individual at a time.

Half an hour later, when he has finished the drinks from the cafeteria, Sturla makes up his mind to go to Druskininkai the next day, however he gets there. He calls the front desk and asks Elena—she says her name; she's the one who welcomed him when he first arrived at the hotel—to find out for him whether any buses go to Druskininkai, and when they leave. While he waits for her to call back with the information, he begins imagining a good-looking woman of around forty, completely unconnected to Elena, who looks out from the dim, first-floor window of a three-story pebbledash house: this woman is a mother, not Norman Bates's mother (which his father Jón had suggested as an interpretation for the mother in Sturla's poem) but his own mother, not at Nýlendugata, but at Mánagata.

DIPLOMATIC DUTIES

"Don't judge a book by its cover," said Hallmundur, who was at the wheel of the dark brown Cortina he and Þeba owned. Hallmundur and Jón, who was sitting in the front passenger seat, had been talking about a movie—the topic of discussion they most enjoyed because they always ended the discussion with different opinions—and Jón answered his brother's proverb with another one:

"But the person who pauses to rest on a rock will be happy twice over."

This wasn't the first time they'd ended a conversation by citing contextless and variously unintelligible proverbs.

Sturla was sitting behind Hallmundur in the car; beside him was Þeba, and next to the window on the other side, folded-up like an insect cocooning itself away from the world, sat Jónas, who during the entire drive along Ártúnsbrekka had been accusing his mother of taking up too much room on the seat and pressing up on him while

"Sturla Jón" (even Jónas had never called him Stulli) had an unfairly large amount of room on his side. Jónas complained so much that Þeba asked Hallmundur to stop the car at Litla kaffistofan, the coffee shop on Hellisheiði, where she changed seats with her son, so he was sitting next to Sturla. That arrangement didn't work any better; Jónas soon began pinching Sturla's leg, and when Sturla called out in pain, having endured his cousin's torture as long as possible, the car was approaching the ski lodge at Hveradalir; Þeba took the opportunity to ask Hallmundur to stop in the lodge's car park so that she could change seats again with "the monster," his son.

They had driven to Hveragerði, where Sturla and Jónas had had their hopes dashed: the monkey at Eden "was being fixed" (as Jón thought he'd heard), and then, on the way home, it had started pouring rain, provoking Jónas's whining about being squeezed in the back seat. That led to his mother getting genuinely angry. As a result, Hallmundur had asked his brother Jón to drive the car, and he himself got in back, between Þeba and Sturla, while the grumbling Jónas was seated up front where he started to read a manual about the car he had found in the glove compartment; this finally quieted him down.

While the rearrangements in the car took place by the side of the road, shortly after they had driven up Kambarnir, Sturla hoped they'd forget to fasten Jónas's seatbelt. Then he asked why his mom, Fanný, had not come along with them instead of Jónas, who didn't even want to go for a drive out of town. Jónas pretended not to hear his cousin's remark—he seemed absorbed in teaching himself about the technical details of the Cortina—and so Hallmundur began describing how he'd wanted them all to go, that it was possible to fit six people in the car (a peculiar assertion in light of the difficulty they'd only just managed to solve with this new seating arrangement), but Þeba had disagreed, insisting that it was a non-negotiable rule: no more than five people could travel in this type of car at once, and to suggest otherwise was not only illegal but also irresponsible. Jón didn't defend Hallmundur; he knew all too well the real reason Fanný hadn't come with them on the trip was because she couldn't stand Þeba. For her part Þeba, who wasn't blind to Fanný's feelings about her, had no particular interest in spending time with her sister-in-law.

When Sturla emerges from his recollections of that car trip from long ago and looks out the window of the stationary bus, he immediately notices an old, bent over woman who he saw a little earlier in the bus station. She is wearing a baggy, dark blue coat and standing outside the bus holding a jam jar with a white lid. She stares at him with a wrinkled brow, and just as Sturla is waiting for the half-full bus to depart for Druskininkai, the woman seems to be waiting for something—perhaps the same thing as Sturla.

The clock shows 10:15. The bus, which has been idling since Sturla sat down, was supposed to leave at 10:00. For a moment, Sturla feels that the vanished communist past is looking at him from this old woman's eyes. Suddenly a couple of lines of poetry begin to form in his head, but he immediately reminds himself that the publication of *assertions* marks the end of his poetry writing, period, and that a fitting punishment for such behavior should, at the least, be losing one's head. With that decision, familiar pictures play through his thoughts: an image of a decapitated head, rolling on cobblestones; a wrinkled old woman with a bottle of sunflower oil in her hand; and a neurotic poet who has bid farewell to poetry.

He waves at the woman with the jam jar, who continues looking at him without taking note of the greeting. And just then the driver sets the bus in gear, and it crawls away from the station.

Sturla suddenly regrets returning the white shirt to the black suitcase—it would have gone well with the dark jacket he is wearing, though it wouldn't work with the overcoat. As he realizes how stupid returning the shirt was, having come into possession of it, he recalls the rule, "first thought equals best thought," which is as true for other activities as it is for writing and poetry. The owner of the suitcase wouldn't be surprised that a single shirt had gone missing, nor could he make a fuss about it. The situation with the American's overcoat is entirely different, thinks Sturla. But even if it turns out today that "the artistically-savvy enthusiast" is somehow connected with the festival—which right now is only two hours distance away—there is nothing to connect Sturla to the disappearance of the overcoat, in much the same way as a tree that falls in a forest doesn't make a sound when no one is near enough to hear it fall.

When Sturla came down to the front desk on the way to breakfast, the dwarf Henryk had told him that someone had called from the poetry festival the previous evening to ask after him. Sturla had wondered then if the call had something to do with the overcoat—perhaps someone from the festival had heard how the American had clutched thin air when he went to fetch his overcoat from the coat hooks, and had made some ridiculous leap, assuming a link between the lost overcoat and the fact that the Icelander hadn't met up with the bus—but now Sturla is convinced that Gintaras (the main organizer, the one who'd called) had only wanted to let him know he was missed. Henryk had been especially friendly to Sturla when he booked himself out of the hotel (again) after breakfast. Henryk told him that he also knew someone named Gintaras—he didn't know the guy well, but well enough to know that he reminded him of his cousin in Poland, a man who reminded him of the man in that famous August Sander photograph, the one of the fancily dressed young farmers on their way to a dance, the man with a cigarette between his lips.

Sturla was a little surprised that Henryk should reference that particular artwork—and as part of such a tenuous link—but he knew the picture Henryk had mentioned; he'd seen it in one of his father's books at Skólavörðustígur. And while it gave him no small amount of pleasure to have a factually-based conversation about the picture by the German Sander with the dwarfish hotel employee, he imagined his neighbor Áslákur was one of the three farmers in the picture: instead of a walking stick, he held the broom from the laundry room; he wasn't on the way to a dance but rather going to tidy up his life—hence, the broom.

Countless things go through Sturla's mind during the two hour journey. But what Hulda said about his mother, or rather what his mother said to Hulda, causes him the most speculation. He considers his mother's words from various different perspectives. He wonders if Brynjólfur Madsen, who appeared to have known Jónas best of all, might hold the key to the mystery, and he imagines the reason Brynjólfur had asked for Sturla's e-mail address was because he intended to shut "the courtroom door" and write to him. Sturla thought over the events of the last few days, and "the poet's situation," which, thanks to his own words, had led to this moment in his life, led him to borrow the broom from Áslákur and brush his confused ruminations under the carpet so that he could instead think about Liliya, the person who most lit up his world.

He imagines her inside with the other temporary guests in Druskininkai, but he feels sure that underneath her friendly manner, as she sits having coffee (or cherry brandy and beer) and talking with Roger and the other poets, whatever their names are, she worries about the congenial poet from Iceland (for that's the picture of himself he sees reflected in Liliya's eyes): Where is Sturla Jón? Has she said or done something to offend him and cause him to vanish? He knows that their short acquaintance isn't really reason enough for her to imagine him in this way. Wouldn't it be more likely that when the poets' names were read from a register on arrival—to make sure none of the poets had gotten separated from the group—Liliya wouldn't even have remembered his name if she hadn't translated his poem?

But what would a person like Liliya think of the American, the one who'd hung his overcoat on a hook in Literatu Svetainé? Sturla suspects (based on an interpretation of his clothes and appearance) that this man is a parasite on the body of art. He's one of those people who over time had come to accept that they will not be artists themselves, and so they get themselves into a position, through tricks and swindles, to skim the cream off the work of those who struggle with their bare hands to make their names, as the saying goes. But in using a metaphor from the world of home cooking, Sturla has included himself in that group which he looks down upon. And he wonders if Liliya—who no doubt grew up in an atmosphere of shortage, of antipathy towards ideas of individual liberty—looks up to and respects people who come from a culture of excess where there is unfettered competition in all fields, not least poetry, which Sturla isn't ashamed to call high art. And with a sneer in his own direction, he thinks about his article on the poetry festival; there you have some progressive art, at least in the sense that it takes its material from the future, a future awaiting the author when he steps out of the rather slow-moving bus in an hour or so.

The sun suddenly bursts from the shadows and lights up the landscape, and just as suddenly Sturla remembers the place he's come from; how different it is from where he lives.

Or lived.

He regrets not having brought a bottle or two of beer with him. He remembers the ice-cold beer he drank at Literatu Svetainė, and in his imagination he looks towards the table where the American and his female friends had sat. Was it possible they'd noticed him sitting at the bar near their table? Is he the type of man who sticks in strangers' minds? When he tries to picture how an American, like the one he has just described for himself, sees the Lithuanian countryside, he is suddenly afraid of going in the front door of the poetry festival at Druskininkai, in case the first person who meets his eyes there is the owner of the overcoat which rests at the bottom of his suitcase. He tries to convince himself that it doesn't matter if the American is in the village; he can't prevent Sturla from the task at hand, from attending to his diplomatic duties, as someone in diplomatic service should: the duties one is entrusted with undertaking after he has delivered his diplomatic credentials as the ambassador of one nation who has come to work in another country, credentials which in this case mean Sturla himself, credentials which he has already delivered by arriving in the country. He has undertaken to greet the other foreign ambassadors, the poets of the other nations, who have all assembled in the spa town of Druskininkai, and who are at this very moment (Sturla imagines) speculating as to why the Icelandic delegate hasn't arrived. They don't know that he is halfway there, having just passed a sign for the town of Dzukijos.

THE DARKNESS OF THE SHADOWS

The taxi which Sturla takes from the bus stop is the same type of car he'd taken from the airport with the poet Jonas and the woman in sunglasses: a red Datsun, though a little newer and more spick-and-span than the one in Vilnius. It smells of musk oil, which Sturla is sure the driver, a woman in her late twenties, will also smell of when she gets out of the car. When Sturla gives her the address of the festival residence, 16 Maironio Street, she asks whether he is headed to The Season of Poetry, and when he replies that yes, he is on the way to "the poetry festival"—he can't bring himself to use the official title—the woman tells him she is a poet herself: she is an artist (watercolors) but composes poetry a lot when she's not painting, chiefly nature poems.

The clothing store employee on Bankastræti; Áslakur in the elevator; the pot-bellied Russian in the Old Town Erotic Center; and now a taxi driver in Druskininkai. Sturla looks at the woman's attractive profile and reminds himself once again that a poet ought to be observant, ought to have his eyes wide open when he's in new surroundings.

From the time he stepped off the bus, Sturla hasn't once thought about how the appearance of Druskininkai compares to other urban areas in the world. But he also argues with himself that maybe he hasn't seen anything worth noticing; the only thing that he remembers is the place's name. And he begins to wonder what sort of nature the driver's poems deal with: he doesn't know about the picturesque river which runs through the town and won't associate the name with natural beauty until Liliya tells him, in a phone call twenty-four hours later, about the matchless fall beauty of the riverbank—about how she feels bad that they can't go there together in the afternoon sun. Sturla will interpret this as a revealing confession, something he's longed to hear but hadn't dared expect he actually would.

"And you aren't taking part in the festival yourself?" Sturla asks.

He doesn't mind hearing a resident of the town telling him that The Season of Poetry is for established writers ("professionals," as she puts it in English, which Sturla thinks is a strange way to describe poets), but he doesn't know if it's appropriate to compare himself to the woman when she adds that employed folk like herself aren't usually invited to such festivals. She works as a janitor in the apartment block where she lives and is only driving the car for her father while he is sick; working as a janitor gives her plenty of time to paint and write. But when she asks Sturla where he is from and tells him she won't charge him for the ride since he is from Iceland, which was the first country to recognize Lithuania's independence, Sturla feels it is only fair to let her know that he also works as a janitor in the apartment block where he lives, adding that no one in the building knew he was a poet.

"No? Then you're probably less well-known than I am," the woman replies, smiling in the direction of the passenger seat. "They post my poems next to the mailslots in the building," she continues, and Sturla remembers he saw some low-rise apartments shortly before getting off the bus at the bus shelter.

Although he repeatedly insists that she take his money, the woman flatly refuses to charge him a fare. She says it is impossible for her to charge the first Icelander she's ever met just for driving him a few meters in her father's car. When she says, as if compensating Sturla for not getting his way, that she's called Loreta, he asks for her address so that he can send her his book, and a translation, when he gets back to Iceland; he doesn't have any copies on him.

The sun gleams brightly as Sturla takes Loreta's hand and thanks her. He wants to suggest that they sit down together at the table in front of the residence, the one with the patio umbrella bearing the logo of one of the domestic beer companies, and drink the first beers of the day together before he hands himself over to Gintaras and the rest of the people at the festival. But the way she lets go of his hand suggests that she is in a hurry; perhaps she isn't especially eager, Sturla thinks, to associate with a guy in his fifties who is, like her, a super, and probably therefore a part-time poet, and who, against her own wishes, managed to make her give him her home address.

Although he's never seen a Chekhov play staged, Sturla can well imagine that he's standing before the shuttered set of *The Cherry Orchard*: he's just about to go for a walk through Madame Ranevskaya's rural estate and to take a teacup (not a beer glass) from the hand of Firs the butler. The three-story wooden house is a pale pink color, with white window frames. A handsome gable rises from the middle, with a window that has a small balcony extending from its left side; both wings of the residence have ornately decorated verandas, which emphasizes the poetry of the image.

Inside, however, the residence looks like a ski lodge. On the left side is a raised, dark-paneled room, but the main room's walls are covered with black-and-white photographs; looking at them, Sturla suspects that his face will be added to the wall at the conclusion of the festival. Off of the breakfast room on the right, there is a wine bar that looks promising: the lone person at the bar (other than the female bartender) is holding a huge glass of beer, something Sturla really wants right now. He figures that the festival participants are assembled somewhere else for one of the events in the program—an event he is probably too late to attend—and shortly the group will meet here in the breakfast room for nourishment and to gather their strength for the next activity. He rolls his suitcase over the broad floorboards towards the bar (which is cozy, even if it does look like a ski lodge) and he nods his head to the pink-haired bartender and the man with the beer glass—a stout, swarthy man Sturla guesses is from Southern Europe.

He orders a shot of cold vodka with his beer.

"I'll have one of those as well," he hears the stout man ask in English, and Sturla thinks he can immediately detect a Spanish accent.

The man lifts his beer glass towards Sturla and asks if he's one of the poets. He introduces himself as Rolf once Sturla answers and explains he's the poet from Iceland. Rolf is Argentinean and hasn't come to Lithuania to listen to some lecture about European poetry through a headset. Everyone else is in the next building attending some debate which is taking place in Lithuanian and being simultaneously translated into English and piped into individual headphones. "It doesn't have anything to do with poetry," he says, shaking his head, as he takes one of the two vodka shots the woman with pink hair has slid along the bar to them.

Sturla likes him. They clink vodka glasses as the pink-haired woman smiles at them. Sturla begs the man's forgiveness, but he doesn't remember reading about an Argentinean participant in the festival description.

"No, until I got here there wasn't one," the man replies, explaining: Rolf isn't, of course, an especially Latin name (as he puts it) and nor is his last name, Tuzenbach; on his father's side, he was from Germany, and he actually lives in Sweden, in Gothenburg, where he knows a few Icelanders fairly well. The reason why he isn't on the list of participants was because a Greenlander who had been invited had been unable to attend, and he'd been invited instead; he'd needed to decide with just a week's notice and "threw his lot in, not having anything better to do."

When Sturla says he remembers the Greenlander's name from the festival's information packet, Rolf is mid-swallow, and he struggles to avoid laughing through his beer; he'd been told the news yesterday, by a guy who was somehow connected to the festival, that the Greenlander had been imprisoned for a serious armed assault in Copenhagen. Therefore they'd called up the Argentinean poet instead, looking for any poet who wasn't from Denmark, Norway, or Sweden but who nevertheless lived in Scandinavia—providing he had a clean criminal record.

"I have great difficulty imagining that gun-toting guy at this event we were invited to yesterday," continues the Argentine poet Rolf with a smile. Sturla thanks his lucky stars that this man, rather than some bore, had been waiting for him at the start of his three-day sojourn in Druskininkai. "After dinner yesterday—I'm not going to tell you how it tasted—we were led by our reins into some old bath house at the back of the lot." Rolf points towards the back door in the middle of the room. "And then some kind of lyrical play was performed for us, some highfalutin play that had so little to do with reality—I don't know what your opinion of poetry is—that we would have needed a gunshot from the Greenlander to bring the spectators, or even better the performers, back down to earth—and I bet that's exactly what the Greenlander would have done: he'd never have sat quietly in his seat through the whole debacle."

It occurs to Sturla that it's a little unfair of the half-German Argentinean to direct his sarcasm at a festival to which he's been invited in good faith; while such a character could be entertaining to pass a little time with, it could be risky to show him too much attention; he might start taking advantage of this attention to get his interlocutor on his side, so to speak. When irony becomes someone's habitual way of expressing themselves, then they are quick to lose sight of how uniform the stance has become—and how tiring. But hadn't Sturla done the same thing, or worse, in his article against the festival? Would his readers—if the article was printed in Jónatan's magazine (not that it looked likely at the moment)—recognize that his irony wasn't meant to be hostile? It was used, rather, to incite the reader to re-consider how a festival of this caliber might best succeed. But Sturla is beginning now to feel like he might expect to spend a few enjoyable days with some stimulating company; even just Liliya, and now this lively guy Rolf, would be enough.

After they talk a little more—a conversation which convinces Sturla he doesn't need to fear that the Argentinean will become a nuisance—Rolf proposes that they head to the main building, where the lecture- and dining-room are housed. And he advises Sturla to leave his luggage at the bar; he will get the key to his room once he has met Gintaras. The pink-haired woman overhears the conversation and corrects Rolf; she has the keys to the rooms. Sturla can leave the case in his room before they go to Dainava, which Rolf tells him is the name of the main building.

Sturla's room turns out to be in the next building, a building which reminds him even more of Madame Ranevskaya's country estate because it hasn't been contaminated by the Scandinavian ski-lodge style. His room is small but pristine and neatly decorated: he describes it to Rolf when he returns to the bar as being "like a woman's powder room from the turn of the nineteenth century, provided, of course, you take away the television." Rolf, who says that he hasn't been quite so lucky with his room, which is in some Stalinesque industrial-era block next to the Dainava building, has ordered another round of beer, and fifteen minutes later as they stroll out the back door, the same door Sturla used on his way to his building, Sturla notices that Mister Tuzenbach is more than a little drunk. It isn't even a minute's walk to Dainava, a strikingly ugly concrete house with four floors, nothing at all like the amenable set for *The Cherry Orchard*.

Despite the mostly mild weather this October morning, a whole row of coats is hanging on the coat rack inside the building. The babble of voices carries down from the upper stories, which Rolf takes to indicate that the lecture is over and that it is now time for lunch; he feels sure that the events have been arranged around the meals, rather than the meals arranged to accommodate the length of the lectures.

As the group comes down the stairs towards the entrance, one of the first people Rolf points out to Sturla is Gintaras; "You should watch out for that one," he whispers. "Although he looks like your typical, dull office worker, at the welcoming ceremony last night, he was trying to pour down his throat, and the throats of everyone around him, about as many vodka shots as there were minutes." Rolf introduces Sturla to Gintaras when he has come down the stairs, and as Sturla stumbles for words to explain why he didn't get on the bus the day before, he sees Roger the Dane. Roger is supporting himself on the banister in the middle of the staircase, looking pale and sickly, and he seems to be in need of help, like he won't be able to make it to the lobby on his own. Sturla can't decide whether Gintaras completely believes his excuse about having arrived too late for the bus, and he looks stunned when Sturla begs his forgiveness: "Roger, the Dane," needs someone to hold onto. And as Sturla and Rolf hurry up the stairs, Liliya suddenly appears along with some other people on the landing of the staircase, and at the same moment Sturla and Liliya's eyes meet, Roger draws everyone's undivided attention by sinking down and sitting on the stairs, groaning either from exhaustion or effort.

Liliya has a sheer yellow scarf bound around her head, and despite the dramatic circumstances Sturla gets a warm feeling when he looks at her. They immediately go to Roger and nod to each other—which Sturla thinks apt in front of the Dane. Rolf and the others who have followed Liliya are standing a few steps away, and Gintaras comes to help Sturla and Liliya, first in making sure that Roger is showing all the usual signs of being alive, and then by helping him onto his feet and supporting him the rest of the way down the stairs. Liliya smiles tenderly at Sturla, and she says she will meet him in the dining room soon; she and Gintaras will see to Roger, who has been somewhat feeble since they arrived, the poor man.

"Too much poetic strain," Rolf whispers to Sturla with a smile, and

Sturla is about to give him an explanation for the Dane's exhaustion—that he'd nodded his head too fast, and too often, during the lecture—but he decides against it; he realizes that irony shouldn't take up too much room in this early stage of their acquaintance. The two of them, he thinks, are probably the only participants who've had two beers and two shots of vodkas before noon.

They come into the huge, rather unpleasant hall where tables have been set for more than a hundred people, and they sit at the round table nearest the door, so that they are easy to spot and "Liliya, my friend, the one in the yellow scarf, won't need to look for us when she comes in," as Sturla tells Rolf. They have their backs to the bright windows, which reach to the floor, and people of a similar age sit at the table that's facing the two companions—which is how Sturla has begun describing the two of them in his mind, after their hour-long friendship. It quickly becomes clear that they need to get their food from a long table that is out of sight behind a stout column, but just as they stand up with their plates, Liliya appears in the door. She is resting her hand on Roger's shoulder; he looks much better now than he had a few minutes before. They sit down next to Sturla and Rolf, Liliya beside Sturla and Roger by Rolf, and Sturla considers his physical proximity to Liliya a real reason to be happy.

She places a hand on his shoulder and plants a kiss on both cheeks, although not a third, like the greeting the American got from the two women in front of the Novotel Hotel.

"It's good to see you again. I thought you'd gone back to Iceland."

"I'm not too sure I'll be going there again," Sturla blurts out without thinking; he knows himself well enough to recognize that repaying Liliya's confession with the same words (saying that he's happy to see her, too) would reflect badly on his character. On the other hand, that's how he feels right now, and he wonders whether the day before yesterday they'd experienced something which another kind of person might call love at first sight (or friendship at first meeting). A word he's always considered rather lackluster pops into this mind, the word *union*, and when he applies it to the two of them, it's as though he's come across it in a novel: he isn't at all convinced by the idea that they've become infatuated with each other, after having met just three times (especially when he's fled without fail on every occasion, or so it seems). He always vanishes for some reason just when they are about to talk.

"What do you mean by that?" asks Liliya, and she nods to Rolf, who she's clearly met before.

"It seems to be a rule these days that wherever I'm meant to go, I'm not there—and vice versa."

"But you're flying to Iceland the day after we return to Vilnius, didn't you tell me that?"

"Strictly speaking, I've only booked a flight for that day," says Sturla, and asks Liliya how the lecture was.

"Nothing especially exciting," replies Liliya, smiling impishly. "Or yes, perhaps it was a little exciting. I counted at least three sleeping poets during the last part. I thought, at one point, that one of them had died, a man I actually know (or knew); he is from Ukraine. Then one of the speakers, a Lithuanian, spilled his coffee over the papers of the next speaker. So, all in all, it was rather exciting."

Rolf, who's begun talking with Roger, can't help but hear what Liliya says, and her words spark a burst of laughter in him, which in turn somehow arouses his thirst, so he offers to get in a round of drinks for everyone. There is an open bar beside the food table, and Sturla can see that the line is ten or fifteen meters long.

Based on Liliya's account of the day before, she seems to be enjoying her stay in Druskininkai. But as they put food on their plates—and offer to take Rolf's spot in line for the bar—she is curious to know why Sturla, as opposed to some other Icelander (that is exactly how she puts it), was sent to the festival. What were the reasons behind the choice—she'd heard (perhaps the evening before, at the welcome reception) that everyone in Iceland is a poet or musician—and how was he funding his journey since this festival didn't, of course, pay travel expenses?

"What mainly counts is that the poet in question has published something which . . ." Sturla stops himself from continuing; he can hear how dry and rote he sounds. Instead, he corrects Liliya's notion about the creative talents of his people: in Iceland everyone is a poet *and* a musician, as well as working in a bank or even managing a bank. And he adds that the Writers' Union is generally in charge of selecting who goes to what festival, and in his case the state was paying his travel expenses. In that sense, he really is the face of his nation abroad, her symbol to another nation, no different than when one country sends a carefully-chosen delegate to this or that management or business meeting across the world.

Liliya nudges Sturla and points out to him a pale-looking, long-haired man who's wearing some kind of burlap coat which looks rather like a bathrobe. He is holding a plate heaped with potatoes, green beans and boiled carrots, and with his other hand he pours himself an orange-colored drink from the faucet of a machine. "That, then, is the face of Norway," she whispers to him, smiling.

"And yet they haven't always looked like that," replied Sturla. "I know that because my grandfather was once ambassador to Norway."

Rolf returns, bringing a tray with eight beer bottles, shortly after Sturla, Liliya and Roger have sat down with their food-laden plates, and he goes to get himself some pork and potatoes which he says looked rather promising. Sturla has no sooner popped the first bite into his mouth then Gintaras—who Sturla has managed to forget he'd been talking to in the lobby when the confusion over Roger broke out—suddenly comes up to him and politely asks him to come over to the lobby; he needs to have a few words with him. Sturla takes one of the beer bottles and apologizes to Liliya.

"You're here, at least," Gintaras says, in his strong accent, when they reach the chilly entryway to the building. Sturla is having difficulty working out why this conversation couldn't wait until after the meal. "You say you took the bus?"

Sturla gives him the obvious answer—realizing that he isn't fishing to find out if Sturla had taken a taxi and was expecting the festival to pay—but as he's about to explain why he didn't come the day before, he decides not to. There is something about Gintaras's demeanor he doesn't like, and he decides to let him direct the conversation.

"I'm disturbing your dinner because it is necessary for me to carry out certain inquiries which possibly concern you," says Gintaras, and for a moment Sturla thinks the man is joking.

"I don't mind about the food," Sturla replies. "There's time enough for eating that, right?"

"Yes, yes. Yes, yes," replies Gintaras, evidently not entirely at ease. "But tell me: do you know the restaurant Literatu Svetainė? In Vilnius?"

Sturla looks into the eyes of this man who, instead of offering to assist Sturla (who has only just arrived), is interrupting his lunch. "Literatu? Is that the restaurant in the Writers' Union building?"

"No, it is on the same street as the hotel you stayed at. On Gedimino. At the corner of the church square."

"I don't know the name," replies Sturla. "Literatu what?"

"Svetainė. There is an American woman poet here" (he uses the word *poetess*) "named Jenny Lipp. She talked to me just now because she recognized you when she saw you in line for food, but didn't remember you from yesterday, and . . ."

"I wasn't here yesterday," Sturla interjects, letting the organizer irritate him even more.

"No, no. No, no. I know that. But she asked me if you were a participant in the festival and . . . she also said she'd seen you in the restaurant I named, two days ago, I believe she said."

"It seems unlikely to me," answers Sturla. "And what is the reason for that . . . ? Why is she telling you that she *believes* she recognizes me from some restaurant? I don't fully understand."

"Well, I really don't know what to say," replies Gintaras, and it is clear that he has painted himself into a corner. "But you say you don't know this restaurant in Vilnius?"

"No, I haven't been to any restaurant by the church tower. I know exactly where the tower is. I did go, on the other hand, to a restaurant which Jokûbas guided me to, in—what was the street called? . . . Pilies . . . and . . . you know Jokûbas Daugirdas, don't you?" Sturla makes sure to keep quiet about the overcoat which was stolen from him there; he wants to connect his acquaintance, Jokûbas, with that loss, but he knows all too well that another man's overcoat is foremost in Gintaras's thoughts, a man who hasn't thought about why the word of an American poetess suffices to disturb a poet from Iceland during his dinner. "And I can't say that I would recommend the restaurant," continues Sturla.

"No, no. I'm only asking you about it now because our Jenny was curious," says Gintaras, a little embarrassed, and then he explains, as though Sturla has asked about it, that they'd nicknamed her *our* Jenny because she lives in Vilnius half the year.

"All right," says Sturla, then he asks in passing if Jenny didn't live in Kaunas; he had heard that she came from Kansas but lived in Kaunas.

"No that's Daniella. Daniella Goldblum. She's also a guest of the festival this year. But please excuse me," asks Gintaras, and Sturla assures him it's no problem; he even tries to look friendly. Although the organizer has certainly allowed the American poet to speak badly of him, Sturla figures he owes him something for having played hooky on the first day of the festival.

When he sits back down between Liliya and Rolf the latter is only just beginning to eat while Liliya has cleaned her plate.

"He has very particular consultation hours," Liliya says playfully, and she apologizes for having stolen some things off Sturla's plate. She is going to get a very little more, and she asks Sturla and Rolf if she shouldn't get some more beers on the way.

Sturla finds Liliya's confession turns him on a little, but he is also irritated by Gintaras's over-officiousness, and no less by this so-called Jenny Lipp. Was she the one in the suit or in the white coat? He takes off his scarf, which he's been wearing since he got off the bus. He slips out of his jacket and lets it rest on his chair back. As he watches Liliya move away from the table with her plate, he listens to Roger tell Rolf, in Danish, about his high opinion of the English poet Keats.

This, then, is what a Belarusian really looks like, thinks Sturla, as he imagines how time might have treated the body Liliya conceals in light-blue jeans and a black tunic, a body which has endured a similar length of time as his own, a body about which he hasn't yet wondered if it has reproduced or if it is "in someone else's possession," as he phrases it to himself; he is amazed that he hasn't yet considered whether Liliya is married or in a relationship. He doesn't remember having seen a ring on her finger, but he does remember that she knows nothing about him—not that he is the divorced father of five children, the same number as his grandfather Benedikt had, a man who around the middle of last century was the official face of the Icelandic people in two countries, first in Sweden, then in Norway.

Just as Rolf said, the food tastes good, "even better than the day before." But Sturla doesn't get much time to enjoy his meal; he has only half-finished the meager portion he'd gotten for himself when Gintaras comes back to the table and asks Sturla to accompany him into the lobby again. This time, there is no apology for the disturbance.

"You know who she is, Jenny Lipp, don't you?" he asks when they get to the lobby, and the determination he tries to manifest is evidently unnatural to him.

"Like I said, I just got here this morning," Sturla answers curtly.

"You must have seen her at the reading" says Gintaras, and his assertive tone persuades Sturla that the invisible Jenny, who in all likelihood is right now enjoying her midday meal in peace, is certain of her accusation: it was definitely him, the Icelander— who, ever-so-humbly, had only now arrived at the festival—who'd been sitting at the bar in the restaurant on Gedimino. She isn't just "wondering" if it was the case, as her messenger, Gintaras, put it earlier.

"Although you didn't make it to Druskininkai on time," Gintaras says, "you had already arrived in Vilnius by the time the Americans' reading took place."

"You have to excuse me," says Sturla, "but I am having no small amount of difficulty understanding why it is that I ought to recognize this Jenny Lipp." He tries to use as formal a wording as possible in order to underscore the absurdity of the topic of discussion, and he recognizes at once how peculiar it is that the two of them, adult men from different countries who are meeting for the first time, are having this conversation.

"She says she is certain that she saw you at the restaurant I mentioned before," replies Gintaras, "and the waiter said that . . ."

"You can tell her from me," interrupts Sturla, "that I am certain I have never seen *her* before. I do not know what this person looks like. And that is the end of the matter."

"You say you are certain you never went to the restaurant?"

Sturla tries to use his eyes to make clear to Gintaras that he is done answering questions. "As I told you, and as I thought you understood," he says, "I have only been into one restaurant in Vilnius, and one alone; it was a place on Pilies Street. And in case you want to know, I didn't get to finish any of the food I ordered there. Which it looks like is going to happen here too."

"She told me that the waiter at the restaurant had confirmed that . . ."

"I can only add," Sturla says firmly, "that the scarf you saw me wearing just a moment ago was bought in Vilnius because my overcoat was stolen in the restaurant I was telling you about. And now you are talking to me as though I have committed a crime! 'But someone saw you in some place!' As far as I know, I've been seen by other people all my life—except, perhaps, the occasional times when I've been in the toilet."

"I am not accusing you of anything," Gintaras attempts to assure Sturla. "For my part, it is a pain to have to trouble you with all this, but as the organizer and guarantor of this festival, it is my duty to attend to all matters which concern our guests. And she, this Jenny Lipp, has, as I said, asked me to investigate whether . . ."

"To *investigate*?" interrupts Sturla, and he gets an affirmative answer to his question about whether she, Jenny, had herself used the word "investigate."

"She thinks you took Darryl Rothman's overcoat from the coat rack in the restaurant she saw you in."

Sturla looks at Gintaras for a few moments, then replies: "Forgive me, Gintaras. It is *Gintaras*, isn't it?" And when Gintaras nods his head, wearing an anxious expression, Sturla continues: "Should I know who Darryl Rothman is? Wasn't I just telling you how *my* overcoat had been stolen from a restaurant in Vilnius? And do you know who runs that restaurant? It is the brother of a man from here, a man called Jokûbas who works with this festival. You know Jokûbas Daugirdas, don't you?"

"It shouldn't make any difference who Darryl Rothman is," replies Gintaras. "What Jenny was concerned about is that . . . you . . ."—he hesitates and looks around uneasily—"that perhaps you have . . . inadvertently . . . taken his overcoat with you from the place."

While Sturla repeats his question about who Darryl Rothman is, saying that he has a right to know, he looks towards the dining room and sees that Liliya has sat back down and is hunched over her food.

"Darryl Rothman is an art dealer from America who subsidizes our festival. He is actually headed to Tallinn on a rather similar business trip right now . . ."

"And this Jenny said I'd *inadvertently* taken some overcoat?" asks Sturla as he praises himself for having correctly guessed the conceited overcoat owner's profession. "Are you sure she used the word "inadvertently"?" he adds, and he continues, after Gintaras admits that perhaps she hadn't used the word "inadvertently," "It seems to me that she is actually accusing me of having stolen some overcoat from some American guy I've never seen, from some restaurant I've never been to—and now it occurs to me that maybe this American you named is the person who stole *my* overcoat. All I have to say is that I don't care for accusations by a woman from America who I have never heard reading her poetry and whose lousy poetry I never want to hear read. You can tell her to go to hell!" And when it is evident that the fury behind his words is enough to silence the organizer, Sturla storms out of the place towards the dining hall but stops when he reaches the door and turns back to Gintaras. "In fact, I've got a better idea," he says. "You can tell her to go back to America!" He pushes open the door and heads as coolly as he can manage over to the table by the window.

"Don't tell me he's been scolding you for arriving late?" Liliya says when Sturla sits down beside her and begins prodding at his food with his fork. "Isn't he going to leave you alone to enjoy your lunch?" But she seems to suddenly notice that her lunch companion is upset; she puts her hand on his shoulder and asks whether something is bothering him—he looks like something bad has happened.

"No, everything's the way it should be," Sturla replies, using the English words "perfectly fine."

"I can clearly see that he said something to you," Liliya insists, and Sturla is momentarily unsure what to make of her concern.

"Do you know this Jenny Lipp?" he asks as he watches Gintaras return to the hall and apologize to a middle-aged man at a table in the middle of the hall who tries to speak to him.

"No, only from the interview I told you about the other day. That she flew from Kansas to Kaunas. And that I listened to her reading; I rather liked it."

"She's not the one who lives in Kaunas," Sturla contradicts her as he puts on his jacket.

"No? I read that in the interview with her."

"That is Daniella." Sturla puts his scarf on, and Liliya looks at him, amazed.

"Who told you that?" she asks. "Are you going?"

"The man I was talking to. Gintaras."

"Then I suspect he knows less about things than I do."

"I think this man generally knows less than the next man," says Sturla, and asks Liliya to forgive him; he needs to go to his room and make a call.

Liliya asks whether he isn't going to finish his food first, and as much as Sturla knows she means well, he finds her concern suddenly irritating; he shakes his head and says he will meet her later. When he gets up from the table and pushes the chair back under, neither Rolf nor Roger seems to notice—they are completely occupied with each other. On the other hand, it seems clear that Sturla's impromptu decision has worried Liliya, as if she realizes that he isn't going to turn back—or perhaps she simply feels that it is boring to be left behind with Roger and Rolf, who have evidently found a common interest: the English Romantic poets.

After about ten minutes have passed Liliya decides to go over to Gintaras, to where he sits talking to Jenny Lipp and Kelly Fransesca, and ask whether something in his conversation with Sturla Jón had insulted him. She seems considerably worried that Sturla had immediately rushed from his table, so to speak, without giving a credible reason. To Liliya's surprise, Jenny looks at her with obvious disdain, as though she's heard something disreputable about her. When Gintaras gets up from his seat to have a few words with Liliya a little apart from the others, Jenny follows him and whispers something in his ear, which leads to him asking Liliya to excuse him and leaving the hall.

A few seconds later she sees him heading across the lawn towards the building where Sturla is staying.

At this moment Sturla is sitting in his room with a beer glass and a shot of cherry brandy, which he'd bought at the bar after leaving the lunch hall. He'd found a place for the overcoat in a separate compartment in his suitcase, a compartment for clothes that shouldn't get creased, and he is talking on the phone to his father Jón, who called while Sturla was standing at the bar in the Ranevskaya-like house and ordering drinks from the pink-haired server. Jón informs Sturla that, according to his publisher, Gústaf, Brynjólfur has decided to do everything in his power to "call off" the unfair media discussion of Sturla's "manuscript theft," as the journalist termed it. He has sent Sturla an e-mail, and Sturla should try to access the Internet as soon as possible. Sturla's concern about his reputation at home, however, clearly isn't all that great, because when the knocking on his room door starts he is in the middle of asking his father whether he managed to retrieve the VCR from the repair shop, and whether the vanished Iranian movie caused major chaos at the library.

"Is someone knocking?" asks Jón, and Sturla tells him that there is never any peace; he'd never in his wildest dreams imagined how busy he would be at this "jamboree."

"Is everything OK?"

"OK with *me*?" asks Sturla, doing his best to sound astonished at his father's question while he opens the door and looks at Gintaras, who is standing outside. "I'll call you later, father. I'm just about to take part in a discussion about the influence of overcoats on modernist poetry in Lithuania." And he looks impassively into Gintaras's eyes while he hangs up the phone and replaces it in the breast pocket of his jacket.

"I only wanted to let you know about this," says Gintaras, "that the book that was published on the occasion of the festival has been set out in front of the library in Dainava."

"Thank you."

"There's a reading this evening; you know about it, don't you?"

"I have a program, so yes."

"Then everything should be clear." It is obvious that the organizer has not knocked on the door with this information alone, and it takes him a great deal of effort to pass on his actual message:

"She has let him know you are here," he says, leaning on the doorframe.

"She who? Let who know what?"

"Jenny."

"Let who know what?"

"Jenny is calling Darryl."

"I don't know what you're talking about," says Sturla, realizing that they've reached the same place as they had gotten to in their conversation outside the lunch hall.

"I am talking about the overcoat which they are sure you took."

"Which *they* are sure? So you are talking about *her*, this American poet who evidently doesn't want to come face to face with *me*, the criminal mastermind, since she always sends you on her behalf, and *he*, this man who has . . ."

"Pardon me," interrupts Gintaras, and Sturla suspects he can't remember his name, "but I am not suggesting that you have stolen anything; this is a question about whether you may have taken something by mistake."

"But *she* is obviously suggesting something," answers Sturla, and adds calmly that he doesn't care one bit for coming in good faith to a poetry festival in a distant country, and being called a thief instead of being welcomed.

"She told me that the waiter was sure that it was you who . . ."

"Who what?"

"She is certain that she saw you at the place and that you are also the person the waiter described."

With those words Sturla has had enough; he goes into his room, opens his suitcase, and tears all his clothes out of it, scattering them across the floor, and he asks Gintaras, who stands motionless in the doorway, whether he sees an overcoat. Then he opens the closet by the bathroom door, grabs the coat hangers, and places them on the bed.

"Is the overcoat you're talking about here?" he asks, pointing to the empty wooden hangers.

Gintaras looks down and glances briefly, with a moralizing expression, at the beer glass and the shot on the table. The only solution to the impasse is for Sturla to talk to Jenny. He should come with him to the office in the next building, and he will then go and get Jenny from the dining room.

"I don't intend to talk to this woman," answers Sturla.

"Why not?" asks Gintaras.

"Because, like I said, I haven't come here to some poetry festival to be accused of being a thief. I came here to read my poems."

Gintaras shuffles his feet in the hallway outside the room and mumbles into his chest that Sturla has to make up his own mind; he doesn't want to force him to meet other people. Without answering, Sturla shuts the door on him and then places his ear against it. He hears Gintaras going briskly down the hallway and waits until he hears a door shut. Then he gulps down the remnants of the beer and brandy, crams the clothes back into the suitcase, and puts the key in the lock before he leaves the room. He checks that no one is around as he goes out of the building and along the sidewalk, from where he looks back up at the wall; he is, despite everything that has happened at the place since he came to town, full of admiration for the building's appearance, and a little disappointed that he won't get to enjoy a night's sleep here. He feels sure that all the other festival guests will still be in the dining hall, and he wonders for a moment whether he should head to the bar in the building and ask the pink-haired woman to call him a cab. But he decides not to take the risk that someone connected with the festival will see him—he half-expects that Gintaras will suddenly appear with his paranoid protégé—and he sets off along the sidewalk with his suitcase, heading away from where the poets are staying.

He hasn't been walking for more than a few minutes when a black Volkswagen with a cab sign drives at a slow crawl down the street, clearly hoping to be hailed. Sturla waves and asks the driver, a gray-haired man in a sports jacket who materializes from behind the dark window, whether he would drive him to the bus station, and make a detour via a supermarket.

The modern feel of the supermarket the driver brings him to after a few minutes drive surprises Sturla. As he carefully regards the selection of goods he thinks about Símon, Hulda's partner in Egilsstaðir, and while he joins two teenage boys standing in front of the beer section in the liquor department he resolves to tell his son Gunnar, when the two next meet or speak on the phone, about his experience going through this huge supermarket in a tiny town in Lithuania, a town which, in proportion to the capital city, could be compared to Egilsstaðir. He selects a small bottle of cherry brandy and a cold white wine bottle he finds stacked with the beer cans and vodka coolers in the cold storage. He then grabs some crackers and potato chips and he smiles to himself at how cheap things are.

Although the taxi driver drives at about thirty kilometers an hour, as though he wants to keep hold of his passenger as long as possible, the bus station is only two or three minutes from the supermarket, and fortunately the next bus to Vilnius is scheduled to leave in half an hour. Assuming there will be a delay like the one in Vilnius, Sturla expects he won't have to stay in Druskininkai for more than forty-five minutes longer.

He is looking forward to the journey: two hours where he will be left alone to himself, free from the atmosphere of misapprehension that arises when poetry is made into a team sport. He comforts himself by imagining that Liliya Boguinskaia will take up his cause and give Gintaras and his cheerleaders the finger by sneaking out of the gloomy dining hall, a place which reminds Sturla of the fish processing room at the trawling company in Neskaupstaður where he worked as a teenager. And his thoughts are already leaping ahead to the journey to Vilnius; he warms at the idea of a drive back in late-afternoon twilight, with Baudelaire's "symbol forests" rushing by as the bus hurries back; the "dim temple" whose living colonnades breathe into his ears the mystic speech where all things watch him with familiar eyes: the stain on the carpet, the hazelnut from the airport parking lot, the dwarf at the front desk, the darkness of the shadows of the mother.

He remembers a quotation he noted down in his black notebook shortly before leaving Iceland, a quotation he'd come across by chance, (not long after he received the invitation to go to Lithuania) in a book which contained the musings of poets on their duty to explain the meaning of their poems. And when he opens his notebook as he sits there on the hard wooden bench outside the bus station, waiting for the driver to go into the parking lot and open the doors of the bus, he feels as if these words by the English poet Donald Davie, published in 1959, are his own. If one excluded the title of Donald's poem, you could easily convince yourself that it was pure coincidence that they'd been printed in a book in England before Sturla's handwriting had fixed the lines in a black notebook:

> This poem I call mine, "The Forests of Lithuania," has revealed to me some new sides of this poet who bears my name. I am glad to see, for instance (what I had almost despaired of) that he is capable of breaking out of the circle of his private agonies and dilemmas, in order to acknowledge that there are other people in the world besides himself, very different but just as interesting.

Nýjar hliðar á ljóðskáldinu sem ber mitt eigið nafn; allt hitt fólkið sem ekki er síður áhugavert. New sides of the poet who bears my name; all the other people who are no less interesting.

What had gone through Liliya's mind as she translated his poem, other than the poem itself? Are those same thoughts going through her head again now, as she sits in her room on Maironio Street and notes his absence in the mirror, or has she entirely forgotten him thanks to a conversation with the next interesting poet who she comes across on her way out of the dining hall, a conversation about yet another interesting poet who during his life has revealed some fresh and unexpected sides of himself, and proudly bears his name up until the moment that name passes away at the same time as he does.

When the driver comes walking towards the bus, Sturla can't help but notice that the man is quite drunk. He all but staggers off the sidewalk and loses his footing right before reaching the bus—and he then blames the bus for this mistake by kicking the tire. On the other hand, Sturla can't tell whether this corpulent, angry man smells of liquor or not: as Sturla carries his bags past him, the very smell he's trying to detect is coming from his own mouth.

THE LESSON
by Sturla Jón Jónsson

that I won't live long
in others' lives

that was what I learned at school

neither dying of old age
when young
nor reaching a childlike old age

When the teacher asked
how many Westman Islanders there were
before the eruption

and were
after that

and when he received
all the wrong answers
he had expected to receive

I began to suspect
as I looked out the window
of the classroom

at the viscous traffic trickling down Lækjargata

that I would soon
rush ahead

and when he asked
this teacher
how many were buried

when the devil pumped
his satanic slag
across the islands

I knew the substance
I was made from
was not meant to last

it wouldn't survive
a lifetime

PART FOUR

THE AMBASSADOR HOTEL

ON THE EDGE OF THE CITY

"Ms. Sturla Jón."

So begins Brynjólfur Madsen's e-mail to Sturla Jón, a letter which is otherwise free of typos and grammatical mistakes. There is no other explanation for the mistake than that, while writing, he'd used the feminine honorific out of habit since, as Sturla has to admit, he'd been writing two names that are both grammatically feminine: Sturla and Jón. That must have been what happened.

He has installed himself in a little boarding house in the northern part of Vilnius, close to the edge of the city. The place is run by an old woman and occupies a soot-gray, two story stone house which, if you forget about the immediate context of the street, looks like something you'd find in the middle of a war zone. The room is minute but relatively neat; there is a narrow bed with faded but clean linen, an iron table and chair, and a bathroom in the corridor for Sturla and the other guests (there don't seem to be any). Sturla spotted an advertisement for the boarding house at the bus station when he arrived in Vilnius the evening before, dog-tired and somewhat fuzzy-headed from drinking. He knew that above all he had to avoid returning to the Ambassador Hotel or sitting down at Literatu Svetainé: he needed to find himself some inexpensive lodgings and maintain his distance from Gedimino Prospektas. He'd taken a cab from the bus station and, though it wasn't yet nine o'clock when he reached the boarding house, he'd nonetheless needed to wake up the old woman, who seemed at first sight to be the same woman he'd seen that morning on the street holding the jam jar, though that surely wasn't the case.

He has a sore back when he wakes up in the rather uncomfortable bed, and despite having slept for a long time his body isn't restored to its usual balance. Normally, Sturla's first waking thought is coffee, but as he drags himself out of bed and checks that he is in OK shape, he decides to ask the old woman for tea, providing she offers him a hot drink. She greets him with a smile and tells him to sit down at a table in a room off the hall, and after she brings him tea, there is a little wait for the rest of the food and drink. Sturla isn't in the habit of eating much for breakfast, but today he gulps down everything the woman brings to the table, totally unbidden, during the meal: thick sourdough bread with salami and cucumbers; yogurt, banana, and apricots; little oat biscuits with cheese. He hasn't eaten anything since midday the day before, other than some crackers and chips on the bus.

Sturla remembers having checked into the boarding house under a Greek name which he made up while he was filling out the form at check-in. It'd occurred to him—more out of fun than in earnest—that he would be hunted in all the city's boarding houses: thanks to his enthusiastic cultural investment in the Baltic countries, Darryl Rothman has acquired a right to the Lithuanian police's personal assistance if he feels he had been violated, no matter how insignificantly, as small as it is, and for her part Jenny Lipp won't let the hullabaloo die down before the organizer of the festival, Gintaras (who was, according to himself, formally responsible for the welfare and the property of the participants), has managed to hand back the item whose disappearance has so unnerved her fellow countryman, even though Darryl Rothman isn't actually a participant in the festival. Sturla hadn't expected the old woman to ask to see his passport, but when she did—very courteously—he'd tried to describe to her that he had dual citizenship. He had no need to, as her sole interest in the passport was looking at the photograph of the holder, which could easily have been taken to be a photograph of a different man than the one who was standing in front of her, smiling apologetically.

"You are another," Sturla thought he heard the old woman say, and he'd chosen to understand from that comment that she thought it was time to update the photograph; it was no longer a picture of the person standing before her.

But had she really said those three words? Given the poverty of her English, Sturla suspects it unlikely that the word "another" was in her lexicon, but his image of her changes soon enough, once he's finished breakfast: the word "cybercafé" comes out of her mouth when he asks her to help him to find a coffee shop which offers a connection to the internet. He is getting impatient to check his e-mail account.

Although he knows he needs to be careful with the money which he has left—not counting the slot-machine money he has earmarked for something special—he takes a taxi to midtown, and soon after midday he's retrieved Brynjólfur's letter, printed it out (it stretches to three pages), and is sitting at a pub downtown, reading the letter over and over. He is concertedly trying to figure out the motives behind the information—or invention?—he finds in it.

Brynjólfur begins his letter by apologizing for "the mess he's caused" by "spilling the beans to the media about his discovery" that Sturla's poems reminded him of poems by his cousin Jónas. He says he deeply regrets that the journalist he'd talked with, a man he knew very well "but no longer thought much of," hadn't let him read the article about Sturla's book and Jónas's manuscript before it went to print. He would never have agreed to the ideas the journalist put in his mouth. But having said this—and not before—Brynjólfur wanted to introduce himself a little: he said he was a district court lawyer in Reykjavík and he'd known Jónas since their first year in Grammar School. They had quickly become good friends, not least because of their shared love of poetry, something which, for his part, he isn't yet cured of, which was why, for example, he'd been browsing through Sturla's new book. He and Jónas had distanced themselves from one another soon after graduation. Brynjólfur had become tired of Jónas's outlook on life, his view that everything a person learned was dangerous, except for the things he learned from himself. Perhaps the idea had been amusing at first, while they were still young men, but it had quickly lost its creative potential when the learning Jónas most wanted to experience for himself mostly concerned life's undergrowth.

In the last six months of his life, Jónas and he had had a few conversations, but their relationship had never been natural or relaxed: Brynjólfur had started a family, and Jónas wasn't at that time a popular guest at any home with children, given his habits and behavior. Brynjólfur had on the other hand clearly perceived that Jónas was asking him for help, without saying so directly; although he'd demanded considerable attention and time, Jónas had never asked him for money. "What's more, I certainly wouldn't have given him money," writes Brynjólfur, and he allows himself to dwell on his "home-brewed philosophy" that if a person really wants to help others, he'll give them his time; if, on the other hand, a person wants to ruin someone, he gives him money. The idea that time is money amounts to a grave misunderstanding: while you can buy time with money, earning the money to buy the time takes so long that the investment doesn't pay dividends.

Jónas got his money from the bank employee on Austurstræti, thinks Sturla, and smiles at the printout, which he has decorated with two beautiful rings from his beer glass and a sprinkle of cigarette ash. And as he lights another cigarette, he shakes his head over Brynjólfur's smug posturing about time.

Many of Brynjólfur's memories about their shared acquaintance, Jónas, found their way into his poetry manuscript. For example, Brynjólfur says, he can remember Armann Valur's Icelandic lesson at the

Grammar School very well, the lesson Jónas had recalled in his poem titled "Icelandic Lesson," an obvious allusion to Dagur Sigurðarson's prose poem "English Lesson," from which Jónas had swiped a few words. Sturla had re-named the same poem "the lesson" in his book, and Brynjólfur actually praised him for the poem's closing lines (as they appeared in *assertions*), lines which suggest that the speaker of the poem is made from materials that are not meant to last, and won't survive, a lifetime. He recognizes that these lines are an addition to Jónas's poem, that they come from Sturla himself and "had had the effect on him" as though Sturla had composed an obituary for his unfortunate cousin. Brynjólfur had always had the feeling that Jónas "would soon rush ahead;" he'd never been like "those folk who let the time go by on this earth, just waiting for it to pass," as Jónas described it in one of the typed poems he'd given Brynjólfur. Brynjólfur was, in truth, amazed that Sturla hadn't used that poem in his book.

The way Brynjólfur's letter discusses Sturla's alleged theft of his cousin's manuscript as though it is an entirely natural thing—the exact opposite of the discussion he'd started in the newspaper—greatly surprises Sturla. But right now, as tired as he is from yesterday's exertions, he knows he doesn't have the powers of concentration to determine whether this overly-industrious attorney's presentation of his case is motivated by sincerity or sarcasm.

At the same time, Sturla thinks it likely that the narrative at the heart of the letter—"something which Jónas trusted to me (Brynjólfur) three days before he died"—is meant as some kind of poetic compensation for having involved Sturla in this damaging newspaper scandal. Alternatively, it isn't out of the question that Brynjólfur was deliberately telling Sturla something that he knew ought to be left forgotten and buried—that Jónas's old schoolmate knew very well the identity of the person who Jónas hadn't wanted to expose.

"Perhaps no good can come from blowing the dust from the past." This is the way Brynjólfur prefaces his recollection, followed by a quotation from Friedrich Dürrenmatt (of all people): "Those who try to unveil the secrets of the dead belong to the dead themselves" (something Sturla finds totally predictable from the type of man who is a district court attorney). "But still," the letter continues, "I think it is best if I tell you something I believe hastened the death of your friend Jónas, something that led him to despair."

Can it be, thinks Sturla, that despair comes after death?

According to the letter writer, Jónas had been dropping in on a married woman of around forty for close to three months, a woman he was too closely-connected to for it to be appropriate of him to visit her when not in the company of their other relatives, "whatever that signifies"—or so Brynjólfur had phrased it. The visits had started one day when he was coming from the State Liquor Store on Snorrabraut and decided to go a different route through Norðurmýri than he usually took on his way home to Meðalholt. And as he was going past the woman's house, and was in fact wondering whether she was home—he knew that she didn't have a job—she had knocked on her kitchen window. It seemed she had happened to be standing there as Jónas was going past, and she indicated through the window that he should stop walking and come to the front door. Jónas had felt like he had to obey, and when the woman opened the door she asked him if she couldn't invite him in for a cup of coffee; she also wanted to ask for his help with something, if he could get a nail out of the wall for her and then nail another in its place. He sat down in the kitchen with her and when she started asking what Jónas had in his black plastic bag—as though she hadn't figured it out—he fished out his recently purchased bottle of Black Death schnapps and they both took some in their coffee, though it wasn't past one in the afternoon. The repair work was soon forgotten in favor of drinking, and the woman craftily tricked Jónas into her bedroom, where she as good as violated him: he hadn't been able to put up any meaningful resistance because of the drinking.

He was a little over twenty; she was close to forty.

Sturla looks at the printout, takes a swig of beer, lights himself another cigarette, and convinces himself that a story of the sort he is now reading for the fifth or sixth time couldn't originally have come from someone who was despairing over a doomed love affair, unless you imagined the whole thing playing out in some people's court on television. The person recalling the story—this guy who calls himself Madsen—must have added some color to it himself. He'd used material from someone who was no longer able to give his own report and reshaped it himself. Was this Brynjólfur doing the same thing to Sturla's family that he'd managed to get Sturla accused of a few days ago: taking advantage of Jónas Hallmundursson's experiences and memories for his own sake?

Was Brynjólfur Madsen adding himself to the group of individuals who indulge in the peculiar need to let Sturla know that they, no less than Sturla, have a talent for creating art? Sturla's suspicion doesn't lessen as he looks further down Brynjólfur's e-mail:

Two days after Jónas had been seduced by the woman in Norðurmýri, he had been on Laugavegur, on his way home, and instead of going past the Station and taking the route which went up Meðalholt, he'd decided to turn onto Snorrabraut and then onto Mánagata. He had promised himself not to go anywhere near that street (except when necessity demanded, that is), given his unavoidable relationship to the woman—when "other related folk" were present—but, as if some alien power was working on him, he found himself going along Snorrabraut, against his own wishes, and before he knew it he was knocking on the door in Mánagata.

And Jónas had afterwards decided to make a third visit to her and they'd indulged themselves with an illicit love affair, which Brynjólfur wanted to believe symbolized his friend's unhappy ending. But as often as Sturla reads Brynjólfur's petty retelling of Jónas's confession in the e-mail, he isn't bothered by it, except when he starts thinking back to the past which "that damn Brynjólfur" has now muddied with his gossip. And Sturla's thoughts turn to what his mother is doing at the moment on Nýlendugata: has she perhaps invited her neighbors' daughter down from upstairs, and is she showing her the picture of her breasts? Or is she sitting by herself, alone with her memories in her minute but finely decorated living-room, sipping on the calm promise of wine which is the same color as the upholstery of her furniture?

Why should he be bothered by what his dead cousin and his still-alive mother had gotten up to together in a life lived thirty years ago? The imagery of that life had, Sturla thinks, been described plenty of times in books and songs; these new descriptions in an e-mail did nothing to alter it.

Sturla blows the ashes off the printout and runs his fingers over the beer stains. He folds the pages together and puts them in his overcoat pocket. And when he stands up from the table he decides, out of nowhere, to buy Liliya something with his slot-machine winnings; he wants to offer her some little token of his gratitude for the friendly way she'd treated him in the short time since they'd met—some tangible object to take the place of what he'd been unable to give her: namely, something of himself.

And he walks all the way back to the boarding house.

For the rest of the day he stays in his little room and reads the detective story that he'd bought in an airport bookstore in Copenhagen. He is so absorbed that he doesn't stop reading except to briefly run out to a nearby supermarket for a sandwich and a bottle of red wine, and lets a character in this thick book, the mother of one of the main characters, remind him about what this complete stranger, Brynjólfur, has just told him. He wonders to himself if it wasn't a bit callous not to let it affect him, this new knowledge that Fanný Alexson, the alcoholic woman in the cellar on Nýlendugata, was the last woman in the life of his similarly-aged cousin—and possibly the only one: Sturla had never known Jónas to be in a relationship with any woman, although various poems in his manuscript gave the impression that he was.

THE FALL LEAVES

When Sturla wakes up the next day and opens the window in the room that looks onto a desolate street, he finds it noticeably cooler than the day before; it is without doubt weather for both an overcoat and a scarf. He decides to go into town, and to go ahead and wear the overcoat without fear. But just before he is about to leave, he makes the decision to try to reach Liliya in Druskininkai; he feels that she deserves it, after he let himself disappear in such a sudden fashion the day before. He asks the old woman if he could use her phone to make a domestic call; she directs him to a room off of the living room and brings him tea shortly after he begins to talk.

He doesn't have much hope that he'll reach his female Belarusian friend—he is expecting her to be busy with the events in the festival program—but when his hope is rewarded just two minutes after he asks to speak with Liliya Boguinskaia, participant in the festival, Sturla figures that it is most likely the greatest *succès* of his whole stay in the land of the Lithuanians. He gets through to the office at the residences on Mairono Street, and he says he is Liliya's relative and needs to speak to her urgently.

Liliya is, naturally, worried when she comes to the phone.

"Hello," she says, questioningly.

"Hello," replies Sturla and it takes Liliya a moment to work out who she is speaking to.

"Is everything OK?" she asks, and he answers by saying that this is precisely why he called: he wants to let her know that everything is indeed OK; he regretted not having been able to fully explain his sudden departure to her.

"Where did you go?" As Liliya tells him he was sorely missed at the performance the evening before, especially by the "Swedish Rolf" (Sturla interjects to say he is from Argentina), he realizes that she seems to think he is still in Druskininkai.

"I am not used to being labeled an out-and-out criminal," he replies. "Especially at a poetry festival. Though no one over five or six years old is totally free from guilt, my experience at other similar festivals has been that participants are treated as innocent."

"I know what happened," says Liliya in a whisper, and Sturla asks what she means: What happened where?

"I spoke to Gintaras."

"And what did he say? What did that courteous fellow say?"

"He told me what Jenny told him."

"Then you don't know anything about what happened," said Sturla, and realizes right away that he sounds unnecessarily certain in his accusation; he doesn't know Liliya well enough to tell her what she does and doesn't know. "I have to let you know you can't trust what those people tell you." He feels like he's stolen the line from a B-movie script.

"No," replies Liliya, uncertainly.

"I'm asking you not to trust them."

"Yes."

Sturla expects Liliya to offer him more support, but when she doesn't he asks whether she'd talked with "that Jenny Lipp."

"Not about that."

"Not about what?"

"The overcoat?"

"What then?"

"I talked to them a lot yesterday, Jenny, Daniella, and Kelly. You know who they are, don't you? Daniella and Kelly?

"No, I don't know who they are. When does a person know who someone is?"

"You know who *I* am," says Liliya, playfully.

"I don't know *who* you are."

"But do you like me?"

Sturla pauses for a moment—he never expected a question like this—before replying affirmatively: "Yes, I like you very much."

"That's good," says Liliya, and Sturla doesn't fully understand the sense behind her assertion. "That Jenny is a total cow," she continues, and Sturla begins to laugh; he feels like he is speaking to a teenage girl who is jealous of her girlfriends.

"But why?" he asks.

"She and this guy Darryl are totally worthless idiots," she replies, and she makes it sound like she is well within her rights to say such things about people she doesn't really know. "Daniella and Kelly are fine. I've got nothing against Americans—I'm actually quite taken with Americans, partly because they once made entertaining movies—but Jenny isn't worth the clothes she wears."

Sturla hasn't ever heard the saying Liliya uses. "I thought you said Jenny read well the day before yesterday. But Darryl? Is he worth the clothes he wears?"

"I don't know how nice or expensive the overcoat was which you . . . which was stolen from him. But I doubt that he is worth as much as that garment." After having heard Liliya use the words "human being" instead of "person" once before, it doesn't surprise him that she should talk about the overcoat as a "garment;" he finds it both funny and sweet.

Suddenly the door to the room where Sturla sits on the phone is pushed open and the old woman enters, carrying a steaming cup of tea on a floral tray, and some biscuits with marmalade. She places the tray beside the phone and says something to which Sturla nods his head in reply.

"You telephone Greek?" she asks and gives him a sharp look.

Sturla asks Liliya to excuse him and explains to his host that he is still on a call to Druskininkai; it is the same number as she'd dialed for him. And the woman pats Sturla on the shoulder in a friendly way and points the teacup out to him.

"But is it true you stole the overcoat?" Liliya asks when Sturla asks her to forgive the interruption. And there is such expectation in her voice that Sturla longs to confess his crime to her.

"Tell me that you stole it," she commands, adding, "I expect you did."

"But why do you expect that?" asks Sturla, completely amazed by Liliya's thoughts.

"Because."

"OK," says Sturla, instead of telling her that "because" is not an answer. He looks around the room at the old woman's world, which smells of tea, preserves, and old, dry paper, though there is little in the room made of paper besides the phone book. He clears his throat. "I stole the overcoat from Darryl Hoffman."

"*Hoffman?*"

"Rothman."

"Are you lying to me?" There is excitement in Liliya's voice. "Are you only telling me what I wanted to hear?"

"You wanted to hear that I am a thief?"

"You aren't a thief."

"No, I am telling you the truth," adds Sturla. "Or half of it. The other half is this: The brand new overcoat I bought myself right before coming here was stolen from a coat hook in the restaurant which Jokûbas's brother runs—he directed you there too, didn't he?—and though

I don't subscribe to either a philosophy or an economics in which those who have been stolen from have permission to do the same to the next man, nevertheless I felt a little justified in taking the overcoat of this 'Darryl' for myself. I hadn't at the time thought that he might in fact be somehow connected to the festival."

"But still, you did very well," says Liliya playfully, and Sturla asks her why she is so against the American art dealer.

She tells him that Darryl Rothman came to Minsk a few years ago in order to buy some antiques, but everyone he met with considered him so arrogant and egotistical that they collectively decided to refuse to do business with him. And then all kinds of stories began spreading about this unwelcome guest, who mostly went around showing off his expensive clothes, including a fur coat which was destroyed by some street urchin with a spray can in front of the State Art Gallery on Lenin Street. Sturla imagines that Liliya mentions this particular location to add to the irony of what had happened to Darryl the aesthete. "In other words, you're not the first person who has taken a coat from him in this part of the world," she continues; Sturla can feel her smiling into the phone. "But even so, it looks like he has become some kind of patron in the Baltic States, pumping money into all kinds of cultural activities—money which he no doubt earns from dealing drugs and from prostitution—and leaving overpriced items of clothing behind on coat racks. Or wasn't it a very nice overcoat?"

Sturla laughs and answers Liliya that yes, it was a *very* fine overcoat. He is filled for a moment with exultation over not being where he should be at this moment: he experiences his telephone connection to Liliya as a real presence, and has the strong sensation that the twenty-four hours they have together in the capital city before he flies home will not be their only time together, although nothing supports this idea. "So I will be sauntering the streets of Vilnius in a coat that belongs to an antiques and drugs dealer who has turned the whole of Minsk against him."

"You say you're in Vilnius *now*?"

"Where else?"

"I thought perhaps you were still in Druskininkai. That you were sitting in some health-spa and letting a middle-aged woman get you peppermint tea and East Indian plant cigarettes."

"East Indian plant cigarettes?" Sturla laughs. "I am in fact drinking freshly-made tea, but the only cigarettes I smoke are my industrial chemical cigarettes. I took the bus back to Vilnius once Gintaras threatened that he and Jenny would look in my suitcase."

"Are you at the Ambassador?"

"No, I'm at some tiny boarding house on the outskirts of the city. I am going by the name Stavros Monopolous."

Liliya laughs warmly, and Sturla is as much amused by the comedy of his description as she is. Once he has described the persecution theory he'd come up with for Darryl and Jenny, and got her to laugh even more, he asks what she'd meant by saying that the Americans had once made entertaining movies. She says she is a great admirer of American movies from the end of their golden age until the sixties, and she names a few titles. When she lists *Sabrina* as one of her favorite movies, Sturla asks if she's seen *The Apartment*; he'd noticed it on DVD in a record store in Vilnius. It turns out that the movie is one of the few well-known Billy Wilder movies she hasn't seen, and then she answers Sturla's question about whether she owns a DVD-player affirmatively: the two of them, mother and daughter, have "that contraption" in Minsk. Sturla immediately makes up his mind to buy *The Apartment* for her out of his slot-machine winnings, along with some other movies. He figures this gift won't seem pushy or inappropriate—it is just something that came to mind because she'd started talking about movies.

"We were also talking about movies yesterday," says Liliya, and she tells him that Jenny had sat down at their table after the reading and put on a haughty expression when they began discussing the lightweight and worthless Oscar-winning movies. Rolf had given an entire speech about "the crazy heifer (or, in English, 'the mad cow from

Kansas')" as he called her once she'd gone to bed (long before the others), and he'd described how Jenny had personally declared war upon him as a poet with her perfectly tasteless last poem earlier that evening, a poem about Israel's invasion of Lebanon and American support for child murderers and needless destruction: she had earned gaping admiration from everyone with some showy bravado, having recited some endless nonsense about the life of an American poetess in Lithuania.

As he listens to Liliya talk about people interacting at the festival, Sturla realizes suddenly that he wishes he was there; he wants to take part in these lively conversations—arguments, even—with informed and entertaining people. They say goodbye, promising to meet the next evening, once Liliya has returned to the city and they can get together at the coffee house on Pilies Street, where Sturla intends to go himself after their phone conversation. Liliya says she wants to show him the bar she wrote about in her poem, and Sturla feels that it is apt, a kind of postscript to their phone call, to tell her about the clever license he took in breaking her word "language," "tungumál" in Icelandic, across two lines. Tungu, the first part of the word, means "tongue" in English, and mál, the second part, can mean almost anything, from a court sentence to needing to pee.

"But it doesn't mean anything rude, does it?" asks Liliya, and Sturla is a little surprised to hear that she's clearly ambivalent about him adding to the poem an ambiguity which wasn't originally there.

And then she tells him about the walk she went on the day before. Shortly after he disappeared from the dining hall she'd walked along the river that ran through town, and the fall had been so beautiful that she couldn't trust herself to put it into words. He is ashamed that they can't go there together later in the day, as there will be such beautiful afternoon sun.

Sturla is a fraction of a second away from asking Liliya if she has experienced The Season of Poetry, as the festival organizers had envisaged it, but he realizes in time that such oafish humor would only offend Liliya's feelings, feelings he thought he'd sensed in her wish that they could enjoy beautiful things together.

And so they say goodbye to each other.

When Sturla has thanked the old woman for the use of her phone, and offered her payment, which she refuses, he feels bad for having deceived her about his name the previous evening, and he decides to correct matters.

"I have to apologize for not giving you the correct name yesterday. I am not Stavros Monopolous."

But she doesn't seem to understand what he is driving at. "Why not?" she asks, after Sturla has put no small amount of effort into explaining his meaning to her in English.

"My name is Sturla Jón. Sturla Jón Jónsson. I come from Iceland."

And the woman shrugs her shoulders and pats Sturla's upper arm in a friendly way. "You like coffee?" she asks.

"Yes, but the tea was very nice."

And she waves him away good-naturedly with a few words in her own language as if to underline that she also knows something *he* doesn't understand.

Sturla looks optimistic when he emerges onto the street in the overcoat, his scarf wrapped around his neck. He is feeling good; he decides that whatever happens over the next few hours shouldn't be determined in advance—he won't plan more than an hour ahead. The only thing he knows he is going to do is buy a few movies for Liliya; he will play the role of Rastignac, the student, to her Madame de Lucingen.

She said she lives with her mother, Sturla thinks as he begins walking along the street in the direction—as far as he can tell—of midtown. As he contemplates the fall in the city he remembers Miroslav Holub's feelings about poetry and uses those words as a justification for being alone, walking through Vilnius when he ought to be working on behalf of poetry with the crowd in Druskininkai. If it is true that poetry can be found in all things, then it's just as true of the hazelnut he now catches sight of and picks up from among the fallen leaves on the sidewalk as it is of the large, concrete lecture hall.

But that doesn't mean I'm going to celebrate this nut, Sturla thinks as he looks at the beautifully created natural specimen in the palm of his hand; then he throws the hazelnut out onto the broad lawn beside the sidewalk and keeps on going.

He buys four DVDs in the record store. In addition to the film starring Jack Lemmon and Shirley MacLaine, he chooses *Sunset Boulevard*, which is by the same director; *Night at the Opera*, by the Marx brothers; and *Made For Each Other* starring James Stewart and Carole Lombard. He thinks long and hard about this last one, since Liliya might misunderstand his choice and think that the title is meant to reveal his actual feelings. He buys three new CDs for himself: one by Kate McGarrigle, the newest release from Maria Muldaur, and the compilation *Sing it Again, Rod* by Rod Stewart. By the time he's concluded his transactions, only a thousand Icelandic kronur remains of his slot-machine winnings.

The restaurant where Liliya and he had talked about meeting the following day is the same one Sturla had briefly sat down at before deciding to follow Jokûbas's advice; it is about midway between the town hall and the little traffic circle which opens into Pilies Street and several other streets. Sturla is quite warm from walking, so he decides to sit down at a sidewalk table and get some coffee and some whisky, that long-awaited combination he'd never managed to get on his first evening in the hotel. They are digging up the section of the street nearest the town hall, and as Sturla waits at the table for his drinks he watches the workmen, who are in blue, labor with drills and shovels, and he allows himself to believe that he could happily do a job like that for a while: rising early in the morning, spending time in the carefree company of sturdy men during the day, and heading home tired in the evening, perhaps with every part of his body feeling like he'd achieved something, something which you could literally call a foundation.

Sturla is lost in thought when he suddenly notices the bass player in the black hat enter the traffic circle from a little side street. He starts; he feels a stab in his gut as though he's seen something terrible. Perhaps Sturla wouldn't have recognized the guy if he'd been wearing the overcoat, but when he saunters onto the sidewalk he is wearing the same clothes as when Sturla first saw him: a well-worn jacket, black jeans, and cowboy boots, and he is holding an instrument case. Although one could say fall has arrived today, the bass player has certainly not let the season dictate the way he dresses; he clearly couldn't expect a warm day if he was planning to spend it outside playing his instrument.

It occurs to Sturla to go straight up to this man who has made him far more angry than everyone else over the past days put together, and let him know that he can't expect to get away with robbing people of their winter clothes. He is about to leap from his chair when he pauses because he realizes that *he*, and not the bass player, is wearing the same kind of overcoat he suspects the stranger of having stolen. And he makes up his mind to let the bass player go about his business in peace because he should, in fact, be satisfied with the way things are turning out. He watches the man in black walk along Pilies Street: after going a few meters along the street he stops suddenly beneath a giant shop sign which sticks out from the wall of one of the stores; he looks up at the sign, turns around just as suddenly as he'd stopped, and goes back up the street. Then he pauses at the corner of the street where Sturla first saw him, puts his case on the ground, and takes out his instrument.

When the waiter has brought Sturla his coffee and whisky, and after Sturla has tasted each of them and lit himself a cigarette, he can hear the man in black playing his bass on the street corner. Listening along, Sturla has the following conversation in his head:

STURLA: You know who I am, don't you?
BASS PLAYER: Yes. You're the guy in the overcoat.

Sturla: What did you do with it?

Bass Player: With what?

Sturla: The overcoat.

Bass Player: What overcoat?

Sturla: The one you stole from me.

Bass Player: The one you're wearing?

Sturla: No. The one I left on the coat hook.

Bass Player: I don't remember being near any coat hook. But I do remember that you're headed to Druskininkai.

Sturla: I went to Druskininkai.

Bass Player: And came back already?

Sturla: Gone and returned. But what did you do with the overcoat?

Bass Player: What did you do in Druskininkai?

Sturla: I asked first.

Bass Player: I answered with a question.

Sturla: I discovered that one has to hide the truth from those who want to build their lives on lies. So as not to prevent them from achieving their goals. And that leads me to ask: What did you do with the overcoat? Do you have any idea that it cost me the equivalent of three months wages for a Lithuanian workman?

Bass Player: I gave it to a Lithuanian workman who has been out of work for three months. I don't have anything to complain about myself. What's more, I'm allowed to bed down at night in the warm kitchen run by the Daugirdas brothers. Oh, that's let the cat out of the bag. Yes, I know Gintaras really well, through Jokûbas. He once let me play some numbers in his poetry festival. I even know that you've just come from there.

Sturla: Who told you that?

Bass Player: You told me when we last met that you were heading to Druskininkai. And I simply put two and two together: someone headed to Druskininkai in October, wearing a quality overcoat like the one you wore—I see you've got a brand new one—well, that sort of person, someone who has grown very pale from staying indoors with European poetry, he must be taking part in The Season of Poetry.

STURLA: This new overcoat is not . . .

BASS PLAYER: *(interrupting him)*: I'll never forget how nervous I was at the festival immediately before I got up on stage, following a reading by some famous American poet. It was like I was standing huddled in a group with the lambs in the slaughter house, with the feeling that the slaughterer couldn't tell the difference between bass players and lambs, that he suffered from the same weakness as de Selby, who, in Flann O'Brien's story, makes no distinction between men and women.

As soon as the bass player winds up his latest tune, Sturla imagines himself getting up on stage in the recital hall in Druskininkai, and he begins to contemplate using the little time he has left in Vilnius to write another article for Jónatan Jóhannsson's magazine. This one will also be about his experience at the same poetry festival he'd written about in the earlier article, except now the festival won't be part of the author's future but his present; and, twenty-four hours later (when he has finished writing the piece), his past. This idea gives Sturla an excuse to order another round of drinks, and before he knows it he is beginning to really enjoy sitting in the cool and listening to the musician in black play from a comfortable distance, alongside the rumbling sounds of the jack-hammers working further down the street, and he amuses himself with the thought that perhaps he would have ended up in the same situation as the bass player if he had chosen music instead of poetry.

Poetry has at least brought him here.

As Sturla is drinking his third shot of whisky, which this time he washes down with beer rather than coffee, the bass player decides to move on, and he saunters along Pilies Street, somewhat hunched over, while the rock song *You Wear It Well* chimes in Sturla's head, not because the man had played it but because it is connected to the song

Mandolin Wind, which he had played outside the restaurant three days earlier.

It is close to two in the afternoon when Sturla pays the bill and gets up from the table. As he did the day before, he walks back to the guest house from downtown, and as he walks he tries to shape this new article in his head, an article which he feels fairly sure will satisfy Jónatan's expectations of what an article about a literature festival ought to look like. Instead of shooting darts at something he has yet to experience—which he had done in the article by quoting from his earlier experiences in analogous situations—he decides to be very tough on himself in this version: to use his words to show himself none of the mercy he'd shown himself by running away like he did.

A SINGLE BED

And the noose is waiting to snag the neck on which it rests.

When Sturla awakes on his second morning at the old woman's boarding house the sun in shining through the windows. He feels much better than the previous morning, yet despite his good mood the first thing he hears in his head on this, his next-to-last day in Lithuania, is the above sentence. It is from the article he wrote the evening before, a piece which he feels quite satisfied with; he makes up his mind to go to the same coffee shop where he received Brynjólfur's e-mail and send the piece to Jónatan, letting him know it is a replacement for the earlier article.

After breakfast, which Sturla silently spends in the company of a man who supposedly checked himself in the day before, a rather mysterious traveling salesman who introduces himself by telling Sturla what line of work he is in, without showing any interest in getting similar information from his fellow boarder, and who afterwards shows no interest in having a conversation, Sturla lies down in his room so that he can finish reading the last chapters of the detective story he began yesterday, and also read over his completed article. And after half an hour has passed, when he's finished the book and set it down on the nightstand, he promises himself that this is the last thriller he will read; from now on, he will write them. He wants to show the reader of this very book, a book he's already beginning to forget, that thrillers don't need a robbery or a murder to hold your attention. They just need to create some uncertainty about whether or not the protagonist will make his Big Decision. Right from the start of the story, the reader knows that the protagonist has booked a flight home—but will he take that flight, or does the aircraft take to the skies with an empty seat (an empty seat paid for by the Icelandic Ministry of Education and Culture)?

Sturla takes a shower and shaves. He folds up the overcoat and places it in the locked extra compartment in the suitcase; he will let his jacket and scarf suffice for his trip into town. As he heads towards the entrance he sees the traveling salesman is still sitting at the breakfast table—he seems deep in thought—and the old woman is watching him with some anxiety. Sturla imagines that when he comes back that evening—or whenever it is he returns—some kind of business will have taken place between this old woman and the silent traveling salesman, something which a person usually only experiences in contemporary American movies.

If yesterday was fall, today it's summer again: for most of his walk to the downtown Sturla doesn't need to wear the scarf around his neck, and he flips his jacket over his shoulder.

He spends the time until midday—Sturla calculates that Liliya will get to the city four or five hours later—typing up the text of his new article in the internet café, and he then sends it to Jónatan. After he's done this, he is even more sure than he was the evening before that this new article surpasses the earlier version, both in style and content. He rewards himself with a cold beer at the same place he'd sat down the day before. Today, there are no sounds on the street other than the noise of cars and of pedestrians walking past.

For the next three hours Sturla sits in the sun and loses himself in the activity that occupies anyone who is facing certain death: recalling his life, from his first memories to the current moment. And he makes sure he doesn't drink too quickly, since he doesn't want to be drunk when he finally meets Liliya. He decides to go for a little walk before they meet up at this same place, but while he is waiting for the waiter to bring the bill his phone rings—but only twice, too quick for him to answer. He sees his father's number on the screen, and when the waiter appears with the bill, Sturla asks him for another beer. He wants to hear his father Jón's news, this character who played a starring role in the trip down memory lane he's spent the past hours taking: the cuckolded movie director on Mánagata who is now a librarian on Skólavörðustígur.

"I wanted to call Örn," replies Jón when Sturla asks him whether he'd meant to call him. "I wanted to let him know that I've managed to get a commitment from this guy Alfreð about the grant."

"For the movie?" Sturla remembers his father telling him not long ago about how an old friend of his from school had promised to finance the movie that he and Örn Featherby had long been planning to make together, as director and scriptwriter. "Who is this Alfreð?"

"Alfreð Thorarensen. Alfreð Leó Thorarensen. We went to school together. He's a chemist and a businessman. And a complete villain."

"And you intend to collaborate with this villain?"

"A man needs to look past the hand that feeds him," replies Jón, and Sturla regurgitates the phrase:

"Look past the hand that feeds him?"

"I was going to tell Örn all about it," Jón presses on, "but there was no answer at his house; he's not the sort of person who has a cell phone."

"Smokes a pipe and won't use a cell phone? Congratulations on the grant."

"Thank you. You've got a reason to be happy, too."

"I do?"

"Do you still have the money you won at the University games room?"

"It so happens I've just spent it."

"Did you meet up with a woman?"

"I bought some movies."

"That reminds me: you don't need to worry about the movie I loaned you. I've already ordered it . . ."

"I'm not worried about the movie you loaned me," interrupts Sturla, a little irritated about how distracted and self-centered his father is being. "But why should I be happy?"

"Didn't you get the e-mail from that . . . what was he called, that . . . ?" Jón had obviously expected Brynjólfur to let Sturla know about the "letter of apology" which, he says, appeared in yesterday's paper, but he is so "completely wrapped up in himself over the chemist's dirty money" (as Sturla phrases it to himself) that he doesn't hear Sturla when he says he has no idea about any "letter of apology": Brynjólfur had briefly talked about the "mess" he'd caused the book, but he was more concerned with dredging up the family's past and telling some of the strangest stories Sturla has heard in a long time.

But Jón doesn't have any interest in finding out the details of these stories; instead, he asks Sturla which movies he bought (if it is actually possible to buy movies in Vilnius) and, after praising the choice of *Night at the Opera*, Jón asks his son whether he ever told him about his and Örn's ideas for the scene in which pandemonium breaks out in a restaurant—it now looks more likely than not that the movie will get made.

"Yes, Dad, you told me all about it," replies Sturla, although he doesn't remember any particular details about the idea; instead, he conjures up a memory of *Pelléas and Mélisande* and what commotion that piece of music had caused on Mánagata, a memory he has just spent a good amount of time recalling.

After Sturla has said goodbye to his father, he still doesn't know why he has any reason to be happy about this item in the paper—this news—which, according to Jón, has been published and which claims that people were too quick to accuse Sturla of plagiarism: the theft was more a matter of personal opinion than had been first described. Although you might say that the judgment has been reversed on appeal, Sturla still feels the image of him that will linger in people's minds—people interested in poetry and perhaps even people whose interests leant *against* poetry—will be of an author who forgot to cite the sources he'd used—and intentionally so.

Sturla drains what's left in the beer glass before strolling in the direction of Pilies Street. The sun has disappeared behind the clouds and it is getting chilly when he turns into a street called Latako, intending to keep a safe distance from Gedimino Prospektas. He starts imagining that he's on Mánagata. He imagines that he has just come out of the long-gone branch of the State Liquor and Tobacco shop, where the wine bottles were kept on high shelves behind the employees and sold over the counter. He is holding a heavy, black plastic bag which clinks when he weaves around the traffic on the wide Snorrabraut, and he eases himself round the corner of Mánagata, making sure the contents of the bag don't make a sound as he goes past the second house on the street from the corner of Snorrabraut number 4, which is where one of his best friends lived. When he reaches his childhood home, on the corner of Gunnarsbraut, he stops and looks towards the kitchen window with the light yellow curtains—which used to be white—drawn across it. There's nothing in the window, nothing except shadows; indeed, there's nothing in the other windows, and no one on the street—unlike the riot of colors that is the foot traffic on the corner of Latako and Rusu (the street which meets Latako), and it's not until Sturla has reached Héðinsgata, which goes all the way up to Rauðarárstígur, that some signs of life can be seen in Norðurmýri; there is a young woman standing with a used dark blue Silver Cross buggy, rocking the buggy with one hand and holding a lit cigarette in the other, and as Sturla goes past she blows smoke from the cigarette and smiles at him as though she knows him—maybe she's read something by him—and at the next moment Sturla is walking up in Rauðarárstígur, where the pharmacy advertises itself in a red house, and he crosses the street, past the fishmongers on the corner on the same side as the pharmacy, and up Háteigsvegur and from there into Einholt, which is a narrower street than Maironio, which takes over from Rusu—Maironio, which Sturla remembers is the name of the street in Druskininkai—and when he has gone a few meters down that street, a street as long as it is from Einholt to the north corner of Meðalholt, the hotel whose card Darryl Rothman had in his overcoat pocket is right in front of his eyes: the Mabre Residence Hotel, a stately white structure which might recall an orthodox Russian monastery with its four wide pillars that stretch over two stories up to the roof. It's a completely different image from the pebbledash houses of Meðalholt, where piebald laundry flutters on a washing line in a front yard, beside a light blue trampoline, and where he can see the window of the basement apartment where the student Jónas ended his life.

When Sturla walks up to the hotel the sun has come back out from the clouds, and he catches sight of himself in a little pond in the car park. He looks at himself on the reflective surface, among the fall leaves that look like they have been specially arranged on the surface of the water by hotel employees. And he is content with what he sees. He decides not to go into the hotel to take a look around, as he intended, and instead walks in the opposite direction; it won't be long before he and Liliya meet up. He goes down to the river which gave its name to the city and enjoys wandering the streets, wearing the face he saw in the hotel pond.

When he approaches the bar half an hour later, a bar which has become quite a familiar sight, he sees Liliya from behind; she's standing by the door and seems to be examining the menu. He stops at the table nearest the road and watches her. She is wearing the same tunic as when he last saw her, but different pants, and her hair is tied in a knot at the neck; she lifts one of her feet to scratch her calf, and then, as though she can feel someone watching her, she turns round and looks straight at Sturla.

"Welcome back," he says, and she nods her head, smiling. She gives him three kisses on the cheeks; has she learned that from Darryl's girlfriends?

"I feel like I've come to your home town!" she says and she looks him up and down as though she'd expected him to have changed during "his urban seclusion, following the rebellion in the countryside," or so he imagines her describing it.

"I'm just a guy who's not made for the countryside," Sturla replies comically, and Liliya laughs. She hits him playfully on his forearm then takes hold of it, the way he remembers her doing when they first met in the lobby of the Ambassador Hotel.

"I brought you something from the festival," she says, smiling, and he beckons towards a table, asking if they shouldn't sit down.

The same waiter who served Sturla earlier comes over to the table, and they order beer and cherry brandy. Liliya fetches a thick white paperback from her suitcase, and hands it to him, remarking that if Sturla had stopped less briefly in Druskininkai he would have received a copy himself. It is the collected poetry of all the participants; which hadn't arrived from the printer before Sturla left the festival, having (briefly) turned up in Druskininkai. She also gives him a little book of her own, a beautiful, signed edition which he responds to by kissing her and saying that he has his new book at the hotel—at the boarding house, he corrects himself—which he wants to give her.

"I also bought a little something I wanted to give you," he adds, and he immediately gets the feeling that he has no business giving a person he hardly knows something he has bought specially. "Just so you can get over the poetry debates from the last few days," he adds, apologetically.

"For me?" Liliya takes a sip of brandy and follows it with a sip of beer. "You shouldn't have done that . . ."

He hands her the plastic bag from the store.

"You shouldn't have bought me something, Sturla."

"Too late," Sturla replies. "I saw this in the store when I was getting something for myself, and for some reason you came to mind."

Liliya looks in the bag and her face breaks into an embarrassed smile. "*I* came to mind?" She takes the DVD cases out and examines them one by one—wearing an expression of genuine astonishment—while Sturla explains how he'd been planning to use a small amount of money he'd won in an arcade games hall shortly before he left Iceland in order to buy something that would always remind him of his trip—he jokes that he is an incorrigible gambler—but he hadn't found anything he particularly wanted to buy. He had thought about buying a Russian Babushka from a street vendor but he'd changed his mind: it didn't seemed right to buy something Russian in a country that was not Russia.

"And hates Russia," adds Liliya, without taking her eyes off the DVD cases which contain the movies. "But you must watch these with me, then" she says, putting her arms around Sturla and giving him a long kiss on one cheek. "You'll have to come back to Belarus and watch these with me and Mommy. She loves this sort of movie."

Sturla smiles, but he feels uneasy; what if he reacted to her unexpectedly, responding positively to her frivolous suggestion?

"Anyway, you must come back to the hotel," says Liliya, continuing to read the back of the cases. "I just need to pop into my room before we go to the restaurant."

Had they talked about going to a restaurant? Sturla tries to remember.

Then she thanks him again and calls the waiter over to ask for another round.

"I probably managed to ruin my liver back there in the spa town," she says, smiling, as she watches the waiter, and when Sturla asks whether he was by any chance missed at the reading she'd told him about, she answers by saying—and he feels she's being candid—that the three people he'd left behind at the dinner table after lunch (Roger, Rolf, and her) had regretted his sudden departure. By yesterday evening

Rolf had been on the verge of "beating the brains out of that hellish imperial cow, Ms. Lipp," after Liliya told him about the overcoat situation, but Roger, as delicate and weak as he was, had managed to cool him down, "doubtlessly with some unexpected quotation from the English Lake Poets; they didn't spend a moment of their time together talking about anything else."

The more important things Sturla and Liliya learn about each other over the next hour, on the other hand, as they sit in the warm afternoon sun outside the bar, are that she has a grown son who lives in Switzerland and she earns a living as a translator from English and German; he (who omits to mention his work as a super) is the divorced father of five children who at the moment—as far as he knows—are all in Iceland; one of them lives in London these days.

Afterwards, they walk together towards the Ambassador Hotel, stopping in the supermarket to buy themselves a cold bottle of white wine and a small bottle of cherry brandy, which Liliya confesses she has become "horribly dependent on" during her brief stay in Lithuania. She suggests that Sturla should put a paper bag on his head before they enter the hotel, but when he says he will (although he will have to use a plastic bag, as paper bags aren't easy to find these days) Liliya shoves him out of the store, laughing out loud, and promising to take responsibility for him; she will defend him if any "of the ambassadors from poetry-land starts asking what became of him and why he vanished so suddenly from Druskininkai."

It turns out that there is no one at the front desk when they enter the hotel. Liliya hurries Sturla up the stairs holding the bag from the supermarket—he isn't prepared for how determined she is—and she tells him to wait outside room number 411; she needs to get the key. It isn't until Sturla reaches the door of the room that he realizes Liliya is staying in the same room as he had; he's probably drunk too much to remember numbers properly. He hears a toilet flush in the next room, and as he stands with his ear to the door from which the sound came, looking along the corridor towards the stairs, Liliya suddenly appears on the landing with her suitcase, rattling the key in the same hand she uses to point at Sturla as she calls out:

"Are you eavesdropping?" Then she laughs and tiptoes along the corridor as though she thinks it is the middle of the night and she doesn't want to wake up any of the hotel guests.

Liliya has a hard time opening the door to the room, and she eventually has to ask Sturla to help her. And at the very moment they enter the room, Sturla's phone rings. He apologizes formally in English ("If you will excuse me," and so on); Liliya nods in reply and tells him she will open the bottle "while he attends to his business affairs."

It was Jónatan Jóhansson calling. He gets right down to the matter at hand, which is Sturla's article, "The Rain Seen Through a Man's Fingers," and the editor's unexpected enthusiasm over "this progress from the last article," as he describes it. He absolutely wants to publish it; does Sturla think he needs to see a proof? The magazine is about to go to the printer. That being dealt with, Jónatan delivers another message while Sturla lights a cigarette and takes a water glass full of white wine from Liliya's hand: perhaps Sturla could write an article for him—maybe even a book—about his half-brother N. Pietur, the visual-artist and musician, an acquaintance and former colleague of Sturla's father. This project might mean Sturla will have to follow Níels on a trip abroad; Níels has recently booked a two-month stay in Kjarvalsstofa in Paris, which Jónatan explains is a kind of studio apartment for visual artists that the city of Reykjavík owns in an art center called Cité Internationale Des Arts (he takes every opportunity to show off his limited French, Sturla thinks). Would he be interested in the project at all?

"I'll let you know," Sturla replies in English, and he smiles impishly at Liliya who is holding her glass at head height and seems like she can hardly wait for Sturla to conclude his business on the phone. He thanks Jónatan for the praise and the offer: he feels good that he appreciated the article and he will consider the offer; it's just that he isn't sure he is heading home in the short term.

"No? Jón told me you were coming back tomorrow," says Jónatan, and Sturla replies that he isn't sure he'll be able to make the airplane tomorrow morning: "I've gotten used to waking up late."

Liliya congratulates Sturla on the offer which he briefly explains to her. Then they open the brandy bottle from the supermarket and toast in little plastic shot glasses which Liliya gets out of her suitcase, and Liliya says she's just listened to Icelandic spoken for the first time. Would he be willing to show her some written Icelandic? She hasn't ever seen it written down.

"Have you lipstick?" Sturla asks her; and in his euphoria he recalls an English translation of a line of poetry by Alfred de Musset: "Julie, have you Spanish wine?" And when Liliya looks confused and tells him she has a pen, he repeats his question: "Liliya, have you lipstick from Belarus?"

Liliya shakes her head, smiling; she doesn't have any lipstick from her home country, but she rummages around in her suitcase and pulls out some lipstick in a gold-colored holder from a pretty cosmetics case. When she opens it and holds it out as though she is going to put it on him, he grabs the stick from her and asks her to wait while he goes into the bathroom briefly. Then he takes his half-full glass of white wine with him, and after a short while he calls Liliya into the bathroom.

When she comes in, Sturla is standing in the bathtub and smiling, his glass in his hand; with a winning grin, he points out some dark violet letters on the white wall above the bathtub:

MÓÐIR BARNANNA MINNA HEFUR
MYRT BARNIÐ Í FÖÐUR ÞEIRRA

Liliya grabs the lipstick back from Sturla and looks astonished at how little is left. She seems about to say something about it, but stops herself and asks what the sentence means in English.

"The mother—" Sturla thinks for a moment. Then he points to the first word, *móðir*, says that it means "mother," and translates the rest of the sentence as "If I may, then I will happily visit your mother."

"If you *may*?" Liliya turns to Sturla, clearly amazed by his request. She starts to say something but stops and asks why the last word she heard in the English version of the sentence was the first word in the Icelandic version.

"The mother always comes first in Icelandic," replies Sturla without hesitation. Then he smiles and waits for Liliya's reaction.

"Of course," she says, looking at him tenderly.

"Of course what?" asks Sturla.

"You can visit my mother."

He strokes his chin and tries to look contemplative. "What is her name?"

"Galina. She is called Galina."

Their eyes meet. Liliya takes a sip of her white wine and Sturla sips his.

"Do you think she's at home?" he asks.

"She never leaves the apartment."

Liliya suddenly turns away and goes out of the bathroom. Sturla watches her; he feels like she has become sad all of a sudden, and he places his glass down on the edge of the sink and goes after her, leaving the writing on the wall: "The mother of my children has / murdered the child in their father." He watches her set her glass down on the table beneath the mirror and lift the bottle of white wine as though she is going to pour some for herself. She looks at herself for a moment, and before Sturla knows what is happening she has come up to him: she places both hands around his head and clumsily presses her mouth onto his—any more clumsily and she might have injured him. He responds by putting his hands on her waist, and the next moment they collapse onto the single bed. Liliya tears his shirt out of his trousers, slips her hand inside, and pulls him to her.

*

Two hours later they sit facing each other in a restaurant in the old downtown with menus in front of them, waiting for their drinks to appear. Liliya, who has untied her hair and let it hang free about her head, is telling Sturla about a Dutch woman in her fifties, a participant in the festival, who had told her in confidence how she died at six years old, while on a walking tour with her father, but had come back to life again three years ago, when she went into an electric appliance store in her hometown of Maastricht. In exchange for that story Sturla tells her about the latest obsession of his youngest son Grettir: European lieder singers; he is nineteen years old and is listening to Gérard Souzay and Hans Hotter. But Liliya's only reaction to this information is to say that she owns an old record by Gérard Souzay: her former husband had been in such a hurry to leave that he'd left behind his record collection, a very large classical music collection which Sturla will definitely have fun flicking through, as long as he likes classical music.

"It's chiefly folk music in here," says Sturla, and he smiles as he points to his head.

Two more hours have passed by the time they return to the hotel room. This time it takes even longer to get the room door open, even though Liliya has given Sturla the key rather than trying to open the door herself.

The air in the room is stale; they hadn't thought to air the room out when they left, and it smells like cigarette smoke and wine. While Sturla opens the window out onto the street Liliya begins to run a hot bath. Sturla calls the old woman at the boarding house to let her know he will be back the next day to get his suitcase; he will pay for a third night, of course, she doesn't need to worry about that. And a few minutes later, when he has finally managed get his meaning across to the woman—Liliya is standing in the doorway to the bathroom, her sides beginning to ache from laughter—he ends the telephone call and the world outside the door fades away as Sturla and Liliya's swimming eyes meet across the floor.

THE RAIN SEEN THROUGH A MAN'S FINGERS

by Sturla Jón Jónsson

> "To yoke poetry to science or morality is nothing less than to ask for death or banishment; the object of Poetry is not Truth but rather Poetry itself."—Charles Baudelaire

"When the poet is just five minutes from his time at the lectern he recalls the rain that he looked at through his fingers earlier that day. He thinks about Vitezslav Nezval's words about his hometown, Prague, which he looked at through fingers of rain, and it occurs to the poet that understanding Nezval's images will mean turning them on their head.

A poet who travels from his country to another place in order to give a reading of his poems has important work at hand.

No less important than the poet Egill Skallagrímsson, who saved himself from being decapitated by the axe of king Eiríkur Bloodaxe when he composed his poem "Head's Ransom," twenty stanzas praising the king.

But today there are no Norwegian kings in the hall. Still, when the poet stands at the pulpit the audience facing him will have just as much power as Eiríkur Bloodaxe. And this audience has probably never before heard poems from the poet's country.

So he waits nervously. He is present in the hall to hear some new things and to discover some things he didn't know before.

This particular audience is perhaps Estonian. And in all likelihood many of them have come to recite poems they themselves have composed.

But there are many people in the hall who have either come to recite their poems or to listen, or maybe even to do both. They've come from Denmark. Or Russia. From England. And Argentina. They've come from neighboring Poland. And over the Atlantic Ocean from the United States of North America. And Italy. One of the audience members is from Afghanistan, another from Iran. A third from Norway, a fourth from Sweden. Two came from Latvia. Only one from Germany. And from Holland likewise. One audience member in the hall is Belarusian. And another, the same gender as the Belarusian—a woman—comes from Finland. One traveled from Switzerland, another came from the Ukraine, but most of those present haven't had to travel further than from within Lithuania to get to the lecture hall in Druskininkai.

For it is in Druskininkai, a spa town in the southern part of Lithuania, that people from many countries have gathered together to let each other hear their poems.

And at the moment there are only four minutes left until the delegate from Iceland takes the lectern. In three and a half minutes he must get up from his chair in the front row of seats by the stage, giving himself half a minute to go to the pulpit and compose himself behind it.

The feeling the poet carries inside him is nothing less than pride at having been invited. Someone has paid for all of the three thousand kilometers that led to the pulpit and has taken care of his hotel bill; he has been fed and even been encouraged to drink alcoholic drinks.

At the same time, the poet is quaking inside, out of fear that he won't be able to stand up to the expectations that go hand in hand with the invitation. In his last moments he wonders again whether the poems he is planning to recite have been carefully chosen, whether he's decided on the order with good reason.

And the poet scolds himself for choosing reason as his guiding light.

The poet has other guides than reason.

But suddenly a new sensation is aroused in the Icelander's heart when the preceding poet, from the United States of North America, more specifically from Kansas City, introduces her last poem and offers a kind of preface: this poem was composed on the occasion of some unforgivable actions by her powerful and great nation on foreign soil.

A murmur goes around the packed hall as the first words of the poem conjure the image of a prosperous nation in fancy dress, a nation which doesn't bother to look around itself before she squats down and "goes to the toilet" in her neighbor's yard. And the murmuring, which the Icelandic poet knows signifies enthusiasm, accompanies the reading of this female poet from Kansas through the final minutes which she has at her disposal, and for two or three minutes more, because the meaning hidden behind the poem's words is now plainly boiling over.

And when the American poet sends a metal dragon rattling from her lips over the sun-baked cradle of civilization, and drops bombs on apartment blocks full of life, she reaps genuine admiration and congratulatory applause, which follows her all the way back through the hall of spectators and continues while the poet from Iceland, crippled by his own inferiority complex, slides out of his seat and walks on unsteady feet up to the execution platform, holding his white sheets.

And given the implicit debate which has undeniably been thrust onto the agenda in the hall, the poet from Iceland has nothing to add, nothing except an impenetrable description of the architecture of his own lodgings in Reykjavík; joy at seeing a mountain from a peaceful valley; the shadows which stretch over quiet streets and sidewalks; and the occasional images which touch no one and nothing but the paper they are written on.

And the poet's mouth has gone dry. The silence that faces him in the room is much the same as the silence that obscures the destruction of Christian and Jewish invading armies.

And as the poet gets close to the end of the poem which has a theme addressing the slipshod material the self is made from, how that material doesn't last a lifetime, he feels the noose of international opinion in the hall tightening around his neck. And the poet still has four or five more poems to read, poems which make no mention of the atrocity of young and healthy men killing children and old people, so long as it's done in God's name, and he knows that the poetic silence which his poems are trying to describe is nowhere near as profound as the silence which they will receive.

And the noose is waiting to snag the neck on which it rests.

But what happens in someone's last moments when they are hung? Perhaps he dances a few steps in the air or sticks out his tongue at the onlookers. If the person in question is lucky enough, and the drop from the gallows is sufficiently fast enough, he might only have to live until his neck breaks at the exact moment the noose snags him, and so meet his end without delay.

But just as the fingernails continue to grow after the body has died, the inevitable conclusion of the hanged man's time on earth is this: he "goes to the toilet" even though there isn't a toilet nearby.

And that is something no one wants to be remembered for, neither the poet nor the audience.

And that is why the Icelandic poet flees his fate. He leaves it to others to compose their own Head's Ransoms.

After all, you can't hang a headless man.

He slips out of the lecture hall and loiters a while under the heavy rain on the sidewalk outside. And before killing his sodden cigarette and vanishing, he looks at the rain through his fingers and finds that it runs down the back of his hands and into his jacket sleeves.

And the waxy texture of the poet's overcoat, which is meant to repel the rain, offers about as much protection as a dust jacket offers against criticism."

PART FIVE

MINSK

PILIES STREET

The train leaves at 3:15 in the afternoon.

The mirror behind the bar shows Sturla standing on his own amidst the bottles of liquor, whisky, vodka, and cognac, and in front of him on the bar are two half-full beer glasses and two large shots of untouched cherry brandy.

How alone can a person be? Sturla asks himself, and smiles at how wearily he looks back out from the mirror.

How alone is Liliya, powdering her nose in the bathroom?

He picks up the black faux-leather case which she left on the bar stool and peeps into it. Before he takes two rather thick books out of it he glances quickly towards the bathroom door, then reads Jokûbas's name on the front of the second book, which is unusually thick for a poetry collection. The other book is his own *assertions*, which he gave Liliya after he'd collected his suitcase from the old woman at the boarding house earlier that morning. He flicks through to the title page of Jokûbas's book and sees that the author has written an inscription to her in his language, and below some long handwritten text he has splashed his name—very carelessly written—and scrawled three big x's after it.

Sturla sticks the books back in the bag and gets out one of the movies he gave Liliya: *The Apartment*. He looks at the still from the movie on the case: Shirley MacLaine holds out a playing card—the Queen of Spades—for Jack Lemmon; they are sitting on a sofa, seemingly outside a window with gray Venetian blinds, Shirley has a string of white pearls around her neck and is wearing a flowing white dress, and Jack is in a white shirt with a black, loosely knotted tie, an indication that something big happened before Shirley held out the Queen of Spades.

Sturla turns the case over to look at another picture of the actors, a black-and-white head-shot. Shirley is in a white blouse beneath a light-gray suit, and Jack is in a black jacket and a white shirt with a tightly-knotted black tie. Some writing to the left of the picture describes how the movie won five Oscars, including Best Picture. And it adds: "C.C. 'Bud' Baxter (Jack Lemmon) knows the way to success in business . . . it's through the door of his apartment!"

Sturla looks up from the case towards the bathroom door of the restaurant, and he begins to wonder what the door to Liliya's mother's apartment in Minsk looks like. He imagines a pale yellow door made out of some kind of wooden material that's long overdue for a coat of paint, if not for replacing. There is a peephole and below the hole a faded card in a rusted iron frame displays the typed names of Liliya and her mother Galina. Sturla turns the knob and forces the door. It opens into the living room. Before he takes a step onto the linoleum floor he breathes in the heavy air, saturated with meat fat or potato-and-cabbage stock—he cannot decide which. He closes the door after himself, takes off his overcoat and hangs it on the hook beside an oval spot which is lighter than the color of the wall, a stain from beneath the mirror which hung there for many years.

Then he turns to the living room. Galina is sitting there on a green sofa looking towards the television, at something moving there. She nods to him, and while Sturla watches, the newsreader reels off something that causes a smile to cross Galina's face. She stands up—with considerable difficulty—and gets *The Apartment* DVD case which is lying on the DVD player inside the television cabinet. She points towards Sturla and makes a motion with her index finger which is meant to suggest movement, something budging forward. Sturla smiles at her and gets a smile in return. He asks where Liliya is, in English first and then by mentioning her name in a questioning tone. She is in the bathroom. He takes the case from Galina's hand; then he remembers that the disc is in the machine from the evening before. He switches it on and indicates to Galina that she should sit down on the sofa. And he contemplates the five little bears that Liliya's mother arranged on the television after she learned that Sturla was the father of five children. Then he goes into the kitchen and opens the refrigerator.

While the lion sighs under the Metro-Goldwyn-Mayer logo, Sturla takes a half-liter of vodka from the freezer and picks up a wooden cutting board, on which there is some cheese and some slices of paprika. When he comes back into the room with the cutting board in one hand and two water glasses and the vodka bottle in the other, the names of the actors in the movie are on the screen.

He remembers the name Johnny Seven from the previous evening, but he sees that he hasn't correctly remembered the name of the composer: it was Adolph Deutsch, not Alfred Deutsch. Next comes the name of the director and producer: Billy Wilder.

Sturla begins thinking about his father. And then the images on the screen change: instead of the grayish row of houses which served as the background for the names of the people in the movie, an aerial view of New York appears and you hear the voice of Jack Lemmon: "November first, 1959: the population of New York City is 8,420,782."

Jack's character says he works for the insurance company Consolidated Life. And then we get to see him in person; he is at his job, at a little desk in a hall that stretches on like the open spaces in Iceland. He tells us he sits at desk number 861 and is called C.C. Baxter, nicknamed Bud. We see the clock on the wall shows 4:41 and when it has counted off another nineteen minutes, a loud bell rings and the employees of Consolidated Life get up from their chairs and leave the room, following an intricate system which has evolved in order to avoid blocking up the narrow walkways between the work desks as they leave. The only person who doesn't go anywhere is C.C. Baxter, and he explains why: he has loaned his apartment to his boss—for a date with a mistress—and because he needs to kill time while his boss is in the apartment with the woman, Bud works overtime.

He indicates that this is something he does quite often. We accompany him on his way home; he goes past a row of houses on the street where he lives. It's nearly the end of the period of time for which he agreed to stay away from his boss and the woman.

Bud says he lives a short walk from Central Park. The weather is bad, and he's wearing a hat and a light-colored duster that he buttons up to his neck. The way he braces his shoulders, walking along all hunched up, indicates that he is cold, that he is looking forward to getting home. But when he is nearly at the front steps, he sees that the light is still on in the window, and the music which he can hear from there conveys only one message: Bud can't go home yet.

The perspective of the movie leaves Bud back on the sidewalk as it heads inside the apartment. A middle-aged man is knotting his tie inside the room; a woman who is considerably younger than him zips up her dress and puts her necklace on. The man informs her that they have to leave the apartment, that he told the apartment's owner to come back at eight o'clock, but the woman wants to have one more martini. And then we get to see Bud again; he is loitering outside, having lit himself a cigarette. At the moment it seems like his overcoat isn't warm enough to cover him; it looks cheaper than it had seemed in the last frame.

Bud's landlord, who according to his account is called Mrs. Lieberman, returns to the house with her dog on a leash and bids good evening to Bud. She asks if he has locked himself out but he says he is waiting for a friend. He continues to trot up and down the sidewalk and smoke. After a little while the door to the house opens and Bud's boss and his girlfriend appear on the stairs. As they depart with the following exchange, Bud crouches out of sight by the stairway; in front of him on the sidewalk are five trashcans that are waiting to be emptied.

"Where do you live?" the boss asks.

"I told you. With my mother," answers the woman.

"Where does she live?"

"179th Street, the Bronx."

"OK. I'll walk you down to the subway."

"I don't think so!" the woman bursts out. "You'll pay for my cab."

"Why do you dames always got to live in the Bronx?"

"Are you telling me you have other dames you meet up with here?"

"Absolutely not. I'm a happily married man."

They walk briskly away, and Bud, who's turned his back to the street so that the bickering pair don't notice him, hurries up the stairs and through the door. As he gets his mail from the mailbox in the lobby Sturla scrutinizes his overcoat, sitting there on the green sofa with Galina. A few moments ago the overcoat had seemed cheap and of inferior quality, but now, inside the house, it looks more like a well-made piece. It's not quite an Aquascutum overcoat—it isn't laminated like a dust jacket, like the wrapping around some worthless poetry. The overcoat is from Brooks Brothers, a design from 1959 made by the oldest, most respected gentleman's clothing retailer in the U.S. (Sturla had read that on the net, after sending the article to Jónatan). The flagship store is on Madison Avenue in New York City, and the retailer has been known for its first class products since 1818. Bud's overcoat is made of thinner and lighter material than the one that you'd find in the locked compartment in Sturla's suitcase.

He pours more vodka into his and Galina's water glasses and as he screws the cap back on the bottle Liliya comes out of the bathroom and into the living room. The image on the television suddenly freezes, and Liliya's mother vanishes from Sturla's thoughts. He is no longer sitting beside her on the sofa; he has returned to the bar in Pilies Street. Instead of a vodka bottle on a cloth-covered side table, he has two beer glasses, one half-full and the other empty, and two generous full measures of cherry brandy on the dark brown wooden surface of the bar. He puts the DVD case back in Liliya's bag and places it on the bar. Then he taps a cigarette out of the packet.

When Liliya sits back down beside him he has lit the cigarette; he first blows smoke across the bar, then takes Liliya's left hand tenderly and smiles at her. Her hand is cold, and Sturla Jón imagines that in order to shorten the time she spent in the bathroom, Liliya hadn't waited for the water to get warm before washing her hands.

"You're ice cold," says Sturla, leaving his cigarette between his lips while he strokes both Liliya's hands.

"Then I should drink some more," she answers, repaying Sturla's concern by taking his hands. "And so should you. I am not certain you'll want to be sober when you get to Minsk. At least by the time we reach the stairs up to the apartment."

They let go of each other and raise their shots of cherry brandy.

"To Minsk," says Sturla.

"To Minsk," says Liliya, and they both smile. "To Mommy's apartment block."

And they down their drinks.

Translator's Acknowledgements

Grateful thanks to all at Open Letter, especially Chad Post, who has the best ideas, and E.J. Van Lanen, whose eagle-eyed attention made this a better translation. Thanks to Bragi Ólafsson for patience, enthusiasm, and volcano trips. Thanks to David Megathlin, Alyssa McDonald, and Lisa Levinson, early adventurers in Iceland(ic), and to Richard North, who pointed me towards and first taught me about Icelandic language and literature. Thanks to Jess, for encouraging and supporting me in this, as in all things. Lastly, abiding gratitude to my parents, Brian and Heather Smith, thanks to whom I grew up among many languages.

Bragi Ólafsson was born in Reykjavik and is the author of several books of poetry, short stories, and four novels, including *Party Games*, for which he received the DV Cultural Prize in 2004. *The Ambassador* was a finalist for the 2008 Nordic Literature Prize and received the Icelandic Bookseller's Award as best novel of the year. He is also a founder of the publishing company Smekkleysa (Bad Taste), and has translated Paul Auster's *City of Glass* into Icelandic.

Lytton Smith was born in Galleywood, England, and lives in New York City, where he is a founding member of Blind Tiger Poetry, a group which aims to find innovative ways to promote contemporary poetry. His book, *The All-Purpose Magical Tent* was selected by Terrance Hayes for the Nightboat Prize. His poems and reviews have appeared in *American Letters & Commentary*, *The Atlantic*, *The Believer*, *Boston Review*, *Tin House*, *Verse*, and the anthology *All That Mighty Heart: London Poems*.

Open Letter—the University of Rochester's nonprofit, literary translation press—is one of only a handful of publishing houses dedicated to increasing access to world literature for English readers. Publishing ten titles in translation each year, Open Letter searches for works that are extraordinary and influential, works that we hope will become the classics of tomorrow.

Making world literature available in English is crucial to opening our cultural borders, and its availability plays a vital role in maintaining a healthy and vibrant book culture. Open Letter strives to cultivate an audience for these works by helping readers discover imaginative, stunning works of fiction and by creating a constellation of international writing that is engaging, stimulating, and enduring.

Current and forthcoming titles from Open Letter include works from Argentina, Catalonia, France, Poland, and numerous other countries.

www.openletterbooks.org